THE SAGA:

DRAGON

HEART

STONE WILL

BOOK I

By Kirill Klevanski

Introduced by Valeria Kornosenko.
Translated by J. Kharkova, R. Mansurova, E. Kornilova
Edited by Damir Isovic
Cover designed by Vitaly Lepestkov
Illustrations by Valery Spitsyn

 Blue eyes peered at two yellow stars.

Instead of pupils, he had sharp spindles.

A man and a dragon looked at each other.

The creature, which had been alive for millions of years, had spent its most recent ones in a tomb. Unable to move its tail or claws, it gazed into the infinite emptiness of its soul.

The man had lived but one life in the prison of his own body, and then continued to exist in the same prison during his second one.

The amazing dragon, whose beauty had been praised in a thousand and one songs... The legendary conqueror of heaven and the Lord of Starlight had been cast down like a simple mortal.

The young man was disgusting to behold. His hands twisted at unnatural angles. He also had skin covered in scabs, a scarred face, an almost white, bald scalp and purulent blisters. Instead of legs— mere wooden stumps.

He'd been one of the most brilliant masters of his time, who'd reached the pinnacle of the martial arts practiced in his country.

The once-talented Prince was now trapped in a body that was incapable of even running, not to mention practicing the art.

In a dark cave, amidst ancient chains, sealed away with energy so dense that it could even be felt, touched, they lay in front of each other.

A bug, and a monster the size of a mountain.

Whether Fate, Chance or Ridiculous Coincidence had brought them together—nobody knew.

The dragon was so bored, he wanted to devour this disgusting mortal, but suddenly noticed the look in his eyes. Those intense, azure eyes. Despite everything that had happened, there was no despair to be found in that gaze, no regret, no fear.

Only the body was rotten, the gaze had remained clear and ferocious. So ferocious that if it were to be manifested, it could split the heavens and bring them down, to the ground itself.

"What is your name, little bug?"

"Hadjar Duran. And what's your name, scaly face?"

The dragon was about to dissolve the insolent whelp with a thought, but then he suddenly laughed, and his laughter made the thousand-year-old chains shake and the stones of the dungeon crack.

"My name is Traves."

They looked at each other. One a prisoner of the impregnable dungeon, one the prisoner of his own body and fate.

Traves knew that, even without being chained down, no mortal could escape this place. What puzzled him was how the ant had managed to end up in here.

This 'Hadjar' couldn't help him, couldn't tell the world that the Great Traves was still alive. Now they were locked in here together. Forever, or until the mortal died of starvation.

And so, Traves' revenge would never come to pass.

Hadjar didn't understand how lucky he'd been—he hadn't drowned in the underwater current, the endless rapids hadn't broken his head open, he hadn't drowned in the waterfall nor broken his body going down it, nor had he been shot by the archers. How had he managed to escape from the city on his improvised, artificial limbs?!

And yet, after only one glance at the whirlpool that had spat him out into this underwater grotto, it became clear that he would die of starvation here.

And so, Hadjar Duran's revenge would never come to pass, either.

The dragon looked at the bug's fierce gaze. He didn't flinch, didn't let go of his rage, even after realizing that it was all completely hopeless.

"I've lived a long life, Hadjar Duran. I've seen empires built. I've seen eternal cities collapse. I've fought with geniuses and defeated immortals. I've created Techniques so complex that many adepts are still, to this day, racking their brains over them. And yet, Hadjar Duran, I remain only a small spark in the world of martial arts.

'A small spark'? Hadjar hummed mentally and invoked one of the few functions that his neuronet was still capable of.

Name	Traves
Level of Cultivation	???????????????
Strength	???????????????
Dexterity	???????????????
Physique	???????????????
Energy points	???????????????

If 'a small spark' looked like that, then what had the hell of all the adepts he had previously met been? What was he, for that matter? A microbe? Mere dust? A recollection?

"I have lived two lives," if Duran had had the strength for it, he would have given the dragon a smug grin. "And so, I'm cooler than you."

All he had left now were stupid jokes and bravado. Well, to be honest, that was all he'd ever had, in principle. Jokes, bravado and an indomitable will.

"Hadjar Duran, will you make a deal with me? One which, most likely, will lead to you dying in such agony that children, listening to stories about you, will pass out from fear?"

"You would make a 'deal' with me? Even idiots would laugh at you if you were to do so."

The dragon laughed. Today was a good day for him to die, and to begin exacting his revenge. Finally...

"Move under my claw, bug."

Hadjar didn't argue. If it had wanted to do so, this creature would've already split him in half. And so, Duran, gritting his teeth, crawled over. The scabs and blisters, irritated by the stone floor, caused him unbearable suffering.

But he still crawled.

The steel claw was the size of a windmill and resembled a guillotine.

Undaunted, he crawled. Toward his death. Toward his revenge.

The ten yards became his own personal green mile.

Traves lifted the claw with visible effort. Not very high, just a little (for the dragon's size), but enough that the little bug could crawl under it.

"Are you ready, Hadjar Duran?"

"Come on, you bastard. Do whatever you need to..."

And then the cave was flooded with the man's cries of anguish and the dragon's roars.

[Urgent message for the user! Unauthorized changes to the owner's body detected! One of the vital organs has been replaced!]

The old heart of Hadjar, who had endured so much pain and despair, was sinking into a whirlpool. The dragon's heart was now beating in his own chest. It had been created by Traves, using a drop of his blood and all the willpower that he'd been able to find in himself.

The dragon died, and the man was reborn.

The age-old chains were crumbling, the ancient dungeon was collapsing, and the streams of water enveloping the body that was writhing in agony were carrying it towards the sunlight flickering above the surface.

The question remains, how had the man with the neuronet found himself in front of the dragon and how did he get his heart?

Chapter 1

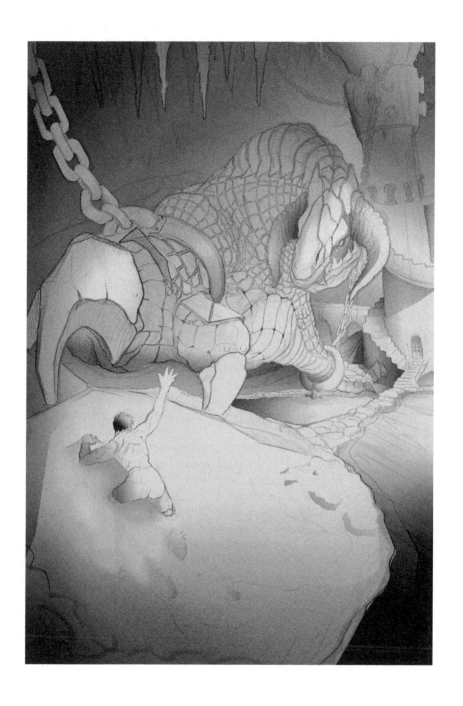

 He was never a lucky man. Many stories begin like this, and this one is no exception. He was born on Friday the 13th. That day, sheets of rain poured down, accompanied by hale. Only this fact hinted that his destiny wouldn't be an ordinary one.

His mother apparently thought the same.

Typical gutter trash, she became pregnant with a street tough's baby. They abandoned him on the threshold of a local hospital. They didn't put him down on it, but instead threw him away out of the car window as they drove by. They'd been afraid of being noticed, or something like that. No wonder he was bedridden literally from birth, able to move only his right hand.

He probably shouldn't have lived long with a broken backbone and craniocerebral injuries. But he decided to disregard that. He chose to live. He was housed in a special orphanage. He lived there until he was twelve. Always alone, cooped up in a small room. Sometimes, the other wards of the orphanage toyed with him.

They thought they were good at making fun of him. They were amused by how he couldn't talk, and could just move the only hand weirdly when they played their cruel games.

Needless to say, he never won one of those games.

Except for the children, a nurse came to him twice a day. She washed him, cleaned, changed his clothes, and often cursed. She complained about her life and the fact that she had to take care of a 'vegetable'. Sometimes, when she was in a foul mood, she used to beat him.

But he was still determined to survive.

In spite of it all, in spite of all of them.

When he was twelve, his life became much better. The delegation of a well-known magnate came to the orphanage. He immediately decided to use the "vegetable" for his own purposes. He placed him in the best hospital, the ward of which exceeded the size of many apartments. He visited him once a month or so, with the press in tow, bringing gifts and probably avoiding taxes very successfully.

So, his life changed.

He was fed delicious meals, smiling psychologists talked to him and other patients often visited him. Some of them were terminally ill, others had recently lost someone. He was able to listen well, although he wasn't able to speak.

Nevertheless, music remained his only friend. He listened to it all the time. When he ate, when he read, even while someone was confiding in him yet again.

When he was sixteen, a hi-tech laptop with special software was given to him. Now he could communicate. He would type, and the laptop would talk for him. The visitors began to come less often. Only the tired but smiling orderlies remained.

Then he started writing. Not books. He wrote music. Of course, the magnate did everything possible in order for the paralyzed musician to become a star.

When he was eighteen, a hundred thousand people would download his music every day. He didn't need the money, and the magnate was all too happy to dispose of it. He said he was using it for charity. But that was unlikely.

Everything changed that fateful day. He was lying in bed, without feeling himself doing so. He turned his own head toward the window with his right hand. The city lights glittered at the foot of the hill in the distance.

"Aren't you sleeping?" The voice sounded like it was very close.

He turned his head back around. New visitors would always shudder upon seeing that, but not this man. He was forty or maybe older, with a strong chin and clear, bright eyes.

"Who are you?" A mechanical voice asked. "Who let you to come in?"

He hated when somebody came in without knocking. It made him feel even more helpless.

"Oh, don't worry, I work here," the man sat down on the edge of the huge bed. This irritated him even more. "I'm from the seventh floor."

"The Department of Neurosurgery?"

"And bio-engineering."

The people working there were called 'Frankensteins'. He wondered what one of those scientists wanted from a simple cripple, just a little bit more famous than the others.

"I'm a chief physician too," the snow-white smile didn't appeal to him either. "Dr. Paul Kowal."

Paul held out his hand. He shook it.

"A strong handshake," the doctor muttered, rubbing his palm slightly.

He smiled inwardly. When you do everything, absolutely everything, with just one hand, it becomes much stronger than other people's hands. The same as blind people who have particularly sensitive hearing.

"Please, get to the point," the mechanical voice said. "I'm not a big fan of... small talk."

He should've said that he wasn't a big fan of people either. A troubled childhood and stuff like that.

"I'm glad to hear it." The man's blindingly white smile could compete even with the whiteness of the walls. "I have an offer for you".

"Sorry, I haven't thought about marriage yet. Plus, you're not my type."

Stupid jokes had always been his defense mechanism. They pushed people away better than anything else. No one liked it when someone made a silly and clumsy joke. However, the doctor just laughed.

He wanted Paul to leave the room as soon as possible. He had to finish a set in time for his new release.

"What do you know about neural networks?" Mr. Koval asked him.

"Just what's written in fiction," the special emoticon shrugged on the screen. "It's a kind of neural interface."

"Only partially," the doctor nodded. "It's more like an extra nervous system."

The emoticon raised its eyebrows on the screen.

"Do you think…"

"That if the surgery is successful, you might be able to walk and talk? Not immediately, you'll have to go through a long and painful rehabilitation. It may take a few years, but…"

"I agree."

"But…"

"I agree!" the metallic voice shouted.

Mr Koval looked into the bottomless, determined eyes of a man who hadn't even been able to turn his head. And there wasn't a hint of hesitation in his eyes.

"Then, as soon as we're done with all the bureaucracy, we can proceed."

The long and very crowded days he spent waiting felt like an eternity. Various specialists visited him. They covered his head with different sensors and did specific tests, or checked some obscure parameters.

So many tests were done on him that astronauts would have probably sympathized with him. It was absurd they'd taken a piece of his nail. And they'd sent in a special person with laser scissors to do it. This, perhaps, had been the only entertaining event.

Various psychologists also came to talk to him. There were even more of them than the ordinary doctors. They, as always, asked absolutely stupid questions, and each time, he graced them with the same smiling emoticon face. When he really got tired of them, he began to tell inappropriate jokes.

It seemed that he'd even managed to offend one of the graduate students. She'd asked him what he wanted to get out of the neural network in the immediate future. He answered her almost honestly. He wished to have the opportunity to invite her to dinner and then get her laid.

She had, probably, wanted to say something unpleasant in reply, but she stopped herself from doing so and just walked away in silence.

He laughed for a long time. It was funny that the psychologist hadn't understood that he, someone who'd never felt anything but his hand, had never experienced sexual attraction, even a mental one. He didn't know what it was.

Then the journalists came to interview him. They interrogated him for a long time, under the greedy supervision of the magnate. He was surely the sponsor of this operation, and had already calculated his future profits. He must've been thanking his lucky stars that he'd decided to take the disabled orphan under his wing.

Finally, he was dressed in a special robe, some muck was injected into his veins and he was sent down a long corridor. He was slowly losing consciousness, disappearing into a deep, viscous lake in his mind. For the first time in his life, he wasn't trying to resist that feeling. On the contrary, he opened his arms to embrace the deep. The last thing he saw was the worried face of the young nurse.

He was dreaming.

He was flying over the vast expanse of a smooth, green sea. Well, he'd thought it was smooth at first, and then, looking closer, he saw the huge mountains propping up the sky that were in the sea. The beautiful cities were so big that they could've fit the entire territory of some countries within them.

Strange animals were soaring in the sky.

They looked like dragons.

The green sea turned out to be the endless forests, valleys, and meadows. The blue veins were the broad rivers that looked more like elongated oceans. And the seas were the size of a starry sky.

The wind was blowing.

It was a pleasant wind, a wind that promised to grant him his only wish—to be free.

What a stupid dream it was, but so enjoyable.

His old friend, pain, brought him back to reality. He knew it better than he did most people. He was burning up and his body was contorting. A scorching hot metal rod was being attached to his nerves, and molten iron was being poured into every cell of his body.

"The pressure's increasing!"

"The neural activity is spiking."

"His pulse is at 250 BPM!"

"We're losing him!"

He heard all these voices as if from far away. There was also a distant, muffled and almost inaudible cry. That's how he first heard his own voice. Among the blurry individuals, the unclear outlines of the variety of instruments and mirrors in which his split open head was being reflected, he saw the information window.

He'd used to see those windows on the screen of his laptop.

[The network is activated. Version 0.17.6. Condition is critical!]

"He's going into cardiac arrest!"

Everything had faded. There was only one sense left to him, which made him laugh. Someone must've opened the door to the operating room and the wind was blowing in, reaching his heels.

He hadn't known something could be so funny.

Chapter 2

\He wasn't one of those people who were interested in death. He didn't care about what came after one's path ended. He was simply too busy fighting for that very life, every day.

And so, he'd expected neither a harem of virgins nor an eternal feast among soldiers, neither Seraphim nor the Golden Gate. Instead, there was only darkness.

It was warm and tender.

He was fine with it.

He didn't want to leave it. For the first time in his life, he felt neither anxiety nor unease. That's why he'd been so unhappy when the bright light appeared at the end of the narrowing tunnel.

He didn't want to leave this intimate darkness. But it forced him out, pushing him closer to the scorching circle of the white flame.

Finally, the light flooded everything around him, and then pouring down inside him as well. He felt a burning sensation in his chest. He shouted. Not from the pain, he knew how to endure that. He'd done it just to make sure he was truly alive. But instead of screaming, all he heard was a nasty squeak.

"Dat har herieon."

He heard an unfamiliar, gruff language. He opened his eyes with great difficulty and saw... An incomprehensible, blurry, clearly inverted, black-and-white spot. Out of habit, he reached out his hand toward the keyboard to type "What the hell". But instead of the keyboard, he ended up squeezing something soft. At first, he thought it was someone's hand, but, looking at it closer, he recognized... a finger.

How huge that finger must've been, if he'd held it with his whole palm!

Wait... Wait a minute...

[Reconfiguring the interface. Correcting the original error. The host's age is 35 seconds.]

What?!

Suddenly, the black-and-white image was filled with color and returned to normal, changing the perspective back as well. Finally, he saw the face... of a woman. Or even a young girl. She was about twenty. Certainly not any older. Her lustrous, black hair, which was in a thick braid, lay on her narrow, elegant shoulder. Her clear, green eyes glowed with happiness.

Her round, tired, sweat-covered face was perhaps the most beautiful thing he'd ever seen. He didn't see the environment—not the huge stone chamber, decorated with velvet and gold; not the painted walls: nor the girls in light leather armor who were standing around them. He looked only into the depth of her shiny eyes.

She stroked his cheek gently and said, "Dlahi Hadjar. Dlahi Hadjar."

***

"Look, Nanny," Elizabeth smiled.

She stroked the crying baby's cheek. She wasn't alone on the damp sheets now, rocking her newborn son in her arms. The nanny bustled around her. She gave orders to the women and they immediately ran into the depths of the Palace corridors.

"My dear Hadjar," the queen lulled the little Prince to sleep. "Dear Hadjar."

A kind smile was on her tired face.

"My Queen," the plump, kind Nanny came up to her. "Look how tightly he is holding onto you."

Elizabeth only then noticed that Hadjar had been squeezing her finger tightly. In his clear, blue eyes, she suddenly saw the reflection of something that the baby should not have been able to feel.

It was confusion.

"A son?!" Suddenly, there was an almost bestial roar.

In the corridor, she heard the tramping of a dozen feet. The gigantic doors opened wide and a tall, broad-shouldered man flew into the hall. Wearing golden, comfortable clothes, with a sash at his belt, he was an impressive man, and he was also taller than his warriors by two heads.

He had light brown, shoulder-length hair and a leather strap with metal inserts covered his forehead.

"My King," the nurse immediately bowed low.

The armored girls, who had returned to the chamber, did the same.

"Darling," Elizabeth's smile became even brighter than it had been before.

"I have a son, brother!" The King grabbed the man standing next to him by the shoulders.

He looked like the King, but was even taller and a little older. His black beard had some gray in it. A golden medallion was fastened to his heavy fur cloak.

"Congratulations, brother," the man answered in a deep baritone voice.

The King shook him a little and almost jumped onto the bed. He embraced his wife and touched his firstborn gently, a little wary of harming him. The baby was warm.

"Why isn't he crying?" The King asked worriedly. "Call the doctor! Quickly!"

"Calm down, Haver," the Queen laughed, and her gaze stopped the knights. "He's cried. He's just... stopped now."

"Stopped crying?" Haver was surprised. "Is that at all normal?"

This time, the question was addressed to the nurse that had straightened up.

"No, Your Majesty. You cried for almost four hours after your birth."

Haver wanted to scold the grumpy old woman, but he remembered that his newborn son was next to him, just in time to stop himself. Could he hear him?

"Don't worry, brother," the tall man came closer. "Look at how tightly he's holding Elizabeth's finger and how hard his eyes are."

The King turned back to his son, and for the first time, a feeling of pride flared up in his chest. He held out his own finger, and the baby grabbed it with his other hand. Tightly. Very tightly.

"The gods know," the smiling King whispered, "He will be a great general and..."

"A scholar, dear," Elizabeth interrupted him. "We agreed that if a boy was born, he would become a scholar."

"But, my love, look at him! He weighs as much as a young ScaryWolf!"

Elizabeth's look hardened. The warriors tensed up.

The King frowned.

"What is going on here?!" The Nanny suddenly shouted. "You can argue later! The child needs a rest now."

After saying that, she went to the Prince and wrapped him in a gold-covered veil, then carried him to a small comforter.

The Queen fell back onto the pillows with a sigh of relief. Breathing heavily, she stroked her husband's arm. Despite their quarrels, which were legendary throughout the whole country, she loved Haver with all her heart. And he loved her in return.

"Congratulations, brother," the man bowed. "But, my Queen, I beg that you forgive us, we need to attend the War Council."

"Just a couple of minutes, Primus," the weakened Elizabeth whispered. "Let me spend a bit more time with my husband."

The King's brother bowed once more, and then went out into the corridor, donning his cloak. He was followed by all the soldiers. Both the knights and bodyguards of the Queen. Finally, the new mother and father were left alone. The royal couple had precious few moments they could just spend with each other, basking in their love and devotion to each other.

The governing of the country demanded their full attention. It often happened that they couldn't see each other for several weeks at a time. It was a great mystery how they'd managed to conceive a child in such conditions. But taking into account the timing, it had most likely happened during the feast in honor of the Harvest Festival.

Haver sat down next to his wife and she lowered her head to his mighty, scarred chest.

"Stay with me this time, darling," she whispered

"The war's starting, dear," the King stroked his wife's hair. Silky and thick, it smelled like jasmine. Untouched by any gray, the same as the day they'd met, almost 70 years ago.

"This one will end, another will begin, and so on, endlessly. Wars never stop."

Elizabeth put her hand gently on the scars. There were more and more of them marring the body of her lover each time they met.

"I was born a King and warrior, this is my fate."

"That is why I want our son to become a scholar," the Queen's voice trembled. "Let's not allow the martial arts world to touch him."

"Will he live a mortal life, then?" The King sighed. "In forty years, his hair will turn gray, in sixty—his teeth will fall out, and in ninety years, if he lives, he won't even be able to remember your name. And you'll still be young and beautiful."

The Queen had celebrated her 90th birthday last month, but she didn't look a day over twenty. The King had ruled the country for almost three centuries. By the standards of the cultivators, they were still young. And compared to those who'd reached the level of The Heaven Soldier and had touched the edge of eternity and immortality, they weren't that different from their newborn son.

"But it will be a full life," Elizabeth whispered, falling asleep. "He will have no hardships, no troubles. He will marry, have children, and live happily, like all the mortals. He won't know the horrors of this world. About needing to fight for a place in the sun. About the enmity of the practitioners of the Art. He will never be drawn into the endless conflict of the strong sects. He won't be taken away from us by the Academy of Martial Arts, where he will forget all about the joys of life. He won't be, like many others are, obsessed with his cultivation. He will live a good, peaceful, happy life. You can make our next son a warrior."

"We can't hide him forever..."

"But we can do it until he's old enough."

Elizabeth ran a hand over his scarred, powerful chest once again and finally fell asleep.

Haver sat next to his beloved wife for a short time, and only after he was convinced that she'd fallen asleep did he get out of her embrace. He covered her with a blanket, closed the door and went out into the corridor. His elder brother, Primus, the First Warlord of the Kingdom, was already waiting for him.

"Does she still dream that he'll be a scholar?"

They walked toward the small throne room, where the generals and senior officers had already gathered. A new war was coming, although, admittedly, Haver didn't remember a time when one wasn't being fought.

"I can understand her," the King sighed and rubbed his numb neck. "Her whole family died when she was little."

"Have you seen little Hadjar? He looks like a scholar about as much as a Heaven Tiger looks like a tame kitten."

Haver smiled proudly and stopped near the window. He looked at his golden-domed capital, which stretched out for miles around. Almost thirty million people lived just in this city. Overall, more than two billion people lived in his Kingdom, which occupied a large swathe of land.

The King shook his head—his Kingdom, Lidus, was very small, almost imperceptible on a country map. Maybe that's why they had to fight so often.

Maybe Elizabeth was right, and Hadjar's fate was to be a scholar.

At that exact moment, he didn't know how wrong his wife was or how right his brother was.

Chapter 3

Much had changed in Hadjar's life over the past year. He wasn't bedridden now, at least. However—that bed had been so multifunctional that it had even massaged him.

And now he was forced to accept the fact that, in the future, he wouldn't only have to sleep on a cold mattress, with preheated coals in an iron box stuffed underneath for warmth, but also... that he'd have to pee in a wooden outhouse. Upholstered in velvet, decorated with mosaics, but still wooden!

Life hadn't prepared him for this…

It hadn't prepared him for the fact that, after his death, he would find himself in another world, either. Fortunately, he wasn't a farmer, but a Prince. Still, he wasn't sure about what awaited him in the future. There were some strange rules regarding inheritance and the throne of his country.

"...but our northern neighbor, the Kingdom of Balium," a white-haired old man was standing near the huge map which covered the entire wall. He delineated the boundaries of different states with a pointer and explained something to the children of the nobles. They were sitting at their desks and sketching something, using feathers to write on scrolls. "... is under the protection of 'The Black Gates', and that's why we're not at war with them. It would be tantamount to suicide."

"Record," Hadjar ordered mentally.

[Processing the request... The request has been processed. The data has been included in the database 'General information about the world']

"Why don't they attack us?" The owner of the surprisingly beautiful eyes and thin wrists raised her hand to ask.

"What could a vassal of 'The Black Gates' possibly need from a small kingdom such as ours?"

Hadjar, lurking in the corner of the hall, tried to roll his eyes, but his body didn't obey him. In addition, it had taken him almost two hours to crawl from his chambers to the hall with the map, where the lessons for future officials and scholars were being held. Not because he'd crawled slowly, he'd just fallen asleep periodically.

The neural network would inform him about his lack of energy, and then he would fall asleep.

Now he understood why babies loved to sleep; crawling a few yards had taken a lot out of him.

"We're all within the sphere of influence of The Darnassus Empire..."

The first court Scholar continued speaking, but Hadjar was looking at the map greedily. He'd almost fainted when he'd first seen it. His mother had been holding him in her arms at the moment. Admittedly, he'd probably just gone back to sleep, but it didn't matter.

In general, the Palace alone was larger than several city blocks. The city blocks back in his old world, of course. Furthermore, the ceilings were so high and the walls were so long that he often felt his head spin. And the map, sewn from the skins of various beasts, was stretched along the width of the entire marble wall, which looked like the wall of a fortress.

The seams were the mountains, and the veins were rivers. This didn't mean that barbarians lived in Lidus, just that the map was very old. It was extremely old, even by the standards of the locals: several million years old. And yes, the lifespan of people was abnormally long here.

And so, new areas would be sewn into the map, to honor the memory of the ancestors. Since Hadjar had been a highly educated man, he'd used his knowledge of geometry to calculate that Lidus was three times larger than the Eurasian continent.

Surely, this had to be a huge piece of land, even gigantic, right? But it was impossible to find the Kingdom on the map, at least without using a magnifying glass. It looked like nothing more than a village, and was just a small piece of land in this vast, titanic world.

Even with the help of his neural network, Hadjar couldn't understand why the day lasted the same 24 hours, on such a different world. He'd lost most of the functions it had. All that was left after his rebirth was the ability to record and play those recordings back, as well as very basic analytical mechanisms.

Still, he wasn't complaining, since he shouldn't even have that much.

"Which sect's sphere of influence is our Kingdom in?" the impudent-looking boy asked.

"That is a very good question," the Scholar put the pointer down and returned to the Department. "The sects aren't interested in us for exactly the same reason that the Kingdom of Balium doesn't attack us. The level of martial arts in our lands is very low. For example, to become just an outer disciple of 'The Black Gates,' one should have reached no less than the 8th stage of the Bodily Rivers."

The students all exhaled at once, and Hadjar gave the neural network an order to record this. The locals had some strange, fetishistic obsession regarding the subject of martial arts, which the local magic had probably been transformed into sometime in the past.

And yet, he still believed that living in a world of might and magic was better than being a 'vegetable'.

This strange quirk in the evolutionary path of these people could be explained by the fact that war, and the constant struggle for survival in general, were more common here than a trip to the store on a Friday had been, back in his old world.

"And that isn't even the most difficult part," the Scholar continued, "it needs to be reached by the time they turn 16, otherwise the cultivator won't even be accepted."

A wave of gasps swept through the classroom again, if this room could even be called that.

"I have to remind you that this path of cultivation is a long and winding one. Each disciple begins at the level of the Bodily Nodes, which is divided into nine levels. Then you advance to the level of the Bodily Rivers with its twelve stages. And only after you step over that threshold, which separates the mortal from the cultivator, will you reach the stage of Formation, when you become a cultivator and a part of the world of martial arts."

All of them were sitting with their mouths wide open in

astonishment. They had certainly already known these facts, but the Scholar was able to convey the information in a manner that made the old subject seem very interesting, especially to Hadjar. Every ounce of knowledge was important for him.

"Can anyone tell me at what level a warrior can become a junior officer in our army?"

A lot of the disciples raised their hands, wanting to answer the question. Almost half of the two hundred children knew the answer.

"Please, Viscount Vale," the scholar nodded.

A red-haired boy, about ten years old, stood up. Hadjar himself was only a year and two weeks old.

"At the eighth stage of the Bodily Nodes."

"That's right, sit down," and the boy lowered himself back onto the stool, looking at his companions rather arrogantly. "And this is considered to be a good level. To become a mid-level officer, you need to cross the threshold and reach the level of the Bodily Rivers. The ones who become senior officers in the army are the few who've managed to reach its third stage. Our generals are at the fifth stage of the Bodily Rivers."

The children scribbled with their feathers on the scrolls and listened to the mentor carefully. Now, in their crazy fantasies, they were probably dreaming about becoming the strongest cultivators of the Kingdom. Fortunately, there were no inequalities between the genders here. Hadjar saw a charming lady, wearing armor and with the regalia of a general.

If you can do it, if you know how, if you want to, go ahead—all the roads are open to you. And why shouldn't you? After all, this lady could not only easily stop a running horse, but also lift said horse with one hand and then throw it a couple of yards away.

"So, you can imagine how difficult it is to reach the required level of cultivation, not only so that 'The Black Gates' will be interested in you, but to even be allowed to take part in their entrance exam."

"You said 'an outer disciple'. Are there any other types?"

"Of course," the scholar nodded. "In most sects, disciples are divided into the following groups: the external or 'outer'—there are a lot of these."

The children looked at each other. So many young boys and girls were at the 8th step of the Bodily Rivers?! But they hadn't even started to train, because their bodies were too weak for it. And that was in spite of all the stimulants and drugs which they'd been crammed full of since birth.

"Next are the students of the inner circle, or the 'inner'. I don't know about other sects, as they are either too far away or aren't interested in us at all."

Hadjar whistled mentally. 'Too far' in this world was approximately the distance from Earth to Mars.

"But in 'The Black Gates', only those who have reached the Formation stage before the age of twenty are allowed to take part in the inner circle exam. For the sake of comparison, our two strongest fighters—King Haver IV and his brother, Warlord Primus, reached that stage by the age of sixty. And they are considered to be the strongest warriors of their generation and the whole country."

This time, the wave of sighs turned into a tsunami of whispers, and Hadjar tried to keep his mind from experiencing cognitive dissonance. A year ago, he'd thought his mother was only twenty years old. But, as it turned out later (when, thanks to the help of the neuronet, he'd been able to understand the local language), she was about a hundred. As for his father, he was about three centuries old.

It was scary to think about how old Primus was, considering the gray hair in his beard.

"So, what's next?" The girl with the beautiful wrists asked.

"Next come the core disciples. These are the ones who deserve personal attention from the teachers in the sect. To get this honor, you need to be an extraordinary person. I know of only one such cultivator. And by the age of twenty-five, he was at the level of the Heaven Soldier."

This time, the children couldn't resist asking their questions all at once. Is it true that a Heaven Soldier can fly? That with a wave of their hand, they can create fire? That their sword can cut an enemy from a distance of two hundred steps? That they can send an arrow through the slot on a helmet from a distance of 3 miles? That for a Heaven Soldier to live a hundred years in solitude while meditating is as easy as living for a day is to a simple mortal?

"Silence," the Scholar slapped his hand down on the pulpit.

And this slap produced a wave of air, which overturned some scrolls and ruffled the hair of even the children in the back rows. The children immediately fell silent.

"That's right, children," the Scholar nodded. "After a cultivator passes the Formation and Transformation stages, and manages to break through the second serious barrier between the stages, they will be able to reach the real level of a cultivator. They'll cease to be an ordinary mortal, and will touch eternity, becoming a Heaven Soldier. And, according to many, only then can a person really be considered a cultivator."

The kid from before raised his hand again, but he had, probably, been planning to ask a stupid question. Since it was that arrogant Viscount, most likely something about the bedroom prowess of a Heaven Soldier.

Hadjar, forgetting himself, raised his stubby hand and asked, "And what exactly should be formed and transformed? What are these 'nodes' and 'rivers'? What kind of sick fantasies did the creator of all this have?!"

The classroom got very quiet.

Standing on all fours, dressed in silk and velvet, Hajar slowly lowered his hand back down on the floor. He'd forgotten that his questions sounded more like: "Agu-gaga-gu? Aglu am saaaaaa-Maglu? Ha-ha-gagumaaaa-g."

[The host's level of speech distortion: 100%. Possibility of correction: 0%]

Some of the smart ones jumped to their feet and, pressing their hands to their chest, bowed. These were the most notable—the children of the dukes. The ordinary nobles collapsed to one knee, and the future ladies sank into deep curtsies.

The Scholar bowed deeply.

"Your Highness," he said. "How did you…"

The doors of the classroom opened, and the person that even some generals were afraid of appeared on the threshold. The elderly, but very energetic royal Nanny. She was called 'royal' because she'd once nursed Haver IV and his brother. There were legends that, before that, she'd been a general in the cavalry. The elite among the elites.

"Your Highness!" She roared with such force that the giant map began to shake. "How have you managed to escape again?!"

Hadjar wanted to answer that, for a week now, he'd been able to use a hole in the door to his chambers, but, most likely, they would guess that on their own later. Also, he couldn't answer, despite the fact he wanted to.

"I beg your pardon, professor South Wind." The names were kind of ridiculous around here.

The nanny held Hadjar in her arms. Despite her stern expression, she did it as carefully as if he were not a human, but a fragile vase. She wrapped him in the blanket she'd prepared. Hadjar protested, but couldn't deal with her. And as soon as he was back in its warmth and comfort, he couldn't resist his natural desires and immediately fell asleep.

The soldiers had already appeared from the hall by then. They surrounded the nanny in a ring of bodies and left the room with her, leaving the shocked disciples and the professor alone with their thoughts.

The nurse sighed, imagining how the King and Queen would surely make a big deal out of this. No wonder the soldiers were checking their armor and shields. If Elizabeth started throwing plates again, it would be necessary to call the architects and builders to take them out of the walls.

Chapter 4

Hadjar was sitting at the table and playing with wooden knights, or so everyone thought. In fact, he was carefully studying the open scroll left there by the King. Frankly speaking, he'd allowed the neuronet to copy everything into its database. He couldn't read the strange squiggles yet, but he'd realized that the drawings were associated with martial arts, or, to be more exact, with palm strikes.
In the Prince's opinion, it was quite corny. Thankfully, nobody was interested in his opinion.

In fact, he was seated at the Royal table with only one purpose in mind - to prevent the Palace from needing costly repairs again.

"Record," Hadjar said for the umpteenth time.

[Processing the request... the request has been processed. The data has been included in the special database " Information about Techniques"]

The King and the Queen didn't quarrel in the presence of their son. They probably only interacted pleasantly on rare occasions. When they were trying to make a brother or sister for Hadjar, when he was sitting next to them, or when they were in different parts of the country.

Oftentimes, their very similar temperaments gave rise to some legendary scenes. And what else could you expect from two cultivators at the level of Transformation? Moreover, Elizabeth loved to bring this topic up, using her characteristic, scathing sarcasm. She often reminded Haver that she was three times younger than him, but had already reached the same stage of cultivation.

The most sensitive topic for a man wasn't the organ in his pants, but his personal strength and age. Which was surprising, considering the lifespan of these cultivators.

"I don't understand why you're so upset—there weren't that many people in the office"

Nanny (despite her low status, she secretly remained one of the most powerful people of the Kingdom) was there, along with Primus, the King and Queen, as well as the court Scholar and the Master. This short, gray-haired (though it was difficult to call him that) old man taught the nobles the arts. He trained them hard and without mercy. For his services, he received so much money from their parents that a large merchant guild would envy him.

"Don't you care that our son was crawling around the Palace alone?"

Haver looked at his son. He was playing with his toys and not paying any attention to the adults.

"It's hard to find a safer place in the country than the Palace," the King shrugged.

"He's tiny!" Elizabeth raised her voice.

The nurse covered the nearby dishes, and Primus clenched his fists. The air around him swirled slightly. It was hard to notice, but it hadn't been hidden from the neuronet and, therefore, from Hadjar.

[Message to Host! Power has been activated in the vicinity!]

This was a message that Hadjar had seen before. He'd decided to call the local magic by a name he'd taken from a franchise back home, simply naming it—'Power'.

"He's a little boy," Haver corrected her. "I remember that I used to crawl around everywhere in my childhood, too."

"I have to say, your Majesty," the nurse coughed, "You only went out if you were accompanied by the late Queen till you were seven years old."

Haver snorted at the bitchy old woman, but didn't answer her.

"And what if he'd fallen and hurt himself?!"

Primus rolled his eyes. In his opinion, Queen Elizabeth cared for the Prince with a bit too much intensity.

"In my opinion, Elizabeth, you're trying to make a hare out of a wolf. It'll lead to trouble"

"No one is interested in your opinion!" The Queen barked. "And what are you doing here anyway? Some war council, hunt, feast, brothel or whatever else you do is surely waiting for you. You know, the stuff you call national administration!"

Primus looked at his brother, raised his palms and, murmuring something, left the office.

"Honey, let's calm down—nothing bad happened."

"But it could have!"

The situation was clearly heated. The neuronet was pouring out messages about potential threats to its carrier.

"Please, let me tell you something, your Majesty," the Scholar bowed.

Elizabeth glanced menacingly at the old man, but soon enough, the fire in her eyes went out.

"Please, honorable professor South Wind, go ahead."

The old man bowed again.

"I may be wrong, but it seems like the fate of the young Prince has already been written down in the hall of Mysteries. It seemed to me, during our classes today, that he wasn't just crying, but had in fact wanted to ask a question."

"A question?" Nanny snorted. "Have you completely lost your mind because of your scrolls, South Wind? You should take more walks. The baby can't even talk yet."

Even the King and the Queen didn't allow themselves such liberties when dealing with the scholars. There was only one person in the entire Kingdom who didn't watch her tone and words in front of Master South Wind.

"It's easy enough to check," the Sholar suddenly came over to the table. He took out some parchment, a quill and an inkwell. He put them in front of Hadjar and said, "Draw me the map of our Kingdom, disciple."

They were taken aback at the word 'disciple'. The nobles who attended his lectures weren't his 'disciples'. They were only the children of those who'd paid the tuition, and the Scholar considered them merely a source of income. Regardless, the King hadn't heard about South Wind taking somebody as a disciple in ages.

"Thank you for the honor, venerable Scholar," Elizabeth suddenly bowed. The Queen had bowed to the commoner! "But my son…"

Silence descended on the study.

Hadjar hadn't needed to think about it for long. What was his purpose in this new world and his new body? The dream he hadn't been able to realize before. When he'd watched TV, or videos on the Internet where people traveled the world, he could only envy them. They were climbers, divers, simple tourists. They could feel and embrace that seemingly large, expansive world.

He lived in this new world now, which was huge, full of danger and puzzling opportunities. And he had to be strong, in order to be able to discover them all, to be free from the shackles of his fate. He had to be much stronger than his father and mother, and much more powerful than his uncle.

His first goal was 'the Black Gates' sect, and in order to get there, he needed to reach the eighth stage of the Bodily Rivers by the age of sixteen. How could he do that, with the meager resources of the Kingdom? He would succeed only if all of those limited resources were devoted to his personal cultivation.

And so, Hadjar gave the order to his neural network and it projected the map onto the parchment. Of course, the projection was only visible to Hadjar himself, but it was enough for him to start tracing the contours with the quill.

"That's incredible," Nanny exhaled.

"This child can't speak, but he can understand us," South Wind seemed to be surprised, too. "Tell me, disciple, what change will you get if you pay two hundred gold coins for a sword worth one hundred and eighty."

"Scholar, don't joke," the Master spoke for the first time. "He can't possibly know about…"

Hadjar slapped his face mentally. He had never gone to school, but if the same 'smart' questions were asked there, it wasn't surprising at all that very few people liked to go to school.

He raised ten fingers. The people sighed disappointedly, and then sank back into their chairs, stunned.

Hadjar had squeezed his fingers and spread them again.

"... this," the Master finished his sentence, incredulous.

"Where can you find the Grass of Seventeen Rays?"

That time, no one tried to argue with the Scholar. And they were very surprised when the Prince pointed his finger at the correct hill on the map he'd drawn earlier.

"How many grams of this herb and how many grams of the Old Soul Powder would it take to make a cure for the Blue Scorpion poison?"

That question was so complex that the King, Queen or the Nanny wouldn't have known the answer. Only the Master and the Scholar knew what the correct answer was.

Hadjar knew the answer to that question, too, or, rather, the neural network did. He was very pleased with the fact that the neural network recorded not only books, but also the lectures he'd overheard. Fortunately, South Wind had given a lecture on this topic just a month ago.

"Amazing," the Master gasped, when he saw two fingers of one hand and four of the other raised.

"It seems, your Highness, that the heavens have blessed you with a genius."

Everyone was silent, and Hadjar was looking at the Master. They used to say, back on Earth, that if a young man wanted to get a beautiful girl in bed, he needed to get closer to her friends first.

No, the Prince wasn't going to sleep with the Master, but the path to his discipleship was through the South Wind's lectures.

"What do you say, dear?" Elizabeth asked the King.

"Esteemed South Wind," the King addressed the old man meaningfully, "are you really going to take Hadjar as your student?"

The old man nodded. "He'll be my first disciple in the last two thousand years that I've been alive."

Well, the old man's two thousand years old. Nothing surprising there. Hadjar thought sarcastically; he no longer doubted that this was a different world entirely.

"Analyze," he ordered, looking at South Wind.

[The request is being processed... The request has been processed. The table is being generated]

Name	South Wind
Level of cultivation	???????????????

Strength	????????????????
Dexterity	????????????????
Physique	????????????????
Energy points	????????????????

[The request cannot be processed... There is insufficient data for an analytical comparison]

"It's settled, then," Haver nodded. "From this day onward, you can visit Hadjar's apartments at any time convenient to you."

"But, pardon the intrusion," Elizabeth added suddenly. "Nanny will be present during your classes.

At first, South Wind wanted to argue that his knowledge couldn't be shared with the clumsy old lady as well, but then he looked into those clear, blue eyes. Those weren't the eyes of an ordinary child.

Was the Scholar that eager to become one of the teachers of a future luminary of the Sacraments? Well, he could make the sacrifice and let Nanny attend his classes as well.

That was the beginning of Hadjar's studies. That was how his devious plan was set in motion.

Chapter 5

Another year of Hadjar's life passed. At the banquet organized to celebrate his birthday, he was introduced to his future... wife. She was only four days old. The Prince, to put it mildly, had been shocked, even though he'd already known that these kinds of marriages were quite a normal thing amongst the nobility.

The girl was the daughter of the head of a large Trade Cartel. Well, 'large' by the standards of the Kingdom. But South Wind had said that the merchant fleet numbering seven hundred ships was a beggarly business.

Fortunately, in addition to his wife, the Prince was also presented with a good amount of all sorts of other 'things'. Well, Hadjar called them 'things'. Scholars would call them very pathetic artifacts. However, all these swords, bows, sabers, books, etc. were at the level of Mortal artifacts. The next level were Spiritual artifacts, which would've cost almost as much as the entire Royal Palace.

No wonder that only Haver and Primus had those. Each of them owned a special Spiritual blade. Hadjar didn't know yet how artifacts differed in the power they could exert (the neuronet had again complained about having too small an amount of data to work with—a useless piece of iron), but he was definitely going to find out.

Actually, that was one of the questions that he was going to ask South Wind in the near future. Fortunately, he'd learned the local language six months ago and could now speak it fluently. And he'd learned to read quite well.

The Scholar complained that, despite his genius, learning to speak and read had taken Hadjar too much time. Well, of course it had. In comparison to the earthly ones, these local squiggles had little resemblance to a normal language. Who knew how long it would've taken him without the help of the neuronet.

Now, swinging his legs, Hadjar was sitting in the corridor with his father, uncle and a dozen warriors. Each of them was able to lift a stone that weighed 700 pounds, throw a spear four hundred yards and split a thick oak with their sword.

The main thing was to get a good sword.

They were at the fourth stage of the Bodily Rivers.

Previously, Hadjar had thought they were insanely strong. But memories of his time on Earth faded more and more over time, with the help of South Wind's lectures. Now, Hadjar knew that a Heavenly Soldier wasn't the pinnacle of cultivation. Stronger cultivators existed.

Those who were almost immortal. Those who could move seas and mountains with a wave of their hand. And it frightened and fascinated him at the same time, the fact that Hadjar didn't know whether this was an exaggeration or not.

And a week ago, he'd been taken outside. Well, 'outside' was just the balcony. From atop it, he'd been able to see the almost boundless city and valley, stretching out beyond the titanic walls.

The wind blew, tousling his wavy black hair.

The wind called to him.

"Which do you want more? A brother or a sister?" His father asked again.

Hadjar pondered the choice again. Each of the options had its advantages.

Haver laughed and ruffled his son's hair, as was his habit.

"South Wind says that you can already pass the exam to be an official, but you can't answer my question for some reason."

"It's too complicated, Dad," Hadjar said. "If I have a brother, I can play with him. And if I have a sister, I can protect her. Plus, a sister will clearly be more beautiful than a brother."

"Well, who can say," the King smiled. "Going by what Nanny's told me, the ladies of the court cuddle you every day. The healers say that, in future, you will break a lot of girls' hearts."

Hadjar barely kept a smug smile off his face. By local standards, he was a very handsome young man. However, what else could you expect from such good genetics and such amazing parents?

"I hate girls. And why have you given me a wife? It would've been better if she'd been a boat."

The King laughed and ruffled his hair again.

"When you grow up, I'll definitely teach you some secrets."

"South Wind's already teaching me!"

"Oh, believe me, the old man won't teach you about this. I'm afraid that this area is one of those where he only has theoretical knowledge."

The warriors laughed quietly, and the King winked at his son. Hadjar made a confused face, which elicited a new bout of laughter. Fortunately, he was a great actor. He had to play the role of a two-year-old child. Ingenious, but still a child.

After all, it's the squeaky wheel that gets the grease.

Finally, the doors opened and Nanny came out.

"It's a daughter," she smiled.

Haver picked up his son and rushed off to his chambers. This time, they burst in there without Primus. His uncle had gone to the southern borders on a military campaign. Nomadic tribes had plundered the villages and towns there.

Hadjar hugged his mother quickly and sat down beside a small, pink, crying lump. His... sister had already been wrapped up in golden blankets. She looked quite ordinary, but something in the Prince's chest tightened.

Sitting on the bed, next to his mother and father, looking at his newborn sister, he suddenly realized what he'd been deprived of back on Earth. It hadn't been the ability to walk and talk. No. Something much more vital had been taken from him.

Since childhood, he'd been deprived of this very feeling.

The warmth of a family.

"And we'd been expecting a son," the tired Elizabeth smiled.

Two years had passed and she hadn't changed at all. Not a single wrinkle had appeared on her beautiful face. Not a single gray in her thick, black hair.

"What should we name our daughter?" The King rocked the little bundle tenderly.

"Elaine," Hadjar said. "Let's name her Elaine."

The parents looked at each other and nodded.

And so, Hadjar now had his forever crying, but already beloved, little sister Elaine. And she changed something deep within him. Without noticing it, he suddenly realized that his performance, his 'I can protect her' act, had stopped being a performance.

***

Just a month after Elaine was born, Hadjar was able to obtain permission to visit the training grounds. It would've been difficult to get in there, the most sacred part of the Palace complex, even if he'd been the son of not Haver IV, but the son of James Bond himself.

The grounds were guarded even better than the chambers of some of the high officials. The Master taught the future elite of the country there, and he couldn't allow his knowledge to be stolen by someone.

He'd had to work hard to earn the trust of South Wind and to make him work on his cultivation. The cultivation of his martial arts, of course. The Scholar, in principle, didn't like this field of study very much. Hadjar learned from his Nanny that once upon a time, the old man could've been admitted to 'The Black Gates', but his meridians had been damaged during the exam . The meridians were the channels in the body through which Force flowed.

So, while he was healthy outwardly, he remained a cripple for life, internally.

As for meridians, Hadjar managed to find out some details about the stages of their cultivation.

The first stage was called 'Bodily Nodes'. There were nine steps in this stage. Special passages, invisible to the eye, were opened in the body of the practitioner at this stage. They used some kind of acupuncture. The warrior could then absorb energy through them; the local air was full of it.

After accumulating the energy in their centers, they directed it through the veins, opening the meridians, which were normally sealed from birth. This stage was called 'The Level of Bodily Rivers'.

When all the points were opened, and all the meridians were saturated, the practitioner came across the first so-called 'threshold'. It was a state where the nearest level was so very close, but it was incredibly difficult to reach it.

Many people couldn't handle it at all.

They simply couldn't condense the energy and reach the Formation Stage. The first level was when The Seed, woven from force, would form inside the soul of a person (and not only there, but we'll talk about that later.)

Then it was necessary to split The Seed into several parts. This was the Fragment Level.

And in the end, it was necessary to gather the fragments back together and create The Core. This was the third level of the Formation Stage.

The Transformation Stage followed next. This was when a person's soul adapted, but not their strength or body. The mortal shell, the Awakened spirit, and the New soul.

Hadjar knew nothing about them, because South Wind had no information on the subject. According to him, only the King himself could teach his son how to progress past these stages.

And as for the transition from a mortal to a cultivator, there wasn't a single person in the entire Kingdom that knew how to make the transition between the Transformation and the Heaven Soldier stages.

Those who knew how to do so lived only in sects or in larger states.

"Anyway," Hadjar spoke to himself aloud, "I've already taken the first step."

He stood on the edge of the grounds where the soldiers trained. He'd made a cunning plan a long time ago. He only had to implement it. And that's how his cultivation would begin.

Chapter 6

The site resembled a sandy parade ground. It was a huge, sandy parade ground. Thousands of soldiers trained here, sparring. They were tirelessly beating each other up under the scorching sun, wearing only short pants (sometimes with a bandaged chest, in the case of the women) under the guidance of the Master walking around.

Someone moved his arms like a whirlwind, parodying the famous Chinese fantasy movies. Crazy jumps, contrary to the laws of physics, were the norm here. Someone stopped falling as easily as a feather on the wind, by pushing off the earth using just a single palm. Others were easily shattering wooden shields.

Others fought with a variety of weapons. Their diversity was impressive. Hadjar didn't know the names of most of these weapons, and he was glad that the familiar staves, wands, swords, bows, swords, axes and hammers were at least there. Some of the girls sometimes waved ribbons around.

It might've looked funny, but not when those ribbons left scratches on the stone walls.

And, of course, all of their characteristics were gradually being studied by the neuronet, gaining enough information to be able to perform a detailed analysis.

For example, it could produce something like:

Name	Training Sword
Quality Grade	Non-artifactual Weapon
Endurance	????? (lack of data)
Damage	????? (lack of data)
Energy points	0

The Prince walked along the edge of the parade ground, listening to the Master's shouts. He constantly repeated obscure phrases, like 'energy circulation', 'external Techniques', 'internal Techniques' and so on.

Sometimes, the old man stopped duos that were training together and showed them how to do something properly. Then, an unlucky disciple found themselves flung, crashing into the wall, and they'd be considered lucky if they didn't leave a dent behind.

A new wall was probably erected here every season, because, at that moment, it looked like it had withstood a shelling.

When someone noticed Hadjar, they stopped training and bowed. This continued until the Master noticed a toddler walking around the court.

"Your Highness," he bowed slightly. "May I ask who let you in and where your Nanny is?"

"I asked for permission from South Wind," Hadjar replied. Judging by the old man's face, he was interested to know where the scholar had gotten the ability to give such permission. "And Nanny is busy with Elaine."

"And did you decide to come to visit us since you were feeling abandoned?"

Hadjar bowed his head in annoyance. Despite all of his peculiarities, the Master still treated him like a small child. A child whose uncle and father had gone to war (and how could they cover such vast distances so quickly?!), whose mother had gone to a nearby town to execute some corrupt governor, whose Nanny was busy with his sister, and whose teacher wouldn't be coming out of seclusion for another month.

South Wind was currently working on a new medicine that he was going to use to speed up the cultivation of the nobles. If he got lucky, it would probably bring him a lot of money and, more importantly, fame.

The Scholar, even being a cripple, didn't refuse his attempts to get the attention of the sect.

So, to the Master, he looked like a lost child.

"No, Master, I've come to study."

"Study?" the old man was surprised. He scratched his long, thin beard. "And what are you planning to study here?"

"Martial arts," Hadjar said proudly. The old man should've known better than to ask.

The Master laughed, and a few dozen soldiers that had been standing nearby laughed with him.

"Why do you, your Highness, think that you can study martial arts?"

"Because I've decided to do so."

The old man twitched slightly, having glanced into the child's deep blue eyes. Damn it, he could've sworn that he'd seen a look that could bend iron.

"Your determination is worthy of praise, my Prince," the Master nodded. "But…"

The martial artist came closer and touched the child's wrist. He listened for a second, and then opened his eyes and shook his head.

"While you do undoubtedly possess some talent…" the Master sighed, "It isn't strong enough to achieve true greatness on the path. Perhaps you should go back to South Wind's scrolls."

This news could've broken another man, but Hadjar was adamant. He had heard, all his life, that he couldn't do anything or couldn't handle anything. But in spite of everyone's words, he'd used to achieve his goals and deal with his problems, punching through any obstacles. He knew that hard work and diligence produced much better results than mere talent.

"I've decided to do it," Hadjar repeated.

Suddenly, the Master realized that he couldn't convince this two-year-old boy to give up.

"I'll take you on as a disciple, then," the old man stood up, blocking the sun.

The court grew silent. The silence hung heavily on the shoulders of the people. They froze, remaining in poses that they'd been in a moment ago. Some of the disciples were even standing with their feet raised above their heads.

First was South Wind, who had been alive for two thousand years, and had never taken a disciple before, and now the Master, who was almost twice as old as him, and had also never taught anyone personally before.

To tell the truth, luck was part of it. Hadjar had been born the son of the King, and had then expressed a desire to study and then become a disciple of the Master. He was quite a lucky boy.

"But you have to pass one small test, first."

"What kind of test, Master?"

The old man smiled and pointed to the opposite side of the court. There was a large barrel of water there, on the surface of which floated a wooden cup. Soldiers often went there to rinse their mouths. They were allowed to drink only a few times during training, and the Master oversaw them very strictly.

He would say that nobody was allowed to mix... He said that one couldn't mix the energy of the sun (fire), with the energy of water. Whatever that meant.

"Do you see that barrel over there, my Prince?"

"Yeah."

"Then your test shall be this: you need to pour water from that barrel into this one here," he patted a barrel next to him that was exactly the same as the other one, only this one was empty. "You mustn't spill a single drop."

Hadjar estimated the distance that he needed to cross. It was about fifteen hundred feet from one end of the parade ground to the other. Given the fact that it was difficult for him to take even a hundred steps, it was daunting to imagine having to walk so much more than that. The task was further complicated by the scorching sun, as well as the large size of the barrels; he needed to pour a whole barrel of water.

The warriors hid their smiles behind their fists. Well, they loved their King, who was strict, strong and fair. And yet, they were glad that the little Prince had been put in his place. They hoped that he, being a well-bred boy, would turn around and leave, offended, but without making a scene, as the spoiled children of petty nobles usually did. Neither Nanny nor the Queen would approve of that kind of behavior.

"Well," Hadjar nodded, clenching his fists.

Nobody had expected this. They also hadn't expected that the boy would lift a heavy barrel and drag it through the parade ground.

The Master blinked a few times, rubbed his beard and screamed: "What are you staring at?! Keep working!"

No one moved, because the Prince, Haver and Elizabeth's son, was walking among them. The very thought of touching him caused them to tremble, they were afraid of hurting him accidentally while sparring.

"But, Master, we could..."

"The Prince is doing his job, and you have to do yours as well. Those of you who are going to take a break can forget the way here! Whoever pauses to cool off, they can forget the way here as well!"

Forgetting the way to the parade ground meant missing out on the opportunity to train with the best instructor in the country. No practitioner could allow himself such a thing.

They all craved strength and they weren't afraid of the danger along the path of cultivation, the complexity of it only fueled their excitement. So it wasn't surprising that, just a minute later, Hadjar found himself having to dodge other people's heels and hide his eyes so sand wouldn't get in them.

He was dragging the heavy cup, looking at the barrel ahead of him intently.

The Master looked at the little Prince. He was ready to save the child's life at any moment if the need arose, but the disciples whom he was training were also trying not to injure the boy. And so, their movements became calmer, more measured, more reasonable.

Well, little Hadjar's stubbornness had produced a lot of benefits. He, the Master smirked inwardly, was an excellent training obstacle. Maybe someone would get so deeply immersed in their movements today that they'd be able to get some inspiration and get to the next level.

It would hardly be that beneficial, but who knows.

The Master wondered how long the Prince's willpower would last. Could he reach the barrel?

It was extremely difficult for a two-year-old child to overcome five hundred yards under the scorching sun, among all the flickering bodies. And what if a heavy cup and hot sand were added to the mix?

However, Hadjar overcame the first hundred yards, then two hundred, and after a quarter of an hour, all five hundred of them. He'd already surprised the Master. But a simple surprise wasn't enough to force the old man to take him on as a disciple.

And as soon as Hadjar scooped up the first cup and went back, he would understand that it was impossible, at his age, to pour fifty gallons of water without spilling a drop. This wasn't just difficult for two-year-olds, this kind of exam was used in the army, for people being recruited into the common infantry. And not even every adult could handle it.

And yet, the Prince got to the 2-foot barrel. He puffed and dragged over a small ladder, putting the cup in. It was small for an adult and huge for a baby.

Climbing on the ladder, he scooped up the cup and carefully went back down. Turning around, he walked back.

The Master saw how difficult it was for the boy. He was almost on the verge of fainting, but his eyes... These blue eyes made the Master, who had thousands of life and death struggles, shiver. There was something inflexible and endless, like heaven itself, in them.

The boy went back. Staggering, almost falling, he held the cup with both hands, not allowing a drop to fall onto the sand.

"Hadjar!" Came a cry from behind his back.

The Master turned around and froze. On the stairs leading into the Palace, the Queen was standing. Her spacious, amber-colored robes fluttered in the wind. Her hair framed her beautiful face, and a fire burned in her lovely green eyes.

"Careful, Hadjar!" Elizabeth pushed off the stairs.

It was about twenty yards from her to the ground. For an cultivator of her level, it was no more than a step was to a common man. And yet, no matter how swift and powerful the Queen's movement was, the lingering warrior's leg was much closer.

The Master barely managed to turn back and stretch out his power toward the clumsy disciple. He threw him aside with only an effort of strength and will, but it was too late. Hadjar had been hit with the full force of the blow.

Like a limp doll, the boy was thrown into the air and slammed right into the rack of swords.

The Master and the Queen hurried after him, but it was obvious that they wouldn't get there in time.

Chapter 7

Hadjar had understood from the very beginning that things had gotten out of hand, and his plan wouldn't be easy to implement. It had been foolish to expect that he could just become a disciple of the Master, the same way he'd done with South Wind.

You could 'talk' to scholars, prove you were intelligent, but warriors were people of action. They required a demonstration of something else.

Alas, in that regard, the Prince had nothing to give. He didn't possess innate martial arts skills. He wasn't one of the legendary cultivators who'd been born with their meridians or nodes already open.

He didn't have one of those divine physiques that would allow a five-year-old child to lift a grown horse into the air. And, of course, he hadn't been born with innate Techniques, whatever the word "Technique" even meant.

Nevertheless, he'd hoped that he would be able to overcome these obstacles using sheer stubbornness. As he'd always done. Stubbornness was Hadjar's main strength. He'd never stopped until he'd reached his goal in his previous life, and he wasn't going to stop now. Pain, boredom or loneliness didn't matter. If he had a goal, he would find a way to achieve it.

That was why, feeling the tidal wave of pain in his chest, he regretted only the cup that had fallen. Some water had leaked out and onto the sand, which meant he'd have to do everything over, from the beginning. Only after thinking about this did he pay attention to the messages from the neuronet.

[Critical message: ...]

It was urgently warning him about a danger to the host, in the form of sharp pieces of metal.

Wait, what? Pieces of metal?!

Hadjar, twisting his head, noticed that he was flying directly toward the sword rack. Damn it, he might not get his second chance now! He was going to become a bloody kebab, and not the adept hero he'd fantasized about!

The Prince waved his hands as hard as he could, but this obviously didn't halt his flight. The swords, reflecting the sun's rays, were already close to his face, when suddenly, he felt a gust of wind.

It got tangled in his clothes, then rested in his hair. What had it brought him this time? The story of some distant country; the shadow of many great battles; perhaps the tale of amazing heroes and villains alike?

No, this time, it brought him peace.

If, at that moment, someone had been looking not at the Master or the Queen, but at Hadjar, they would've seen a complete absence of fear on the boy's face. He flew towards the swords as calmly as a sparrow would toward the branch of a birch tree on a clear summer's day.

When he landed right on the blades of all those swords, Elizabeth's cry flooded the parade ground. The Master could already hear the executioner sharpening the guillotine which would cut off his head. Or the angry Queen would just finish him off herself, right then and there. It didn't matter that she was weaker than him. An angry mother who'd lost her child was easily as scary as a wounded tigress.

And yet, the Master was unable to see the inevitable fountain of blood. He couldn't even see one drop.

The swords fell to the sand with a ringing noise, and Hadjar stood among them as if they were merely a harmless rain. He looked at the falling blades and couldn't help but feel surprised. The sunlight ran along the polished blades and it was a beautiful sight to behold. The ringing of steel sounded better than his music back on Earth ever had.

Suddenly, he stretched out his hand, and the handle of the lightest and thinnest dagger rested itself in his palm. It was a flexible, short cutlass.

This 'toothpick' seemed like a gigantic broadsword, in the grip a two-year-old boy. However, Hadjar took hold of it firmly, and at the same time, he did so with ease, his grip both careful and powerful.

The Master and the Queen stood nearby. They froze, trying to understand what they'd seen.

The warriors stopped in their tracks, as well. Even the clumsy soldier who had kicked the Prince could come away from the wall and look at what was happening, though blood was running down his face.

The swords fell to the ground, but not a drop of blood left Hadjar's body. He stood, lost somewhere deep within himself, holding the dagger which had become his first sword.

Elizabeth had wanted to go to her child, but the Master stopped her in time.

"A moment of inspiration." He whispered, as if that meant something.

But since these few words stopped the angry and worried mother in her tracks, they must've carried a really amazing meaning. More than a thousand people watched the young boy. He stood there calmly, serenely turning his face toward the east wind.

Suddenly, Hadjar opened his eyes, and they lit up for a moment with a beautiful, clear light. Afterward, he took a small step forward and swung his blade lightly. In response, the wind blew and a crescent moon, barely perceptible to the eye, rushed out from the tip of the blade. It was only visible thanks to the windswept sand.

The sword strike hit the wall and left a small cut on it. It was no longer than Hadjar's little finger and no thicker than a woman's hair. But it was still there.

That strike had been performed at a distance of two steps.

By a two-year-old child who hadn't touched a sword before.

[Attack made: ... analysis of the attack is not possible... recording the attack is not possible... error: 1434@%!/5]

"Let the demons curse me," the Master exhaled. "And let the center of my power go back to the endless universe if that isn't 'One with the Sword'."

"One with the Sword," Elizabeth repeated. "Is my son at the One with the Sword Stage?"

Suddenly, the old man fell to his knees and touched the Queen's feet with his forehead.

"Your Highness, please let me take the Prince as my disciple."

This time, none of the soldiers allowed themselves to even think about class inequality. Who would dare call it such, after what had happened? To do so would mean that such a person lacked not only a heart, but also a brain as well.

Many of those who walked the Way of the Sword spent decades to acquire the skill 'One with the Sword'. Only a second and a threat to his life had been enough for Hadjar. If geniuses existed, Hadjar wasn't one.

He was a monster, hiding in the body of a two-year-old.

Alarm, followed by resignation, and then determination all quickly flitted across Elizabeth's face.

"If a carp has turned into a dragon, it is impossible to turn that dragon back into a carp again", she said, quoting the old saying of her people sorrowfully. "Rise, venerable Master."

The old man stood up, but didn't dare to look back at Elizabeth.

"I think South Wind is going to try and stop this, but if you can work it out with him, then you have my permission to teach Hadjar."

After speaking, the Queen ran to her son and scooped him up in a crushing embrace. The boy, dropping the dagger, closed his eyes and... fell asleep. It had been too hard for his body and mind to bear this exhausting adventure. And though he didn't fully understand what had happened, at that moment, while falling asleep, Hadjar knew one thing—he'd achieved his goal.

Now, not only would the best scholar of the Kingdom be teaching him, but also the best martial arts instructor as well!

**

Four years passed, seemingly in the blink of an eye. Hadjar lay on the hot sand, enthusiastically doing push-ups with two boulders weighing a bit over 20 pounds each on his back.

South Wind sat in the shade. He was fanning himself with a white fan and constantly adjusting his white robes.

"Where can I find the trees of Five Lives?"

"In the valley near the river Buffalo," Hadjar replied, mentally counting his third set of ten repetitions.

"Which star will lead you to the mountain of Loud Whispers?"

"The fifth one from the constellation of the Bow."

South Wind nodded and turned to the nearby Master. He closed his eyes, muttering something under his breath.

"Now it's your turn," the Scholar said, hurrying him along.

He couldn't wait to continue his examination, but he could only do it when it was his turn. That was their agreement.

"How many have you done, Prince?" The old man asked as he approached the sweaty boy who was grinding his teeth from the strain.

"Thirty-two... three-and-and--and-and-and thirty three-eee," Hadjar counted out, barely able to do so.

"Excellent," the Master nodded.

He walked over to the flat cobblestones, which were the same as the two that were currently on the Prince's back. The Master had personally carved them out of stone that the northern wind had batted against for two hundred years. Its energy permeated the rock and that would supposedly strengthen the Prince's weak body.

No matter how proud the Master was of his apprentice, he had to admit this simple fact. As strong as Hadjar's spirit and skills with the sword were, his body was equally weak.

As if a hero's soul had been placed in a peasant's body.

The heavens had been surprisingly unfair to the Prince, but his tenacity could overcome even their will.

"Then you could probably use a little help," and then, saying that, the Master put another cobblestone on Hadjar's back.

The weight of the stones was over sixty pounds now, and sweat rolled down the Prince's forehead. His elbows were trembling, and each new repetition caused him unthinkable pain. But this was the only way he could reach the required level by the age of sixteen and take the exam of

'The Black Gates' sect.

Even if he were to take just a moment to relax, he would end up forever stuck as the Prince of a small Kingdom on the outskirts of this boundless world. And he could forget about his freedom, adventure, and the wind that was calling out to him from the distance.

"Name the three stages of sword mastery," the Scholar suddenly asked.

The Master nodded his approval.

"It's 'One with the Sword,' followed by 'One with the World.' Finally, 'Wielder of the Sword.'"

"That is why not everyone can say that they mastered a sword or spear," the Master explained. "Many people are only able to truly master their weapons after reaching the stage of the Heaven Soldier."

Many people had to work hard on their weapon skills, but Hadjar was different. It turned out that he did have one talent. And while Fate had given him a weak body, his talent for the sword arts was difficult to overestimate. At the age of two, he'd been able to reach the 'One with the Sword' stage. He could feel his blade as well as his arms and legs, it was an extension of him.

He had possessed this skill almost from birth, while other people would be forced to study for years and grasp the skill through sweat and pain.

It was kind of funny, since he might never have found this out if it hadn't been for that one event that had left a bruise on his chest.

With his skill, he had earned the envy of many courtiers, who were so-called 'geniuses.' Some of them had also achieved unity with their swords at an early age, that is to say, around the age of twenty.

" 'One with the Sword' can hit an enemy that's up to five steps away," the Master recounted. 'One with the World' can use the energy of the world itself, and combine it with a blade to hit an enemy at a distance of twenty steps. Those who have fully mastered the sword no longer have need of it. The sword is in them, and everything around them becomes a sword. They see the Spirit of the Sword everywhere, even in a leaf or a drop of water. And they can hit an enemy with that Spirit at a distance of fifty paces."

It sounded like an old, Eastern fairy tale from back on Earth, but this was actually an achievable goal for Hadjar. After all, he'd seen with his own eyes how the Master's sword strike had cut a wooden doll at a distance of sixteen steps.

And so, combining his lectures with physical exercise, Hadjar spent the rest of the day trying to grow stronger. And the next day mimicked the previous one. And the day that came after it was also the same.

In any case, this was how it had to be.

Meanwhile, Primus rode in on a horse, passing by the 600-feet-tall lion-guards (majestic statues of stone and copper) at the Palace gates.

He was in a hurry to deliver some wonderful news. News that promised many riches, news that would bring great trouble with them, and change Hadjar's fate and the destiny of the whole Kingdom forever.

Chapter 8

"Repeat what you just said, but in more detail this time," the King requested.

It was unusually crowded in his cabinet today. Almost all of the top officials had gathered by the Kingdom map: the generals, South Wind, the Master, a few dukes, the chief justice, and someone else that Hadjar didn't know.

He had built a system of mirrors, and was now using it to watch the scene from the ventilation duct. It was quite convenient, but a bit risky as well. If someone were to inspect his hiding place, he would immediately be discovered. It was called Feeling. And, if one were to believe the Master, a Heaven Soldier was able to feel and see an ant at a distance of five miles away.

The locals didn't have such abilities, but each of the people present could've detected the Prince in the ventilation shaft. Luckily, they were too busy discussing the news Primus had brought to bother doing so.

"We've crushed the Bajek tribe," the man reported. "But an enemy cultivator's wounded General Lasset. I don't know how, but the Bajeks managed to send an cultivator at the level of Transformation against us."

The assembled people shook their heads, the younger ones even whistled. This stage was very impressive, by the standards of these backwoods. However, Hadjar wasn't impressed. As his Master often said, the whole sect of 'The Black Gates' was no more than a bunch of country bumpkins, when compared to the children of the Empire's nobles. In the Empire, a person was required to reach the stage of Transformation by the age of fourteen in order to be trained by a sect or attend one of the Academies.

The Prince simply couldn't reach that level, even if he were to try ten times harder that he already was. Realistically it was impossible. The Darnassus Empire had a lot more resources than were available here, on the outskirts.

"I made the decision to camp near the town of Silent Evening," Primus moved several figures, which served to depict his army, to a point on the map. "We hired the best healers we could find there and waited for any news. Alas, the town is small—four million people live there, no more than that. That's why we didn't ask them for food, as we would've ruined them with a demand to feed the 300,000 strong army."

"Did you have to hunt?" Elizabeth asked.

"Yes, my Queen," Primus nodded. "Fortunately, the local forests aren't able to give birth to strong creatures. We didn't encounter a single monster that was higher than the initial steps of the Awakening of Power."

Well, it would seem humans weren't the only ones in this world who could work on improving themselves. Animals could as well. South Wind had often told about such 'animals' that were actually stronger and smarter than most people. They, like the adepts, have their own paths for cultivation, with different stages, but that's not important right now.

"During one of the hunts, one of the senior officers fell from his horse and into a hole."

"Treasurer," the king called. "Give this officer an estate and a thousand servants. No one else in my kingdom has ever fallen off a horse so successfully."

The treasurer—a man with a simple face, but a very sharp mind—nodded and wrote something down on a scroll.

"Go on, brother."

"Descending into the cave after him, we discovered a vein of Solar ore."

Everyone there exchanged glances once again. Solar metal was made from Solar ore. It was much more durable and lightweight than simple steel or iron. And artifacts, which were a level higher than even Spiritual ones, were also made using Solar metal.

So, to put it simply, the officer had fallen into a hole that didn't contain mere riches, but a vein of ore whose cost exceeded the total value of the whole kingdom.

"How big is the vein?"

They had no reason to rejoice quite yet, maybe there wasn't much ore there. Possibly less than nothing. No one would set up a whole mine there for the sake of four or five pounds. A couple of miners with a military escort would be sent there. They would then bring the ore back to the treasury.

"It's no less than 6 miles deep and a bit less than 250 feet wide."

Everyone quieted down. Only South Wind closed his eyes slightly, and then said, "No less than a thousand tons, then. It's useless to measure its value in gold or in the Azure Coins of the Empire... It's just useless. I don't know how much such a vein could even cost."

"It's priceless," the King concluded. "And we have to do something about it, right now. To begin with, anyone who breathes even a word of this to outsiders will automatically become an enemy of the Kingdom. No one will be leaving the room until they take a blood oath."

No one argued, despite the fact that a blood oath was a rather serious thing to bind yourself to. If a person went back on their word, all the blood in their body instantly caught fire. As a result, their death was terrible and very painful.

"Primus, have your soldiers and that officer already taken the oath?"

"Immediately after the discovery," the Warlord nodded.

Haver sighed with relief. Such news could attract vultures from all around the world. And there were at least a dozen kingdoms, equally strong or even superior to Lidus, that might've tried something. Not to mention the family clans and sects.

"I wouldn't be so happy if I were you, Haver," Primus said. He was the only person in the Kingdom who could say something like that with impunity. "There's no way we'll be able to mine this vein and keep it secret from everyone."

"We will station a garrison there, build a fortress around it. Each soldier will be handpicked and all of them will take the blood oath."

"The Warlord is right," South Wind said. "It'll take at least a month to build a fort. The construction will draw attention, everyone will immediately be interested in it—in why Lidus needs a powerful stronghold so far from the border."

"It's not that far..."

"Four days, if you ride at a gallop," Primus shook his head. "All our outposts are two days away, by road. And this is twice as close."

There was now a heavy, oppressive silence in the room. The situation was a tricky one—they had the wealth, but it was impossible to get to it. They could easily lose their lives and the whole Kingdom if they make a single misstep.

"And what do you suggest?" Haver leaned back and looked pensive.

"We could appeal to 'The Black Gates' for help," South Wind suggested.

"Stop talking about these 'Gates' already," the Master snapped. "It's not their prey. We need to go to the Emperor. We'll be sending him a tribute next week anyway."

"Go to the Emperor," Haver repeated. "To the Emperor, you say, Honorable Master? And do you know that The Darnassus Empire is currently at war with the Lascan Empire?"

Everyone there looked at each other. They hadn't heard the news. Only the King and Queen were aware of such nuances of the world's politics.

"Can you imagine what'll happen if the Emperor finds out about this vein? One of his armies will be sent here! And how many warriors does his army have? One hundred and twenty or one hundred and thirty million? Even if he decides not to install some Governors here, how will we feed them all? Our forests will be completely cut down during their construction. Our cities will lose all their fields and reserves. The whole southern region will be ravaged. And that is the best case scenario, and what might happen in the worst… If worst comes to worst, ordinary people will be sent to do forced labor. They'll be turned into slaves and taken away, and the Imperial Governors will come here. This already happened with one of the other kingdoms, do you remember, Primus?"

The Warlord looked at the dumbfounded Queen and nodded.

"I remember, brother, I remember."

"I would like to point out, my King," one of the Dukes said. "That despite the possible devastation of the area, we will still thrive and…"

"Shut your mouth, Duke, before I shut it for you."

A palpable menace emanated from the King and the speaker instantly subsided and turned pale.

"Brother, calm down and think about this," Primus insisted. "Duke Remein has a point. Just think, what happens if we do give up this southern territory? There's nothing wrong with that! We'll get the peaceful times you and your wife covet so much. After all, who would dare attack us if the Emperor's own army was stationed here? I've heard that all the senior officers are no weaker than the level of the Heaven Soldier. And the generals are the Spirit Knights."

The Spirit Knights—words that inspired awe and disbelief in the hearts of ordinary people. For many, this stage of cultivation was nothing more than a part of the tales told to children at night, to put them to sleep. It was difficult to imagine that such monsters could really be living under the same sky as ordinary people.

"What are you trying to say, brother?"

"We would gain a lot more than we'd lose. If we did it right, we'd be able to get no less than ten, maybe even fifteen percent of the production. Do you have any idea how much money that is? We'd finally be able to build new, large cities, establish schools and invite high-ranking instructors to teach there. Cultivators would flock here, hoping to make a profit or be recruited into the Imperial Army."

Primus looked intently at a point on the map, indicating the place where the Solar ore had come close to the surface.

"We'll be able to acquire Techniques and knowledge that we couldn't have even dreamt of before. You and me, and the others as well… we'll get a chance to become Heaven Soldiers. A chance to grasp eternity—to be eligible for the title of cultivators, no longer mere mortals!"

"What must we sacrifice in return? The destinies of tens of millions of people?"

"The destinies of poor ragamuffins! Of miserable rodents, wallowing in the mud! What are their lives compared to ours? They live for just a century, and no more. On top of that, at the age of fifty, they stop working the fields, they stop being of any use to us. They become useless parasites, ones that waste precious resources. The Kingdom would be better off without them!"

"You forget yourself, brother!"

"No, you forget yourself, Haver! How long can we endure the ceaseless raids of the nomads and the attacks of our neighbors? How long will we be forced to eke out our miserable existence? You don't go to the Empire to pay tribute—I do! I've seen their 'border villages', which are richer and more beautiful than even our capital! I hate the ridicule of their petty nobles who don't even consider us to be peasants! I've seen beardless boys who are several times stronger than me. Why? Because, from the day they're born, they're stuffed full of herbs that we don't grow. They can buy drugs that we don't know how to make. They're taught Techniques we haven't even heard of!"

"Are you worried about the Kingdom, or are you giving in to your envy?" Haver whispered, but the whisper was more powerful than most screams.

Things got heated.

"I don't understand why you're so blind, brother."

"I'm not blind." Haver shook his head. "But you are, Primus. Do you remember what our father used to say? The life of a single peasant, even if they're old and infirm, is worth more than a dozen carts laden with gold. It is an honor to protect their lives. An honor worthy of a king."

"Father was weak and stupid, and so are you. That's why he made you King instead of me."

Haver grabbed the hilt of his sword, but Elizabeth's soothing touch stopped him. She merely shook her head and smiled warmly.

The rage was gone from the King's eyes, and his breathing was once more steady.

"You said it yourself—he made me King. And my Royal decree is as follows—we bury the pit of the Solar ore. We won't talk about it any further. We'll continue to live our lives as if it had never existed. That is all."

Primus hit the table angrily and left the room. A good half of the Dukes followed him out.

At that moment, Hadjar realized that he would have to train even harder (if that was even possible), because he had a gut feeling—it wouldn't end so easily.

Chapter 9

Despite Hadjar's fears, another year passed without incident. A few of his parents' quarrels led to Elaine being moved to his chambers.

Not because they didn't have vacant rooms available, but because it would otherwise have been very difficult for their bodyguards to ensure their safety. Elizabeth had this weird thing about making sure they were safe.

His five-year-old sister, was, in fact, a pain in the ass. She constantly followed him around like a puppy, which irritated the Master and South Wind. But, regardless, that nuisance was his sister, so the Prince endured it. And if the Prince could handle it, then the Scholar and the warrior had to put up with it as well.

And now, after letting all the students who'd paid for their training go home, the Master started working with Hadjar.

They stood on the parade ground.

The Master, moving the blade forward, struck a pose that was vaguely reminiscent of a classic attack stance in fencing. It should be immediately noted that a sword, in Lidus, was short and narrow. It was about a yard in length, and about two or, at most, three fingers in width. The most interesting thing was the weight of the sword, which was concentrated not in the blade itself, but in the handle, thanks to a weighty pommel. The handguard was almost non-existent.

It was easy to see that the Master's Technique would be focusing on speed coupled with thrusts at a distance. The faster the attack, the more elements were added, the more impressive and damaging the attacks would be.

Yesterday, Hadjar personally witnessed the Master behead 17 practice dummies, while remaining in one place. The dummies had been positioned in a semicircle around him, at a distance of 16 paces from the warrior. The local arts were true magic and they were amazing to behold.

And, of course, Hadjar had tried to analyze what he'd seen, using his neural network, but it had once again complained about not having enough data to work with.

"Move more smoothly," the Master instructed, watching Hadjar's movements. "But at the same time, move more swiftly as well."

They were practicing on the parade ground, leaving long, sandy furrows in their wake. From the outside, it might've seemed like just a slow, morning stretch. But in fact, they were practicing the basic Techniques.

"Tell me the first three levels of these Techniques," South Wind demanded.

Today, the Scholar was sitting in the shade again. Fanning himself, he kept adjusting his gold, spacious clothes. They were an interesting mix of a robe and a dressing gown, belted with a wide strap.

"The first is the level of Mortal, then the Spirit, and finally, the Earth."

The Scolar nodded and made a note in his scroll.

"Can you learn the Spirit Technique?"

"No," Hadjar answered. "I need to reach the Heaven Soldier stage before I can do that."

"And that's why a lot of people believe that a practitioner can only be considered a true cultivator once they reach the stage of the Heaven Soldier!"

South Wind was often irritated when someone in the Palace called themselves a cultivator. In his opinion, most of them weren't even close to it.

While the Scholar was grumbling something unintelligible under his breath, the young but already beautiful Elaine was watching her big brother. She noted his black hair, gathered into a tight bun, and his blue eyes; she had a handsome brother. And he was moving around amusingly, a sword in hand.

She'd seen her father moving around, too; he was swift and as sharp as a Death-Tiger. Hadjar floated through the air, moving his sword as if he were guiding a toy boat along the surface of a spring stream.

"Tell me, Hadjar, how do you distinguish a Heaven Soldier from a simple warrior?" the Master asked suddenly.

These kinds of questions were usually asked by the Scholar, not the warrior. Hadjar thought about it for a while, trying to find the catch.

"The Heaven Soldier is able to fly, to summon fire and water. They've grasped eternity and can live for many thousands of years."

"That's right," the old man nodded and stopped demonstrating the Technique.

The Prince stopped practicing as well.

"Now, look at this and tell me what you see."

The Master closed his eyes. His breathing became steady, and the sand under his feet suddenly started to spin, rising higher and higher into the air. A moment later, a faint, sandy tornado was whirling around the Master. It had been summoned by the swirl of unleashed force.

[Urgent message! Activation of force has been detected in your vicinity!]

He'd noticed that on his own. Sometimes, the neural network was more annoying than helpful. But, to the Prince's surprise, that wasn't the last message.

[Expected power: 2 units!]

I'm sorry, what?!

Hadjar didn't get a chance to think about what that message meant. The Master exhaled sharply and swung his sword. Suddenly, a fire sparrow appeared and, leaving a trail of smoke behind it, flew for about forty steps, then crashed into a wall, melting a section of it the size of a tennis ball.

The Prince staggered back and instinctively raised his sword in a defensive position.

Now he saw the Master in a completely different way.

"Are you a Heaven Soldier?!"

After a moment's silence, the sound of two people laughing rang out. Both the old man in short training pants and the old man in the golden clothes were highly amused.

"No, your Highness," the Master shook his head. "I just showed you the Mortal Technique."

The Prince assessed the damage. Perhaps the tennis ball sized amount of damage to the wall didn't look very impressive, but... Hadjar had seen something truly magical for the first time. Despite the fact that he'd been able to cut a dummy with his sword at a distance of three paces, he still sometimes found himself questioning everything around him.

"Venerable Master," Hadjar fell to his knees and lowered his forehead to the sand, "please, teach me!"

The Master lifted the Prince back onto his feet immediately and shook him off. He didn't want the Queen to see that her son was bowing to him.

"Of course I'll teach you, your Highness," the old man smiled.

He went over to a small chest, not far from the barrel that had been pivotal in Hadjar's apprenticeship five years earlier.

The old man put his hand on the lid and it opened. Neither untold treasures nor amazing artifacts were inside. There was only one old, battered scroll. The Master handed it to Hadjar.

Having already given the order to record the scroll to his neural network, the Prince unrolled it.

"The Scorched Falcon Technique", Hadjar read. It was Volume One.

The Scorched Falcon was one of the local fauna's magical birds. Say, for example, that adult birds could've reached the Alpha Level. It was the equivalent of the Spirit Knight among people. One such Falcon, with its wingspan of twelve yards, could've burned down half of their Kingdom.

[Recording information in the 'Detailed description of Techniques'... A register of 'The Scorched Falcon Technique' has been established]

"Is this the right scroll, Master?" Hadjar smiled a little devilishly. "I saw only a Fried Sparrow."

"Shame on you, your Highness," the elder frowned. "You won't find another scroll of the Mortal Technique in this entire Kingdom. I only have this one because I went on an amazing adventure in my youth. And it took me almost two centuries to comprehend it."

Hadjar read the contents of the scroll once more. There was little he understood, but, fortunately, the text was accompanied by detailed drawings. They showed the way in which he needed to circulate his energy, and through which nodes he needed to do it, in order to produce the 'Fried Sparrow.'

"Tell me, Prince," South Wind spoke up again. "What kind of Technique is this?"

"This is a Weapon Technique."

"And what other Techniques do you know?"

"Besides the Weapon Technique?"

The old man nodded, continuing to fan himself.

Hadjar could answer this question even without the help of the neuronet. He remembered it easily enough.

"I know of The Body Techniques, The External Energy Techniques and The Internal Energy Techniques."

"And do you now understand what they're intended for?"

The Prince looked at the scorched wall again.

"Do the Techniques allow us to use the power of the higher stages?"

"Not exactly, Your Highness," the Scholar disagreed. "Mostly, they allow us to use our current level of power better. In other words, a Heaven Soldier doesn't really need any Techniques to create fire."

"But if a Formation practitioner were to create it with the help of a Technique," Hadjar continued, "then their fire would be stronger."

The Scholar and the Master exchanged glances.

"I can say both 'yes' and 'no' to that," the Master sighed, scooping up the cup from the barrel. "The world of martial arts is complex and multifaceted, Your Highness. And you have yet to see even a true glimpse of it, let alone actually scratch the surface. Now, try to memorize the contents of the scroll. It'll take you at least a year."

Hadjar nodded, very glad he had the neuronet since, as it turned out, it was quite useful. Thanks to it, he'd already remembered all of the contents, even the commas. Even if, admittedly, there were no punctuation marks in the local language...

"It says 'Volume One' here," Hadjar pointed to the heading. "Are there any others?"

"The Techniques are often divided into volumes. Their complexity increases with each volume, demanding more from a practitioner with each higher volume," the Master returned the cup to the barrel and washed his face. "I've seen it with my own eyes, Your Highness. A practitioner at the Heaven Soldier level summoned a fiery bird with a wingspan of almost three yards with this Technique. But the Scorched Falcon, it…"

"Adult specimens have a wingspan of twelve yards."

"That's right, Your Highness," the Master nodded. "What you're holding in your hands are just the basics. And yet, you could still count the number of Techniques of the Mortal level in our Kingdom on the fingers of one hand."

"Does that mean that the second scroll would be at the Spiritual Level?"

"Exactly, my Prince."

Hadjar looked at the scroll, then at his teachers, and then again toward the east.

The wind blew. It told him stories. It called to him.

The Prince was weak.

He couldn't answer the call of the wind.

Nevertheless, at that moment, a smile of anticipation spread across his face. Every day, he could see the way forward more clearly. The path leading to his cherished goal and freedom.

The path which would lead him to the vast expanses of this amazing world, to its secrets and dangers, to everything it had to offer, something that Hadjar had been deprived of in his previous life.

And while this brief moment of enlightenment was happening, he didn't know that the wheel of Fate had already spun. That his dreams weren't going to come true.

At that very moment, the Warlord was on his way back to the capital to celebrate his seventh birthday. He was the King's brother and the Tribute Collector for the Empire.

Primus was coming.

Chapter 10

Only a week was left before the celebration, but the atmosphere in the Palace was tense. Primus and Haver pretended that they'd forgotten all the insults they had hurled at one another and ruled the country peacefully, at least in public, but in reality... Everyone felt that they'd had not just a tiff, but a truly horrible argument.

But Hadjar was worried about something else entirely. And it wasn't the fact that he would be introduced to his future wife again. Maybe she'd grow up to become a real beauty. True, her family had a lot of money, but the Prince still felt like a dog, a pet more than a son. As if his own father had gotten him a 'bitch' to 'mate' with.

Of course, for a seven-year-old boy to have such thoughts should've been impossible, but Hadjar had lived another life before his current one. As a legacy of that previous life, he'd inherited the neuronet, which was acting strangely at that moment.

[The interface is being reconfigured. The upgrade to a new version is complete. The current version is 0.18.1!]

Hadjar didn't understand what the hell it had reconfigured and where the update had come from. There weren't even any normal toilets in Lidus, let alone a patch for the neuronet. And yet, the network was miraculously updating itself. Perhaps this was due to the fact that he shouldn't have had it in the first place.

The Prince had been reborn in a new body, with a new nervous system. His old body had remained in the other world, and the neuronet should've been left behind too. So, taking into account the fact that local people not only believed in the existence of a 'soul', but had proved it was actually real, then... Most likely, the neuronet was attached to his soul, as a sort of energy component.

And since Hadjar had been training and had managed to get to the sixth stage of the Bodily Nodes by the age of seven (which was an impressive achievement by the standards of the Kingdom), the network also developed alongside him, absorbing the energy of, as the locals called it, 'heaven and earth'.

[Reconfiguration completed. Ability to process new analytical information has been acquired. How should the new information be displayed?]

Hadjar pondered the question and then decided on to the simplest option.

"In tabular form," he said, deciding to use the format in which the neuronet had initially shown him information.

Immediately, a table appeared before his eyes ...

Name	Hadjar
Level of Cultivation	The Bodily Nodes. The 6th stage.
Strength	0,4
Dexterity	0,7
Physique	0,2
Energy points	0,5

"Fuck..." the Prince said.

The new function of the neuronet more than made up for all its shortcomings.

According to the Master, someone else's level of cultivation was one of the most important secrets anyone had. And no one could find such information out easily. If you knew in advance what your opponent was capable of in battle, you would have an incredible advantage. That's why, according to some rumors, special equipment used to identify the level of enemy power existed.

Hadjar had a clear advantage. He could find out how powerful others were and have it shown to him in great detail, with clear, precise numbers.

This new discovery had to be tested right away!

That's why the Prince ran out into the corridor, rushing toward the parade ground. The warriors were already training, and the Master was sedately pacing around, supervising them. That's who Hadjar ended up scanning.

Name	Master
Level of Cultivation	?????????
Strength	?????????
Dexterity	?????????
Physique	?????????
Energy points	?????????

The Prince slammed his hand against his face in frustration and spent another hour trying to find out why the capabilities of the neuronet were so lackluster. It was only able to analyze someone that didn't exceed his own level of cultivation, or, more precisely, those who were equal to his own level or below it.

"Very well," the Prince sighed, sitting down on the steps. "At least I can monitor my own progress and recognize those who are stronger than me."

Despite these 'clever' words, he'd hoped that the neuronet could show him more about people at a higher level than his. On the other hand, he still didn't even understand what 'Energy Points' meant. Did this mean that the software was able to calculate the power of cultivator?

Taking into account that, during the demonstration of the 'Scorched Falcon' Technique, a message about the '2E units' had popped up, that was most likely the case. This meant that the Master's single strike had been four times stronger than the whole of Hadjar's current level.

You couldn't even call it a one-off trick since the old man hadn't looked at all tired afterward.

"Why," Hadjar shook his head.

His mentors were right—he hadn't even truly seen the martial arts world yet. The fact that he could do twenty push-ups with a weight of 90 pounds on his back at the age of seven didn't mean anything. He was no stronger than an ant.

A long and arduous journey lay before him, but Hadjar refused to give up.

No, he was too motivated…

"Your Highness?"

The Master distracted the Prince from his thoughts. Having noticed his disciple, he'd walked away from the warriors and approached Hadjar.

"I was sure you wouldn't let yourself miss class because of the holiday."

The Prince blinked a few times and berated himself for his laziness. He really had been planning to miss out on training... However, he no longer had any such plans. Not because of his instructor's words, but because he'd realized his own weakness.

"Change clothes and get to the training grounds," the old man hurried him.

The Prince followed him and, after a few moments, was practicing the basic sword technique enthusiastically. Moving from one rack to the next, he fought his shadow, dodging attacks and punches while throwing out his own.

He rarely sparred with someone. None of the warriors could keep up with Hadjar's talent, nor his hard work.

The Master had said that it was a rare phenomenon for a seven-year-old child to be able to start exploring the Mortal technique of the sword. Most warriors were only able to master the main basic skills by the time they turned sixteen.

Many of the warriors present, if put in front of a practice dummy and given a sword, despite their strength, wouldn't always hit their intended target. They wouldn't be able to control the sword like an extension of their body.

Tap, chop, pierce, rising slash, strike on the way down, dodge, parry, sword drawing and sheathing it back—all of these were intertwined in a single web. And if someone else needed years to understand all these basics of handling the 'King of Weapons' (which the sword was), Hadjar... had known how to do so from the very beginning, all thanks to his instincts.

And so, the years passed.

Five years, to be exact.

And if someone performed a hundred strikes, Hadjar performed a thousand.

If someone made a thousand attacks, Hadjar made ten thousand.

If someone drew their sword five hundred times, Hadjar did it five thousand times.

He trained ten times harder than ordinary people because he knew that it was the only way he could achieve his goal in this world. And while the rest of the kids his age had to be forced to train, he would go to the parade ground every day, refusing to take a break. He made his father proud but worried his mother.

"Your Highness," the Master called.

The Prince stopped practicing and turned around.

The old man was carrying a wooden dummy to the parade ground. One that he'd never brought in before. It was the size of an adult and had nine red circles on it, denoting targets to aim for with the sword.

The targets were the throat, heart, joints, abdomen, center of mass and forehead. Most sword strikes should be aimed at these points on the body.

"I haven't missed for a year," Hadjar got angry because the dummy babies practiced with had been brought to him. The Prince ignored a few envious glances that were cast his way.

"That's with a stationary opponent, my Prince," the Master smiled in a slightly bloodthirsty way.

He put the dummy down, then put a wooden sword it in its hands and placed his own hand on the dummy's back. A moment later, Hadjar saw the dummy begin to spin on its own, without any mechanisms, his mouth open in shock.

"Please, your Highness, go right ahead."

Hadjar approached the dummy cautiously at first, and then more confidently. He'd kept his weighted wooden sword used in training. Assessing the speed of the dummy's rotation and the maximum distance it could reach, he rushed in to attack.

He moved, almost touching the sand with his chest as he used a lightning-fast strike, cutting the dummy with an upward slash. Such skill and speed drew astonished gasps from the audience. No one could believe that a seven-year-old boy was capable of such a feat

A breath later, lots of giggling followed the gasps.

The Prince was amazed. Even the paint on the targets had been left untouched. His blow had struck the broad side of the dummy's sword. However, he hadn't just been blocked, but also parried, and the Prince received a painful poke to his chest as a result.

Collapsing on the sand, he growled, sounding like a small wolf, jumped to his feet and rushed in to once again attack it.

Thrusting with his sword, Hadjar moved his wrist, making the tip of the blade twist as he lunged. This time, he easily bypassed the dummy's attempt to block him and almost managed to reach its throat, but then the dummy moved. It lowered its sword slightly, changing the trajectory of his own sword and, with its free hand, tripped him up, once again knocking the Prince down.

The Prince jumped up again and doggedly resumed his assault. Every time, he came up with something new to try. He'd dive under the punches, but then he'd just get pushed away.

He'd go around the blocks, but he'd end up knocked down.

Hadjar was furious, he even ended up using 'One with the Sword' and reached out with it toward the enemy, when he was within range, but he only managed to leave a small scratch on the wooden blade.

The warriors, tired of watching his fruitless attempts, went back to sparring, and Hadjar continued charging the dummy.

He attacked it a hundred, possibly even two hundred times. He didn't care about the bruises and cuts he was receiving, he wasn't planning on going to the feast until he'd defeated the dummy.

And, after he'd once again been thrown to the ground, he suddenly noticed one small detail.

The dummy didn't move.

Yes, it waved its long, wooden arms around, dealing very painful blows, but... it wasn't moving its body. The dummy was stationary, buried in the sand, while Hadjar jumped around it like a crazed insect. It was like a stream trying to cut through rock.

But would the stream even do that? Would it try to break through the mountain, spending billions of years on such a stupid endeavor? Or would it simply overtake the rock and continue forward?

The wind blew.

Hadjar hadn't heard the wind for a long time, but right then, he thought he could discern a little more of his old friend's 'words' than before.

Once again, the same as five years ago, he stood on the sand and listened to the world around him, looking inside himself and trying to feel what he saw there. He tried to feel what had brought him this new inspiration he'd been waiting for while training hard every day.

The warriors stopped to watch again, able to feel that something strange was happening.

The Master opened his eyes slightly. He hadn't hoped that Hadjar would be able to defeat the dummy.

The Prince, shocking everyone at the parade ground, put the sword back into its cloth sheath. And so, the seven-year-old boy went toward the dummy, unarmed. It swung its sword, aiming at his unprotected forehead, but it failed to even touch a hair on his head.

Hadjar made a subtle movement with his feet, moved his center of gravity and walked away from the impact. He dodged the blow smoothly and calmly, like a leaf floating in the spring wind.

The dummy aimed its next attack at his stomach, but it once more struck only air. Hadjar spun on his heel, dodging the blade by a hair's breadth, as it barely missed his back. Then he slipped forward and stopped near his enemy.

His sword flashed and the dummy froze a moment later, as Hadjar's blade had struck all 9 of the vital areas, drawing paint from each of them.

"Congratulations, your Highness," the Master applauded. "Now you can truly be considered 'One with the Sword'."

The Prince was breathing heavily, but he was happy. He now knew what was missing from his swordsmanship; he hadn't been controlling his own body properly.

Before, he'd used to make a dozen unnecessary moves, whereas now he knew that he really only needed one. He'd to make five different attacks, but now he could smoothly position himself and make just the single, necessary attack.

"Really?" Hadjar asked, sheathing his sword.

"I've told you, my Prince, that the world of martial arts is deeper than the boundless cosmos. And if you were to compare a thousand swordsmen who are 'One with the Sword', you wouldn't find two with the same level of skill."

The Prince nodded, understanding what the man was saying. There was always a mountain higher than the one 'just climbed. There was always a practitioner who would be better than you. All these stages and levels gave only an approximate direction to follow, while one's power depended on the person themselves.

"I'll admit, I'm surprised you were able to grasp the basics of the Footsteps Technique so quickly, despite the fact that I haven't taught them to you yet." Then the Master looked around his domain—a sandy parade ground. "I sometimes feel sorry for you, my Prince."

Hadjar raised an eyebrow in surprise.

"If you'd been born on the outskirts of the Empire, or in some strong clan, your name would've been revered in the entire valley, in as little as a hundred or two hundred years. I've lived a long life and will soon go on to my eternity, but I've never seen a swordsman as talented as you," the Master shook his head. "Apparently, that old saying is right: luck is also a strength. And despite the fact that I've had the opportunity to teach a genius, I'll never get to see him bloom and conquer the glory he deserves."

The Prince wanted to argue that he still had a chance to join 'The Black Gates', but then Elizabeth appeared on the stairs.

"Hadjar, the feast has almost begun and you're not dressed!" The

Queen called out to him and turned toward the children of the nobles. "You shouldn't linger either."

"Yes, my Queen!" the kneeling warriors shouted in chorus.

Hadjar looked at his Master who was taking the dummy back to the warehouse. For some reason, he had the strange feeling that he was seeing the old man for the last time.

Chapter 11

 With half an hour left before the feast, Hadjar had to endure being dressed by seven maids at once. After that, he meditated. That's what everyone called it. The Prince had hated using the word at first, but then he got used to it. 'Meditation' was an OK term. On Earth, it had sounded a bit strange and even silly, but here it was appropriate.

What else could you call what he was doing?

He was sitting in the lotus position, breathing steadily, clearing his mind and trying to absorb energy. Fortunately, he could now feel it much better than before. At first, he'd even doubted its existence. Now, after getting to the sixth stage of the Bodily Nodes, with many points on his body open to it, Hadjar could actually feel the energy.

It was like the feeling preceding a thunderstorm. Or when the air is too electrified. Like someone nearby had turned on a huge magnet. It felt like someone sizing you up murderously for half an hour, something even the most skeptical people would notice eventually.

So, something did exist in this world. This something made Hadjar stronger, and at that moment, that was all he cared about.

Hadjar was fully aware that meditating was necessary. That's why, while the rest of the children slept instead of really trying to absorb the energy, he did his best. Although… it was difficult.

It was as difficult as trying to capture wind in a pot or sunlight in a box. The only difference being that he was slowly succeeding, and his level of cultivation was already considered abnormally high for his age. But the Prince knew that, apart from his talent for swordsmanship, he didn't possess any outstanding abilities.

This meant that had the nobles of the Kingdom been raising their children better, they would've been able to achieve the same results.

"Hadjar, honey," the door opened and Elizabeth appeared at the door.

She was wearing a dress embroidered with amber and gold, with a silk belt that emphasized her thin waist. Jade flower buds had been woven into her hair and her eyelashes shimmered with color. Her clear, green eyes glowed with love and warmth.

He had a beautiful mother, whom he probably loved more than anyone else in this world. He'd never had a mother before, nor a father or sister, for that matter. He loved them all.

The Prince ran up to the Queen like a little boy (which he was) and hugged her tightly, leaning his head against her belly.

"That's enough," Elizabeth laughed and smoothed his long hair.

He was wearing black and gold robes, as well as a wreath on his head. All of this was terribly inconvenient, but the Prince had already grown accustomed to such eccentricities, therefore, he wasn't terribly put out.

Calmly ignoring the mocking glances, he walked down the corridor, holding hands with his mother and sister. Many people thought he behaved too 'childishly', in a manner unworthy of a genius swordsman, but Hadjar didn't care. Nobody could forbid him from enjoying this moment.

Alas, it didn't last long. The jasper doors opened and they entered a spacious hall full of pillars. It resembled the feast halls of Scandinavian peoples back on Earth.

It was a spacious room, with a ceiling so high it couldn't be easily seen, and wide columns which were decorated with carved patterns and bas-reliefs. They depicted scenes of heroes fighting huge monsters and beasts, as well as scenes of great battles.

The hall was huge, even by local standards. At least five thousand people were now gathered at its long, wide tables. And at the head of it all were the 'main chairs'—the golden thrones—where the Royal couple were supposed to sit. So far, only Haver IV was there. The King.

As was the tradition in this world, he wore his armor to all celebrations. Not a gilded one, not an armor decorated with expensive stones and silks, but the armor he really used in battle. It carried the smell of combat with it, was covered in many dents and scratches, and made from a special ore. It was said to be an old Mortal artifact that had been inherited by the family.

Wearing it, Hadjar's father looked even more powerful and unapproachable than usual. He looked like a mountain in the face of an impending storm: utterly unaffected by it all.

Forgoing the crown, the King instead wore a leather strap with metal inserts. Haver never wore his crown because he believed that, first and foremost, he was a warrior who defended the country. Being King came after that.

Perhaps he was wrong, but the people only loved him more for it.

"Her Majesty, Queen Elizabeth Sammen!" A majordomo announced the newcomers.

All of the five thousand people stood up and bowed simultaneously. They straightened their backs only after a couple of seconds had passed, and only after the Queen nodded in turn.

"Her Highness, Princess Elaine Durant!"

They didn't bow this time, just lowered their heads. Elaine, embarrassed, hid behind her mother. This earned her a couple of kind smiles and even a few people applauding, which made her even more embarrassed. The royal couple believed in raising their children simply.

They had the best clothes, the best food, and, as much as the knowledge of the kingdom allowed, they were given the best potions. However, they didn't have the nobles' snobbery.

"And now we welcome the man of the hour," this time, the King made the announcement personally. "My son—Prince Hadjar Duran!"

A flurry of applause filled the hall after they gave him a synchronous bow (which hadn't been as low as they'd given the Queen, to be honest). Most of the guests welcomed the Prince honestly, although, for plenty of others, it was just a formality. News of his phenomenal success at such a young age, both as a warrior and as a scholar, had spread throughout the country.

Residents of the outskirts predicted that he would be a king in the future, as Haver wouldn't be able to sit on the throne forever. The people only had good things to say about Hadjar. Everyone knew that he cared about his servants and was always polite and courteous to them. They loved him much more than the haughty children of nobles.

Hadjar, smiling, reached the thrones and sat to his father's left. The Queen and her daughter sat to Haver's right. This was all according to the rules of etiquette.

"Let the feast begin!" The King declared.

Countless servants placed various dishes on the tables. The inhabitants of the Kingdom were also being treated to a feast in the squares of all the Kingdom's cities and were even being served the best vines. The birthdays of the Royals were celebrated by the whole country—they were almost public holidays. The people weren't against plenty of free food and drink.

The fun began. People danced in the squares, and many traveling circuses performed a variety of acts.

Hadjar wasn't paying any attention to the clowns performing for the enjoyment of the guests in the Palace. Their tricks were of little interest to him. After all, he knew a lot about the worth of true cultivators, so the circus didn't impress him.

He just enjoyed his meal. The selection of food on offer was amazing: from simple reindeer to the meat of a fierce-boar, which had been at the stage of Awakening of Power (which is almost the same as the Formation Stage in the human world).

"Slow down, dear," the Queen whispered across the table. "It's not the last time you'll get to eat."

"Okay, ma - ma," Hadjar whispered back, his mouth full.

The Queen and the Princess looked at him as if he were an uncouth barbarian, and his father secretly encouraged him. A warrior had to eat a lot to grow strong. Haver couldn't blame his son for wanting to be powerful.

The only thing that was spoiling the King's mood was the absence of his older brother from the festival. The feast wasn't fun without Primus. Or at least Haver thought so since he'd gotten used to the fact that they were always together. Their different opinions on how to run the country had recently alienated them from each other. But the King still believed they could set aside their differences.

They'd used to argue in the past, but it never stopped them from fighting side by side in thousands of different battles.

"Honey, people are watching," Elizabeth whispered in his ear.

The King snapped out of it and immediately smiled happily while ruffling his son's hair. No one should see the King looking troubled at a feast. You never knew what they might think about it and if it would make them uneasy.

Fortunately, Haver didn't have to worry for long.

"The honorable Warlord, Primus Duran!"

The people stopped eating, stood up, and bowed faintly. Primus was feared and respected, but not that loved. He was too sharp and even dangerous to be loved.

"Brother, I'm glad to see you!" The King rose and spread his hands, beckoning his brother over to embrace him. "What kept you so long?"

Primus came over and the brothers slapped each other on the back. It looked as if mountains were fraternizing, or at least it seemed that way to Hadjar. These two mighty warriors were similar to bears, both scary and exciting to be around.

"I wanted to stop by the castle," Primus moved to the foot of the thrones. "To pick up a gift for the young Prince."

"Son, thank your uncle."

"Thank you, uncle Primus." The Prince bowed his head.

Any normal kid would've just grabbed the gift, but Hadjar wasn't normal. He'd managed to live a life trapped in an unmoving body and had therefore learned to understand people. Though his gut had been dulled by years of living a quiet life, his self-preservation instincts were warning him that something wasn't right.

"Bring the gift!" Primus waved his hand impatiently.

Four soldiers came through the door and their appearance shocked everyone there. The King, who'd been sitting on his throne, rose anxiously.

The four soldiers from the Imperial army, clad in green armor, marched in. Their black cloaks brushed against the floor and their helmets covered their faces, but a single glance at them was enough to tell they were strong practitioners.

"Analyze," Hadjar ordered.

[Processing request ... The request cannot be processed]

They were at the Formation Stage or even the Transformation Stage. They could've been elites in the army of the Kingdom, and yet they were ordinary privates in the Imperial army.

They carried a heavy chest in their hands, and when they reached the King, they set it noisily down on the table, without even bowing.

"What is the meaning of this, brother?" Haver asked quietly.

"A gift for the Prince!" Primus shouted, ignoring the King and opening the chest violently.

There was a sword in a sheath of light inside, on velvet bedding. Grabbing it by the hilt, the warlord pulled the blade out from its sheath, making everyone inhale sharply. The blade glowed with a barely noticeable, dull golden glow in the light of the torches and lamps

"A Spiritual artifact." The people whispered in awe.

"Forged from Solar metal..." The rest of the guests commented.

Hadjar made a barely perceptible step back.

What the hell?! Why would Primus give me such a gift!? That sword's worth a whole Palace! He thought.

"What does this mean, Warlord Primus?!" Haver shouted, resting his hand on the hilt of his own sword.

"It means treason," a quiet voice spoke, and the room plunged into silence once again.

A thin, middle-aged man walked into the hall. He was dressed in simple black robes and had an aura of such great power around him that it was difficult for Hadjar to breathe. He queried the neural network, but it couldnɔt show him anything.

[?????]

With a wave of his hand, he lit up the hall as if it were the middle of the day, and it became clear to Hadjar that he was seeing a Heaven Soldier for the first time in his life.

"The Governor?" Haver seemed to recognize him. "Weɔre happy to welcome an Imperial official to our celebration, but may I ask what youɔre doing here?"

"I came to see the festival," the cultivator grimaced, glancing at the people around him with his most disdainful look. "If that's what you can even call it, Haver... Well, it's not like I'd expected more from your village."

The soldiers grabbed their swords, but the King waved his hand and they froze. Even if the entire army had been there, they would've hardly been able to touch the Heaven Soldier. Of course, it would've been impossible for them to execute him for merely insulting the King.

"Honestly, I hadn't expected such stupidity from you, Haver. For centuries, your... backwoods have paid tribute to us. Sure, it was a pittance, but you paid it on time and without trying to cheat us. And so, you didn't get into any trouble."

"We're still paying it."

"Enough!" the cultivator barely raised his voice, and yet many of those who'd been standing next to him fell unconscious.

A wave of inconceivable power reached Hadjar and almost bent him in half.

Haver made a strange sign and it became easier to breathe. Out of the corner of his eye, the Prince noticed that a slightly shimmering sphere now covered the throne.

"You pretend you don't know you've committed treason!" The cultivator raised his chin proudly. He was clearly mocking what was happening. "You've hidden the Solar ore from us, Haver. And that's a clear betrayal of the Emperor."

The King looked at his brother with disbelief and pain etched on his face, but Primus only gave him a predatory smile in response.

"We are not the subjects of the Empire!"

"Don't kid yourself, Haver," the adept shrugged his words off like a bug. "The Empire simply wasn't interested in you before because... you had nothing. We just maintained a border town at your expense. Your tribute was barely enough to cover the expenses."

'What?! Our entire Kingdom was only able to feed one city of the Empire!' Hadjar had known that he'd been living in a well while an entire ocean raged around him, but he'd had no idea that the ocean was so vast.

"You know the penalty for treason, Haver."

The King grabbed his sword, but the adept just waved his hand and the world froze. The sphere burst like a soap bubble and no one else was able to move; they could only manage to breathe with difficulty.

It was the power of a Heaven Soldier. He'd turned them into weak-willed slaves without any Techniques or artifacts by just using his desire and will.

"Our King has betrayed us!" Primus roared, walking through the rows. "He's weak and stupid! He doesn't want to admit the simple fact that our Kingdom's no more than a village on the outskirts of this world! He had the chance to change that, but he didn't want to... We found a Solar ore vein and it's so large that the Emperor himself would've been interested in us!"

While the Warlord talked, the cultivator stood around and examined his nails idly. He had no interest in what was happening in the room. He thought they were uncouth hillbillies who were wallowing in manure.

"He's a traitor to the Empire, and to his own crown! The only punishment the traitor deserves is death. And because I understand that you were deceived by his weakness, I'm offering you one last chance. Those who wish to serve me, your new King…"

Primus swung his sword, leaving a long, deep furrow in the stone floor.

"… take a step beyond that line."

The cultivator remained motionless, but suddenly, all of the five thousand people were freed. Some of them crawled over the line like beaten dogs while crying in fear.

Some of the people glanced at the Royal family and, after bowing their heads, walked humbly toward the line.

Only a few hundred out of the five thousand people remained motionless.

There were both men and women among them, even children.

They remained faithful to their King, the man who'd devoted his whole life to them.

"The poor fools." Primus sighed and suddenly began to emit the same power the cultivator had been emitting earlier.

Somehow, Hadjar's uncle had reached the stage of the Heaven Soldier, and that could only mean one thing—they didn't stand a chance.

Chapter 12

"Brother," the King's voice showed no fear nor trepidation, only a little bit of hope. "Let my children go."

Primus turned to Haver and Hadjar realized that they couldn't expect anything good to happen here.

The look in the Warlord's eyes was cold. He waved his hand toward the entrance. A black wind gusted out from his fingers. It slammed into the heavy doors and opened them as easily as if they'd been made of paper.

"Greet your new Prince, my son, Eren Duran!"

Once again, the room went silent. No one had known that the Warlord had a son. Eren looked to be at least four years old. He stood at the entrance, looking like a smaller, younger version of his father.

He had a cold look about him. Standing in a haughty pose, wearing black and gold clothes, the same as Hadjar's, he really did look like a Prince.

"Did you really think that Solar ore could've been found with simple luck?" Primus whispered, approaching the thrones. "How easily you believed the fairy tale of a soldier falling into the pit, brother!"

He almost spat out the last word. Primus was so full of hatred and malice that they poured from his mouth.

"All this time.." The King shook his head. "How old is he?"

"Four."

"Four..."Apparently, something had happened four years ago, but the Prince didn't know what. He only remembered that his father and uncle had gone on a campaign at the time. They'd taken almost two hundred warriors with them, but less than half of them had returned.

Hadjar had never been told anything about that trip...

"It was an accident, Primus. Just an accident..."

"Shut up!" The Warlord swung his hand.

The same black wind from before now whirled in his palm. One glance at that miniature tornado was enough to make Hadjar dread what was to come. It had enough concentrated power to destroy the entire hall.

Is this how I die?

"Run!" Haver spread his arms and a powerful rush of force threw his family toward a secret passage hidden behind the wall to the rear of the thrones.

Hadjar felt strong, but gentle hands lifting him up.

Elizabeth, taking the children into her arms, ran down the narrow corridor. She pressed Elaine to her chest and the Prince, because he was rather tall, she carried over her shoulder. This meant that Hadjar saw everything. He didn't want to look but ended up seeing it anyway.

He watched as Primus' hand slowly moved toward the King's neck. Slowly, but with the inevitability of an executioner's ax.

He saw that the King had raised his sword to defend himself, and how it crumbled under the might of the black wind.

He saw blood coat the walls, the leather strap falling to the floor. With a metallic clinking, the inserts rolled along the now scarlet painted boards. Witnessing this, Hadjar felt something break inside him.

"Stop, Your Majesty!" Elizabeth's personal bodyguards appeared ahead. As a matter of fact, all of them were females.

The Queen let out a sigh of relief and stopped, but a moment later, she was cursing the fact she couldn't take out her sword without letting go of one of the children.

The warriors didn't lower their weapons.

They looked at their Queen, their spears and shields held at the ready.

"Please, don't make us do this," the lead bodyguard almost begged her.

"What did he promise you?"

"Please..."

"What did he promise you?!" Elizabeth snarled at them.

Her green eyes burned with a mad rage and despair. Behind her, through the magical seals superimposed on the secret door, soldiers were already making their way through.

"That we'll be able to become stronger," one of the bodyguards said with mild anger coloring his tone.

"Stronger... Damn the world of martial arts! It turns animals into humans and humans into animals."

"That's enough, my Queen. Give it up."

A thunderbolt struck somewhere behind them. Or so it seemed to Hadjar. In reality, Primus had hit the wall with his black wind.

"How long do you think you can elude me, Elizabeth?!" He laughed, moving ahead of the soldiers, now wearing green armor.

The Queen's warriors stood in front of them—all of the fighters she'd personally selected. Behind them were the Empire's soldiers, their curved blades out. Her Majesty stood, paralyzed by indecision. At that moment, Elizabeth was no longer a cultivator or the ruler of a kingdom. She was a mother, and she didn't know which of her children she should put down in order to use her sword.

"Run, mom!" Hadjar shouted.

He wriggled out of Elizabeth's grip. Grabbing his ceremonial sword, which was tied to his belt and too big to be practical, he rushed toward the warriors. They were clearly weaker than the Imperials. In addition, they didn't have a Heaven Soldier with them.

"Hadjar!" Elizabeth roared like a wounded beast, but it was too late.

The Prince slid under the lead bodyguard's spear. What level of cultivation had she achieved? The Bodily Rivers? Maybe the Formation? Possibly the Transformation?

Hadjar didn't care. He had a sword. Uselessly ceremonial or not, he could wield it. The east wind called to him, and his eyes saw the target.

His heart pounding wildly, he called upon his mastery of the sword and swung the blade.

A barely visible strike answered his call. He bypassed her shield, angled himself toward the bodyguard, and sliced through the unprotected, narrow strip of skin between the bib of the helmet and the helmet itself.

The heavy helmet fell to the ground, and a moment after it, painting the floor and walls red fell the warrior. An expression of extreme surprise would forever remain in her glassy eyes.

Not paying any attention to the fact that he'd killed someone, Hadjar continued his crazy, desperate dance. He dived under the spear of the nearest warrior. She'd already recovered from her initial shock and was about to hit the Prince with her shield, but he was faster.

Despite her experience, despite surviving hundreds of deadly fights, she was helpless against Hadjar's talent and fury. He moved as elegantly as a swan across a lake, only needing to swing once.

He flicked his wrist and cut the bodyguard's forearm tendon.

She dropped the shield with a crash, and Hadjar, pushing off of it, soared into the air. He flew over the warrior's head, his blade moving so fast it left an afterimage in its wake.

Another body fell behind him, but the remaining bodyguards had managed to snap out of it.

Seven of them rushed in to attack him. They attacked from all sides, forgetting that they were trying to kill the Prince, not a ferocious tiger cub.

Hadjar jumped. His legs were strong and his body felt light.

He rose into the air again, evading all seven spears. Bouncing off of the spear tips, he once more swung his sword, and a ghostly strike from his blade found its target, going through the eye slits.

Another crimson spray of blood followed. The blinded warrior cried out.

Hadjar landed behind her and used her kneeling body to block several attacks.

Instead of hitting him, their spears embedded themselves in the body of their ally.

Despite how much had happened, all of it took only a couple of seconds. In fact, Hadjar had been moving so quickly that he'd been leaving behind black and gold colored, ghostly silhouettes. A seven-year-old boy managed to kill three experienced practitioners of martial arts with only four strokes of the sword.

"Hadjar!"

The familiar voice tore Hadjar out of his rage and fear-induced trance.

He turned around.

The ceremonial sword fell from his exhausted hands.

There was a lump in his throat.

Heavy, salty tears rolled down his cheeks.

"Hadjar…" A palm, shrouded in the black wind, had been thrust through the Queen's chest. He could see it grasping something red and twitching.

The unconscious Elaine lay on the floor. She looked so small and fragile. Her hair covered her body like a thin, golden blanket.

Elizabeth took a step forward. Her clothes were soaked in blood. Her green eyes grew dim, and a weariness that made her seem older settled over her.

"Mother!"

Hadjar ran up and embraced the fallen Queen.

"Promise me…"

At that moment, all the Prince could manage was to hold onto his mother tightly. He had no idea what was going on. His mind refused to accept reality.

"Promise me that you will never... enter the world... of martial arts." Elizabeth's body trembled as she awkwardly kissed her son on the cheek, and her last words were uttered with a sigh: "It brings only misfortune..."

Hadjar looked at his hands, covered in the blood of his mother.

The body of the woman who'd once given him a whole new world meant the whole world to him… now lay at his feet.

The Prince didn't remember how it happened, but it seemed that he'd growled and rushed at Primus. He didn't need his sword—he was ready to sink his teeth into the warlord's throat. But Primus just grabbed the boy's neck and lifted him into the air.

"I would advise you to kill them, Primus," a dispassionate voice offered.

"They are my family, Governor."

"What about Elizabeth and Haver, then?"

"That had to happen. The country can't have two kings."

Hadjar clawed at his uncle's hand, but no matter how hard he tried, he couldn't even scratch the Heaven Soldier. He didn't have enough air—strange, alarming sounds filled his head and he started to panic as darkness encroached on his vision.

"Did you see his swordsmanship, Primus? If he lives, you can never rule in peace."

Primus looked at his suffocating nephew. It would be so easy to squeeze his hand and send the boy to be with his father and mother again. And yet, he was his flesh and blood.

"Then I'll make sure he never picks up the sword again."

Hadjar, if he'd been able to, would've been screaming in pain.

[Host is in critical condition! Irreversible damage has been dealt to the internal organs! The Meridian and Nodes are being destroyed!]

The Governor watched without any emotion as the black wind tormented the body of the twitching boy. He still didn't care what these cretins did. What mattered was that a steady stream of Solar ore would be sent to the Empire. To be honest, the Solar ore wasn't that rich, and the metal made from it wasn't the best, but…

Resources were very limited in this world and there was a constant struggle for control over them. The metal from the Solar ore was one such resource.

Maybe if he spent a couple of centuries working on it out here in the sticks, he would get the inspiration he needed for a breakthrough and reach the level of the Spirit Knight.

The higher the stage of cultivation was, the more valuable resources it required, resources that were harder and harder to find.

Even while the exhausted son collapsed onto the bloodied corpse of his mother, the Governor could only think about his own future. New horizons had opened up to him thanks to the new King of Lydus—Primus Duran.

Chapter 13

 "Your supper, your Highness," the young guard mocked him, then closed the door.

Hadjar was once again one with the darkness. This cramped stone cell had become his new home. It was designed to ensure that an adult couldn't lie down or stand up straight. Hadjar was lucky in that regard—thanks to his small size, he was quite 'comfortable' in its confines.

He'd already spent a month locked up and what's worse—there was no information in the neuronet's database on how to fix the damage he'd received. Primus had destroyed the very foundation for his cultivation.

The damn Warlord had burned all the meridians in his body and destroyed all the nodes as well. The Prince, although he was no longer a Prince... Hadjar could still feel the energy in the air, but he couldn't harness it.

Besides...

Hadjar crawled to the bucket of dirty water, not trusting the wooden stumps that now served as his legs. A loaf of moldy bread sat beside it.

A beam of light made its way up to the ceiling through a small hole.

Hadjar positioned himself above the bucket and looked at his reflection.

He'd used to think that he was lucky, having great parents he'd inherited good genes from. He'd been a handsome and dignified boy. Now, however...

A face covered in scabs and sores looked back at him. The right eyelid was swollen, covering the eye almost completely. His head was almost bald and his trembling hands smelled of something rotten and musky.

Hadjar drank greedily, gulping down close to half of the bucket. He hadn't been fed for three days, so the boy ate the bread as well, despite its disgusting smell and taste.

Leaning his back against the cold wall, Hadjar looked at the grating. He watched specks of dust spinning in a beam of light.

The wind was blowing again.

It didn't call him anywhere...

"Duke Velen, Earl Vaslia, Primus, the Governor, Viscount..."

The musicians played trumpets, the choirs sang hymns, the bells rang—the coronation of the new King of Lidus was in full swing. But the enthusiastic exclamations of the people were absent.

"Duke Velen, Earl Vaslia, Primus, the Governor, Viscount..."

The funeral processions were probably being held in the small towns and villages that day. People mourned for the dead King and Queen and threw angry glances in the direction of the capital.

But none of them dared to take up arms and rebel. No one was foolish enough to try and fight the Imperial soldiers marching along the roads of the country. Their power was far beyond what the ordinary villagers could even imagine.

The people that had reached the stage of the Bodily Rivers had been great heroes to the common people. And the Imperials surpassed those cultivators in every way.

"Duke Velen, Earl Vaslia, Primus, the Governor, Viscount..."

And yet, there was still some hope in the hearts of the citizens.

Rumors spread.

Few people believed they were true, but they still told the tale, using the cover of night to escape the notice of the authorities. It was about Prince Hadjar. The Prince was said to have slain ten warriors with his sword, then wounded Primus and the Governor, and after that, he escaped from the Palace.

"Duke Velen, Earl Vaslia, Primus, the Governor, Viscount..."

They said that he was now training somewhere in the distant mountains, killing the cruelest, most ferocious animals. He lived in solitude, gaining the kind of power that would make the mountains themselves shudder in terror and the skies above cry from fright.

People wanted to believe that their suffering under the rule of Primus and the Empire would last no more than nine springs. After all, Prince Hadjar would then be sixteen years old. He would have a legal claim to the throne.

Peasants and merchants, warriors and artisans, scholars and ordinary citizens alike all believed that the hour would come, that the bell in the ruined Royal castle would ring again. And when that ringing was heard in all the fields and forests of the Kingdom, the army would rally and overthrow Primus.

They wanted to believe in this comforting, fictional tale. They wanted it more than anything.

But no one knew the truth. The Prince hadn't even seen the sky or breathed fresh air for an entire month.

He could no longer fight anything, neither beasts nor humans.

No one knew that the Prince's legs had been cut off below the knee. No one knew that Hadjar had been deprived of any and all opportunities and chances to develop his power.

But, even now, sitting in a dungeon, crippled, he refused to give up.

He would find a way out of there. Even if he had to sell his soul to the devil, he would find a cure.

And he would get justice for his family so they could rest in peace. Even if he had to slaughter every Imperial warrior and every traitor in the Kingdom to do it.

At that moment, his blue eyes burned with an unyielding, almost palpable light.

And that's why Hadjar was muttering, "Duke Velen, Earl Vaslia, Primus, the Governor, Viscount…"

He repeated the names of the traitors to himself, over and over. There were dozens of them, hundreds, but they'd all pay one day, he didn't doubt it for a second. Even if the sky itself were to stand in his way, he would go to war against it.

His name was Hadjar. They'd taken his power, destroyed his sword, cut off his legs. But his will was indomitable, his determination endless. No one could change that, he would not be broken.

That day, an ancient dragon awoke. He resided in a cave hidden by a waterfall and had been forgotten by all. He was chained down and unable to move, but suddenly, he felt something approaching him from the west.

Something driven by fate.

The dragon thought the feeling must be false, only a remnant of its thousand-year sleep. Such a thing might've happened ten, twenty, fifty thousand years ago. But no one had come to him for countless centuries of his imprisonment in that cave.

No one was coming this time, either.

The dragon only managed to catch a glimpse of two fierce, blue eyes in the reflection of the waterfall.

***

"How much do you want for him?"

Hadjar awoke not because he'd heard a voice, but because this voice was new. For the past year, he'd only heard the mockery of the guard who would bring him moldy bread and a bucket of grimy water.

Once a month, when the cell began to stink so much that even the guard couldn't bear to go in, he would bring him a waste bucket. Then he would ruthlessly beat Hadjar. His warden believed that cleaning up the Half-Prince's shit was beneath him. That was what he called Hadjar: the Half-Prince.

"Five gold coins."

"Five gold coins?! You're insane, Lithium."

Hadjar's guard had a really funny name. Lithium. But, alas, except for the prisoner himself, no one could appreciate the humor behind it. There was no periodic table in this world. Even if there was, it would probably have different elements in it.

"I wish I hadn't met you last night."

"You bought your own ticket to see our freak show, no one forced you."

"What's that got to do with it?"

"If you hadn't offended the owner, no one would've put you in such an awkward situation."

Freak show? Anyone else in Hadjar's position would've been afraid after hearing that, but he only saw a chance at freedom.

"I owe the owner two gold coins, to pay for the tent I ruined," the soldier had apparently gotten drunk and made a mess.

Recently, he would often drink and complain to Hadjar about his life. He'd told the boy about how his wife had left him. She'd abandoned him for a stronger practitioner, a man who'd reached the level of Formation and had attained a high rank in the army of King Primus.

To be honest, Hadjar was glad to see his tormentor suffering.

"Look, you'll give me five coins, I'll give two coins to your boss, and he'll pay you a bonus for the freak. It'll probably be more than five gold coins. We'll both profit from this!"

Someone was hesitating behind the door, shifting uneasily from foot to foot.

"This seems like fraud. And you know what the new laws are like—I'll lose my hand for this, and you'll lose your head."

"No one will notice if this freak disappears. No one but me has come here for a year."

"Who is he?"

Hadjar only pursed his lips. Wow! He costs five gold coins now. Previously, his right shoe alone had cost a hundred times more. But he didn't care about that—the main thing was to get out of here.

"The son of a disgraced nobleman," the soldier lied easily. He'd become so impudent that he was planning to sell the Prince! "His father died long ago and the son's been completely forgotten."

Or he was just a moron.

"Five coins, you said?"

"Yep, five."

The stranger hesitated a bit more.

"Let me look at him, first."

"Yes, please, go right ahead," the soldier agreed easily. "Just try not to breathe. The smell is awful in there."

The sound of footsteps echoed in the corridor and the door was unlocked. Hadjar closed his eyes, unable to handle the bright light. The soldier had previously always come in without a torch, but now he'd brought two oil lamps at once.

For Hadjar, who'd spent a year in the darkness, it was like two midday suns had suddenly appeared in the dungeon.

"What a stench," a tall, thin man in a patched jacket said.

He looked quite unobtrusive. The scars on his face and the burns on his hands hinted at troubled and violent youth.

"By the demons," he breathed, bringing the lamp up to Hadjar's face. The young man almost howled in pain. "You didn't lie to me, Lithium. He's a real freak. The crowd will be delighted to see him."

The soldier just chuckled.

"We have a deal, then?" He asked.

The stranger again hesitated a little and then slapped his outstretched palm.

"Deal. Five gold."

"Good. Just wait a second."

The soldier left the room and returned with a heavy, black blanket.

"Here, let's cover him up," he said, throwing it over Hadjar's shoulders. "He stinks so much that all the other guards will come here. And he hasn't seen any light for a long time. Or, wait, do you need a blind freak?"

"No, we have enough blind freaks already. The owner will find another use for him."

Hadjar was propped up on his 'legs' and he managed to stagger to the exit. Every step he took produced a metallic knocking and made fiery pain shoot up his hips. But Hadjar tolerated it all. He just muttered the names, adding another one to the list—Lithium.

And so, a year later, he left not only the dungeon but also the Palace and the capital, leaving the only home he'd ever known behind.

He rode in a wagon, half-listening to his new 'warden'. They were in a hurry to join up with the wandering freak show to which he'd been sold.

Hadjar barely paid any attention to the boastful man. He kept checking the collar that had been placed on him (it had a magical slave seal on it) and looked at the receding lights of the city.

It was the first time he'd ever gone out into the world. This wasn't how he'd pictured the beginning of his adventures.

What awaited him now?

Slavery, having to entertain crowds?

Hadjar just smiled wickedly.

Chapter 14

 "Come on, stop wasting time and come look at our monstrous freaks!" The crier kept shouting at the top of his lungs.

Hidden under the tarp that covered the cage, Hadjar

could hear the howling of the crowd. He'd gotten used to it after five years, and after two more, he'd even grown to like it. At least it was something different in his otherwise routine life.

"Yes, my lady, that's a good choice! The man-fish!"

And with a clap, the cover was thrown off the neighboring cage. The crowd gasped in horror, the girls screamed, and Leer did his best to perform well, trying to bite someone with his sharpened teeth. He often claimed he hadn't even lost consciousness while they'd been filed.

Hadjar didn't believe it.

"Three silver coins. Just three silver coins!" Stepha repeated as she worked for the crowd.

The girl was 'friendly' with almost every normal-looking employee of the show. However, she was also a very nice person and sometimes even let the 'freaks' out for a walk. She did it at night, hiding them under black cloaks. Because of this, Hadjar was far kinder toward her than the others.

"And now, get ready to see a creature born out of the love between a woman and a wolf!"

This meant Ernesta was being shown to the crowd. She was the girl covered in thick hair from head to toe. She couldn't even speak, and she didn't need to fake her bestial rage. Hadjar once nearly fell victim to her fangs.

She was the result of what happened in this world if a person bred with wolves. Because of the energy in the air, or possibly some other reason, the mutant progeny could grow up and even be mighty. She had the strength of three adult men, not practitioners, of course, but she was still powerful.

"Is she as wild in bed?" One of the assholes asked, laughing as he did so.

"If you're interested in trying it, we could make a deal, but it would cost you ten silver coins," Stepha replied calmly.

The man immediately stopped talking and instead began muttering something unintelligible under his breath.

Stepha knew how to calm the audience down. Frankly speaking, cowardly men, the ones who were all bark and no bite, rarely argued with her. Stepha was very experienced when it came to sex and didn't even try to hide it. Thanks to that, she had this mocking look to her that unnerved and quieted the usual troublemakers.

Hadjar fiddled with the collar around his neck. It was a strip of metal, sealed with magic. The seal itself looked like some sort of eastern figure, and if they activated it—he would receive a very intense and painful electric shock.

It was, quite frankly, a disgusting way to keep someone in line.

"Now! Get ready..." The crier began to speak in a more subdued tone of voice. "We present to you the horror of the Mist. A nightmare from the darkest corners of the Misty Mountains, a place where even the demons hide in their caves at night. I ask that all cowards please leave immediately. Even I'm afraid to look at it sometimes."

Someone from the crowd began to brag, and others stayed quiet. He saw the same thing in every city. Hadjar has already stopped counting the years of his life he'd spent wandering. He'd visited so many places in the country that were the same as this one. Everything was the same everywhere, really. Tired and frightened of the authorities, people were looking for entertainment to help them forget, even for a moment. Something to help them leave their hardships and tribulations behind.

"Are you ready?" The crier whispered to the public.

"Yes!"

"Can we leave?"

"Show us this terror of yours!"

"Darling, please, let's just go."

The crowd cried out, most of them wanting to see this supposed monster. Today was a good day—the Governor had allocated the central square for the circus. They would normally not even be allowed inside the city walls. They'd have to make due and perform in the fields and meadows, which was far from ideal.

When that happened, all sorts of thieves, troublemakers, and people who just plain refused to pay would come out to see their show. However, nobody dared to take liberties inside the cities, under the watchful eye of the guards that'd been trained by the new government. Nobody was eager to receive ten to fifty lashes, lose their property or even their limbs.

"Behold!"

A bright light hit Hadjar's eyes. He was glad for it. He often had nightmares about a small, dark oubliette, about being trapped in it, unable to move or breathe. He would probably remember the dungeon his uncle had thrown him in for the rest of his life.

"Demon!" The girls in the crowd screamed.

"Damn it." The men moaned weakly.

A person that was apparently squeamish hurried to throw up into an urn. Hadjar began to howl and growl like a rabid beast while barely clearing his throat because the popular 'clichés' demanded he do so. The boys and girls that were too cowardly began to move away from the cage and leave.

The soldiers who were standing on the perimeter of the square started reaching for their spears and swords.

"Calm down, beast!" The crier hit the bars of the cage with his iron stick.

Hadjar roared in his direction and then waited for the second blow.

After that, like a thousand times before, he froze.

"Please, don't be afraid." The crier told the people soothingly. "Let me tell you this monster's story. One day, a great hero went to the Misty Mountains. He could cross thousands of miles in one step. He could cut through the whole sea with by swinging his sword once."

"Did he forget something in the Misty mountains?" The people in the crowd laughed.

"His sweetheart!" The crier responded loudly, and Hadjar frowned.

He'd figured out this story three years ago. Thanks to it, he could now eat meat every day. The crowd always paid handsomely to see his performance and the profits made the circus owner happy. This new crier, however, was really messing things up.

"What was she doing there?" The people continued to laugh at the crier while trying not to meet Hadjar's eyes.

"This beast had kidnapped her!" The crier hit the bars of his cage again. "Don't pay attention to his horrid ugliness or the fact he no longer has legs. This monster used to be the size of a mountain! He could create hurricanes and destroy entire countries with his breath alone. One single stomp of his foot could create a tsunami! He'd reached such heights in his cultivation that he was able to turn into a handsome young man. He fell in love with a beautiful and innocent girl, but her heart belonged to another."

The crier was finally starting to sound convincing and wasn't fumbling his replies. People in the crowd began to get interested in this story. The girls clung to their companions tightly, while the men stared at Hadjar angrily. He answered them with the same kind of look. While they were busy listening to the story, all Hadjar could think about was the meat he'd be fed after this.

"Then the beast kidnapped her!" The crier hit the bars again. "The hero immediately went after them. He managed to survive going through even the wildest places, where he fought ancient monsters, the kind whose strength and power we can't even imagine today. He found himself on the verge of death hundreds of times, but love gave him the strength to keep going!"

All the women were listening attentively.

"And so, at the end of his journey, he came upon a Palace of unprecedented beauty, where his beloved was being kept, chained to a huge column. The battle that made even gods and demons quake in terror began! They fought for ten years, day and night."

Everyone had stopped talking. The man's audience was all ears.

"The hero finally defeated the beast, after ten long years. He returned to the palace, but..."

The crier paused.

"But... what?" A guy asked.

"What happened to his lover?" A girl standing in the back asked.

The crier looked around at the crowd and just shook his head sadly. Many sighs and quiet whimpers were heard.

"Their battle had been so fierce that its echo had reached the Palace and stopped the heart of the hero's beloved." Some people were crying now, and it wasn't just the girls. "The hero wanted to kill the beast, but, at that moment, he became enlightened. He now understood all the secrets of this world. He threw away his sword, for he no longer needed a weapon. He'd reached the fourth stage of the sword skills."

"There's only three," the soldier who was the closest to the cells of the circus grumbled.

"Most people think so, yes. The first is 'One with the Sword' when a warrior is able to attack their enemy at a distance of five steps," the crier made a clumsy lunge with his iron stick. He mocked the soldiers but got the attention of the crowd. "The second is 'One with the World' when a warrior can hit their target at a distance of twenty steps. And the third is 'Wielder of the Sword', a practitioner who no longer needs the sword. They themselves, along with their surroundings, become the sword. But..."

The soldiers moved closer in order to hear the story better.

"But there is a fourth one. When a cultivator reaches the highest degree of enlightenment and power, they understand that neither the sword nor the power exists. Then they cast the sword aside and know eternity. And the hero, who had thrown away all his skills and power, knew eternity. Before he returned to the mountain peak so he could stay next to his beloved forever, he decided to give the beast a second chance."

The crowd turned to Hadjar. He pulled at his fake chains sadly. They were lighter than paper, but sounded good and looked heavier than normal ones.

"What kind of second chance did he get?" One of the ladies asked while wiping her tears away.

"He cut off the monster's legs! Then he sealed his power with great spells and turned him into a freak. He gave the beast his favorite Ron'Jah and commanded him to play it in front of people. The only way for the beast to be restored is for him to fall in love with someone who would then return his feelings."

"Who could ever love such a freak?!" Someone in the crowd shouted incredulously.

"That's why the beast's been playing for three million years, no one can love someone like him."

The people looked at each other and smiled. They thought they understood what the hero's intentions had been. Instead of simple revenge and just murdering the beast, he'd instead doomed his enemy for all eternity. It was a sad story, but it had a just end.

"And now, let's enjoy the beast's music," the crier turned toward the cage and struck it with his rod again. "Play, monster! Play!"

Hadjar snarled and took out a musical instrument from his black rags. It looked like a large, round balalaika—it had a round base with two holes in it, a short neck, four strings, and four long pegs. The instrument played mostly high notes, but Hadjar had managed to tweak it a bit and was now able to play a larger range.

And so, he started to play.

The people calmed down, listening to his song in silence, a song which was as old as the world itself.

He'd used to play for a lot of money in his past life, and now he was playing for a piece of meat. Ironically enough, he was back where he'd started. And if, before, it had only been Hadjar's outlet and a way to keep in touch with the world, now it was what kept him going, what gave him hope. He felt lucky for the first time in five whole years.

Chapter 15

"How much?" The first person asked after Stepha approached him.

"Give as much as you think this performance deserves," the girl said, smiling as she did so.

The man, despite wearing simple clothes, appeared to think on it a bit and then gave her nine silver coins. Moving to the side, he winked at Hadjar, who gave him only a brief nod in return.

It was their subtle way of tricking people—they didn't ask for a fixed price, but for "as much as they thought the performance deserved." Tourin, the same man who'd bought Hadjar when he'd still been in the dungeon would always pay first.

The ruse worked and the crowd ended up paying no less than six coins per person. This meant that the owner of the circus had earned a whole one and a half gold from just one of Hadjar's performances. That was a lot of money; a peasant family of five could live off of that for a month.

Hadjar had earned only two silver coins and a piece of meat. Well, the other freaks hadn't earned even that much. They didn't get any money or a hearty dinner. They would just get more abuse. That was why they hated Hadjar, but he didn't really pay much attention to them.

After the performance, Hadjar's cage was covered with a dark blanket. It was then wrapped up in the same fake chains he'd been put in and dragged into a large wagon. At the owner's insistence, they kept up the charade for as long as they were within ten miles of the city. Only after getting far enough away the freaks were allowed their so-called freedom.

The ruse was closely guarded and no unnecessary risks were taken. People could have their suspicions and think whatever they liked, but every measure possible was taken to prevent them from finding out the truth.

Hadjar didn't complain. Truthfully, he couldn't. The owner could electrocute any one of them if they messed anything up or tried to ask for too much. With that kind of threat looming over them, they became much more docile and careful.

They'd been traveling down a bumpy country road for about an hour now. The farther they got from the city, the worse the roads became. Despite the army becoming more powerful, the country itself was falling apart. Entire villages and even small settlements had already disappeared.

People either fled their villages and moved to the cities, where they eked out a miserable existence or were enslaved. The Imperials always needed more labor for the mine, which had become absurdly huge.

Hadjar would often hear about some new pestilence sweeping the country or people starving to death when such news reached the cities. Needless to say, the number of bandits on the roads had increased exponentially.

In the old days, each village, despite the extreme scarcity of resources necessary for their cultivation, always had at least several practitioners. Well, they'd be, at most, at the upper levels of the Bodily Nodes, but that had still been enough to protect people from wild animals and bandits.

Now, with the villages and towns disappearing, these 'warriors' rarely joined the army. More often, they went to pasture and became useless. That's why the circus caravan was being guarded by a group of mercenaries: seven men and five women, to be exact.

They considered themselves a powerful force and couldn't understand why Hadjar didn't fawn over them as everyone else did. He only smirked at their stupidity. If he ever managed to take up the sword again and hear the call of the wind, three minutes would be enough for him to kill all of these arrogant assholes that never missed an opportunity to mock the freaks.

"You can come out now, Hadjar," he heard Stepha's voice and then she pulled the blanket off his cage.

It wasn't surprising that Hadjar hadn't come up with another name for himself. After all, to the locals, his name was quite ordinary. The Queen hadn't been particularly ingenious when naming him, and there were certainly a lot of other Hadjars roaming the world.

The former Prince took off his chains and stretched out his aching arms. An ulcer on his elbow burst due to the motion, which nearly caused Stepha to vomit. Being nice, she tried to hide it but wasn't successful.

"Could you come up with another ending for the story?" She turned away and tried to change the subject, instead.

Hadjar got down from the wagon and found himself in a spacious meadow. The coachmen had already arranged the wagons in a semicircle, and a fire had been lit in the center. The craziest freaks, such as the hairy girl or the birdboy, had been left in their cages. They were mindless, so it was dangerous to let them roam.

The rest huddled around the hastily constructed cesspit. They'd been given a bit of soup with crusts of bread and were now looking at Hadjar enviously. None of them could even dream about talking to Stepha.

"Why? Don't you like the part with the transformation?" Hadjar asked her.

It wasn't difficult to guess what fairy tale he'd used as the inspiration for his 'marketing'. His current goal wasn't only to make as profitable of a story as possible, but also one that was as noticeable as possible. That was the only way he could get what he wanted. He'd succeeded if today was anything to go by.

That old nugget of wisdom was true—People will follow the path of least resistance if they can.

"It's just so... sad," Stepha took his arm, trying not to touch the skin directly.

Hadjar really didn't look good, to put it mildly—he was wearing simple short pants to better show his wooden stumps, along with a shirt with short sleeves, which served the same purpose, and some black cloth, which he would be wrapped in. He wore it when he left the cage. Or, to be more precise, he was made to wear it in order to not ruin the appetite of others.

"People, even if they won't admit it, love tragic endings," Hadjar shrugged. "Compared to those, their own lives don't seem as bad. Especially if there's some hope to go along with the sorrow."

Stepha looked at him oddly, after he said that.

"You're quite good with words, Hadjar."

"Possibly."

She led him away from the central fire. There, the other circus performers were playing musical instruments, drinking, eating and having fun. They were kind of jealous of the freaks, because they brought more money to the circus, despite the regular performers being more numerous. But no one would've let just a crowd of 'monsters' into a city, so the owner kept the regular performers around as well.

Hadjar was given a wooden bowl filled with chowder, that also had a piece of meat in it. It was kind of fatty and far from good, but it was still better than what most of the freaks had.

This time, the former Prince ate slowly and savored his meal. If he'd planned well and calculated everything correctly, then this would be the last time he'd be eating with these vagrants.

"Status," Hadjar ordered. The neural network promptly obeyed.

Name	Hadjar
Level of Cultivation	None
Strength	0,01
Dexterity	0,03
Physique	0,002
Energy points	None

Hadjar just shook his head and continued eating. Despite everything, he'd continued his 'training'. His weak, almost disintegrating body hadn't been capable of much. But, after five years of 'training'— it was a little stronger than before.

He did three pushups every day. A trifle, even for a simple child, but for Hadjar, it was a titanic feat. And he often managed to keep going only thanks the neural network sending him messages like this:

[Physique: +0,0001]

For the sake of these infinitesimal gains, he would torture himself for weeks on end. It was better than simply waiting and hoping that his plan would work.

Whatever the case, it was better to do something than to give up.

"Come on, you can't be serious!" A knife thrower laughed drunkenly.

He was a thin, weak-looking man, but he could throw two dozen blades at once and not miss a single target. Hadjar would've been happy to scan his level of cultivation, but he was too weak to do so.

"I swear it! When I was sixteen, I killed a Fierce-Bull!" The broad-shouldered mercenary roared back.

His name was Brombur or Bromvurd... something like that, and, despite being quite short, he was famous for constantly trying to 'use' someone. Both figuratively and quite literally. He was always trying to trick people and take their money and visited the brothels in the cities whenever possible.

"A Fierce-Bull, even a young one, isn't below the level of Awakening Power!" The thrower continued to argue. "Which is definitely higher than the middle levels of the Bodily Rivers!"

"You don't believe me?" Brom-I-don't-remember-his-name threw a blade in front of the doubting man's feet.

The thrower immediately bent down and picked it up. He was thin, but, nevertheless, was quite powerful. In fact, except for the owner himself, he was the one who visited Stepha the most regularly and stayed with her the longest. Nobody really dared get in his way when he did so.

"Analyze," Hadjar ordered mentally.

Bald Brom, let's call him that, threw off his shirt, exposing his stomach, which was impressively firm. He held a sturdy, curved sword in his hands and wielded it as if he were a windmill and the weapon itself one of the windmill's blades.

Name	Bold Brom
Level of Cultivation	The Bodily Rivers, Stage 3
Strength	1,3
Dexterity	1,24
Physique	1,86
Energy points	1,9

Two 'cultivators', and each of them, according to the neuronet, wasn't below the Bodily Rivers' third stage. They waved their pieces of iron enthusiastically at each other. The loud hooting of the others, the sound of wooden mugs and the rhythmic music of the lute player encouraged them.

The company had nothing to do in the evenings. Everyone had been fucking everyone else for a long time now since there weren't any new people (only the freaks would be new, but no one wanted to go to bed with them). They'd grown tired of frequently getting drunk, so these kinds of scenes weren't rare. The truth was that the fights were mostly to alleviate boredom.

Hadjar looked even at this stupid performance with a slight longing.

Their strikes were slow and inaccurate. They struck at random, without even thinking about it. It was a fight between idiots. A true Master was no dumber than South Wind. Defeating a worthy opponent was only possible if your mind was a few dozen moves ahead.

The way they moved their feet resembled the process of stomping on grapes to make wine. They stayed in the same place and had almost no control over their center of gravity and balance. They possessed neither the grace nor elegance that was so essential to the art of the Sword. The art that, despite being used for murder, had art to its lethality.

It was as beautiful as a soaring falcon that had spotted its prey. It was as elegant as a tiger crawling through the grass, lurking, then pouncing swiftly.

They weren't swordsmen—they were just practitioners who didn't see the forest for the trees.

Most warriors were like that.

The Master had said that even some of the Heaven Soldiers weren't able to grasp the 'peaceful unity' required to truly be at one with their weapons. It was necessary to have both talent and perseverance, as well as a certain worldview to achieve this. Nobody really needed a lot of intelligence to stuff themselves full of precious resources and rely on others' expertise.

Anyway, that's what his mentors had told him.

He wondered what had happened to them and the Nanny, as well.

"What're you grinning at, freak?!"

A slight slap brought Hadjar out of his reminiscing. Falling down and dropping his bowl, along with the half-eaten meat, Hadjar saw the figure of Brom towering above him.

The mercenary could've easily killed him if he'd used even a tenth of his power.

"Nothing, venerable warrior." Hadjar looked down at the soup he'd spilled and tried to look respectful.

He could eat meat that had fallen on the ground. He was hungry, so he decided to try and eat it all.

"Do you think I was lying?!" The mercenary stepped on the meat, flattening it into the ground and mixing it with the sand and dirt. "Look at me when I'm talking to you, freak!"

He lifted Hadjar's chin with his boot. He then staggered back, falling onto his ass comically. For a moment, he'd thought that Hadjar didn't look crippled, but like an ancient, fierce animal. His cold, blue-eyed glance had been frightening.

However, when the people who'd witnessed the incident started laughing a moment later, he stopped seeing the rage and determination that had unbalanced him, and instead only saw subservience and meek deference.

"You think you're better than me, huh?!"

Brom made Hadjar get back on his "feet", then handed his blade to the freak. Someone tried to object to what was happening, but, alas, Stepha was the only one who could've stopped what was happening. Since she was already in the owner's wagon and unlikely to come out in the next hour, Brom kept his abuse up.

"Well, show me what a freak you are, 'legendary beast'!" The mercenary laughed, trying to conceal his fear.

"Damn it, damn it!" Hadjar thought, hardly able to lift the sword, despite the fact it would be light even to a common man. "Not now, not when I'm so close!"

After all, Stepha hadn't gone to visit the owner alone, she'd been accompanied by a person who could bring Hadjar one step closer to his cherished goal—freedom, and justice.

But he was now faced with a new problem.

A problem in the form of an angry, humiliated mercenary who clearly didn't intend to leave things up to chance.

Chapter 16

Despite the absurdity of the situation, Brom had no idea how much danger he was actually in. Despite losing all of his levels and being weaker than most ordinary people, Hadjar was still a threat. His mastery of the blade couldn't be taken away. He was still 'One with the Sword.'

And yet, Hadjar just lifted the blade in a ridiculous manner, almost cutting his own thigh in the process.

This elicited another bout of laughter from everyone.

"Stupid freak!" Brom said derisively.

He took his sword back from the 'enemy' and sent Hadjar back to the ground with a light push to his chest.

Hadjar, however, didn't care and just kept looking at the now inedible meat forlornly. It was silly, but his humiliation really didn't matter to him right then. He was more interested in his hunger. He would have plenty of time to add Brom's name to his 'list' later.

"I want to…" The mercenary swung his blade, but the owner caught his hand in time.

He was a handsome man in his thirties. He had red hair, arranged into several braids. He wore light leather armor and his boots were polished to a shine.

"Think twice, mercenary, before you ruin my property." The practitioner that had reached a high level of the Bodily Rivers said and pinned him with his almost black eyes. The look was so menacing that the man just froze. The sound of laughter suddenly stopped filling the meadow. The music cut off abruptly. It was as if everyone was holding their breath, waiting to see what would happen.

"Sorry, Darnan," Brom mumbled apologetically, looking down.

He pulled his hand back and, literally spitting out insults, went back over to his giggling colleagues. Once he returned, he smacked someone loudly, then yelled at someone else, but no one was really paying any attention to him anymore.

Stepha was standing next to Darnan, who, according to some rumors, had once been an officer in the army. Her beautiful face was framed by her silky brown hair, bound with two jade hairpins. Those were her entire fortune. A strong gust of wind snatched several 'fortune telling cards' from her hands.

They floated around for a while, then one card landed on Hadjar's knee. It had the image of a squirming dragon on it.

"Look, Hadjar," Stepha whispered, helping her friend up and collecting her scattered cards. "It says that fate has something new in store for you."

"Go into the tent, slave," Darnan commanded in a steely tone of voice.

The tent was always placed between the owner's and Stepha's wagons. The circus performers rehearsed there, held meetings to discuss various issues and divided up the money. A strange young woman was sitting at a folding wooden table in the tent as he came in.

She'd covered herself with a red cloak and her face wasn't visible to him, but Hadjar already knew, based on the shape of her figure alone, that she was beautiful; incredibly, abnormally gorgeous, in fact. She had the kind of beauty a woman could only attain after studying techniques for seducing and enthralling others.

[Warning! The host has entered the zone of influence of an aura that affects his perception!]

She probably hadn't tried to seduce the freak. Her aura was probably a sort of passive, magical one. And since Hadjar lacked even the resistance that non-practitioners possessed, he'd easily fallen under her spell.

"Is your name Hadjar, slave?"

"Yes, Milady," Hadjar groaned out, his chest still aching from the blow he'd received earlier. It had felt like a blow to him, at least.

"Play for me."

Darnan handed him the instrument quite carefully. It seemed like he was afraid of accidentally touching the ulcers or scabs covering the skin of his 'property'.

Hadjar took the Ron'Jah with a bow. He asked for permission to sit down on a chair, adjusted the pegs, and played as if his life depended on it. The fact it was true only made it easier to do so.

He ended up not playing for long, only about five minutes.

The stranger stopped him with an authoritative wave of her hand.

"I agree to your price, Darnan."

Saying that she placed a leather pouch on the table. From what he could see, it had no less than forty gold inside it. Wow, Hadjar's worth had increased eightfold in the past five years.

"Take off his collar."

"Are you sure, Senta?"

Senta waved her hand vaguely in response.

"If I can't protect myself from a cripple," she said. "My cultivation has been for nothing."

Darnan just shrugged in response. He made a quick gesture with his hand, folded his fingers into some odd positions and the collar clicked open. The former owner didn't dare approach Hadjar. Stepha had to take off his chains for him.

"Goodbye, Hadjar," she whispered in his ear.

Surprisingly, he detected a hint of sadness in Stepha's voice. Although, it's possible he'd just imagined it. But he had no time to dwell on that. He breathed in deeply, marveling at how much tastier the air had become. And while it may seem that nothing had changed, that he'd only regained a bit of freedom, that was enough to change his perception of reality.

In any case, he now felt more comfortable breathing.

"Let's go," the woman, still wrapped up in her scarlet cloak, exited the tent.

Hadjar 'hurried' after her, hobbling along on his sticks. He cast a farewell glance at the circus troupe with which he'd spent the past five years of his life, touring half the Kingdom. They hadn't been the happiest years, but they were still better than what living in prison would've been like.

Before running off into the night, he threw one last glance at Brom. As if he'd sensed something, Brom turned, then paled and grabbed his sword. But it was too late, the strange creature with the creepy eyes had already disappeared into the darkness.

"Don't you want to know where we're going?

Hadjar could've asked her, but he'd known from the start that he was being purchased for a brothel. And no, not for the sake of pleasuring perverts there. He'd been bought solely because he was an outstanding musician.

"I'm afraid it might all be a dream."

"It's not. I'll take you to the 'Innocent Meadow' and you'll see for yourself," Senta said.

They approached the wagon, which was drawn by tall, gray stallions.

"Are... are these stallions at the Awakening of Power level?!"

"The fifth stage."

Hadjar couldn't utter a word in response. His troupe also had stallions at the Awakening of Power level, but they were only at the first stage. Even then, they could go up to 25 miles per hour and gallop for almost three hours straight.

That was the answer to something Hadjar had wondered over for a long time—how armies and ordinary people managed to cross vast distances. It was apparently possible because there were horses in this world that could be ten times faster than the most sophisticated of sports cars.

Like other animals, the horses could also absorb energy. And they could evolve as follows—first, the simple (or wild) horse. Then a horse would reach the Awakening of Power level, then the Awakening of Mind, then, finally, the Leader. But Hadjar didn't even want to try and imagine the value of a stallion at the Leader rank.

"But first, we will have to clean you up," Senta, the mistress of the brothel, said hoarsely, clutching her nose and not even trying to hide it.

It was her that Hadjar had noticed in the crowd while playing music in the square. In every city, he looked for the owners of brothels, restaurants, taverns, and hotels. And every time, he made sure to play music that, hopefully, would make them want to buy him, despite his appearance.

"Please let me know, Honorable Senta, how much did you pay for me?"

The mistress of 'Innocent Meadow' sat down next to him and took the reins in her hands. She calmly responded:

"Seventy gold coins, Hadjar."

By the demons and gods!

"Now you have to work hard to pay me back."

Chapter 17

The brothel named 'Innocent Meadow' was considered to be the best one in this prefecture. It was right next to the shopping district and as big as the district itself.

Its six buildings formed a kind of hexagon. There was only one entrance if you were coming in off the street, which led to the courtyard. Alongside the gardens and several ponds, there were also shops where the local scientists plied their trade.

They sold a variety of drugs and potions for men. One pill worked wonders on their libido and another helped to ease any tensions. That's how they made their money. Senta, of course, received her fair share of the profits.

They offered a discount to the workers of the 'Meadow', as was stipulated in the contract they'd made with Senta. The discounts were quite hefty, considering how much these potions normally cost in shops that sold medicine.

With red lanterns burning everywhere, the girls were easily visible through their sliding windows. They varied in beauty, and their prices were set accordingly. They were having fun: drinking, sleeping and chatting with various customers.

Most of the buildings were two or three stories high. During one typical evening, thousands of people could end up visiting the 'Meadow'. This was awe-inspiring in a way, since the town itself was rather small, having only three or four million inhabitants. Also, the prices for even the most ordinary of girls were quite high here.

During this 'extravaganza' in the central hall, where the most important city officials were having fun, a figure sat there, covered up completely by its black clothes. Nothing of the figure could be seen, only their white gloves as they ran skillfully along the strings of a musical instrument.

The customers ate and drank, laughed and sang. They kept hugging the giggling girls merrily, reaching under their skirts and kissing their satiny necks with their greedy lips, spilling alcohol all over the silk pillows and fleecy carpets. And the figure just kept on playing as it all happened.

Hadjar had gotten used to it. By now, he'd spent as much time in the brothel as he had in the freak show—five years. Just yesterday, he'd turned seventeen.

He had officially spent seventeen years in this world. Seven of them had been happy and carefree, but the remaining ten, however, hadn't. For ten years now, he'd been living as a powerless freak, unable to take up even a broom, let alone the sword.

"Play louder! I can barely hear you" Some official roared drunkenly and moved his hand back to throw a slipper at Hadjar.

A tiny girl immediately came around the corner. She had red hair, black eyes, and white, almost porcelain skin. Her name was Eina, and she was the daughter of the brothel's mistress. Smiling charmingly, she whispered something into the official's ear, and he calmed down.

Moving back, Eina winked at Hadjar. The former Prince wasn't always able to find company, especially if said company was a cute girl. He was really only friends with one—Stepha. She knew Eina well and had, apparently, put in the right word for him. That's why Hadjar and the red-haired girl were friends, too.

She often gave him extra food or left him way too generous 'tips'. Hadjar saved them carefully. He never forgot his primary goal—finding a potion.

In this world, there were only two ways you could obtain something. Either you took it by force, or you bought it. While the first option wasn't available to Hadjar, he was hoping that the second one would be his salvation.

***

In the darkness of the dungeon, with only a pervasive stench to keep her company, an old woman hung, suspended on thick, iron chains.

Her body was emaciated to the point where she nearly looked like a skeleton. She was covered in numerous cuts, with only a few rags protecting her modesty.

The only sound that disturbed the oppressive silence was the creaking of the unoiled iron hinges.

A broad-shouldered, gray-haired man entered the room. He was wearing a heavy gold crown. Soldiers in blue armor accompanied him, carrying torches. The light from the torches was making him squint.

"Primus," the woman gurgled out. "You're so afraid of me that you've come with a squadron of guards."

Without any hesitation, the King slapped her in the face. He didn't even pause to consider if he should remove his armored glove first. The woman's head swung limply to the left, and scarlet drops fell to the stone floor.

"Where is it?"

"You need to be more specific, Primus."

The woman gave him a toothless, horrible smile and then laughed. It was a wild, almost crazy sound.

"Where is the King's Sword, Nanny?!"

Yes, the Nanny, who had changed so drastically, was the one in the dungeon. Before, it seemed like she practically radiated an aura of health. These days, it was hard to look at her without bursting into tears.

"Didn't I teach you, Primus…" the former nursemaid of the royal brothers barely grunted out. "That it's bad to take someone else's things?"

Another slap to the face, followed by a new cry of pain and a fresh surge of scarlet was Primus' response to her mockery.

"Ten years, Nanny. Ten years of suffering. Maybe it's time to stop resisting? Tell me where the King's Sword is, and it can all end."

Despite her weariness, the pain she was enduring, when she raised her head to look at him, Nanny's gaze had a sliver of sanity.

"And hand you the heirlooms of the royal family? You?! The man who murdered his own brother!"

Primus swung, but the third strike didn't land. He only lowered his hand feebly.

"Haver was weak."

"Like you're so strong. You had to chain me to a wall, coward." The Nanny spat at her former ward. "What about your daughter, Primus? Does she know who she really is? Does she know what actually happened to her parents and brother?"

Primus jerked his head to the side as she'd slapped him.

"You old witch!" He hissed, and, turning around, started walking away from the woman's prison.

"See you next year, Nanny."

He was almost gone when he heard her speak. "It might take a year, maybe two or three...but you can feel it, Primus. Am I wrong? You know your time is running out."

"What do you mean?" Primus turned back.

He only received a dry, croaking laugh in reply. Even the seasoned soldiers shuddered at the sound. It was straight out of a fairytale told to children: the raspy cackle of an evil witch.

"Don't lie to me, Primus. I can't see much, thanks to your torturers, but when I lost my eyesight, I gained something else. And I'm sure you haven't been sleeping much, that you wake up often, drenched in sweat. You can hear him coming to kill you, can't you? The soft sound of his armor as he moves toward you, the rattle of his sword as he pulls it from its sheath. You can feel the ground itself shaking as your doom approaches."

"Shut up, old woman."

"Hadjar is coming." The toothless smile only further disfigured her already deformed face. "The rightful King is coming for you, Primus. His sword is like a river. His power is as endless as the sky. His rage will incinerate your soul."

"Hadjar is dead," Primus growled back. "If he's alive, he's hiding in a hole and waiting for death to take him. He's a freak and a cripple, what could he ever do to me?!"

Nanny only smiled wider.

"Are you trying to convince me or... yourself?"

Primus stood, and the laughter of the witch followed him as he turned around and walked out. He slammed the door forcefully, leaving the woman in complete darkness and solitude once more.

"Hadjar is coming!" He heard her muffled cry from the casemate.

"I warned you..." The Governor was leaning against the wall. He was still as cold and arrogant as ever and kept looking at his nails. "If you had just killed the boy, none of this would be happening."

Primus closed his eyes, then abruptly drew his sword and swung it twice. A barely visible black haze remained in the air after each strike. Four dismembered bodies fell behind him in a shower of gore, dropping their torches. Even their artifact armor, that had been forged for them by order of the King, failed to save them.

"Why did you kill them?" The Governor seemed surprised.

"They would've betrayed me at some point," Primus cleaned the blood off his sword.

They'd seen his weakness, they'd heard about the Prince... Primus was right; they would've betrayed him eventually.

"Why haven't you given up on this King's Sword nonsense by now, Primus? It's just a legend from your village. If such an artifact did exist, Haver would probably have had it. Not that he could've ever understood what it was."

"It's not a legend." The King smoothed his hair down. "I can still remember my great-grandfather giving Nanny a scroll on his deathbed. I noticed that the scroll had a map on it."

"That map could lead you anywhere," the Governor laughed.

Primus, ignoring the Imperial bastard, grabbed a torch from one of the dead men and began climbing back up.

"You should be worrying about the Empire's share of the ore instead! You were nearly 450 pounds short last time."

The King only cursed in response. He wandered through the long, empty Palace corridors. One of his first decrees had been to expel all the minor nobles from the royal residence. Haver might've let them live there, but he had no such plans. The Palace was surprisingly empty without those parasites around to fill it up.

The abandoned classrooms no longer had thousands of disciples in them. The Master, who had used to teach thousands of disciples on the parade ground, was now all alone, fighting wooden dummies all day long.

It was only possible to glimpse pale, frightened maids occasionally. They feared the King and were careful not to upset him in any way.

"We need more slaves," Primus whispered to himself.

The mine needed more laborers and the work there was torturously hard. People were dying at a terrifying rate. There were never enough slaves. It was getting hard to find any suitable people from the southern region to replace the losses with.

Primus didn't notice that he'd come to the lake. The garden in the Palace occupied such a large area that the whole lake fit in there. The mountain where Haver's castle used to stand could be seen in the distance. He almost never visited it, and a squad of soldiers always guarded the ruins.

Primus stood over a nameless and lonely tombstone that had been placed in a rather picturesque place.

"I spared your son," Primus said in a low voice. "For the sake of your memory, I spared him—and now I can't sleep. The guard sold him if you can believe it. He sold your son. I made sure the gold he earned was enough for the rest of his life!"

Primus looked at the golden monument standing in the throne room. Only a few people knew how the sculptor worked—he would pour boiling hot metal directly onto a living person.

"It's such a nice day today, brother," Primus said as he let the wind caress his face.

"Remember how we used to sneak out and go into the city on days like this? We'd play with the local boys, and we never lost a single game, not even once."

Two swans swam along on the placid surface of the lake. They were majestic, beautiful and utterly indifferent to him.

"Do you ever miss those days, brother?" It seemed like Primus was aging noticeably as he stood there. As if the weight of the centuries he'd lived through had fallen on his shoulders, all at once.

"I do. I admit it. But why are you so silent, brother? Answer me."

"Dad!" someone suddenly shouted from behind him.

Primus turned around.

An incredibly beautiful girl was running across the meadow toward him.

Her skin was whiter than snow and her golden hair was so long that it almost brushed against the ground.

She was as tall as any man could ask for. Her breasts, hidden by her chaste dress, were perky, tantalizing people wherever she went. Her long legs were admired by just as many men, even called art by some.

Her waist was so thin that one could wrap their hands around it and almost touch their fingers together.

"Elaine," Primus smiled and suddenly looked reinvigorated.

He hugged the girl that had become his light in the endless darkness.

"Dad," the girl hugged the King back tightly. She hadn't seen her father for almost a month now. "Have you come to visit my uncle's grave again?"

The King nodded.

Elaine looked at the nameless headstone angrily. It was the reason she didn't like this garden.

"You should've had it demolished a long time ago! He killed Mom! He even tried to kill you and my brother! All because he wanted the throne…"

"I know, my daughter, I know," Primus said, stroking Elaine's golden hair. "But he was still my brother."

"And why did you make my brother join the army? Now, who's going to ward off my… suitors?"

Primus smiled kindly at her. There was true tenderness and warmth in his gaze, as he looked at her. A whole ocean of it.

"Maybe you should consider accepting someone's offer."

"Don't even joke about that, dad!" Elaine said menacingly. "They're all stupid and lazy. Not one of them can even hold a normal weapon in their hands. Them being able to actually fight me is out of the question."

Primus only shook his head.

"With every day that passes, I am more and more convinced that letting you train with your brother was a mistake."

Elaine laughed again and clung to her father. When she was with him, she felt so safe, so loved.

Hadjar awoke from a strange dream. It seemed like an old sword, stuck in stone, was illuminating a dark cave somewhere. It seemed to be calling out to him.

What a silly dream... He thought.

He put on some dark clothes, covered his face and head with a black hood, wrapped himself up in his cloak, looking a bit like a bat, and went out into the city.

Chapter 18

 Hadjar plunged into the normal chaos of the city. People were scurrying about everywhere—some were carrying something, others rushing to get to the market that was opening, and a few were just walking around. All in all, it was familiar, almost comforting, despite oddities like the fabrics people wore.

"Look!" someone in the crowd shouted.

Everyone looked up. There was a black line going through the white clouds, and a small boat racing after it. The boat had no sails or masts. It was nothing unusual—just a boat in the sky, moving at great speed as it chased after an adept.

The two silhouettes disappeared behind the clouds soon enough and people went back to what they'd been doing previously.

"Thief!" A soldier roared, grabbing the hand of an old man in the crowd.

This often happened in the market. Hadjar saw these kinds of scenes frequently. He'd used to spend hours wandering around the different stalls, recording bits of conversations with his neural network. Then he would have the network analyze them, hoping to find a hint about the medicine he needed.

Alas, it was all in vain.

"Sorry!" The old man wailed. "Please, forgive me!"

He was brought to the wooden poles, which, for the sake of convenience, had been placed on the square. There were five strong posts arranged on the small podium. Thirsty, chained up men were already occupying two of them.

"Tie him up!" The soldier grunted, hitting the ground lazily with his whip.

"Sorry! I'm so sorry," the old man pleaded, beginning to cry.

His hands were bound tightly with rope, and he was forced to kneel down.

"Honorable guard," the vendor, who sold cookies, turned toward the soldier. "I don't want to punish this man, please let him go."

"That doesn't matter."

"But…"

"Buzz off!" the soldier pushed the salesman away.

He fell and crawled away because he was too scared to say anything else.

The whip whistled as it cut through the air. There was another cry of pain, then a crying child in ragged clothes ran up to the post to try and comfort the old man. The whip, however, didn't stop and now two cries rang out.

The old man shouted something about his family starving to death, but the soldier was adamant. Despite having turned pale, he continued to whip the child and his father. If he stopped, the next person tied to the post would be him.

The people murmured, but no one dared to address the soldier directly. Everyone knew how harsh and cruel Primus' laws were. No one wanted to be sent to the mine, condemning their family to a slow death by starvation.

"What did you just say?!" The soldier suddenly shouted.

The boy, drenched in blood, whispered something.

"What?!"

"Prince Hadjar…" the child whispered, barely audible. "He'll kill you… he'll kill all of you. Prince Had…"

The blade that beheaded him didn't allow the boy to finish speaking.

The silence was broken only by the sounds the head made as it rolled down the wooden steps. The old man howled in anguish, but his cry was also cut off by the blade.

"Prince Hadjar's the son of a traitor to our country!" The soldier recited, wiping his bloody blade off using the clothes of the unlucky thief. "He won't be saving anyone, because there's nothing to save us from! Only under King Primus…"

"Prince Hadjar," someone said timidly, interrupting the man's speech.

"…It's only thanks to his rule that our Kingdom has become strong. So powerful, in fact, that now 'The Black Gates' and other sects like it bow down before us, and not…"

"Prince Hadjar!" Someone shouted.

"…And not vice versa! King Primus is our true ruler! Only he…"

The soldier tried to shout louder than the crowd but it was a useless effort. Ten thousand people were shouting "Prince Hadjar" all at once. No one knew who started it—maybe one of the young soldiers couldn't stand it any longer and drew their sword or, maybe, someone from the crowd threw a stone because they felt angry and powerless.

Regardless, a rebellion broke out in the square that day. It wasn't the first and clearly wouldn't be the last. It was quelled right then and there, flooding the street with blood. But not even that could prevent the common people from spreading the legend.

They spread the news that the Prince was gathering his army somewhere far to the north. And that, very soon, he would take the capital by storm, destroy the mine, and free his people from the tyranny of his murderous uncle.

And none of them knew that Hadjar, feeling ashamed, had actually fled from the square before the sword even killed the boy.

Wrapped up in his black clothes, he returned to the brothel, where he sat in his room until nightfall.

In the evening, the mistress' daughter came to him. Her smell was a combination of a meadow full of flowers and a mountain stream. She sat down on her knees, in front of him.

"Give me your hands, Hadjar," she asked.

"I can do it myself," the cripple said. "You don't have to…"

"I don't mind," the girl's smile was so warm that it could've melted a glacier.

Hadjar moved the edge of his cloak aside. Eina didn't flinch like the rest at the sight of his scabs and ulcers. She gently applied a special cream to his wrists and hands, which kept them healthy

"Thank you," Hadjar said.

"You're welcome," Eina replied. "I owe Stepha."

Hadjar looked out the window.

It was getting dark.

The lights had already been lit and well-dressed officials, as well as ordinary rich people, were already gathering in the courtyard.

"There's no way you owe her enough to justify taking care of me for the past five years."

Eina smiled at him. Sometimes, Hadjar felt that, for the sake of this girl's smile, he would gladly cross even the impenetrable Eternal Mountains to find the potion he needed. He would do anything to insure the horrors of this world never touched her angelic smile.

He wasn't in love with her.

Love was unattainable for someone like him.

But he felt gratitude toward Eina.

During his ten years of wandering, Hadjar had come up with a simple code he would live by. Those who showed him kindness and treated him well would have it repaid a hundredfold. Those who hurt and mistreated him would get a hundred times worse in return.

Unfortunately, not many people were in the former category.

"Would you believe me if I said that my mother asked me to do this?" She pulled a bandage out of a small medical box.

She then carefully wrapped Hadjar's hands with the bandage. She even put his gloves on for him, to spare him the trouble.

"I wouldn't."

They looked at one another for a while. She was a beautiful girl whose mother took care of her and treasured her. Despite the fact that Eina had been living in the brothel since childhood, she hadn't 'slept' with any man.

Few people wanted to get on Senta's bad side. She knew many secrets and a lot of people owed her. On top of that, the mistress of 'Innocent Meadow' was at the Formation stage.

Suddenly, Eina asked: "Is it true that if you love someone and they love you back, you will turn into a beautiful beast?"

Hadjar just laughed.

"That's an old story I made up so I could eat meat for dinner."

The girl laughed as well. Hadjar rubbed his neck mechanically as he watched the tinkling, leaf-shaped pendant on her collar. It was unlikely that he would ever be able to put something around his neck again and not wake up after having a nightmare about being a slave once more.

"I thought so as well," Eina said.

She helped Hadjar stand up and handed him his instrument.

"Mother's asked you to play on the Dream Floor today."

The Dream Floor? That was where 'the crème de la crème' went to have fun. Only the people at the very top of the food chain ever had the opportunity to visit the Dream Floor. Hadjar hadn't played there yet.

"What about Leila?"

"She hurt her throat," Eina sighed, sad about her friend's misfortune.

Hadjar didn't want to know how exactly the singer (and a brothel worker) had hurt her throat. But, because she had, Hadjar would get the chance to play for the elite today. Maybe he'd finally be able to learn something about a potion to restore his nodes and meridians. Maybe there was even another way.

"Will you tell me a new story today?" the redhead asked him.

"Of course," Hadjar answered distractedly.

He often told her fairy tales and stories from Earth, adapted to the local way of thinking, of course. It was the only way he could thank her for her kindness.

As he climbed the stairs, Hadjar missed the sad look Eina gave him.

Chapter 19

Refusing Eina's help, Hadjar climbed the stairs with difficulty. Facing the gates to the 'World of Dreams', he held his breath for a second and tried to calm his wildly pounding heart.

He hadn't experienced the difficulties that came with puberty in his past life because he simply hadn't been able to feel his body. It hadn't been ideal, but it had still been much better than his current situation. Now, living in a brothel, he would constantly find himself desiring something he couldn't afford.

Even if he had a hundred times more savings and suddenly decided to spend it all on indulging his wants—no girl would've agreed to it.

When the doors opened, Hadjar was calm. But he still felt a powerful surge of desire, even through his forced serenity.

Vats of water were positioned along the perimeter of the huge hall. Girls in wet, translucent silk capes danced in them. It would be impossible to call these capes clothes. The girls were graceful and seductive beyond all reason. They weren't naked, but the wet cloth stuck to their bodies and inflamed the imagination. It somehow looked even more alluring than simple nakedness.

The branches of various fruit trees hung from the ceiling. One could just raise their hand and pluck a juicy, sweet fruit right off of one. Other girls smeared the lips of addled guests with this juice, which was full of the fragrant aroma of flowers and fields. Only the highest-ranking officials were in here. Hadjar even noticed the sons of the most important military and economic leaders among them.

They were hugging several of the 'fairies', pushing their hands underneath their clothes and causing them to make languid, sweet sighs in response.

Some officials, unable to endure it any longer, were busy in the corners covered with thick fabrics. There, the things that had made the 'Innocent Meadow' famous were happening.

Half-naked ladies were walking around and lightly kissing men. This ensured even the more reluctant patrons were coaxed into participating. It was all so exciting.

Hadjar closed his eyes and sighed deeply.

He tried his best to calm the surge of heat that had arisen just below his waist.

"As you asked, honorable Eternal Stream, here he is," Senta suddenly appeared in front of the tables.

She was dressed in red, loose clothes and unsettled people with her cold, unapproachable beauty. No one would dare to even think about touching her, let alone trying to paw her like the rest of the girls.

"Is this your best musician?"

Hadjar couldn't believe it, but it seemed like the heavens had finally taken pity on him and had sent a famous Scholar to help him. Eternal Stream had managed to become famous throughout the whole Kingdom in the last six years.

No one knew the true story of this man's life, but it was said that he was the heir of some famous clan that had gone on a journey to learn more about the world and its mysteries.

People said that he could make medicine that cured thousands of diseases and knew the answers to all questions.

He was dressed very plainly, in green clothes that were belted with a simple leather strap. His calm, gray eyes were alert, despite the situation.

There wasn't a single trace of a beard on his face, and his thick hair had been tied into a tight ponytail.

He looked young, but in this world, age was difficult to discern.

"Yes, he is."

"And what is this musician's name?"

"Hadjar, venerable Eternal Stream."

The Scholar immediately looked more interested, even if only for a moment.

"What a simple name, hopefully, the musician is better." He said sluggishly.

No one mentioned that this was the name of the Prince of the Kingdom. Nobody wanted to incur the wrath of the local general, whose son was, at present, groping some of the most desirable women that Hadjar had ever seen in his life. And that was saying a lot, when you took into account that, in his past life, he had practically lived his life on the Internet.

"Can you play 'The Song of Claird'?" The Scholar asked.

Hadjar knew this work well. Men with broken hearts often asked him to play this difficult song, but Hadjar played it skillfully and with ease.

"I can," he nodded.

"Could you play 'A Summer's Day'?"

That was an even more complex piece of music, and few talented musicians would risk playing it without rehearsing it for a long time beforehand.

"I can."

What about 'Six Moments before Life'?"

The hall became a little quieter.

'Six Moments before Life' was a legend about the birth of the world. It told the story of ancient gods that, tired of their loneliness, exhaled their six lives into the vast void, creating this majestic world. They sacrificed their lives to let others live.

A piece of music more complicated than that one would be

impossible to find in this world (at least in the Kingdom itself). And yet, at the same time, this was the easiest task of all for Hadjar.

His mother used to sing that song to him every night before bed. He remembered all the notes and chords easily, but every time Hadjar played the song, he remembered the smiling Queen and her scent... her warm, gentle hands holding him.

"I can." Hadjar sighed forlornly.

Many people took his sigh as a sign of impending disaster. Perhaps the Scholar thought so as well.

"Play." He waved his hand imperiously, leaning back against the pillows.

And so, Hadjar began to play. With each new note, the heat in his heart was quickly replaced by the cold of the desert night. He was no longer interested in the dancing girls or the carnivorous, greedy laughter of the visitors. All that mattered to him in that moment was the memory of his mother.

He remembered her laugh, how she would run after him in the garden, how they'd painted Elaine's nursery together.

What was happening to his sister right now? What horrors was Primus subjecting her to?

And the longer Hadjar played, the quieter it became. The people stopped what they'd been doing before, plunging into the sad music which was full of hope for a new dawn. They listened, but not for long.

Everyone soon resumed laughing, speaking and even yelling. The musician no longer interested them and only the scientist was still listening to the music, as if he were looking for answers to some of his own, hidden questions.

"Did you like it, venerable Scholar?" The Mistress bowed low.

"I'm satisfied," Eternal Stream nodded. "I haven't heard this melody performed so well for a long time. May I ask you for a room where I can talk to Hadjar in private?"

"My musician isn't an employee of this institution, honorable Scholar. But I'm sure that if you look for..."

"And I'm not a fan of men, dear Senta."

She bowed immediately.

"Forgive me!"

The Scholar waved it off casually.

"I want to reward this musician, but to do so, I have to know his desire. So, do you have a spare room we can use?"

Many were now interested in their conversation. They were jealous of Hadjar's luck. Receiving a reward from one of the most famous scientists in recent years was an incredible success.

"Of course," the owner nodded. "Let me show you the way."

They went down a floor, and she opened the doors to a rather spacious room. There were several screens, mattresses and silk sheets there. Nothing superfluous, but still a relaxing enough atmosphere to indulge one's desires in.

Senta, after a quick glance at the musician, went out and closed the door behind her.

Hadjar, without any hesitation, fell to his knees in front of the Scholar and pressed his forehead to the floor.

"Please, venerable Scholar, tell me if there is a cure that can restore meridians and nodes in the human body after they've been destroyed."

The seconds passed as if they were years. Hadjar didn't hear an answer, and the only thing that intruded on the silence were the echoes of the eternal feast in 'Innocent Meadow.'

Suddenly, Hadjar heard the exact same sound that his own forehead had made a few seconds ago.

"Don't you remember my saying?" A voice asked through tears. "Have you forgotten what I've taught you, your Highness?!"

Hadjar slowly looked up.

He saw the haughty scientist kneeling before him in a low bow, in the same pose Hadjar himself had been in.

"I've been looking for you, my Prince... I've been looking for you for so long..." the Scholar sobbed.

"Your saying..." Hadjar repeated.

An almost forgotten scene from his childhood flashed before his eyes. An old, strict man, and his saying, "Southern winds breeze over internal streams bringing cold winters with them."

The First Royal Scholar had called it the eternal cycle of life in the world, where the death of one person always gave birth to another.

"Teacher?!"

Chapter 20

"My Prince," repeated South Wind, who was now named Eternal Stream.

"But how?" Hadjar asked while clumsily attempting to get his Mentor to stand back up.

Finally, after hugging, they sat down on a long, narrow bench. Neither of them wanted to ponder why it had been placed next to the bed and what sort of acts were usually performed on it.

"First, I must tell you a story, my Prince," and so, South Wind began to talk. "I managed to escape from the Palace the same day the coup happened. For six months, I traveled alongside a trade caravan. We went to the Hot Valley…"

Hadjar's eyes opened wide in surprise. The Hot Valley wasn't just far away, it was unimaginably so. How could they have possibly gone there in just half a year? Apparently, South Wind had gotten lucky by joining up with a rich trade caravan that had strong and durable animals who were perhaps more than mere horses.

"What happened to Nanny and the Master?"

"I don't know," the Scholar answered sadly. He continued talking. "A terrible storm struck. The caravan was almost completely destroyed, but some lucky people, including me, managed to hide from it in a cave. Unfortunately, the exit out of the cave ended up completely blocked off, so we ventured deeper into it. We had been walking for almost a month and had run out of food and water, but then we stumbled upon a city."

They walked through the cave's tunnels for a month?! How deep was that cave?! And they found a city? Hadjar thought in astonishment.

"I won't go into all the details, but I've managed to become the disciple of a great Scholar, a cultivator of the Lord Stage."

"The Lord Stage?" Hadjar asked. "What's that?"

"The Stag most Imperial cultivators can only dream of. The level that almost borders on the magical. Look here, my Prince."

The Scholar took a rectangular piece of yellow paper out of his pocket. Unknown symbols were inscribed on it in red ink.

South Wind held it between his index and middle finger and began to murmur something. At some point, the talisman flashed and a ghostly, golden diagram began to circle above their heads.

"Analyze!"

[The request is being processed … The request cannot be processed. Error —'Unknown Object']

"What was that?!"

"Don't be afraid, my Prince, it's only a small spell. You see, even though I've only reached the stage of Transformation, it's not difficult for me to use the knowledge of the great sage."

A spell? There are spells in this world? Fortunately, the neural network had managed to record everything in great detail for later.

"As you can see," South Wind pointed at his strong, young hands and smooth face. "The great Scholar can easily rejuvenate a person. He did it as soon as he accepted me as his disciple. But, alas, I am only talented by the standards of our Kingdom and can't do the same for you."

The Scholar looked longingly in the direction of the east, where the vast desert lay.

"My abilities are below average by the metrics of this world as a whole. I learned only a little from the wise man, and that knowledge was enough to make me the 'Honorable Eternal Stream'."

"And why have you returned?"

"To find you, my Prince," the old man responded with a nod toward Hadjar. Admittedly, he now looked young and was very handsome. "During my apprenticeship, a caravan came to the city. As it turned out, some cunning merchants knew about his existence and had decided to bring him goods that can't be acquired underground. Some of them had heard about the situation in our Kingdom."

There was a pause.

"Please, will you allow me to examine you, my Prince?"

The Scholar reached for the black cloak covering Hadjar. He hesitated but eventually allowed him to pull off his hood.

"I hope demons eat Primus' body and soul!" South Wind breathed out, lowering his hand. "After bribing some greedy officials, I managed to find out about some of the things that happened to you, but this…"

"How did you know where to find me?"

"I didn't," the Scholar smiled for the first time that evening. "But I'd guessed that you would decide to make a living out of this."

"Because music is the only thing I can do now."

"Exactly. And so, for seven years, I wandered around the Kingdom, and everywhere I went, I asked people to play 'Six Moments before Life' for me'."

Hadjar shrugged.

"Well, I would think that, among the millions of musicians, you surely found a few that were capable of performing it."

The smile on the Scholar's face became even wider.

"But no one, except Elizabeth's own son, could've played her version of the song for me."

Hadjar blinked and smiled warmly as well. Even after her death, the Queen was still trying to help him and doing her best to protect him.

"That helped me recognize you. Although, to be honest, finding you wasn't easy. I've heard about almost two dozen different Hadjars. It's like Her Majesty had foreseen the future and thus chosen a suitable name for you."

The former Prince couldn't disagree with that. Walking around the city, he often heard his name being called out multiple times. Perhaps that's why Primus' secret service hadn't been able to find him all these years.

"Esteemed mentor," the smile vanished from Hadjar's face, giving way to a heavy, resigned sigh. "Primus destroyed my nodes and burned the meridians in my body. All this time, I've been trying to find a clue about the potion I need, but..."

"But I got lucky and found it!" And with these words, the Scholar took out a scroll from the depths of his clothes. "Take a look, my Prince."

He unfolded the map. Along with its edge, among the designations for valleys, there were several circles. One circle was quite small, the size of a small coin. The second circle had been drawn around the first one. It was wider, about an inch in diameter.

There were also other 'larger' circles, from one to three inches in diameter.

While Hadjar was examining the map, he gave the order for his neuronet to record it. In this world, maps were valued almost as much as some of the Techniques. It was very difficult to get a hold of some of them.

"That's strange, Teacher," Hadjar suddenly said. "I remember all of your lectures, but I can't remember these designations at all. These mountains, these forests... All of it's foreign to me"

"That's because it's not a map of our Kingdom."

Hadjar looked at him.

"Observe this area," South Wind pointed to the smallest circle, the one that was no larger than a coin.

"Is that Lidus?"

"No," the Scholar shook his head. "That is the Empire of Darnassus."

"The Empire of Darnassus?!" Hadjar practically shouted.

The Darnassus Empire was a huge territory that united numerous sects, family clans, and kingdoms. It was almost endless, but on this map, it had been designated as something small and not worthy of attention.

"What is that around it?" Hadjar pointed at the outer circle, which was several times larger than the Empire itself.

"An organization that controls our Empire and some others as well."

"Others?"

The Scholar sighed.

"This world is truly enormous, my Prince. Living in the Palace, we didn't get to see even its smallest part."

"And the other circles are also organizations?"

"Yes," the Scholar nodded. "The sage gave me this map. He said that it's the simplest one he has. That day, he changed my view of the world by showing me his personal map. It occupied a wall the same size as mine had been, in the palace. But it was on the same scale as this scroll."

Hadjar stopped breathing. How abnormally gigantic was this planet? Or was it even a planet? After all, if the Earth were to become several times larger, it would cease to be 'solid' and would become a gas giant instead. And this world was thousands, no, tens of thousands of times larger than the Earth.

"Now direct your attention here, please," the Scholar moved his finger farther and farther East and then poked at a lake designation. In reality, that lake was probably larger than the ocean. "This is the lake of Forgotten Hopes. The sage told me that the Flower of Hope grows there. If a person picks it during a day when both the sun and the moon have appeared in the sky, then boils it in the lake water and drinks the concoction, they'll be reborn. Their fate will change. Their appearance will change as well. At the same time, their body will be rebuilt, completely."

"So… My nodes and meridians…"

"Will be reborn along with your body," South Wind nodded.

Recording the route in the neuronet's database, Hadjar gave the order to calculate the approximate path length and travel time.

[Estimated time of arrival, excluding possibilities of unforeseen circumstances, is 79 years. The calculation was made with a mode of transport at the Awakening stage of power as the baseline.]

"We have to travel a long way, and, seeing as you're not a practitioner, your main enemy will be time itself," the Scholar said and then took out a flask with several red pills from his pocket. "The alchemists of the underground city made this for me. Each of these pills can extend the life of a mortal by twenty years."

"When are we leaving?"

"Today, my Prince! A wagon drawn by very powerful horses is already waiting for us at the…"

At that moment, a thin arrow pierced the paper partition, flew through the air and stabbed into South Wind's back. Carving a hole through his body, it ended up embedded in the floor, just a few inches from Hadjar's 'legs'.

Chapter 21

The Scholar's spell began to flicker, then exploded into gold dust and disappeared altogether. Hadjar suddenly heard a whole cacophony of new sounds, since South Wind had apparently been keeping a sound barrier up around them.

"Teacher!" Hadjar cried out, ignoring the sound of clashing blades, the crackling of flames, and all the shouting coming from outside.

"My Prince!" Pink foam bubbled at the corners of South Wind's mouth as he spoke. "Take this."

He took out a small notebook from his pocket, his hand trembling all the while. Two flasks full of pills and a map etched in wood, which depicted a road and a horse, were taped to it.

"That's... the spell. And the seal... for ... the wagon."

"Teacher," Hadjar couldn't hold back his tears.

Yet again, a loved one was dying in his arms.

"Good luck... my... Prince," South Wind sighed, and his last words were: "Now I can be at peace."

A great Scholar died in the arms of a freak that day. A man who'd devoted his life to serving the Royal family. And even while dying, he could only think about one thing—how to help the true Prince of Lidus.

Hadjar took the notebook, and then awkwardly jumped to the side.

Breaking the wooden bars and tearing through the paper as he went, a fat, naked official burst into the room. He gasped and pointed at South Wind's back, where the sword was still lodged. Hadjar rose to his 'legs' without hesitation and, after a bit of a struggle, pulled the blade out of his deceased Mentor's body.

"Help..." The official croaked out.

He worked in the local court and had managed to send almost forty thousand people to the mine in less than four years.

"The gods will help you," Hadjar muttered and staggered out, dragging the sword behind him. Naked, screaming girls ran all around the place. Many of them tried to smother the flames that were engulfing everything in sight. Burning debris kept falling from the ceiling and it was difficult to breathe. Black smoke choked anyone that tried to inhale, the smell of burnt flesh and wood permeating everything.

Officials could sometimes be seen—racing for the exit while trampling the prostitutes and anyone else that came close to them. They even cursed the people that got in the way of their mad dash. Hadjar steadily made his way through this nightmare, a stoic patch of calm in a sea of fire and fear.

Unlike the others, he was able to think clearly. He wasn't moving down, where the fire was apparently raging and only getting worse. Instead, he planned to go up, toward the Dream Floor. He hoped he could use the gutter there. It was made of iron and wide enough for a man to use to get down.

Dodging yet another burning wooden beam, Hadjar swore and removed his black clothes. He continued walking upstairs, now dressed in only a light, blue robe. The people who saw him screamed in terror.

It seemed like a demon had come for them, raining fire and brimstone upon their sin to cleanse it.

Hadjar knew about smoke inhalation so he used his sleeve to try and negate it, even as the fire grew so hot that his lungs burned on every inhale. Despite all of this, feeling weak and a bit disoriented, he managed to get to the 'Dream Floor'.

He opened the door, which was untouched by the flames for some reason, and entered. Upon seeing what lay within, he immediately froze up.

In the baths, where lovely girls had once danced, the water had now turned red from all the spilled blood. The girls themselves had been left strewn about, horribly butchered. Their glassy-eyed expressions would forever reflect their horror and disbelief.

The dismembered bodies of officials and even the members of the magistrate lay on the floor, drenched in scarlet.

"Young Master, you have to leave!" A man wearing gray urged the General's son.

The old man, surrounded by several dozen soldiers, stood next to his liege. The General's son was looking into the eyes of a girl pinned to the floor beneath him and moving in a violent, repetitive way. The girl beneath him was still breathing... Eina?

Hadjar didn't immediately notice that the guy was naked below the waist as he lay on top of the screaming and crying girl.

The red hair covered the floor around them. The torn green pendant lay nearby.

She looked at him, her vibrant eyes pleading with him.

"Hadjar!" Eina shouted, continuing to sob.

The soldiers reacted to her exclamation. They turned and shuddered once they caught sight of him. What they saw was a horrible monster standing in the doorway. He held a scorched sword in his hands, heedless of the raging inferno trying to enter this room as well. The old man, a devoted servant of the Garrett family, was using an amulet and that was the only reason why the flames hadn't devoured them yet.

He pressed the glowing sphere to his charge's chest, trying to calm the Genera's son, who'd gone mad with rage and lust.

"Eina!" Hadjar cried out.

At that moment, he wasn't thinking about his cultivation, the map, the flower... He could only see the girl who, for many years, had been his only light in this dark world. And she was suffering.

He saw the kind, sweet Eina being raped.

In that moment, he cared about nothing else. All the rage, all the anger, all the pain and darkness that had been accumulating in Hadjar's heart all these years was unleashed, all at once, in one swift slash of the sword.

Hadjar screamed, his anguish both mental and physical. He was standing at a distance greater than fifty steps.

In fact, the former Prince stood almost seventy steps from the General's son, and yet the ghostly sword strike still landed. It cut open the rapist's cheek.

He screamed and put his hand over the bleeding wound.

He fell off the weeping Eina like a lead weight, then looked toward the doors, where the freak was standing, holding a sword and breathing heavily. Blood flowed from Hadjar's hands, mixing with the pus of his ruptured ulcers. It was an eerie sight that sickened the General's son. Any desire he'd felt vanished instantly...

"Kill him!" the man ordered desperately and, after saying something to Eina, took out a dagger...

"No!" Hadjar screamed, but it was too late.

The blade slit the girl's throat. She tried to stop the blood from seeping out, but her beautiful eyes quickly grew dim and she breathed her last.

An arrow flew toward Hadjar, but it didn't hit him.

Senta, who'd been pierced through with a sword and nailed to the floor, was screaming like a wounded beast. A black light began to radiate from her.

"Protect the young Master!" The servant shouted and the soldiers, not paying any attention to Hadjar, surrounded their lord with their bodies.

They did so just in time, as Senta detonated her own energy a moment later.

The explosion was so powerful that it easily turned the brothel's top floor into a pile of rubble and threw Hadjar around like a ragdoll. He flew through the air, unable to control his fall. However, it seemed like he wouldn't be dying today.

He fell into the gutter and rolled down it, suffering wounds inflicted by the boiling water and scorching hot iron.

Landing on the ground, the scalded Hadjar hurried to crawl away, screaming in pain.

Behind him, clearly visible despite the darkness of the night, the brothel was burning down. He'd considered it his home, even if he'd never felt much love for it.

"Kill him!" the hysterical cry rang out and black arrows thudded into Hadjar's back.

In fact, they'd fired so many that not only were Hadjar's back and arms filled with them, but some arrows had also sunk into the earth all around him.

He vaguely remembered what happened next. Apparently, he fell into the sewers and the water carried him somewhere. Hadjar spun and was tossed about in the filthy, stinking muck.

Then the stream carried him all the way down to the river. It carefully, but swiftly, not letting Hadjar collide with the rocks, carried him further and further from the city and deeper into the forest.

How much time had he spent in that stream?

Hadjar, completely exhausted, had lost track of time long ago. He inhaled desperately whenever he could, filling his lungs with life-giving oxygen.

Then there was a waterfall and an undercurrent drew him into the cave that changed Hadjar's fate.

An ancient dragon was waiting for him there.

***

"Are you ready, Hadjar Duran?"

"Come on, you bastard. Do whatever you need to..."

And then the cave was flooded with the man's cries of anguish and the dragon's roars.

[Urgent message for the user! Unauthorized changes to the owner's body detected! One of the vital organs has been replaced!]

The old heart of Hadjar, who had endured so much pain and despair, was sinking into a whirlpool. The dragon's heart was now beating in his chest instead. It had been created by Traves, using a drop of his blood and all the willpower that he'd been able to muster.

The dragon died, and the man was reborn.

The age-old chains were crumbling, the ancient dungeon was collapsing, and the streams of water enveloping the body that was writhing in agony were carrying it towards the sunlight flickering above the surface.

***

Several people were walking along the lakeshore. A little boy, carrying a bundle of wood on his back and leaning on a frayed, thin staff was among them.

"Grandpa, look!" the boy suddenly cried out.

He was pointing at the center of the lake. Nothing had been there yesterday, but now the waves were pounding against the edge of a cave that had risen above the water.

"Gods and demons," the people in the group gasped.

They were carrying a long pole on their shoulders that had a fat boar tied to it.

A group of hunters looked at the cave and they saw the face of a sleeping man at the entrance of it.

"There's a man in the cave!"

The half-naked young man was lying on the rocks close to the entrance. Water lapped at his feet and his long hair covered his face. Despite his current state, there was something about him that took many people's breath away.

The young man, even while unconscious, seemed to be as mighty as the mountain in the east. Suddenly, a bell started ringing in the ruins of the Royal castle.

Chapter 22

Hadjar was dreaming. He saw a stone inside a cave untouched by the rays of the sun. The cave was within a distant mountain that was shrouded in a dense fog. The stone stood in the middle of pitch-black water. There were symbols on the stone that had been carved out by sword strikes. Seeing these symbols, Hadjar's heart sank.

He felt like they were going to cut him if he looked at them any longer.

He averted his gaze and immediately cried out in horror when he saw a blade that could take his life merely by being in the same room as him.

Hadjar awoke abruptly, taking a half-sitting position. The barely distinguishable images were still flickering in his head.

The cave. The stone. The sword.

Hadjar shook his head in an attempt to ward off the delusion. He even slapped himself on the forehead. However, this only resulted in him feeling an unpleasant stinging sensation.

"What the hell..." Hadjar couldn't believe his own eyes.

He was staring at his hands, marveling at how they'd changed compared to what he'd grown used to over the past decade. There weren't any scabs, nor were there any abscesses or gray scars—only clean, healthy, dark skin that was covered in short, black hair.

He then tossed his blanket aside. He didn't spare a thought about how it had even appeared there in the first place.

With tears in his eyes, Hadjar wiggled his toes. The man now had strong, long legs. He bent his knees and, laughing while he cried, fell back on the bed.

He spent nearly a quarter of an hour laughing hysterically. The laughter only died down toward the end of it, leaving him sobbing quietly.

"South Wind," Hadjar said in a low whisper.

His teacher had given his life in order to help Hadjar be reborn. He'd done so selflessly, doing everything he could to help, expecting no reward.

Another name was now on Hadjar's long list. Correction, a nameless face. Regardless, it was as high up on the list as Primus' own.

One day, the General's son would pay for his transgressions.

Hadjar would make sure that the Scholar could rest in peace.

Sighing, Hadjar got up.

That's when he realized that he was in a wooden hut. There was a bed against the wall of the small room he was in.

Other than the bed, there was a homemade nightstand and a window made from a dried animal gallbladder. The house looked rather shabby, because in normal towns and cities, people could afford glass.

Hadjar tried to take a step toward the door but immediately fell down, gripping his knees tightly.

"Idiot," the young man rebuked himself.

Sure, he had his legs again. However, for the last ten years, he'd been walking around on wooden sticks and was now suddenly much taller than he'd been before.

He would likely have to learn how to walk again.

At that moment, the door opened. More precisely, somebody tried to open it, hitting Hadjar on the head in the process.

"Oh, I'm sorry," a warm voice said. It was like honey in his ears. "Why did you get out of bed?"

A girl entered the room.

Hadjar mentally rolled his eyes.

Was it his fate to always have women nursing him? Or did someone in the sky get confused and, noticing that Hadjar was generally unlucky, had decided to give him some good fortune for a change?

"I'll call my grandfather," the cute girl cooed and ran off down the corridor.

"Well, that was unexpected," Hadjar whistled while trying to get up.

He only managed to sit up and then lean his back against the wooden wall.

"Status," Hadjar ordered.

[Reconfiguring the interface. Error correction has been completed. Host's Age: 9 days!]

Hadjar didn't really show any surprise since he quickly puzzled it out.

It was actually quite logical when he thought about it.

Upon his rebirth in this world, the neuronet's age counter had returned to zero and then began to track it from the beginning. It seemed as though Traves had done something to his body and Hadjar had been reborn for the third time. Or was it the second time? He was rather confused by his obviously broken cycle of rebirth.

Name	Hadjar
Level of cultivation	None
Strength	0.7
Dexterity	0.9
Physique	0.8
Energy points	0.3

"What have you done, young man?" A... Hercules asked as he came into the room.

Hadjar was unable to come up with any other names for this man. He was about seven feet tall and his shoulders were about three feet wide. His mighty hands could've easily turned Hadjar's head into pie dough.

In one gentle motion, the man picked up the Prince with ease and put him back on the bed.

"Thank you, Honorable..."

"Robin," the gray-haired Hercules said. "Call me Robin, wanderer."

'Wanderer'—Hadjar mulled the word over in his head. It sounded quite pompous and yet it was no worse than 'Prince'. In any case, it was more mysterious.

"How long have I been asleep for, Honorable Robin?"

"Just Robin," the 'old man' corrected him with a slight reproach in his tone. "We're common people here, we speak to each other without any formalities."

"Ok."

The Hercules nodded.

"Ten days. We even wanted to send for Gnessa. She's our herbalist. A kind of scholar. We thought she could maybe cure you."

Hadjar's hunch was now confirmed. So, the neuronet wasn't mistaken—he was indeed only nine days old now.

"Would it be possible for you to tell me where I am?"

"Of course, wanderer," Robin continued to nod. "Everything's possible. But you know my name, and I don't know yours yet."

Hadjar mentally slapped himself for his foolishness. He wasn't used to offending people so easily. But, in his defense, he'd just experienced another rebirth, however weird that might sound.

"My name is Hadjar."

The old man tilted his head to the side.

Hadjar rolled his eyes.

"Honestly, my name really is Hadjar."

"You have a very simple name, wanderer."

"You have no idea, Robin," the Prince emphasized the old man's name, "how often I hear that."

The old man laughed, tugged at his beard with his mighty fist and, after going back out into the corridor, returned with a stool in his hands. It honestly wasn't much smaller than Haver's throne had been.

Robin shushed his dark-haired granddaughter that was peeking around the corner. She giggled while covering her mouth and then rushed off into the street.

The gust of wind that blew through the hut pleasantly tousled Hadjar's newly grown hair. But something else was the cause of his joy.

He could hear his old friend's voice again, calling to him, guiding him somewhere toward the east.

"Please, go ahead and ask your questions, wanderer Hadjar."

"Where am I?"

"In my house," Robin glanced around the room. "In my room. In the village..."

"Is the village yours as well?"

"No. I'm simply a hunter here. The chief asked if anyone had some room to spare. And I did. We must help people when we can, wanderer."

"Indeed," Hadjar agreed. Especially since he'd been one of these 'people' Robin was referring to.

"We found you in a cave by the lake that's about a six-day walk from here." Robin went on. "Once you regain your strength, don't be surprised by all the people who'll be whispering behind your back. There were never any caves near that lake. We pulled your body out of a rather unusual grotto. By the time we returned to the shore, the cave had disappeared again, covered in stones."

Six days away? So the hunters had dragged him on their backs for days, putting themselves and others at risk.

"You should've left me behind...."

Robin immediately frowned at that.

"I don't know what kind of people you've met before, stranger, but people from our village don't behave in such a manner. Every person here sincerely believes that we need to look after everyone in our country. Otherwise, we won't survive."

"What about the army?" Hadjar asked, remembering that Primus would take people from the village and force them to work in the mine.

The old man took a moment to think about it and then laughed.

He laughed for a long time and quite sincerely, to boot.

His laughter made Hadjar bounce slightly. It wasn't out of fear, but because the bed was shaking.

"What army, pilgrim Hadjar? Those rocks must have hit you on the head... The nearest town—which is Spring Town—is a month away on foot. And that's assuming that you encounter no trouble going through the Woods."

Spring Town—where the brothel 'Innocent Meadow' had been.

But... that's impossible!

Even if he presumed that the fastest and most powerful river had carried him and he'd somehow survived it... he still couldn't have gotten that far!

Unless, of course, Traves' cave, where Hadjar had been found, had magically appeared near the lake.

"And which forest is this?" the Prince asked.

"Just a forest," Robin shrugged. "There are mountains around it, just ordinary mountains. There are other villages as well. We trade with them sometimes. We live very peacefully here. We don't disturb anyone; we just hunt, fish, work the fields and have children. We're simple people, stranger Hadjar."

He clenched his hands slightly as he said this. They were as thick as a young tree trunk, the skin as tough as tanned leather, and the veins looked more like ropes.

"What's that, then?" Hadjar nodded at Robin's hands. "Scars you earned plowing a field?"

"If someone with evil intentions tries anything, we don't allow them to disturb our peaceful way of life."

They stared at each other in silence for a long time.

Hadjar finally nodded and lay his head back on the pillow. He understood what Robin meant. In addition, his credo made it so he'd have to return the favor. These people had put themselves at risk by helping him for no reason other than to help him.

Hadjar wouldn't be able to sleep properly if he didn't thank them...

"Rest up. My granddaughter's name is Lida. She's a good kid, a bit flighty but reasonable. Sleep well and recover your strength. I'll introduce you to the others later."

After that, Robin used the blanket to cover Hadjar and went out into the living room, gently shutting the creaky door behind him.

Hadjar was alone.

He lay there, staring out the window.

Some clouds were floating in the sky.

He didn't find them irritating anymore. Probably because he was no longer so burdened. Hadjar could once again breathe deeply. Feeling alive for the first time in a long while, Hadjar got out of bed after two minutes.

He fell, but, gritting his teeth and leaning against the wall, he managed to somehow stand up on his wobbly legs. They barely obeyed him. He had to use all his strength in order to stand up straight.

Hadjar came to the door and opened it.

"Robin!" He shouted to the old man who'd gone outside. "Do you have two wooden sticks? I'm tired of just lying in bed! Can I help you with something? I'm not used to doing nothing."

The old man turned around... and smiled warmly at him. He seemed pleased.

Chapter 23

 Two people were standing on a covered bridge that connected two high towers in the Palace. A girl in a gold dress that fluttered in the wind was sitting on the railing. Her hair was the color of the midday sun and her beautiful face reflected her melancholy mood.

A tall young man stood beside her. His black hair lay across his shoulders. Heavy bracelets covered his wrists and, along with his blue, expensive clothes, clearly showed that he was someone important.

"I told you, Elaine, that's what dad decided."

"We can still ask him to change his mind!" The Princess insisted.

"Do you really think that'll accomplish anything?!" He chuckled. The handsome young man was Eren, Primus' son. "He'll just end up giving me a lecture about what I need to do and what my duty is."

"But he wants you to join the army...."

"And what's wrong with that? He doesn't want me to be a scholar. He hates them. Considers them to be spineless worms."

They looked at the garden. The nameless tombstone, illuminated by the sun, stood near the lake. They'd never liked it, but the King hadn't allowed them to demolish it, no matter how much they asked.

"Everything will be fine, Elaine," Eren approached his sister and hugged her tightly. "I'll be back soon, scarred and decorated."

"And all the maidens will be yours!" The Princess smiled sadly, kissing her brother on the cheek.

"You'll find yourself a fiancé, too."

"No, I won't!"

Eren laughed and let go of his sister.

"It's not normal for you to not even be engaged at your age."

"It's fine," Elaine snorted. "Not like I could ever be interested in any of the local weaklings."

"Should I bring you a general then, when I return?"

"And he'll bring a heap of whores and concubines with him. No, thanks!"

"You're too fussy!"

"You're a fool!"

"Goldilocks!"

"Shorty!"

They argued jokingly for some time and then grew quiet. Their faces were caressed by the east wind.

Elaine covered her eyes slightly. The Palace would be even more lonely after her brother left. All she'd have to keep her company would be her dreams. A lonely figure often appeared in them.

It was a man, standing on a hill, his sword drawn, facing a thousand ferocious warriors fearlessly.

The figure was always as calm as the rocks beneath him. His clothes would flutter in the wind, a bottle tucked under his simple rope belt. Rags wound around his feet were the only shoes he had.

But despite all of that, the figure was majestic.

Like the rocks beneath him...

Elaine, for some reason, felt a kinship with this figure. It was strange, but she kept waiting for him to come, and each day, she felt that he was getting closer.

The Princess hoped that her wish would come true and her betrothed would come for her. The one who the heavens themselves had decided she would be with. She heard bits of his name sometimes, in the wind.

If she listened carefully, she could discern some of them,

"H....jar."

***

"Add one more stone, please," Hadjar asked the girl who had surprisingly bright, black hair. It was the color of a crow's wing or a moonless night.

"Don't you have a lot already, Bull?" Lida laughed.

She used a mechanism Hadjar had built, easily bringing over and putting one more flagstone on his back.

Hadjar grunted and continued to do pushups. He'd spent the last week in the village shocking the people with how rapidly he was recovering.

He'd been able to re-learn how to use his legs in just a week. With the help of long meditation, he'd gone further down the path of cultivation in this short period of time than during the five years he'd spent in the Palace.

His body responded to long, strenuous hours of exercise like it craved being pushed beyond its limits.

With six flagstones weighing twenty pounds each and Lida (who hardly weighed more than two of the stones) on his back, Hadjar did three hundred pushups.

Progress gained

Strength	+ 0.01
Physique	+ 0.07

The messages from the neural network motivated Hadjar even more.

"Look! Bull's lifting Lida again," the girls that were on their way to wash clothes in the creek laughed as they went past.

The locals didn't call Hadjar 'Bull' because of his might. There were much stronger people than him around. Some of them could turn a cobblestone into sand by just squeezing it. Hadjar had personally seen Robin amusing the village children by doing that.

Hadjar got that nickname for his... inability to be helpful. The villagers knew he'd been ill and therefore didn't condemn him for staying behind when everyone else was working in the field, crafting or helping the village in other ways.

The former Prince knew that it was wrong to not help them. He owed them his life, after all. And so, one day, he decided to help out in the rice fields.

It was a disaster. Hadjar had had no idea that rice was planted in the water in straight rows, without straightening ones back. That was why the Prince had managed to screw up something that, normally, would be impossible for someone to screw up.

The peasants thanked him for his eagerness to help and then hurriedly escorted him far from the field.

And when Hadjar tried to help the potters... well, it's best not to mention that at all.

The Prince was allowed to work on his recovery, given a not too offensive nickname and never bothered again.

"One more... stone," Hadjar croaked out while moving on to the next set of one hundred pushups.

"As you wish, Bull," Lida laughed and, as if on purpose, got off him way too suddenly.

The Prince's arms nearly buckled because of this. But he managed not to fall. He felt he was now in a better position than when he'd been training in the Palace.

And not because he'd been six then, and was now almost nineteen.

No, it was his body... it had changed a lot. His instincts had become sharper, his vision had improved greatly, his reaction time was much faster, and his strength was noteworthy now. What most people would've achieved after many years of training, Hadjar had gotten after a bit over a decade of suffering and one lucky coincidence...

Lida dragged another stone onto his back and then sat on the pile.

"Is it true that you can play the Ron'Jah?"

"Yes," he replied with difficulty.

"Will you play it for me?"

"In the e-e-evening," he groaned out.

"Great!" Lida clapped her hands and jumped slightly. Hadjar groaned even louder at that, to the amusement of the people passing by.

He mentally ordered the system to show him his status.

Name	Hadjar
Level of cultivation	Bodily Nodes. 8th Stage
Strength	0.9
Dexterity	1.1
Physique	0.9
Energy points	0.7

Despite his love of tables, Hadjar acknowledged the convenience of the default setting, so he left it that way.

His characteristics had been growing at an astonishing rate... in the first few days of training. Now they were improving at a much slower pace. Hadjar was doing pushups, squats and running because he was anxious to get acquainted with his new body and its capabilities, not purely for the improvements.

"Wanderer," the Prince discerned his 'landlord' through the sweat blurring his vision. "Would you like to fight?"

"Lida..." Hadjar's voice sounded hoarse.

"Well then!" The girl sighed in mock annoyance, jumping off of him again.

She removed the stone slabs one by one with the help of ropes and Hadjar, his back creaking, stood up. He took a deep breath and began to warm up.

He suddenly realized that he wasn't much shorter than Robin. Hadjar only came up to the man's chest, but that still meant that the Prince was just shy of six and a half feet tall.

Haver would've been proud... He'd always dreamed of having a tall son.

"I'm ready," Hadjar said with a nod.

They went to the square. About once a week, the villagers measured their strength there. The locals checked how much they'd cultivated since last time when the guys weren't just showing off for the girls, that is. It was spring, after all—everyone was looking for a mate.

They walked along one of the central streets. 'One of?' you might ask. It being a village, usually even one street would be a point of pride. But don't forget that the village was small only by the standards of this world. There were, in fact, almost 150 houses in it, and several thousand people lived there.

Hadjar understood how lucky it was that one of the many hunting squads had noticed him. And that the village chief—a thin old man— had allowed a stranger to stay in the village.

The guys were already at the square, warming up. Compared to them, the slender, elegant Hadjar looked like a reed amongst trees.

Every single one of these young men looked like they could easily crush Hadjar with their bare hands. None of their physiques were inferior to Robin's, and many of them were even more muscular than him. In any case, each of them could have, without any 'Photoshop', been on the front page of a fitness magazine.

"Look, Bull's here," the female spectators laughed.

"Hadjar!" The young men, who sometimes joined the Prince when he trained, waved to him.

He waved back.

Various boulders were rolled out to the central square. A handle had been carved in each of them, making them look like abnormally huge kettlebells.

These kettlebells varied in size—from ones as large as a basketball to ones that were a yard in diameter.

Hadjar hadn't seen anyone lift the biggest one yet. There wasn't an adept here that could hold three tons of weight above their head and stay upright.

"Let's begin!"

Robin went first.

Single guys usually tended to be the ones lifting the stones, as it was something of a local 'courting' ritual. And, besides his granddaughter, Robin was alone—he had lost his family in a forest fire.

At first, he picked up the boulder weighing forty-five pounds, and then he grunted and went for the one which was ten times heavier. Groaning, he put it on his shoulders, and, with a loud "Eh!", he lifted it pretty high up and then dropped it to the ground immediately.

The crowd applauded.

The atmosphere was competitive but very friendly.

After the old man went, the other guys approached the stones one by one. Some of them lifted two hundred and twenty pounds, while others lifted three hundred and thirty pounds. Only a few of them could match Robin. And it was only later that two young men came to the fourth row of the stones and lifted the ones weighing six hundred and sixty pounds. The girls rewarded them with especially enthusiastic applause and exclamations.

Finally, it was Hadjar's turn.

He spat on his palms and went to the second row, where the stones weighing 220 pounds were placed. Groaning under the tension, he lifted the boulder and put it on his shoulders.

He was sweating buckets and gnashing his teeth, but, with a loud "Hoof!", he lifted it pretty high up and then dropped it to the ground immediately.

The observers... laughed and applauded a little.

The locals believed that a boulder from the second row could be lifted by a ten-year-old boy. Hadjar was supposed to begin with the third row.

Of course, none of them knew that Hadjar couldn't have held an empty basket a fortnight ago. So, the speed of his progress and recovery was already abnormal by his standards.

The Prince's eyes were full of joy when he looked at his hands which were trembling from the exertion. He felt alive again.

"You are recovering quickly, like a young dragon," Robin gave the Prince a pat on the back. The old man didn't know how right he was. The fact that a dragon's heart was actually beating in Hadjar's chest made him ... What did that make him, he wondered. He needed to ask someone who knew more about these things.

"But I'm not strong enough yet."

"Well, lifting the stones won't make you stronger. You need something else."

Hadjar turned to the old man.

"What are you talking about, Robin?" the Prince asked.

Robin glanced at the guys standing behind him. They looked at each other and then nodded and smiled kindly at him.

"I've talked to the others—we're going hunting soon. It's not that we need an extra pair of hands, but you strike me as a smart guy. Would you like to join us?"

Join the local hunters? The hunters that kill animals which aren't lower than the fourth stage of the Awakening of Power? Animals that can crush the boulders from the first row with just a single blow of their paws?

"Of course I would!"

Chapter 24

'We're going hunting' meant—get ready to go right away.

Hadjar and the old man returned to the hut. Immediately, Robin went to get his equipment: a light chain armor and a strong hunting bow. It wasn't as big as a military one, but it was bigger than the bows used by the nomadic tribes near the southern border.

Hadjar paced near his bed for some time. All of his possessions amounted to his worn clothes, which he'd gotten from Senta, and what he'd gotten from South Wind. Unfortunately, the book had been destroyed by the river water and Hadjar couldn't take the risk of using the talismans without knowing what they did, why they did it and how.

The map had miraculously survived. It didn't seem as simple as it had looked at first sight. He'd also kept the seal for the carriage. Hadjar didn't know why he had kept it. Maybe as a way to remember someone dear to him.

"Here you are," Robin threw a chain armor and a bunch of darts on the bed. "My son used to wear this."

The old man didn't flinch at these words. Not that he was a heartless monster, just... Life here was like that. Common people rarely lived to be as old as him. There were very few resources available, and a lot was required to overcome the threshold and advance to at least the Bodily Rivers stage.

Hadjar wore a simple shirt with the chainmail over it. It was a little too big for him, but it was better than being gored by a boar.

Hadjar belted his wide strip of leather with a metal plaque, armed himself with darts and left the living room. A crowd of more than twenty people had already gathered on the street.

Hadjar knew some of them, but he rarely hung out with them.

He wasn't particularly sociable.

"Today we shall go to distant streams." Robin began talking first.

They were standing right in the middle of the street. The old man drew a small map on the sandy road by using a long stick.

"Iriy saw deer traces there while he was with his brothers." A mighty guy with scars all over his face came forward.

"They went to the north, to the Depression of Waterfalls."

"Is this herd big?" Someone in the crowd of people that had gathered around asked.

"There are two hundred of them there, or even more than that."

Whistles and whispers were heard.

"We'll capture the weakest ones," Robin told the people reassuringly. "We won't be fighting the Alpha."

Hadjar shuddered.

Fight the Alpha? It was a beast as strong as a Heaven Soldier...

"We'll take enough food for two weeks with us, track them down, and then count the number of those whose level is greater than the Awakening of Power."

"Do we need traps?"

"No, we don't." Robin pulled at his beard with a fist. "Luke's squad saw boar tracks. If they fall into the traps during their migration— the whole forest will ring out with their squealing."

"Shall we get a move on?" Iriy asked.

"Yes, let's get going," Robin nodded.

And so, a little more than two dozen villagers, armed with inferior armor and swords, went hunting. They weren't going to hunt simple animals but those that had the Core of Power. Hadjar hoped he could get a hold of at least one beast—they could easily be sold in the city.

"Are you afraid?" Robin gave Hadjar another pat on the back.

He was about to answer 'of course', but, surprisingly, he realized that he wasn't afraid. His heart was beating as steadily as always, and he was overwhelmed with excitement.

"No."

"That's right. There's nothing to be afraid of. Always aim for the eye of the beast; and, please, don't throw a dart if you aren't sure you won't snag the hide."

"Why do you need the hide?" Hadjar asked for the sake of making conversation.

"We can keep some for ourselves and sell the rest."

"Do you sell the hide to the inhabitants of the other villages?"

"Sometimes we do," Robin answered while chewing a blade of grass. "But more often than not, we sell the hide to some wandering merchants. There's this quirky guy from Spring Town. He's a pipsqueak, but he knows all the trails in our forests. The most interesting thing is that he's never gotten any splinters or even scratches. A lot of people from our village have been wounded by wild animals. Some have drowned in the swamp, some have tripped on rocks or branches, but nothing's ever happened to this guy!"

Hadjar looked at his chainmail once more. Well, now it was clear how the village had gotten their hands on some. It should be noted that the baths, mills and water wheel on the creek were the only benefits of civilization to be found in these parts.

Hadjar was very interested in the fun facts that the merchant might know, and he wondered when he would be coming around again.

"When will he be visiting again?"

"In a month."

A month isn't such a long time.

Hadjar paused and began to ponder this. Robin looked at him, nodded and went over to the other hunters.

They approached the largest and most beautiful house in the village. It looked like the place where Hadjar had grown up.

One would think that the chief lived there, but Hadjar had already seen the house of the local governor. He lived near the river, in a hut that was even smaller than the one belonging to Robin.

The villagers followed a simple logic, according to which the best things were to be shared. It was some sort of medieval fantasy communism.

A fat woman came out of the big house, which they used as both a warehouse and 'club' because they would hold feasts and 'wedding dances' there sometimes. She asked about the supplies they needed and sent several hunters inside. They pulled out large, stitched leather bags. Then, everyone was given a smaller bag, filled with jerky, crackers and a jar of water.

Everything was evenly distributed among the people. The total food supply should be enough for two or three weeks.

Next, Robin was given another bag full of different powders as well as leaves and pills. He would take special care of the 'kit'. The lives of his people depended on it.

"Hadjar!" He heard a familiar voice behind him.

The Prince turned around and saw the black-haired Lida standing before him. She was holding a basket and hurrying toward the stream to wash clothes and exchange gossip with the others.

"Yes?"

"Don't forget that you promised you would play for me." And, after saying what she'd come over to say, she proudly sauntered off.

She looked like a duchess!

How amusing.

Hadjar hurried along behind the group. They went out to a high stockade (there was even a watchtower there, and people were stationed on it and wishing them good luck). Then they came to the edge of the forest.

The village was located on the bank of a stream which resembled a proper river. They were surrounded by mountains. Perhaps that was what had saved the village and allowed its people to live in their own little world, cut off from the rest of civilization.

The hunters stopped, pulled off the rags on their belts and began to fashion their makeshift shoes. Hadjar did the same. They had no boots. They were useless in the woods. They would only do person harm since they were made of heavy, tanned skin; they were smelly and made too much noise. They would scare away all the animals.

Robin stopped to pray after he got dressed.

An idol in the form of a horned bear stood at the gate. A bowl of honey and some berries were offered to it.

With the preparations finished, the squad of hunters entered the endless forest.

Chapter 25

When jogging, the average person might cover three, even six miles. Then they take a taxi home. Or they might do a lap around their local park.

However, back on Earth, there are legends about African and Native American tribes whose inhabitants can run for weeks on end. Not too quickly— just a little faster than their usual walking speed.

The locals, whose bodies were as hardy and powerful as young oaks, did things a little differently. They ran for many hours, at the kinds of speeds cars in cities managed. All in absolute silence. They were like the wind as they rushed beneath the canopy of trees.

Naturally, at first, everyone kept looking askance at Hadjar. He charged through the forest like a rhino—almost knocking the trees down with his forehead. Then, using the navigation function of the neuronet (it looked like a ghostly arrow in front of his eyes) and applying his own understanding, he began to run more quietly.

By the evening of the first day, eliciting yet more shocked whispers, he made as much noise as a snake on the hunt. It was difficult to even sense him.

The people marveled at the wanderer's talent. Hadjar only smiled to himself.

The Master had taught him a lot—he only had to remember it.

And the dragon heart beating in his chest was doing something to him. Hadjar didn't understand what just yet, but he felt it.

In the evening, after running a distance that was inconceivable by the standards of a person from his world, but trifling by the standards of the local hunters, the squad stopped for the day. They climbed up to the second tier of the forest—below the crowns of the trees, but still not on the ground.

After they'd secured themselves to the mighty branches and ate a little of what they'd brought in their bags, the people fell asleep, still as silent as before.

Talking while hunting was seen as something only a complete layman would do. And so they talked rarely, and only by using various hand signs. Each of them knew their business well, and Hadjar just tried to keep up. Fortunately, thanks to his new legs and body, he found it easy to do.

A couple of times, he was pleasantly surprised by the messages of the neural network informing him about the scant increases in his physique.

After everyone fell asleep, Hadjar checked whether the straps were holding him tightly, closed his eyes and concentrated.

Once again, he felt the particles of energy in the air. As usual, he reached out toward them with his mind and 'soul' and began to breathe them in and out just like an ordinary person would air. With each breath, the nodes in his body would burn slightly. When the fever became unbearable, Hadjar held his breath and, mustering all his willpower, pushed the energy in the direction of the sinciput—the last point in his body that was still closed.

The power began to shift around like a hot whirlpool and pierced the 'gates' that had been 'closed' since birth. Thus, Hadjar was able to break through to the last, ninth stage of the 'Bodily Nodes'.

To reach this stage by the age of nineteen was unimpressive, even by the standards of Lidus. However, thanks to the dragon, he was now less than a month old.

"Status."

Name	Hadjar
Level of cultivation	Bodily Nodes. 9th stage
Strength	0.95
Dexterity	1.15
Physique	0.95
Energy points	0.8

Hadjar had changed the settings once again, deciding to display the steps he'd reached within the stages in numbers. The message took up less space this way. It looked like something from an augmented reality device but was still pretty annoying. That's why Hadjar tried to use the neuronet as little as possible.

He was pleased with the increase in his stats and the fact he'd managed to progress to the next stage. He easily fell asleep.

The next four days followed a simple routine:

Run.

Halt.

Run.

Sleep.

Run.

Halt.

Then it all came full circle.

Any other group would've lost their minds by now, but the hunters, who'd covered almost a thousand miles in four days, had only warmed up. Finally, something interesting happened.

Robin gave the signal.

His upraised fist meant "Stop".

They were in a small clearing.

The old man squatted down, ran his hand over the grass, and then made several hand signs.

"Herd. Nearby. Two hours. Run."

One of the hunters came forward. He also used the hand signs that Hadjar had entered into his database beforehand, and could now 'read' easily.

"Ours?"

"I don't know. Herd. Deer. I'm thinking."

There was no democracy in the group. Only harsh totalitarianism—what the leader of the hunt commanded was carried out. They had no time or desire to argue.

Finally, Robin punched his open palm three times.

This signal meant "Getting started".

The hunters moved from a 'gallop' to a 'light trot'. They took their bows off their shoulders and nocked arrows. Looking alert, they moved strictly downwind of the herd. Armed with one of the darts, Hadjar followed them.

The farther north they went, the more clearly Hadjar could hear the sound of falling water.

"Tree. Crown. Scout," Robin showed. He pointed to Hadjar and they climbed a tall, deciduous tree. It was almost as tall as a ten-story house.

After getting through the thick crown, the Prince turned his face toward the east wind. Taking a moment to enjoy himself, feeling refreshed, he opened his eyes and nearly fell.

Not because of the vast expanse of the valley that was covered in thick vegetation. The endless sea of green was lined with blue veins—a huge number of streams and rivers.

Some of them formed waterfalls that plunged into ponds and lakes, then ran farther down until they merged into a single, enormous body of water. Billions of tons of water fell onto a huge giant that was embracing the waterfall.

"Dead" the smiling Robin signaled immediately.

"Who?"

The old man tried to show him something, then waved his hand and got as close as possible to Hadjar.

"The ancient titan," he said in a whisper. "The Lord of this valley. The legends say that he was once so powerful that he lifted a mountain with one hand and threw it into the sky, where it remains to this day. And below, he created our valley."

"The one where you hunt?"

The old man smiled.

"The one where our Kingdom is located, and more besides."

Hadjar looked at the ancient creature again. He noticed that it had turned to stone long ago. The legend was most likely untrue, but the giant, who was the size of the famous tower in Dubai, still inspired awe.

"Look" Robin signaled, pointing at something.

In the meadows on the edge of the forest, a herd of deer grazed. You could only ever see such beasts in pictures. They were all mighty and stately, much larger than their 'ordinary' relatives.

The weakest ones were still a higher level than Robin.

The fallow deer were beautiful. Slender and graceful, they looked like arrows that had been shot from a bow.

Robin came down first, followed by Hadjar.

"Herd. Ours. The first—scare." Robin signaled as briskly as if he were speaking the sign language from Earth. At the same time, he drew something on the ground with an arrowhead. "They'll run. We'll cut off. Old ones. Weak ones. Don't disturb the Alpha."

With a glance, the old man 'asked' the people around him if everything was clear. The hunters responded with quick nods.

Robin jabbed his finger at Hadjar.

"Look. Stay close." That was an order that Hadjar didn't intend to disobey.

The old man took out a bundle from the 'first-aid kit' and handed it to the guy with the scar on his face, who moved the fabric aside to reveal a small, shimmering stone. It was too big and too... alive agate.

Hadjar felt the potent energy emanating from the stone.

It wasn't the same as the one in the air, but it was still energy.

Having tied the strange object around an arrow, the scarred man, Iry, who had also been the one to find the herd, ran ahead.

After patiently waiting for the wind to change direction, he came out of the bushes and fired the arrow. It flew at least five hundred yards and landed next to the herd. The deer with the best senses raised their heads but didn't smell anything. Iry had already hidden in the foliage.

Hadjar looked inquiringly at the old man, but he wasn't paying attention to the newcomer. After a couple of minutes, something in the meadow growled. Hadjar's heart sank, even if he wasn't afraid.

The ghostly figure of a gigantic wolf appeared from the stone that had been tied to the arrow.

Damn! It was the size of a house, and its aura was the same as the Imperial Governor's!

The Wolf-Leader, whose spirit the hunters had called forth, snarled and rushed at the deer. Fleeing from its ghostly fangs, they rushed toward the forest immediately, where the hunters were waiting for them.

The Wolf-Leader growled for just a couple more moments. His spirit disappeared after two heartbeats, but the frightened deer were still running frantically toward the safety of the forest and hills.

"In the eyes!" Robin signed.

Climbing up onto the tree branches, the hunters began to fire one arrow after another. The herd, mad with fear, ran farther and farther without noticing that some of them were falling behind.

The oldest and weakest ones.

The well-aimed shots took them down easily. None of the arrows missed their mark. Every single one hit them exactly in the eyes.

The hunters loosed their arrows calmly. They used their sturdy, heavy bows skillfully and with practiced ease. The bows were small but still required enough strength to use that not every royal archer would've been able to fully pull them back.

When ten deer fell to the ground, Robin raised his fist, signaling for everyone to stop.

There was no point in killing more deer than they could safely carry back to the village. And it could also attract...

Suddenly, a human cried out, and the place where Iry had been sitting in ambush erupted in a column of fire 6 feet tall and 2 feet wide. Hadjar had to close his eyes for a moment.

When he opened them again, he saw a gigantic deer towering over the burnt remains of Iry. It was seven feet at the withers. His majestic horns were adorned with the roaring, scarlet flame.

The Beast was at the Alpha Stage, and he had come to avenge the fallen members of his herd.

"Look out!" Robin shouted, but it was too late.

The rest of the deer, apparently obeying their Alpha's 'orders', had surrounded the clearing. They lowered their horns and stood fast, ready to impale anyone brave enough to try and get past their barrier.

Who are the hunters here? Hadjar asked himself, as he shifted his grip on the dart he was holding. Doesn't look like it's us...

Chapter 26

Without hesitation, Robin shot three arrows at once. Well, not literally at once, of course, he still released them one by one. Each of them was aimed at vital areas—the beast's eyes and heart.

Snorting, the deer stomped. Three fireballs coalesced from the flame circling around its horns. They evaporated the old man's arrows as they flew forward.

"Move!" He shouted and pushed Hadjar away.

The fireballs crashed into a tree, burning several holes through it. With a loud bang, the leafy giant teetered and then collapsed. Right on Robin's leg.

He roared like a wounded bison.

"Run!" He shouted, the pain clear in his voice.

But none of the hunters moved to do so. Instead, each of them loosed two arrows. The forty arrows flying at the deer at once hid it from Hadjar's view.

The Prince hoped that this was enough to bring down the Alpha. But it had other plans.

The deer reared up and then sent the entire column of fire outward. It burned through all the arrows and kept going. Some of the hunters didn't take cover fast enough and now their scorched remnants lay on the ground.

Someone let loose a cry full of pain and despair. Dart in hand, a young man jumped forward, lunging toward the beast frantically. Hadjar recognized him. It was one of Iry's three brothers.

Turning around, the deer struck the man's chest with its back legs.

The force of the impact doubled the man over and sent him flying. He hit a stone that was five yards away with a horrific crunch. A fountain of blood erupted from his throat.

The dead body twitched a little and then stilled.

A heavy silence descended on the clearing.

The deer snorted as it looked at the terrified people surrounding it. Rearing up again, it shook the earth with a powerful stomp and the horned beasts began to move inexorably toward the center.

Watching as the hunters shot arrows and burned in the fire, Hadjar couldn't understand it.

He couldn't understand why he was standing still!

With a loud hoot, he threw one of his darts. It flew like a stone launched from a sling, but that wasn't enough to break through the barrier of fire.

"Damn it!" Hadjar swore, watching as one more hunter fell to the ground.

The cries of the man, powerless against the Alpha's flame, echoed in Hadjar's head.

"Run!" He barely heard Robin's voice through the noise.

The old man looked at the Prince with a sad, regretful look. At that moment, Hadjar realized which fire had killed Robin's son and why he'd been so glad that they'd come across the herd of deer.

The old man wanted revenge...

Gripping his last dart tightly, Hadjar paused to steady himself before throwing it. He knew that he wasn't accurate. In training, he'd been able to hit a coin with a sword, while standing three steps away. Of course, he'd been using a sword then, not a dart.

Suddenly, Hadjar remembered an image he'd all but forgotten.

The Master, standing before his 'disciples'. He was armed with only a stick, but, nevertheless, could've used it at a level far beyond Hadjar's capabilities.

The Prince looked at the dart in his hand once again.

It wasn't a sword. However, that didn't matter. He was about to face his death. The important thing was that he did so with his head held high. Bravely. No chickening out. No hiding or screaming.

His name was Hadjar Duran.

He had spent ten years dreaming about finding a cure.

He had found it.

Many people had sacrificed their lives to help him.

He wouldn't allow this beast with fiery horns to end his life! He didn't care about what his weapon was—a sword or a dart, it was all the same. As long as he could hear the call of the wind, he would keep fighting.

Hadjar pulled an iron arrowhead out of a nearby nest. Then he used it to whittle at the dart, shaping it.

Holding the stem of the dart, he calmly stepped out in front of the deer. He heard Robin's desperate shouts in the background.

The closer Hadjar got to the enemy, the more he felt the heat of the flame. With each step forward, the beast seemed to become larger and more menacing.

The Alpha snorted, and the other deer stopped approaching. It's important to note that, at the Alpha stage, the beast had sufficient intelligence, even if it wasn't as smart as a human, to realize what was happening.

Perhaps, after another thousand years, the deer would've progressed further along the path of cultivation and been able to speak, but luck hadn't been on its side.

It had been unfortunate enough to come across a strange, two-legged monster.

Hadjar's eyes, as blue as the cloudless sky, didn't show an inkling of fear, only his resolve, and an all-consuming fury. And so, the Alpha, upon noticing the look of a worthy opponent, took a step back, startled.

Realizing that it had just shown it was afraid, the deer reared up and sent four fireballs at Hadjar.

"Duke Velen, Earl Vaslia, Primus, the Governor, Viscount..." Hadjar whispered the only prayer he knew.

The prayer that he'd come up with. It was his battle cry.

He wouldn't let some deer get between him and justice.

He hadn't gotten to bury his parents yet. He hadn't found his sister.

It was too early for Hadjar to die.

The fireballs left a heat haze in their wake as they flew toward Hadjar. The hunters were shouting about something, but Hadjar paid them no mind. His homemade sword didn't waver.

Making it look effortless, he dived under the first and then avoided the second fireball. He turned on his heel, skipping over the third one and, barely swinging the dart, struck with the sword. It was weak, not even ghostly—a barely perceptible gust of wind. But it was enough to cut the fireball in half.

Hadjar let the two halves of the fireball pass by him, on either side.

His heart was racing.

His blood boiled. He could fight again. He could breathe again. After so long, he was alive again.

His blue eyes lit up and the deer howled with rage and fear.

The beast lowered its head and launched a burst of fire as wide as the torso of an adult man from its horns. It was the most powerful attack it was capable of.

Hadjar crouched slightly and then suddenly rushed forward. He vanished into thin air, leaving only a black mark behind, leaping over the flames with perhaps an inch of clearance, and feeling his chainmail heating up. He held on to his sword tightly, and when he landed in front of the deer, he swung upward with his 'blade' while straightening his body.

The hunters, who couldn't believe that a man was capable of moving so smoothly and quickly at the same time, thought that they'd heard a roar accompanying the sword strike.

The hunters and silent deer both felt the blood freeze in their veins upon hearing that roar.

It was the roar of a dragon.

The wounded Alpha ran back toward the forest, leaving the meadow covered in its blood. It had been foolish to hope that a practitioner whose cultivation was at the Bodily Nodes stage would be able to defeat an Alpha. But he'd been able to hurt it; hurt it and scare it off.

The nearby people had only heard the roar of a Lord of the Heavens, but the beast had seen the Lord itself. It had seen the flame of power behind those deep, blue eyes and had felt the fang lurking in the sword strike. A fang that could cleave mountains in two.

The other deer ran away, following after their leader.

Exhausted, Hadjar slowly lay down on the grass. He spread his arms out to the side and stared at the boundless sky. The 'sword' in his hand crumbled into dust, unable to withstand the force that had been channeled through it.

"Duke Velen, Earl Vaslia, Primus, the Governor, Viscount…" he repeated, almost inaudibly, and closed his eyes.

He didn't even have enough strength left to breathe. But he could still hear the mighty serpent growling somewhere in the depths of his chest, near his heart.

Chapter 27

 Hadjar awoke with a shout and reached for his sword. Instead, he grabbed someone's wrinkled hand and not the makeshift blade he'd wielded previously.

"I'm too old to fall for such tricks, stranger," a hoarse, raspy voice told him.

The Prince turned his head; amber eyes stared back at him. He was tied up, lying in a large bed in the living room of a rather impressive house. In any case, this room was far more spacious than Robin's entire house had been.

The old woman was sitting by the bed, slathering a fragrant, green goo on his burns. She looked like any other forest witch—fat, with a sharp nose, wearing clean, well-kept clothes with visible patches on them.

There was a wardrobe filled with numerous clay jars behind the sorceress. Hadjar saw a variety of medicines he was familiar with inside the wardrobe, marked with the familiar hieroglyphs.

The Prince inhaled the odor of the goo, recognizing the sharp, slightly putrid smell.

[Swamp Ointment. Healing properties: low]

"Is that Swamp Ointment?" He asked.

The witch looked up. He shivered slightly at her glance.

She was a kind of stereotypical forest 'witch.'

"What's your name, smartass?" The old woman asked him, speaking clearly and precisely, unlike the other villagers.

"Hadjar."

She just shook her head.

"Your name is too dangerous these days."

She was obviously not one of the natives. And her house was

situated on the outskirts, outside the village stockade.

"Is your name Gnessa?"

"You're a quick-witted one." Despite her age, the healer's movements were strong and quick. She easily bandaged his hands and right thigh. "How do you know about the ointment?"

Hadjar stared at the old woman for a while. She finished bandaging his burns, got up and walked over to the wardrobe, where she put away the rest of the ointment. It was a rather rare medicine. It would be possible to buy a horse in the city for a tenth of what Gnessa had just stored.

Scholars manufactured all of the healing concoctions, and there were a lot fewer of them than the practicing warriors. Learning how to do it took too long and was too difficult.

"My teacher told me about it." Hadjar had no reason to lie.

"Teacher?" Gnessa was wiping her hands with a rag towel as she spoke. "Did the river bring you here?"

"How did you guess?"

The witch smiled. She came over to a homemade table (to be fair, everything there was homemade) and picked up a bowl of delicious soup. She handed it, along with a spoon, to Hadjar, and then sat down again.

"It brought me here, too. It's brought many people to this and the other villages in the valley. Sometimes, I even think that it takes away those who have been rejected by the outside world: the runaways, the poor, the ones with broken hearts. They are healed here." Gnessa looked out the window and smiled at the midday sun. "The Forest heals them."

That's right—the word 'Forest" was written with a capital letter. She'd pronounced the word 'Forest' with a lot more respect than the natives had.

Hadjar touched his chest. It was hard to argue with the sorceress; his heart really had been broken.

"I won't ask you to be my disciple," she said suddenly. "You have another fate, stranger Hadjar, one tied to wielding a sword."

She looked at him so pointedly that only an idiot wouldn't have understood— the wise woman knew. But, how...

"The merchant told me about it many times, years ago," she said, answering his unasked question. "And then Lida came back one day, saying that the river had brought a newcomer... Then two worn out hunters came out of the forest with a wild story. Iry and his brothers were dragged back in body bags. We asked the hunters what had happened and they... They told us about the Alpha, about the heroism of the stranger. And, of course, you and Robin were carried back to me on stretchers."

"Does anyone else know?" Hadjar asked.

He appeared calm. He was eating soup and talking peacefully with the harmless, old lady. But he was ready for anything. He'd already found at least four escape routes out of this room and a few items that he could use as weapons.

"Do you mean the natives?" Gnessa laughed. "I love them, of course, but they're like pets. They're simple, harmless. They'll never guess the truth."

Hadjar remembered the powerful bodies of the native men and the explosive tempers of the women. He could've argued with the healer but said nothing. Regardless of the situation, it was always better to listen more than you spoke.

"I'm so sorry about your parents, Hadjar," Gnessa took the empty bowl from him. "I didn't know them. I was just a simple student of the Scholar back then. The royal treatments were beyond me, but... They were good people. Yes, the Kingdom had been poor under their rule, but the people... were happy. And now…"

She waved her hand as if to dismiss the thought, stood up, and took out another jar that was full of simple forest berries. The witch offered them to Hadjar, and when he refused, began to eat them with gusto. The native's way of life could probably still affect even the most enlightened people.

"The merchant said that there are no settlements left in the south and the cities are empty. All the people have been taken to mine. Is that true?"

"It's true," Hadjar nodded. "Primus signed a treaty with The Darnassus Empire, which is at war with The Lascan Empire. If Primus delays the delivery of Ore even a little, we'll be wiped off the map. A legion of Imperial soldiers has been stationed in our country."

"The Warlord has his reasons, surely you can sympathize."

"I can?!" Hadjar felt furious.

"Yes, calm yourself, Prince without a crown," her amber eyes lit up. "Or do you not know the story of what happened fifteen years ago? When your father and uncle went off to yet another war?"

Hadjar stood still. Even if he wanted to, he could never forget the day his parents died. What had his father said before he'd died? "It was an accident."

What's the story? What happened at the border?

Gnessa paused and then shook her head.

"I mustn't tell you. I didn't see it for myself. My teacher had been a military doctor back then. One of the injured officers told him. One of the commanders had told that story to the officer. And my teacher's maid told it to me. I don't know how much truth and how much falsehood was in that story. But know this—your uncle had a good reason for what he did."

"What?"

The sorceress was about to say something, but then she smiled slyly instead.

"I'm a witch of the forest, aren't I?" She slapped her knees. "You'll find everything out on your own, Hadjar. And now, take this."

She pulled out another drawer that had a lot of parcels inside. They resembled the one Iry had tied to an arrow and shot near the deer. She pulled one out and put it on the table next to Hadjar's bed. He immediately concentrated and felt the aura emanating from it. It was the aura of a beast at the Alpha stage.

Such a stone would cost at least five hundred gold coins in the city. It was a huge amount of money, even for a nobleman.

However, these stones weren't used for trade around here.

They were used in hunting.

"I can't accept that," Hadjar protested immediately.

The villagers had already done too much for him. The fact that he'd helped the hunters had just been payback, nothing more.

"Accept this gift, stranger," Gnessa slammed the drawer shut and pushed it back under the bed. "I told you, the people here are simple. Don't offend them with your refusal. They wouldn't understand your reasons."

Hadjar sighed and nodded. It would be stupid to deny that he wanted to have the stone. It would greatly increase his chances of breaking through to the next stage— The Stage of the 'Bodily Rivers'.

He would have to open his meridians and allow energy to circulate through his body in order to open up new horizons.

"I want to give you one bit of advice before we part, Prince Hadjar," the witch stood at the door, her head turned away. "Don't seek revenge. It'll burn you from the inside until there's nothing left and you're a shell of your former self, wandering the world."

Don't seek revenge?

For his father's death?

For his mother, who died in his arms?

For his sister, who still didn't know what had happened?

For the ten years, he'd spent living as a persecuted freak?

For the people who'd spent all this time enslaved?

For a country that had become not even a vassal, but a slave to the Empire?

"I'm not looking for revenge," Hadjar could hardly restrain his fury. Gnessa took a step back because his blue eyes were blazing with the force of his wrath. "I'm not going to the capital for revenge. I'm going there for justice."

"There is no justice in this world, Prince. And if there are other worlds, then there is no justice there, either. People don't know how to be fair."

Hadjar chuckled and lay back on his cushions.

The wise woman shook her head with a heavy sigh and walked out the door.

Maybe people didn't know how to be fair, but Hadjar strongly doubted that, after recent events, he was still a man. In any case, his heart was clearly from another tribe.

Chapter 28

Hadjar rested and slept until the evening, and then decided to work on his cultivation. He sat down in the lotus position, crossed his fingers and began to breathe evenly. He absorbed more and more energy with each breath, a lot more than he could've managed back when he'd lived in the Palace.

It could've been the result of growing older, his body getting stronger naturally, or maybe it was because of the dragon heart. It was useless for him to try and guess his own age: the neural network stubbornly kept track of it only from the day Traves had died and Hadjar had been reborn.

The Prince continued to breathe. The amount of energy in his nodes kept increasing. It burned and raged in every center and at every point, he'd opened during his training.

Someone's talent for cultivation was determined by how long they were able to keep the power contained in these 'bodily nodes'. The longer a person was able to hold the power in, the more they were capable of improving their martial arts.

Hadjar had never achieved much in this field. His talent had always been below average. That changed for the better, of course, after his rebirth, but not by very much.

Now he could hold more power, but there were still many practitioners, even in the Palace, among the children of the nobles, who could surpass him in this art.

The dragon hadn't been able to produce a miracle and Hadjar was still totally average, even if a bit above pure mediocrity.

The energy kept accumulating. The burn of it grew more painful by the second. It raged in his nodes violently and chaotically. His body felt like he was on fire. Sweat was pouring from his forehead.

If someone had come into the room at that very moment, they would've seen clouds of steam rising from the body of the young man sitting on the bed.

But no matter how much it hurt, Hadjar continued to absorb energy from the world around him. He knew that if he stopped the process of evolution at that moment, the energy would burn through his 'inner body', setting his cultivation back by a couple of months, at least.

That was the reason why many practitioners hesitated—the fear of failing to transition from one level to another. After all, it was relatively easy to go from one stage of the Bodily Nodes to another. The same could even be said about the Transformation level. Who would want to revert back to the initial stage of the Heaven Soldier for a whole decade after feeling its very peak?

That's why the practitioners needed a variety of resources. They helped them cross the boundaries of the levels without fear of 'rollback'. There was an endless struggle for these resources. Of course, the 'core' of the Alpha Stage beast was not the most coveted of trophies, but it could still help Hadjar.

Therefore, when his nodes were overwhelmed by the energy and seemed as if they might collapse at any moment, the Prince reached for the parcel. He felt the power of the beast's aura; after Hadjar managed to withstand the blow, he took another breath.

This time, he didn't draw on the energy of the world, but the power coming from the beast Core. And if the energy that was always present around him could be considered peaceful and calm, the one that rushed to answer the call of the Core...

It was fierce and not at all malleable. It didn't want to quietly assimilate into his nodes. It raged at them like a storm.

It was battering the walls of the nodes, tearing them apart, inflicting hellish torment upon him. Hadjar still kept quiet. He only clenched his teeth tightly, summoned up all his courage and began to pull in the energy that answered the call of the beast core.

The Prince manipulated the energy in the decaying thread and tried to 'push' it into his body. He did it over and over: once, twice, ten times, a hundred times, a thousand times. Another flash of agonizing pain and a new round of struggling with the power of the beast awaited him after each failure. Hadjar thought about only one thing—whether the power contained in the Core would be enough.

He could not afford to fail.

He spent the whole night struggling to advance, but, by morning, he'd finally succeeded. A thin, blue thread flickered within his body, and energy now flowed through it from his nodes.

Hadjar, exhausted, fell back on the bed.

The pain gradually receded. He felt immensely proud at the fact he'd succeeded and he also felt a lot stronger than before.

"Status," Hadjar groaned out.

The Prince could see, in digital form, the things that other people could only feel. It was his little advantage.

Name	Hadjar
Level of cultivation	Bodily Rivers (1)
Strength	1.1
Dexterity	1.3
Physique	1.01
Energy points	1.7

Hadjar read the message from the neural network. There was nothing unusual and extraordinary to be found. Surely there should've been more...

"What?!" Hadjar exclaimed, instantly jumping up out of bed.

He read it again... and again... and again, but he hadn't been mistaken. His energy points were pathetically low.

At some point, Hadjar realized that those were really his stats and burst out laughing. You're a damn dragon, he thought to himself and laughed. So, that's what you meant, you winged bastard! Damn you to hell!

What a pathetic sight! Any normal practitioner of the Bodily Rivers would've had at least one and a half times more energy at the first stage.

The Master had told him that such a practitioner should've been able to use the 'Scorched Falcon' Technique almost five times. Hadjar wouldn't be able to use even the 'Fried Sparrow' thrice. He was almost one and a half times weaker than any other, even the most unlucky, practitioner.

Hadjar shrugged off the message after he recovered.

Don't look a gift horse in the mouth. It's better than being crippled. And who said it would be easy? Even if he had ten times less power, he would still have arms and legs and a good head on his shoulder—he wouldn't complain. He would keep plowing ahead, never slowing down.

Writhing in pain from his aching wounds, Hadjar left Gnessa's house. She'd already gone off somewhere.

He reached the village by following the trail—fortunately, there weren't any wild animals in this part of the forest. The ones that were so powerful that they could've leveled the village to the ground weren't interested in this settlement and its inhabitants.

They were busy fighting for territory and resources: all sorts of magical roots, herbs, and stones, just like humans.

The whole world was constantly struggling to gain more power.

If the piece of music titled 'Six Moments before Life' was true, then, in Hadjar's opinion, the native gods had created a very ugly system.

"Hadjar," as soon as he went through the gate, the villagers ran up to him.

"How are you?"

"Have your wounds healed?"

"Was Gnessa really scary?"

"Will you have lunch with us?"

"Let's go to the river."

People swarmed him, eager for his attention. Hadjar was no longer a 'wanderer' or 'Bull' after what the hunters had told them. Now he was one of them. Someone who had risked his life for the others. There were husbands, sons, grandsons, and fathers that hadn't died in the forest thanks to him.

Hadjar smiled.

It had been a long time since he'd felt like he belonged anywhere. Like someone who would always be welcome.

"I've promised to play the Ron'Jah," he reminded Lida.

"Then let's go to the meadow. You can play for everyone there."

And so the crowd moved toward the creek, everyone voicing their approval in a hum. In the meantime, on the other side of the village, the merchant had arrived. He was leading a donkey loaded with bales behind him. He kept his goods and other various knick-knacks in those bales. But apart from them, he also had news from the outside world.

Chapter 29

 In the evening, some of the men from the village gathered in the central square, by the fire. There were about seventy people present, sitting on the makeshift log benches. This was the local Council that ruled the village, second only to the chief in authority.

There were no women there.

The natives hadn't heard anything about feminism, and the enlightened customs of the outside world didn't matter in this village. They lived according to an ancient creed: 'the husband says it—his wife does it.' As for the women, they did their best to subtly 'set their obnoxious husbands on the right path'.

Hadjar, who'd never really gotten a chance to do something like this back on Earth, was content. He was feeling particularly comfortable thanks to the pipe of strong tobacco he'd bought from the merchant.

However, the reason why this meeting had been called was the merchant, and not the men's desire to sit around and smoke.

The pipe was the only thing Hadjar had bought, apart from an inferior, rusty sword. He'd gotten a whole deer skin after the hunt, as part of his reward. He'd bought a sword and a pipe with the money he'd earned from the sale of the skin, and received a few silver coins as change.

Hadjar had often smoked back on Earth because it had been one of the few activities that his body was capable of. In this new world, he'd managed to forget about the habit. But now he could afford to start smoking again because his practicing body had the endurance needed to do so safely.

After thanking Robin for the honor of being allowed to attend the Council, he sat there, silently smoking and inspecting the sword lying on his knees. Honestly, the misshapen hunk of metal was unworthy of even being called a kitchen knife, but since he didn't have anything better…

Robin sat down carefully due to his bandaged foot, setting aside something that was all too familiar to Hadjar. It was a wooden crutch, similar to the ones that had replaced his legs for a long time.

"You live in a blessed place, it's much better than the outside world," the merchant said, wiping at his lips with his sleeve.

He was small, with a sparse beard, slim as a rake, wiry, and had bright eyes. He looked like one of the pickpockets Hadjar had seen plenty of at the fair.

"What's going on out there?" The chief decided to ask immediately.

The old man, despite his deceptively simple appearance, was tenacious and meticulous, as a ruler should be, delving into all the details and not leaving anything to chance. He approached this the same way he'd gone about training Robin, who was to take his place in the future. Hadjar learned about all this from the villagers with whom he'd spent the whole day.

When night fell, everyone went home to try and show off their new purchases.

"War," the merchant replied immediately. "Admittedly, there's always a war going on out there. But this time, his Majesty is very angry. The Empire won't help him, so he's gathering troops to fend off the nomads."

"Are they attacking from the south?" Hadjar asked, after raising his hand.

No one took any liberties here. Everyone could only speak after the elder's permission.

"From the south, yes," the merchant agreed. "They attacked from the south before. But now they're attacking from the east, coming down from the mountain tops. There are no Imperial legions stationed there, so they come in and freely rob, rape, burn, and ravage the settlements."

"And what about the King?" The elder asked.

"They say that the King even sent his own son to join the army. He doesn't love him, but he adores his daughter. People tell amazing tales about her clothes and servants."

"The King has a daughter?" Hadjar raised his hand again and asked, feeling confused.

"Don't you know anything, kid? For sure he does. She's the most beautiful girl in the Kingdom. Her hair is pure gold. Her eyes are like emeralds. Her skin is whiter than snow. And if she's wielding a sword, you're better off burying yourself in the ground than facing her. Everybody's waiting for the day when Elaine becomes a Heaven Soldier."

Hadjar choked on the smoke he'd inhaled, dropped his sword, cutting himself on it, and then barely managed to ask his question: "Sorry, merchant, what?"

"Yes, you heard right, everyone expects her to become a Heaven Soldier. Primus has hired teachers from the Empire and used the best resources to help her advance to that stage…"

"No, you don't understand." Hadjar interrupted him, "What's her name?"

"Elaine."

Elaine... Was it really his sister? No, absolutely not. Why would Primus adopt someone who could one day stab him in the back? But why, then, did Hadjar feel that it was really her, deep in his heart? How could she have forgotten their mother and father? But the description of her hair and eyes fit—it was all exactly as he remembered.

His beloved, flighty little sister was now the daughter of Primus.

No, he couldn't believe it.

But his heart told him he'd be wrong to deny it.

"So, right now, they're actively recruiting people for the army."

And again, Hadjar flinched.

"Do many people join the army?" He asked.

"Enough of them do," the merchant shrugged, gratefully accepting another bowl of stew. After all, he would be setting out toward a new village tomorrow. "There are a lot of people who sign up to ensure that they and their families definitely won't be taken to the mine. They'll also be paid better than most can hope for. The food is decent. They will even be given a chance to advance further in stages, if they have the talent to do so. And, accordingly, they'll be rewarded with promotions. What kind of soldier doesn't dream of becoming a general?"

The merchant laughed and Hadjar pondered his words.

"How long will they be recruiting for?"

"Well, the recruitment will be completed at the end of the month. The nearest station is in Spring Town. I don't think they'll take you, young man. You're too... sleek. You look like you've never even held a sword in your hands before. It's necessary to pass an exam, once you get there. Your level must be no lower than the sixth stage, and the nodes must be no older than eighteen years."

The other men looked at each other and grinned. No one told the 'stranger' about Hadjar's recent deeds. Meanwhile, he was estimating if he could make it.

Less than three weeks remain, and according to Robin, I need more than a month to travel on foot to Spring Town, even without any trouble along the way.

Elaine...

***

Hadjar stood on a cliff, wrapped up in a cloak Robin had given him. He looked at the water streaming from the cliff, deep in thought. He wondered what lay ahead. How could he find justice in this harsh world? How could he bring peace to the spirits of his father and mother, whose bodies had been buried in the middle of nowhere?

He could become a mercenary and work for many different people in the hope that, someday, he would be able to do more than just mention the King in his prayer. And then he would break through the Palace guard, after hundreds of years of training. This was a very dangerous idea, but it could be implemented...

But there was another way. Much more difficult and bloody, but a lot faster. He could've gone to...

"Are you thinking about what you should do?" Robin walked up to him quietly and asked.

Hadjar almost fell off the cliff in surprise.

"Yea, I am!" He nodded.

The old man, groaning from fatigue, stood next to him.

"You'll go to join the army," the old man didn't ask but claimed. "I remember how much you don't like soldiers. Why you're going there is a mystery to me. But I'll tell you something. No matter what you have to do there, no matter how hard your journey is, I know you'll get through it. And when you're done with all that..."

Robin turned and hugged Hadjar so tightly that the younger man felt his bones crack.

"You know you have a home here. You will always be welcome here and there will always be a bed and a hut ready for you to use. Don't get lost, Hadjar. We'll be waiting for you."

The Prince hugged the villager back, swallowed the unwelcome lump in his throat, picked up the bag he'd packed, and set forth through the forest.

He left without turning around because he was afraid that if he did, he would end up staying.

Chapter 30

Today, on the outskirts of Spring Town—a town with a population of several million—it was surprisingly busy. For two months now, one of the King's armies had been encamped there. Every morning, at the central square, a crier would invite everyone to come to try their hand at the exam.

There were a lot of people that did just that.

All sorts of individuals were represented among the men and women streaming toward the center of the army camp—from ordinary vagabonds, who expected to be fed for free, all the way to dashing adventurers. But, mostly, they were either the younger sons and daughters of large families or those who hadn't found something else to do in town.

Some were motivated by their hunger or poverty. Some had been lured in by the promise of power or by the prospect of advancing in the ranks, as the crier had described. He'd promised that anyone who signed up could have general's armor and regular dinners in the capital in a couple of years.

Alas, only a few of those who wanted to join the military could pass the entrance exam.

A tall, young man stood in line, slowly moving in the direction of a huge parade ground in the center of the army camp that resembled a labyrinth of tents. He towered over the others around him, which surprised him a little.

His long, thick black hair had been gathered into a ponytail and fastened with a leather strap. He was garbed in plain, blue clothes instead of a shirt or a jacket, like most of the other men wore. They were dirty, torn and didn't look like noble robes. Instead of a belt, he had a rope, with a wooden bottle filled with water tucked into it.

He didn't wear any proper shoes or boots. Instead, he wore strips of cloth wound around bast shoes, fastened there with wide ribbons. He held a rusty sword and was smoking a pipe. A wide straw hat covered his face.

"Is your tobacco from the western plantations?" Somebody asked.

Hadjar turned toward the speaker. Next to him was the only other person as tall as he was.

The young man was dressed decently—a leather jacket, high boots, black pants made from a durable fabric. However, he didn't have any weapons, or even a knife.

He was quite handsome—wide cheekbones, a strong chin, with a determined and calm look in his gray eyes. Like Hadjar, he had long hair, but had elected not to tie it into a ponytail.

The young man held a pipe as well. But the smoke coming from it was completely different.

"Probably," Hadjar shrugged.

The young man blinked several times.

"Don't you know what you're smoking?"

The Prince only smiled inwardly. Back on Earth, he would've just left a cigarette smoldering next to his bed. So it was hard to say that he had ever truly 'smoked'.

"My name is Nero," the young man introduced himself, holding out his hand.

"Hadjar."

The young man's handshake was firm, but his skin was soft. Judging by his appearance and the absence of any calluses, he was probably the youngest son of a merchant. Or a young nobleman who had escaped from overly protective parents.

"I see you've brought your own weapon," Nero nodded toward the rusty sword.

Hadjar noticed a slight hint of mockery in his companion's calm gaze.

"The road was long, so I had to defend myself from bandits."

"Hmm... " The young man said. "You mean they saw how poor you were and ran away immediately?"

The Prince laughed.

"No, they gave me some money and bread first," Hadjar added, snorting.

Nero chuckled, and then they both started laughing loudly, which annoyed the people around them.

"Where are you from?" Nero asked, putting the pipe back in his pocket.

"From a village. It's about a month away on foot. And you?"

"I'm a local," Nero waved his hand around. "From Spring Town."

Hadjar looked at the parade ground. Another group of people who wanted to try out was being gathered there. According to his more optimistic estimates, it would be at least another quarter of an hour before it was his turn.

Some friendly banter would hopefully make the time fly by.

"Have you run away from your bride?" Hadjar smirked, putting his pipe away as well.

"I wouldn't run away from my bride... I would..." Nero sighed dreamily. "By the way, who runs away from a woman? Women... No, Hadjar of the village, I haven't run away from anyone."

"Why then do you want to join the army?"

"My family's making me," Nero shrugged. "It' what my kin do - serving."

"As part of the fighting forces?"

"As an official. A low-ranking one, but an official. Some of my family work in the court, others in the port's administration. Apparently, there wasn't a civilian job available for me. And so they sent me to the army."

"Well, it's always good when there's a military officer in a family of officials. You always know who to bribe."

Nero squinted at him and smiled.

"Did you say you were 'from a village'? What kind of village do you come from, Hadjar, that you would think like that?"

The Prince shrugged.

"Well, I did travel for a month to get here. I've managed to learn all about the urban lifestyle."

They looked at each other and smiled again. Sometimes, you may feel like you've met a kindred spirit. You chat, laugh, part and then never remember that other person again. But while you're talking to them, it seems like you've known this person your entire life and even longer than that.

Such people are said to be connected by the 'red thread'—the thread of fate woven around everything in this world, be it living or not.

"Why do you want to join the army, Hadjar? Do you think that the army, like those bandits, will feed you for free?"

"Not just feed me," Hadjar corrected him, "but also dress me, give me a roof over my head and replace this sword."

Nero stretched his neck slightly and looked at the tents all around them. They were simple, one-person tents, and all of them were white. A few of the officers had more luxurious shelters, and some even had large enough tents that they had actual entrances.

If one squinted, it was possible to spot the tents of the top commanders and the largest one, which belonged to the general.

"I also heard that they have women of easy virtue on Fridays," Nero smacked his lips.

Hadjar laughed again.

"Do you want to join the army because of your family or because of women?"

"In this life, everything I do is because of women, my new friend.

What is the point of living, if not for the sake of enjoying women? Their magnificent and firm breasts, their long legs, those wide hips, that satiny skin..."

The young man licked his lips and made some girls, who were standing nearby, blush.

Unlike the villages, the world, in general, wasn't sexist. If a person was good enough at cultivating their martial arts, then their gender wasn't important.

"If you hold me, Hadjar of the village, you'll be sleeping in not just a soft but also a warm bed."

They turned and looked at the ladies behind them. The girls blushed and almost growled in annoyance. "Bastard!"

"Me or him?" Nero asked immediately. "I want to emphasize that my incomparable handsomeness is known throughout Spring Town."

"And I was the best catch in my village."

"That doesn't matter, my new friend. Spring Town is much bigger than a village. Therefore, my good looks are more objective."

"But the girls are prettier in our village."

Nero clutched his chest.

"The girls are more beautiful than the ones in Spring Town? You must take me to your homeland!"

"I'm afraid you would end up stoned if you went there..."

"So be it! Even the threat of such a cruel fate will not deter me! I must get to these fabulous creatures!"

The ladies behind them were already reaching for the canes tied to their belts. They'd probably brought those canes with them to avoid feeling 'inferior to the men'. Or maybe they just couldn't manage without a cane...

Hadjar shook off these thoughts. I'd best avoid that particular rabbit hole.

"Hey, you two!" A soldier in black armor barked.

Exhausted from the heat, he was trying with all his might to move the breastplate away from his body and looked silly doing it.

"Go to the parade ground! Damn, why is it so hot..."

"Well, it was nice meeting you, Hadjar," Nero extended his hand.

"You too," Hadjar shook it.

Then they went in different directions.

There were too many people interested in joining the army, so the parade ground had been divided into four parts. In each of them, separate groups took the same tests. Hadjar went up to the table where four people who looked like Scholars were sitting.

Just 'looked like', mind you, because compared to South Wind, they were ordinary quacks. They had big bellies, shifty eyes, and fat fingers. The Scholars showed Hajjar the large skull of some creature.

"Put your hand in there," one of them said. "If it doesn't bite your hand off, your age and stage are suitable."

"What are the requirements?" Hadjar asked, to make sure.

In all honesty, he was simply stalling for time, because he wasn't sure how the skull might react to his neural network.

"To become a private, you should be no lower than the sixth stage of the Bodily Nodes. And under the age of eighteen."

"How do you check that?"

The Scholar was about to answer when his colleague interrupted him.

"Peasant! Don't delay the queue! And you! Put your stinking stump in the skull or get out of here."

Hadjar shrugged and put his hand inside the mouth of it, feeling a small, cold, stone sphere in there.

"The Bodily Rivers, the first stage. The age is under eighteen." The third and most sensible of the Scholars wrote this down in a huge scroll immediately. "Name?"

"Hadjar."

"Full name?"

"Hadjar... Traves."

"Listen to me carefully, Hadjar," the Scholar made his well-rehearsed speech in a bored tone. "Your level of cultivation allows you to take an officer's exam. It's much more complicated than a private's exam, but your salary will be higher and the conditions will be... better. You'll start with a low rank—junior lieutenant. Of course, you won't have anyone to command straight away."

"And if I fail?"

"Then you'll be a private."

Apparently, he wouldn't lose anything if he tried to become an officer.

"I accept," Hadjar answered without hesitation.

Chapter 31

"Then I'll administer the first part of your exam. If you pass, I'll tell you where you should go next. Agreed?"

Hadjar nodded.

"In that case, draw the hieroglyphs for 'house', 'sword' and 'light' in the air."

Apparently, this was how they'd test his literacy. Hadjar drew the required hieroglyphs immediately. Even without the neuronet and its database, he was still a literate man. Well, as far as anyone can be a 'man' with a dragon's heart beating in his chest.

That's why Hadjar had chosen the dragon's name as his surname...

"Tell me, what herb should I apply to a wound to ensure a speedy recovery?"

He wanted to answer 'plantain' at first, but that didn't exist in this world.

"A leaf from the Yellow tree dipped in water."

"How much will I have to pay back if I take out a loan from the moneylender at twenty percent interest?"

What a stupid trap. Nevertheless, the Scholars smiled, enjoying the free show. After all, what they saw wasn't the Prince of Lidus, but an ordinary boy from some backwoods village, with a rusty sword as his greatest treasure. And, admittedly, with a decent level of cultivation considering where he'd come from.

He'd probably been lucky enough to stumble upon some rare plant or some other means of getting so far.

"How much would you borrow?"

"One gold coin."

"In that case, you'd need to repay one gold and twenty silver coins."

The Scholar nodded, wrote something down in the scroll and pointed toward the path leading to another parade ground. There was no queue there since it was five times bigger.

"Take this," the Scholar held out a wooden plate with his name and 'signature' on it. "Good luck."

"Thank you," Hadjar nodded again.

Moving away from the table, the young man turned around. He saw a profusely sweating Nero holding a huge tub. Its weight was obviously more than one hundred pounds. Clenching his teeth, he straightened his legs and held the tub in the air for almost ten seconds, and then threw it back on the ground. The officer overseeing the exam roared something and Nero went to another section—some people had been paired up and were already fighting there.

Judging by his shrewd gaze, Nero was trying to join the queue in a spot that ensured he'd be fighting a woman, not a man.

Hadjar wished his new friend good luck.

Bypassing several tents, Hadjar approached the huge parade ground.

He was stopped by an officer in fairly standard metal armor, without any patterns or silly frills like the armor of ordinary privates had. The quality of the armor was also much higher.

"The seal," he extended his hand.

Hadjar handed him the plate.

"The first stage of the 'Rivers'..." The officer snorted with displeasure. "And you look scrawny. Will the wind carry you away?"

"Only if I don't have breakfast."

"Funny," the officer nodded. "If you break your legs or arms, the army isn't responsible. If you get cut and bleed out, the army isn't responsible. If your guts fall out onto the sand…"

"The army isn't responsible."

"But we will provide a healer. Is that clear?"

"Yes, sir."

"Then throw your stuff away here," the soldier pointed to a bunch of the same 'weapons' as Hadjar had—rusty swords, sabers, knives, daggers, even a couple of spears. All this had been dumped into one pile of scrap metal.

Hadjar hesitated to part with the sword that he'd bought with honestly earned money. Even if it was rather bad.

"It's actually worth a bit of money."

"If you pass the exam, you'll get a normal one. If not, privates also get something."

Hadjar didn't like the sound of 'something', but seeing the officer's unyielding gaze, he decided not to argue. He untied his sword and threw it on the pile, shuddering from the metallic rumble that ensued. A small piece of his blade seemed to break off.

Well, he had been lucky enough to not encounter any animals on the way to town. Perhaps the sharpened dart had been a better weapon than what the merchant had sold him.

There were about a hundred people at the parade ground, which was the size of an ordinary square. There were also several officers. A senior officer was present as well. He wore a white cloak made from a mountain tiger's skin, which was a beast at the 'Awakening of the Mind' stage.

Hadjar wondered if the officer felt hot under such a thick cloak. Or was demonstrating his high status more important than comfort?

"Now that there's exactly one hundred of you, we can start."

An officer with a truly great beard came forward. His beard reminded Hadjar of movie adaptations made based on Dumas' work.

"First, we'll test your strength. This part of the exam is a little different from what the ordinary warriors have to do. Four of you step forward."

Four people came up to stand on the sandy surface of the parade ground. There were three guys and one girl. It would be hard to call her frail or slim, but she didn't appear to be fat, either. Instead, the girl had a powerful build.

Weights lay before them, instead of the metal tubs Hadjar had seen before. Stone weights. They were ridiculously reminiscent of the ones that the villagers in the Valley of Streams used. However, they were much smaller, which was also true for the people themselves. During the month he'd spent in the village, Hadjar had gotten used to being a man of 'average height.' And now he towered above all of them, looking like a veritable giant.

The first examinee couldn't lift even the smallest of the weights. He was immediately sent over to where the ordinary warriors were being tested. He asked for a second chance but immediately retreated as soon as one of the officers put his hand on the hilt of his sword.

Among the first four people, only the woman managed to lift the lightest of the weights.

The girl, after dealing with the first weight, immediately went over to the second one.

She gave up only when she got to the fourth.

The officers wrote something down in their scrolls and asked her to wait on the sidelines. The woman sank down on the bench made of boards, sweating and panting.

The queue began to thin out pretty quickly. About twenty out of a hundred failed to lift the first weight and they were sent back. Both the people sent back and the officers supervising everything seemed disappointed in the results.

How was it possible for people at about the same stage of cultivation to show such wildly different results? That's because the stages were only a superficial measurement. Only if you dug deeper did the real differences become evident—talent, willpower and the effort put in.

Finally, it was Hadjar's turn.

He had been the last to enter the parade ground.

Spitting in his palms out of habit, he went over to the first weight.

He planted his feet, straightened his back and with a jerk... almost threw the weight into the sky.

It must've weighed more than two hundred pounds, and not long ago, that kind of weight would've been an issue for him. This time, he picked it up a lot more easily than he'd expected, albeit with some effort.

"Go on," the officer hurried Hadjar along.

The Prince approached the second weight. It was the size of a soccer ball, but apparently made from a different material than the weights he'd trained with before. Weighing about three hundred pounds, it became a serious challenge for Hadjar to overcome.

Feeling his muscles straining so hard that his veins popped out, he first lifted it up to the level of his waist. After gathering all his strength and willpower, Hadjar raised the weight over his head and then immediately dropped it.

Breathing heavily, he came up to the next weight, without waiting for the command.

Four hundred pounds. It was an almost impossible task for his current body. And yet, he was still able to lift it. Well, not completely—he couldn't get it above his head. Regardless, he'd been able to raise the weight to the level of his waist.

"You have fifteen minutes to rest and then we'll check your dexterity and reaction time," the officer instructed.

While the rank and file warriors were setting up a portable obstacle course on the parade ground, Hadjar was staring at his trembling hands.

What the hell was going on with him?!

He had been sure that having one unit of strength meant he would be able to lift approximately 200 pounds. With the abilities he had, Hadjar shouldn't have been able to lift the second weight.

"Status," he ordered.

Name	Hadjar
Level of Cultivation	Bodily Rivers (1)
Strength	1,1
Dexterity	1,3
Physique	1,01
Energy Points	1,7

After reading the message several times, Hadjar didn't find anything new that could explain his feat. Then he looked at the girl sitting a good distance away from him, the one that had been able to lift the third weight.

"Scan."

Name	Ariel
Level of Cultivation	Bodily Rivers (5)
Strength	1,8
Dexterity	1,5
Physique	1,99
Energy Points	2, 3

Apparently, the neural network, which was constantly collecting information, had somehow managed to find the girl's name out. She might have told someone her name, or it could've appeared in some scroll. Hadjar was always eager to get more information into the database so that he could increase the analytical abilities of his neural network.

At that moment, however, he didn't understand whether he was being an idiot, or something had happened to the computing abilities of the network.

Why was the system that had worked so well thus far beginning to bug out?

He felt that it must've had something to do with the heart beating quietly in his chest.

"Continue!" the officer barked.

Chapter 32

The next test involved training dummies, which made Hadjar feel nostalgic. The dummies were positioned on the edges of a trampled, winding path. Each of the dummies was armed with a knife and red paint had been applied to the edge of each blade.

"Your task is to get through the entire course without getting hit more than twice," the officer announced. "The knives have been blunted, but if the blow is strong enough, you'll still get badly injured, which will have to be sewn up. Those of you who aren't confident in your abilities better leave at once. What you've shown in the last test is enough to get you into the army as an ordinary warrior. You'll be able to repeat this exam next year if you're nineteen years old or less."

The officer made sure everyone had time to think about the situation, but no one gave up. Those who'd reached the stage of the Bodily Rivers already saw themselves as future cultivators. And it was very difficult to become a cultivator without proper dedication and motivation. In fact, it was almost impossible.

That meant all of the people trying out had enough willpower to not be tempted by a bird in the hand.

"Well then, go ahead. This time we'll start from the back of the line."

The officer pointed at Hadjar. He stood up, a little disappointed that he wouldn't be going last this time. He hadn't had much time to rest.

Hadjar dusted his clothes off and walked over to the obstacle course. While standing next to the course, the officers made several gestures with their hands. A dull, gray glow covered their palms and the dummies sprang into action.

They spun at different heights. Some dummies aimed at the knees, others at the ankles, but the majority was targeting the chest and neck. Sometimes, they changed their speed or the direction of their movements. The mechanical bodies also went up and down in an effort to confuse the person running the course.

Hadjar sighed and closed his eyes.

He could use the neural network. If he asked for a hint, it would instantly determine the best route to take. The neural network would display the pattern and Hadjar would simply need to follow the proposed hologram.

But it wouldn't be his, Hadjar's, own skill.

He could have used the help of his neural network, as he'd done more than once during his training. But this time, he wanted to test himself. He didn't care about joining the army. Instead, he wished to see what months of training in the village had done for his skills and to test his new body.

Opening his eyes, Hadjar went forward.

What the audience saw had no logical explanation. Even the senior officer forgot about his glass of cold, diluted wine, and watched the examinee with a slightly open mouth.

What could they have expected from a person trying to pass this test? Well, if the first dummy didn't "hurt" the person, they were supposed to get through by jumping, dodging and falling down comically, all the while twitching like a crazy person. The audience clearly hadn't expected to see what they were witnessing right now.

Hadjar was walking along as calmly as if he were wandering along the lakeshore on a fine day. His long hair was fluttering in the wind and his loose, ragged clothes were buffeted by it.

The movement of his legs was the only thing that attracted the attention of the people watching the testing process. Hadjar's feet were not 'walking,' but 'floating' on the sand, leaving barely visible footprints behind.

"The Measured Footsteps Technique," the highest-ranking officer whispered in amazement.

He'd mastered it only a year ago and it was one of the reasons why he'd been able to move up the career ladder. 'The Measured Footsteps Technique' was nothing complicated: it was the simple ability to move without any unnecessary movements, as silly as that may sound.

In fact, to master this Technique at a level before the Transformation stage, a practitioner needed to be very talented. Not at cultivation, but at the very essence of martial arts-battle.

By all outward appearances, Hadjar was calm, but inside, he was almost groaning with the unbearable effort needed to maintain his concentration. Using all his senses, he monitored every movement within a radius of about three feet. Hadjar would foresee the attacks of the dummies and then take the single step he needed to avoid everything coming at him.

This test was like playing chess against hundreds of people at once.

That was what 'The Measured Footsteps Technique' actually meant. It wasn't just moving correctly (although that was a fundamental part of it), but the ability to react and think quickly. A focused and clear Mind was the main weapon of a martial artist.

After five minutes of slow walking, Hadjar stepped out at the other side of the obstacle course. He examined himself and found only one red mark at the level of his ankle.

His initial use of 'The Measured Footsteps Technique' had not been perfect. Hadjar's mind wasn't in full sync with his body and that was the reason why the dummies had been able to hurt him.

If the Master had gone through that course, the dummies' knives wouldn't have even come close to his body.

"You've passed the test," the officer who'd explained everything earlier came to his senses and wrote something down in his scroll again.

Hadjar sat back down. His legs and arms trembled slightly, so he closed his eyes and began to breathe evenly, absorbing the energy of the world. It wasn't just suitable for cultivation, but for recovery as well. Some even said that true adepts didn't need to eat or drink for years on end-they used only the energy of the world to sustain themselves.

Hadjar didn't really believe it.

Judging by the sounds, as well as the awkward attempts to ask for a second chance, a lot of the applicants hadn't completed the task.

As a result, when Hadjar opened his eyes, he saw that only half the people remained after the second round of testing. They were all smeared with red paint. Only one short, a thin boy had been left unpainted by the dummies.

The proverb was correct—there's always someone better. Hadjar was eager to compete, relishing the challenge, and he was glad to see someone could provide him with a goal to strive toward.

"The next stage will be the last one," the officer announced, while ordinary soldiers were taking the dummies away and cleaning up the parade ground.

They created some sort of arena in the sand and set up some stands with a variety of weapons along the perimeter of it. These weapons were much better than the one Hadjar had used for the last month but much worse than the ones the Master had owned.

However, comparing the Royal Palace and a mobile army camp didn't make any sense.

"We will pair you up for sparring. You'll fight until first blood or until one of you gives up. But remember that victory is not the main goal. Your task is to demonstrate all of your skills. There are twenty people left, and we'll choose only five of the winners to become officers. So, even if you manage to defeat your enemy, but you do it simply and without showing any real skill, you can feel free to go and sign up as a private."

The examinees looked at each other. All of them were clearly ready to fight, determined to give it their all.

"The first pair…"

"The General!" the senior officer exclaimed as he fell to one knee.

He put his fist against his breastplate and bowed his head along with the other officers.

The examinees gave a low bow, bending forward almost a full ninety degrees.

Hair fell over Hadjar's face as he hunched over. It hid his spiteful gaze.

He saw a fragile-looking blonde woman. Her hair was in a tight, thick braid and she was walking beside two tall officers who were clad in heavy armor. Dressed in simple clothes, she only wore half-armor. Apparently, she'd taken off her neck guard, but had kept the gloves and a 'lower corset', which was like a metal skirt that reached up to the hips.

Women being in the army was completely normal, so female armor had been invented long ago.

The General wore a funny metal crown with three leaf-shaped spikes. The central spike covered her slightly snub nose, and the other two framed the sides of her beautiful, oval face.

The General was beautiful enough to break even a cold, withered heart. And, apparently, despite her seeming fragility, she was amazingly powerful. In her right hand, she held a siege spear that was almost twice her height.

But the beautiful woman in armor and with a General's seal hadn't been the one to draw Hadjar's attention.

The man swaggering next to her, smirking confidently, was who Hadjar focused on. A man whose face he would never forget.

He was the one who'd burned the 'Innocent Meadow' down. The one who'd killed Eina, Senta, and everyone else that Hadjar had lived with for the last five years.

The son of a local chief General.

"You can't run away this time," Hadjar growled faintly, dropping his gaze.

A half-mad smile was on his face as flames surged up from within the dragon heart.

Chapter 33

The General greeted the soldiers with a gentle nod. She was immediately offered a fairly comfortable, hand-carved chair. After placing her spear beside her, she lowered herself into it, and with a wave of her hand, allowed the examination to continue.

She looked calm, confident and imperious, as befitted a General. Seeing a woman in such a high position was unusual to Hadjar, but wasn't anything new to the locals.

And yet, he wasn't looking at her, but at the son of the official-bribe-taker. The man looked the same as when Hadjar had last seen him. Except for the long, straight scar that now marred his cheek. He constantly tried to cover it up, but it was quite difficult to hide such a mark.

A white, thick line ran down his handsome face, and then further still, hidden under his expensive clothes. They were worth a lot more than what the General wore. This was probably why her son looked at the General with smug superiority whenever he was sure she couldn't see him.

He clearly felt that he deserved to be the one commanding everything.

The first pair faced off in the makeshift arena. They were the girl, Ariel, who'd managed to pass the second trial by the skin of her teeth, despite being the most rested, and the undersized young man, who'd done the best of all of them.

The girl chose a heavy war hammer, and her opponent decided to fight with two daggers. He looked and moved in a way that left no doubts about his past. The former bandit had decided to join the army's officer ranks. Maybe he'd been kicked out of the gang. Or they'd just decided to have one of theirs join the army.

That was something taken for granted around here. Large gangs would sometimes become official groups. They would just start to call themselves sects, and if they were organized like the mafia, they would be called family clans. One never knew whether a sect or a clan was of the ordinary kind, or whether it was an ex, or even an active, gang.

"Begin!"

The General crossed her arms. If she hadn't been wearing so much armor, her pose would've probably looked a bit seductive. But at that moment, she looked completely serious and businesslike.

Ariel, after taking a deep breath, rushed forward like a battering ram. The hammer didn't look like a clumsy pile of metal in her hands, but a rather formidable weapon. When she swung it down with all her might, the powerful impact shook the ground, scattering sand everywhere. But the nimble boy wasn't anywhere near the spot she'd struck.

He was ostentatiously picking his teeth with one dagger, while the second one was pointed at the girl's throat as he stood behind Ariel. Most people hadn't even seen him move.

Only a few of them had been able to discern the vague silhouette that looked like a gray shadow.

Hadjar saw more: despite how ordinary the trick turned out to be, he was still impressed. Thanks to being at the eighth stage of the Bodily Rivers, the smaller man had been able to redirect all of his energy into his legs.

That allowed for The Measured Footsteps Technique to, even if for just a few moments, gain the properties of the Mortal Technique. This helped him increase his speed, and the young man was able to win the fight in seconds.

After all, no matter how strong your enemy was, if you were faster than them, you'd always have an advantage. Unless, of course, you got hit.

"Next!"

The next pair entered the arena after Ariel put the hammer back on the improvised weapons rack and walked dejectedly back to the area designated for the new privates. The second fight was quite long. One guy was wielding a shield and a mace, and the second one had a halberd. They'd already been fighting for over ten minutes before the officer stopped them.

In the end, they both joined Ariel.

Then came an archer, who was admitted to the officer ranks as soon as he fired the first arrow.

The army always lacked good archer practitioners, so they were very appreciated and valued highly. They were so welcome, in fact, that even the General awarded the guy a private nod of her head. Apparently, a very bright future awaited him.

People chose to use the staff a couple of times. It was a weapon the people from the villages and small towns used quite often. It was usually difficult to find good iron, and thus iron weapons cost a lot of money, which peasants rarely had. It was much easier to carve out staff and learn how to swing it. However, one should not underestimate the real masters of the staff.

"Your turn," the officer pointed at Hadjar.

A slender guy was chosen to be his opponent. Their fight was among the last ones. By then, the sand in the arena had already been scattered in places, exposing the trampled ground. Grass would probably not grow there in the next few years.

Blood stained the sand. Some of the competing people, who hadn't blocked or dodged in time, had needed healers. They'd been taken to the large tents that served as the army hospital. Most of the time, the healers ended up dealing with open fractures and having to bandage deep cuts.

Various hammers, staffs, batons, and maces were the most popular choice. In second place were spears, throwing knives and daggers. The least popular were bows and swords. Those two were the most difficult to master and the most expensive weapons.

The two undisputed kings of the battlefield.

Hadjar and his opponent had been the first ones to choose a sword as their weapon. That intrigued all the spectators, whose number had, surprisingly, increased by that time.

The officers and soldiers alike had come to the arena as soon as they were able. Each of them, upon arrival, would kneel and greet the General. She rarely answered with a nod, mostly not noticing the people around her. She was too busy spectating the fights.

Hadjar's opponent picked his weapon first. That immediately put Hadjar at a disadvantage, because the other combatant had had the chance to choose the best sword. In fact, it turned out that, among a dozen blades that hung by their cross-guards, Hadjar could not find a single sword of outstanding quality. They were all on the same level. Enough to swing around in a normal battle between two armies, but... no more than that.

Those blades would be of no interest to a cultivator. However, it was said that real cultivators could make do even without a sword. It was widely known that a person who had gone beyond the level of The Spirit Knight would gain the ability to concentrate energy so tightly that it was enough for them to move their index and middle finger together to make a phantom blade appear.

That kind of sword was much weaker than a real weapon but still allowed a practitioner to use sword Techniques.

Hadjar chose a classic sword. It had a narrow blade with two sharp edges. The blade was long and had an almost invisible, rectangular cross-guard. The handle, wrapped in calfskin, felt right in his hand.

Hadjar, walking around in a circle, swung his blade a couple of times, getting used to its balance and weight.

The enemy in front of him assumed a standard stance. His left hand used both for balance and to help his aim, froze in the very gesture mentioned before. His index and middle finger were pointing upward and the rest were clenched in a fist.

Hadjar stood there casually, not assuming any of the ten stances he knew.

Ignoring his skillful opponent's condescending smile, he closed his eyes and felt the east wind caress his face.

How many years had it been since he'd last fought with a sword? It was probably in his past life. In one of his many lives.

"Begin!" came the familiar command.

Unlike the others, the swordsmen didn't run around the arena like rabbits. They didn't yell at or taunt each other.

Hadjar remained in the same spot, enjoying the cool breeze blowing across his sweaty skin. He was standing with his eyes closed, having dropped his sword to the ground.

The enemy was approaching him slowly. Amusingly enough, he looked like a crab as he moved around on widely spaced legs, staying in his previously adopted position. His right hand was extended forward, exposing the blade of the sword like a scorpion's sting. His left hand was raised above his head.

His opponent thought that he was facing an upstart peasant. Admittedly, one that had mastered The Measured Footsteps Technique. Apparently having some middling talent, he'd been able to learn it by spending time catching snakes. Probably considered himself a genius, after doing well in fights against the other villagers. That was the reason why the poor peasant couldn't even hold a sword properly.

He was different, however. He'd spent the last ten years attending the best fencing school in Spring Town. The Master there had even praised him and said that he was talented with the sword!

Hadjar's opponent didn't notice the spectators' mocking glances at all. They had already named him Crab in their minds.

Crab, as he'd been taught in school, moved his center of gravity to where the sword's pommel was and immediately lunged forward. The tip of the blade whizzed through the air, flying at Hadjar who was still standing with his eyes closed.

Chapter 34

Crab could already see the blade slicing through the rags that served as clothes for this stupid peasant. He felt like he could sense it as it crushed the weakling's bones. In his mind, he'd heard the enemy take his final breath.

Most of the other examinees had left the arena with minor wounds or fractures. But in a battle of swordsmen, death was commonplace. The weapon was too cruel and served only one purpose—murder.

Sword wielders could die even while training with blunt blades and the battle for an officer's position was a much more serious affair.

Crab would finally be able to help his family move out of their tiny home on the outskirts of town when he won the fight (he had no doubts he would). They'd buy a nice house, right in the center of town, to live in. His sister would find a good husband. His father could stop working in the market and his mother could stop sewing. And, well, he himself would finally be able to enjoy plenty of female attention. He'd be an officer in the army, after all.

The dreamy smile that had adorned his face immediately faded when the enemy opened his eyes.

He saw a coiled, fierce beast in that blue, bottomless gaze. It was like staring into the abyss.

Hadjar didn't even move from his spot. He only turned slightly, letting Crab's sword pass an inch away from his body.

The attacker flew past, but, managing to right himself, he planted his foot and turned. Using the momentum of his rotation, he swung his blade in a vertical arc at Hadjar, hoping to split him in half, right down the middle.

If Hadjar had been a little slower, he might've even succeeded. Unfortunately for Crab, Hadjar seemed like he didn't even know what the word "slow" meant. He remained in place, tilted his body back, and after the blade whistled through the air harmlessly, he pushed the attacker in the chest with the hilt of his sword.

Crab lost his balance and landed on the ground. He rolled to the side immediately, got up, and swung his sword once more. This time, Hadjar swayed back to avoid the impact as gracefully as a branch in the wind. Once he was back in the safe zone behind the center of Crab's blade, Hadjar again threw him to the ground with a casual push.

The Prince stood there, looking quite calm and serene.

Preoccupied with the fight, he didn't notice that the audience couldn't take their eyes off of him. The hillbilly who had, until recently, appeared even more ridiculous than Crab had changed suddenly. After taking up the sword, he'd gained... no, not greatness. Something far more terrifying than greatness.

Many people gripped the hilts of their weapons involuntarily. Someone had, without realizing it, began checking if their armor was properly adjusted.

It seemed to them like something other than a man was standing in the arena. A wild beast, dangerous and ferocious. Ready to tear you apart if you dared encroach on his territory. An area that was almost plainly visible to all.

It was a circle, about a yard in diameter, in the center of which stood a tall man wearing a ragged coat instead of robes. It was a boundary which very few of the spectators would've dared to cross.

"What's your name?" Crab asked as he was getting back on his feet.

He took a strange stance. It was as if he were trying to parody a sleeping heron, his leg bent oddly.

"Hadjar," came the quiet answer.

"Then pay your attention, Hadjar. The best swordsman in Spring Town taught me this Technique. However, in your village, you probably haven't even heard about Sword Techniques yet. Let me show you how vast this world is, and that your Steps are nothing more than child's play."

Crab exhaled and a blue glow surrounded his blade. It shook as if trying to get away from the blade but still remained in place. The audience almost took a step forward to get a better look at what was happening.

Ten years ago, this kind of Mortal Technique would've been considered something incredible and even mystical in the Kingdom of Lidus. Nowadays, thanks to the Empire, even schools in backwoods like Spring Town had access to them.

But, judging by the intensity of the glow and how the blade was acting, Crab wasn't all that good at it yet. Maybe he was still at the initial levels of the Technique. All the same, not all of the officers in the lower ranks could've boasted about mastering a Mortal Technique like that, not even its most basic form.

Hadjar, while outwardly calm, was now on edge. Well, he knew a Mortal Technique, too. The Technique he'd named "Fried Sparrow." Unfortunately for him, Primus was no fool, and all his agents already knew about it. That was why Hadjar would never use it before the time was right.

The Technique that his opponent was about to use was indeed beyond the realm of the Footsteps. Raw speed couldn't always counter overwhelming force. This Death Technique was exactly that kind of force when compared to the conventional Technique of movement.

"Awakening Heron!" Crab cried out, confirming Hadjar's guess.

Awakening Heron:

Energy Points	0.32
Threat Level	Medium

His adversary swung his sword and the people heard the cry of a heron. It pierced their ears, and then a blue blade flew toward Hadjar. Crab hadn't reached the level of 'One with the Sword', rather, the Technique allowed him to hit a target at a distance of seven steps. Even if Hadjar had been in full armor, the attack would've still gone through him like a hot knife through butter.

The attack was fast. So fast that it left a ghostly, blue afterimage in its wake.

Someone was already calling for a healer.

And then there was silence.

For the first time since the fight began, the hillbilly used his sword. However, he didn't use the blade itself, only the crossguard and the hilt.

Faced with the Mortal Technique, Hadjar remained as calm as if he were reacting to a pillow thrown in jest.

Well, Hadjar did end up having to step back. Without lifting his feet from the sand, he drew his right leg back, leaving a wide arc in the sand. Putting the crossguard and the hilt forward, Hadjar clasped his right wrist with his left hand and took up a defensive stance.

The strike slammed into his sword like an ax trying to split a log.

But instead of splinters, it produced some sparks and a few drops of blood. Those scarlet drops shot into the sky and then fell to the sand. The cuts on Hadjar's wrists were bleeding, but the wounds were negligible.

And, more importantly, that was the only damage the Technique had managed to do.

Crab couldn't believe his eyes.

That Technique had helped him win the tournament at the fencing school. Using it, he'd become famous as one of the most talented swordsmen of his generation. It was supposed to have been the foundation of his legend. And it had been absolutely useless against some random hillbilly.

"What the hell!" Crab screamed. "He's using some kind of artifact! He must be cheating! Check if he's cheating!"

Crab tried to approach Hadjar but tripped and fell face down in the sand. He didn't even have the strength to stand back up. And so, unable to comprehend what was going on, he sat there, looking at his own trembling hands.

"Hadjar Traves," the senior officer's voice sounded.

"Yes, sir?" the young man turned and bowed, lowering his blade.

"Why didn't you use your sword? Do you have any bodily Techniques? Or are you just skilled in the 'Footsteps' Technique? That alone is not enough to become an officer in our army."

Hadjar turned to his opponent, who still seemed unable to comprehend what had happened to him. Why hadn't he used his sword? The answer was very simple.

"I don't know this man. He hasn't done me any harm. Why should I kill him?"

"Kill him?" The surprised officer asked again. He even awkwardly adjusted his animal skin cloak. "You think you're so skilled with a sword that you would've killed him?"

"I wasn't sure that my opponent could survive even a single strike, sir," not straightening his back, Hadjar continued the conversation. "That is why I only defended myself, waiting for my opponent to tire himself out and lose his will to fight. I think my approach was the correct one. It seems to me that I've won fairly and deserve to be an officer in our army."

The officer had started to reply when a cry full of disgust and arrogance sounded, cutting him off.

"Who are you, you bastard, to make any kind of decisions around here?"

Hadjar, still bowing, turned around and saw the screaming man through his long hair. Even if he hadn't been able to see him, he'd recognized his voice easily enough. It was the son of general Larvie. Wearing expensive clothes, polished armor and carrying a blade that must have cost as much as the whole of 'Innocent Meadow' had once been worth.

"Officer Colin," the senior officer spoke in a fawning voice but with hatred in his eyes. "The fact that you've become, for reasons unknown to me, an adjutant, does not give you the right to interfere in the exam."

"I'll intervene when I see fit, and where I think it's needed," Colin chuckled. Hadjar was delighted to find out his name. "And you, officer, should be punishing this miscreant. Didn't you hear? He dared to tell us what we should do with him."

Hadjar remained silent. If he'd been a Prince, the whole army would've been kneeling before him. But he was a 'hillbilly.' Someone who had no right to even breathe in the presence of the esteemed officers. He couldn't even think of trying to influence his own future.

Only powerful men and women could forge their own destiny in this world. The rest had to rely on the decisions and will of their superiors. It had been like that even during the reign of Haver and Elizabeth.

"This young man is right," the senior officer stood his ground.

It was unlikely that he was worried about Hadjar's future, he probably just wanted to annoy Colin. Or maybe he was doing this out of envy-he'd been serving as a senior officer for half a century, but that eighteen-year-old boy had already become an adjutant.

"Are you braindead, officer? A fraud is standing right in front of you, and you want to make him a junior officer in our grand army!"

Colin snorted and took off his silk cloak. It slowly fell to the ground, but before it finished its journey, Colin was already standing in front of Hadjar.

"While you might've been able to trick this poor citizen, you peasant, I can see you're holding a sword for almost the first time in your life. Talk all you want, you won't fool me. Your death is nigh."

Colin unbuckled his sword belt defiantly and threw it aside. He kept only the scabbard, holding it in his left hand and standing as proudly as if he were a mountain, not a mere man.

Everyone looked at the General. They spent ten seconds waiting in silence, and then she waved her hand to signal for the fight to begin.

"Say goodbye to your life, peasant!"

Chapter 35

"Don't be hasty, Colin," the general finally spoke. She had a very warm, quite an ordinary female voice. She sounded friendly, more like a woman that sold fruit at the market than a stern general. "You are at the Transformation stage, aren't you?"

Colin turned to the General and replied, teeth grinding as he did so, "Yes." After a pause, he added a very reluctant "Sir."

In this world, 'sir' was used to address superior officers of both sexes.

"This fight will be meaningless," the General responded, completely ignoring his hesitation, "if you use all of your power."

"This bastard needs to be taught a lesson!"

After a few more seconds of silence, she went on. "Adjutant, heed my order," she said, in the same exact tone as before, but Hadjar immediately wanted to bow down and apologize to her. The other soldiers and officers were already on their knees, trying to look inconspicuous. Even Colin bowed low but didn't kneel. "You may not use a level of power higher than the 'Bodily Rivers'. I forbid it."

"I shall obey your order," the General's son said through clenched teeth and saluted her by banging his fist against his chest.

He straightened up, turned toward Hadjar again, and closed his eyes. When he opened them, his aura became... calmer and weaker.

Hadjar just shook his head. Colin hadn't done much. Limiting his power like this only influenced the amount of energy that he could use. But as Hadjar already knew, each new stage a practitioner reached not only increased the amount of energy available to them but also transformed their body.

The neural network couldn't scan Colin, but it was clear that he was at least four times stronger than Hadjar in every way.

And that didn't even make it the same as fighting against four people who were as strong as him. It was much more difficult. Hadjar had fought such an opponent only once in the past— when he'd fought the Alpha of the deer. At the time, Hadjar, using all of his power, had only managed to injure the beast.

Now he had to contend with a human practitioner who was possibly even more powerful than the deer had been. One wielding a sword. Oh, joy.

"Thank the general," Colin hissed, "for dying slowly."

He drew his blade, unsheathing it in a flash of movement. He held it tightly, too tightly. His stance and grip showed Hadjar that his opponent wasn't particularly good at wielding the magnificent weapon. But the difference in their levels of cultivation easily made up for Colin's lack of skill.

Did that stop Hadjar?

Did any fear or hesitation show in his gaze?

No, everyone watching could still see both the human and the... beast in the center of the arena. A cautious beast that bided its time and waited for the perfect moment to strike. They were still unnerved by the sight, forcing them to grip the hilts of their weapons for comfort.

Hadjar charged his foe, his blade out, moving unpredictably and trying to come at him from the side. Colin charged in as well.

Despite being pompous and arrogant, he wasn't a fool. He didn't actually intend to blindly rush at an enemy, who, while only being at the first stage of the 'Bodily Rivers', had stopped a Mortal Technique attack.

The General watched it all with an unchanging, stoic expression. Only by watching closely could one spot a mild flicker of interest in her gaze.

Colin attacked first.

His sword was longer than Hadjar's, allowing him to do so with impunity.

His blade shot forward as an arrow fired from a siege bow. It whizzed toward Hadjar's belly, leaving a dark, smoky trail in its wake. It wouldn't be a fatal strike. Not immediately fatal, anyway. Its victim would have enough time to try and pull his intestines back into his body.

Repeating what he'd done in his fight against Crab, Hadjar unsheathed his sword and stepped aside smoothly, turning his body slightly. It looked slow, but in reality, he'd moved with the speed and grace of a predator—fast as a bolt of lightning and not wasting a single action.

Hadjar's clothes fluttered, hiding Colin's blade from view for a moment.

When everything was still again, the spectators saw some rags falling to the sand. They had a few drops of blood on them. The beast pressed a paw to his wounded side.

Colin chuckled haughtily and swung his sword around, painting the sand purple and getting the blood off the blade.

"If you immediately fall to your knees," he pointed at the ground with a smug grin, "and crawl, like the worm you are, over to me—I'll let you live."

The onlookers glanced at each other. Everyone knew how nasty Colin was and doing this wouldn't shame the newcomer. How could a simple country boy ever defeat a military officer? Even if he was a stupid and lazy one, like Colin. Still, years of training and a rich family had provided him with undeniable advantages.

But they hadn't taken into account the fact that it wasn't just any ordinary man standing in front of them, sword in hand, and with his clothes torn.

It was Hadjar.

Colin flinched. The senior officer unsheathed his sword slightly. The General stretched her hand out toward her spear.

For a moment, they'd seen... not a swordsman, but a dragon standing in front of Colin. It had been there for a fraction of a second. It went by so quickly that they didn't even notice it consciously. Their subconscious, however, did.

"Idiot!" Colin laughed, but his knuckles turned white from how tightly he was gripping his sword.

Without knowing why he wanted to get rid of this annoying ant as quickly as possible. His goal was to demonstrate his strength in front of the other officers and put that deluded daughter of an insignificant merchant in her place. In his father's Palace, she would've been just a common servant, the kind of nobody he would've fucked whenever he felt like it.

Why did he have to obey a commoner?!

Colin was going to take out all his rage on this talented countryman.

Hadjar took a few practice swings with his blade, testing the feel of it. He took the sword in both hands, raising it to eye level and turning the tip of it toward his enemy. He bent his legs slightly, ready to keep fighting.

In front of him was an enemy who was only four times stronger than him. Could they have made it any more unfair? Of course, it was unfair to his foe, not Hadjar.

Even if the devil himself were to stand before him, Hadjar would kill him too. As long as he held a sword, no one would stop him!

Colin swung at Hadjar. Once again, his sword whistled as it cut through the air. But this time, it swerved and went from side to side as it was swung, leaving a ghostly zigzag in its wake. The speed of the strike was incredible, despite the complicated pattern it was tracing.

Such an attack could've easily broken through the guard of most senior officers, but not Hadjar's. He ducked beneath the strike but slipped on the sand as he was trying to attack Colin's legs. The powerful counterattack, which had been capable of crushing the arrogant man's ankle, only kicked up a lot of sand, instead.

The very next instant, Hadjar had to roll in order to avoid a follow-up attack which would've most likely ended with him skewered and pinned to the ground.

"You pathetic worm!" Colin laughed, lunging forward.

He tried to find a gap in Hadjar's defense. And he did. Hadjar, despite all his speed and dexterity, was always a little slower than the enemy's attacks.

Small cuts covered his arms and torso.

Colin wasn't going to forgive this arrogant commoner. During his next lunge, he aimed for the stomach again. But this time, instead of feeling his blade cutting through the yokel's flesh, he felt it strike... another blade.

Hadjar had managed to block the deadly attack.

The vibrations caused by the blades crashing against each other made him wobble unsteadily. Trying to keep his balance, he took five steps back, almost ending up outside the arena. An imperceptibly angled shield kept him from falling. The officer who'd helped him stay on his feet also pushed Hadjar back toward the center of the circle. His expression didn't change, as he was afraid that even the smallest hint would give away that he'd helped the newcomer.

Hadjar cracked his neck and approached his hated foe once again.

He caught on to the enemy's fighting style. He saw the general outlines of Colin's Technique, which were based on impetuous, thrusting attacks, almost as if he were wielding a spear. It was like fighting against a scorpion or a wasp. Lots of deadly, quick strikes, followed by an immediate retreat.

That's why Hadjar didn't block the next attack. Instead, he rushed toward it. It looked like the poor country boy had gone crazy and was going to impale himself on his opponent's blade in a desperate gamble, but...

The tip of Colin's blade grazed Hadjar's shoulder. A few drops of blood fell to the sands. But Hadjar was already in the safe zone where he couldn't be hit by his enemy's sword. This was the biggest disadvantage of Colin's lunging attacks—if they didn't hit the target, they'd leave a large gap in his defense. A skillful warrior could've compensated for this using raw speed, but he was far from one.

To the spectators, it seemed like Hadjar's blade didn't whistle, but growled instead. Some of them thought he was wielding a white fang instead of a sword.

Hadjar slashed Colin's chest.

But instead of blood, he only saw sparks.

Colin dodged aside and put some distance between them.

He felt his chest incredulously. Under his shredded silk robes, white armor could be seen. Obviously, it wasn't ordinary armor, as most kinds of armor wouldn't have stopped such a powerful attack, especially at point blank range. However, Colin had remained completely unharmed, despite his armor being destroyed.

"Oh, you stinking bastard!" He growled.

The black fire flared up around his sword.

"Scorpion's breath!" Colin shouted.

Scorpion's breath

Energy Points	1.01
Threat Level	High

This time, as he lunged forward, an actual stinger rushed toward Hadjar. A scorpion's stinger that had been woven together from a ghostly, almost imperceptible flame. This attack was over three times more powerful than the 'heron' that Hadjar had managed to block, and that was just the energy level.

The audience didn't even bother to send for a healer this time. They knew that no one at the 'Bodily Rivers' level, especially at its initial stages, could block this Technique. Despite being technically at the 'Mortal' level, it was used by practitioners at the 'Transformation' level.

And yet, Hadjar didn't get out of the way.

He got a more comfortable grip on his blade and, half-turning, swung it. It all looked so casual as if he were doing some morning practice.

And yet, it was this very ordinary-looking slash that finally caught the General's interest. She even leaned forward slightly, but the conjured scorpion's stinger obscured her view. It covered Hadjar with a fiery veil.

Wiping the sweat off his forehead, Colin smiled haughtily and was about to sheathe his sword, when he saw it...

On the sand, with his left hand behind his back, Hadjar stood, unharmed. There was no hole in his chest, as there should've been. But two of the tents behind him had been slashed and set on fire.

The Technique had been split in two, not harming a hair on Hadjar's head.

"You eat far too much spicy food," Hadjar commented dryly.

"One with the Sword," the audience whispered.

Some of them even gulped nervously. This level of skill was much more frightening than any Technique. After all, to use any Technique, you had to spend the energy you'd accumulated in your body. How many stings could Colin create? Five? Ten maybe?

The calm countryman could simply split them all with a single slash. His strikes, made at a distance of several steps, didn't require a single drop of energy from him. He would just use his skill and a sword.

"That's impossible..." Colin gaped in astonishment.

Even his father had only recently reached this stage, and he was considered to be the best swordsman in the whole prefecture.

For a moment, Colin thought he'd heard the bumpkin utter a name. A name that he'd already heard somewhere before.

Who was this Eina?

Colin didn't have the time to try and remember.

For the first time since the fight had begun, Hadjar pressed the attack. But he didn't just lunge forward like Colin had—at every step, he swung his blade in a wide arc. And with each sweeping motion, a phantasm was conjured at the edge of the blade, like a shimmering mirage, ready to disperse at any moment, but somehow still visible to the naked eye.

Merging into one ghostly attack, they flew at the shocked Colin. By the time he'd come to his senses, it was already too late.

The ten attacks became one. One strike, which had absorbed the power of ten, and was no longer just a ghostly mirage. The spectators saw a huge crescent, ready to sever Colin's unprotected neck.

This crescent was held back, however. It covered the sword, emanating a smooth, blue light.

Hadjar wouldn't rely on his luck and a ranged attack. He chained the strikes to his sword, reinforcing them further with cold iron and his own strength.

"Stop!" The senior officer, who had started the whole argument, shouted.

He knew what fate awaited the man who would kill Colin, the son of the prefecture's General. It was not a fate to be envied.

However, Hadjar didn't slow down. His sword didn't waver.

In his blue eyes, the burning rage of a dragon smoldered.

General Larvie's son?

Ha!

He could've been the Emperor's own son and Hadjar wouldn't have cared!

The blue crescent on the sword crashed… into a spear.

Hadjar was flung ten yards away, like an ordinary ragdoll. He crashed through several tents and rolled on the ground.

The General stood in front of him.

She held her siege spear, which now had a black scratch on it.

"How dare you threaten the life of an officer?" she snarled.

The officers and soldiers pressed their fists to their hearts and bowed simultaneously. Each of them knew that this misconduct wouldn't go over well for the newcomer. They also knew that, perhaps, the general had just saved not only Colin's life, but the countryman's as well.

But Hadjar didn't think about that.

They'd taken his prey away from him, and an animalistic roar almost tore out of his throat.

After regaining his senses, Hadjar knelt and pressed his forehead to the ground.

A real storm raged inside him, but outwardly, he was more submissive than a sheep. "Please, forgive your unworthy servant," he lifted his head, and then, forcefully, lowered it back into the sand.

As he did so, he would repeat the plea every time: "Please, forgive..."

With every humiliating repetition, the storm in his chest grew more turbulent.

Hadjar was able to bow to anyone, as long as he knew that, in the future, his sword could drink the blood of someone from his list. And now he knew where to find one of the people for whom the goddess of justice had been waiting far too long.

"You've passed the officer's exam," the General sat back. "But your behavior demonstrates that you don't know how to follow orders, nor the army's laws. Perhaps it would be worthwhile to ensure that you won't negatively affect others in the army. Senior Officer Dogar?!"

"Yes, General!" a mighty man fell to one knee.

Compared to him, the General looked like a little girl. Admittedly, compared to this bear of a man, any other officer would've looked the same as well.

"You've been asking for an assistant. Here he is—your new assistant."

"Thank you, my General."

The spectators exchanged glances again.

Dogar's squad? No one survived there for more than a year! Even a penal battalion would've been a milder punishment than Dogar's squad!

Chapter 36

 Senior Officer Dogar, in Hadjar's opinion, was even more impressive than the residents of the Valley of Streams had been. He was almost eight feet tall and nearly five feet wide at the shoulders. He truly looked like a bear that had shed its fur.

He could've probably crushed rocks in his massive jaws and smashed the city gates to pieces with just a glance. He used military gloves as weapons. Apparently, this was due to the fact that it was impossible to find a weapon he could wield comfortably, as his arms and hands were too big (one of his biceps alone was as big around as Hadjar's waist).

It seemed to Hadjar like the earth shook slightly when Dogar walked. Though, admittedly, he could have been imagining it...

The neural network, of course, reported only the following details when asked to analyze Dogar:

Name	Dogar
Level of cultivation	???
Strength	???
Dexterity	???
Physique	???
Energy points	???

The senior officer was much stronger than his new subordinate, so it wasn't possible to 'scan' him. Hadjar didn't exactly look presentable. Thanks to the General, he was covered in bruises and cuts. He limped along, leaning heavily on his sword, which served as a makeshift crutch.

"Go to the warehouse and leave your toothpick there," the officer's voice was quiet and even slightly high-pitched, despite the man's mighty appearance.

"Yes, sir, senior officer Dogar."

"Just sir will do."

They left the main camp area and headed toward the outskirts. There wasn't even a parade ground there. Just lots of tents and marquees, standing in the high, uncut grass. It looked like a backwater village or some sort of 'refuge for exiles'. But, nevertheless, Hadjar could feel the unique military atmosphere of the place, one that he hadn't been able to sense in the main camp.

It had seemed to Hadjar, back at the main camp, that he had not come to an army camp, but to an ordinary tent city. The only difference was that the people had worn armor instead of clothes, nothing else.

"Here's your tent," Dogar pointed to a tent in the center of the area. It was spacious enough to accommodate several people. He stood next to the bigger one that was right next to Hadjar's own tent. "You're my new assistant, so we'll live near each other."

"Yes, sir."

Dogar turned to Hadjar for the first time. He appraised him coolly, then pointed his finger at his subordinate's chest. The newly instated officer of the Royal army swayed from the force of the accidental poke but did not fall over.

"You're fragile," Dogar could hardly stop himself from spitting the words out. "I watched your fight. Your speed and reaction time are great, but you have the body of a frail little girl."

Hadjar didn't argue or try to prove anything because he felt that the officer was telling the truth.

"Well, since you're my assistant, you'll train ten times harder than my other subordinates. Any objections?"

"No, sir."

"I'll send you to the healer afterward. You'll sleep all night, and you'll come to training in the morning. If you come to training lame, with a runny nose or a headache—I'll kill you and then tell everybody that you attempted to desert the army. Any objections?"

"No, sir," Hadjar repeated.

Dogar stood there for a short time, towering over Hadjar like a mountain, and then nodded. He took Hadjar to one of the most spacious tents in the whole camp—the Healer's tent. The Prince counted all the tents on the way over—there weren't many of them—approximately enough for a thousand people. In all honesty, it was a very small camp.

In an army of several million soldiers, a tithe, which had ten thousand soldiers, was considered the smallest unit. This camp was like a tithe that had been formed from a tithe. What does the General use Dogar and his people for?

The healer was a quite pleasant man of indeterminate age.

He had Hadjar lie down on a foldable bed. There were about three dozen of them in the tent. The tent itself was full of pained groaning, howling and bandaged bodies resting on each of the beds.

"Was the battle fought recently?" Hadjar asked while the healer was coating his wounds in an ointment.

"The battle?" the scholar was distracted for a moment, looked around, and then smiled. "Oh, no. This was just training."

Training? This is how they look after training! What did they do to end up like this?

"I heard about your fight."

Hadjar's eyebrows shot up in surprise.

"Just some rumors," the healer explained. "Half of the camp is talking about the hick swordsman who beat adjutant Colin. But don't get a big head. There are plenty of great swordsmen in the army. There is a great number of those who are 'One with something' too. I want you to keep this in mind—a girl came here at the beginning of the last month. She was at the 'One with the World' level of swordsmanship. She defeated four senior officers like they were helpless kittens."

Hadjar blinked a couple of times and leaned back against his pillow. Every time he felt like he had made a little progress on the path of cultivation, it turned out that the world was much more complicated than he'd previously thought. To reach 'One with the World' before the age of eighteen... Who was this monster in a skirt?

However, it wasn't at all surprising to see such immense power in such a young practitioner. No wonder that the various sects, clans, Academies, and even the army, had introduced the age limit. Simply put, as somebody matured and aged, they were less likely to move on to the next stage.

If a practitioner hadn't managed to reach the stage of the Heaven Soldier by the beginning of their third century of life, they would never reach it. The same law was also applied during the transition to other stages.

That was why the fastest and most active cultivation occurred in the early years of a practitioner's life. It was also why the children of the Empire had stood out so much when compared to the children of the Lidus Kingdom.

The situation changed a little when Primus came to power. Now, once mythical Mortal Techniques had become quite commonplace. And not only those Techniques, either…

"Don't be angry at the General." The doctor had a slightly rural accent that Hadjar found made him sound kind. He put aside the ointment and placed a green pill on a spoon for Hadjar to consume. It tasted vile, but the pain gradually faded away. "She saved your life."

"No, she probably saved Colin's life."

"Don't be silly, officer Hadjar. The adjutant had, after all, only been using power at the level of the Bodily Rivers against you. Do you really think he would've followed the General's orders in the face of death?"

Perhaps he wouldn't have. But Hadjar was still sure that he would have cut off his head before Colin could've used all his strength.

"Besides, even if you'd killed him, you wouldn't have been prosecuted. His father is very dangerous. The laws mean nothing to him. I'd be willing to bet my soul on it—you wouldn't have woken up tomorrow morning, after killing him. And that's the best case scenario. At worst, you'd have spent the rest of your life in his torture chambers. And trust me, the torture chambers of General Larvie are known throughout the Prefecture."

Hadjar understood that there was at least a grain of truth in the words he'd just heard, but it was still a hard pill to swallow.

"Moreover, Dogar's group is a punishment only for the weak of spirit and the weak of body," the healer continued. "For people like you, however, there's no better place in the whole army. You'll see for yourself, in time."

Hadjar looked at all the wounded, groaning men around him... He wasn't quite sure he could agree with that.

"Drink this," the doctor ordered and held out a wooden mug with a sweet-smelling, scarlet drink inside.

[Object: unknown. Properties: unknown. Initiating analysis...

Visual data is not enough to complete analysis. Analysis process has been halted.]

"What is this?"

"Definitely not poison. It is a mixture of berries and sleeping pills, designed to help someone sleep soundly and restfully."

Hadjar sniffed it and didn't detect any toxins... He scanned the drink with his neural network one more time. Just for sure.

There was nothing dangerous in it.

Nothing that his extensive database of the smells, colors, and textures of various poisons and other nasty things could detect, anyway.

Hadjar thought the taste of the drink was quite pleasant as he chugged the entire mug. A minute later, he was sleeping peacefully, wrapped in a blanket the healer had brought. Cheap healing ointments always caused people to feel a bit cold.

Hadjar didn't know that he would soon get used to this feeling and to the company of the talkative healer.

Chapter 37

Hadjar woke up because he'd felt like someone was staring at him.

He opened his eyes and immediately reached behind the headboard, where he always kept his sword, but Hadjar's grasping hand found only empty air.

"Good reflexes," Dogar nodded.

The senior officer was standing next to Hadjar's bed. With his arms crossed over his powerful, naked chest, he looked even more like a bear than he had previously. He was covered in scars and black tattoos, with sinewy, steel hard muscles.

In addition to his military gloves, Dogar was wearing only a pair of pants made from high-quality leather and high boots that didn't have hard soles. The soles had been replaced with several layers of the same leather the pants were made from.

Hadjar looked around—there was no one else besides them in the tent. The scarlet rays of the dawn were piercing through the cover that fluttered in the wind, acting as the door.

"Sir, I was sedated and…"

"I was informed," the man interrupted him. "Otherwise, you wouldn't have woken up at all. You have twenty seconds to get ready, officer."

It didn't take Hadjar twenty seconds. Ignoring the slight pain from his bruises and cuts, he managed to get ready in seven seconds. Dogar counted down loudly and demonstratively, playing with his huge muscles as he did so.

Hadjar didn't know what stage this bear of a man was currently at, but he assumed that it was the Transformation stage, at least.

"You are slow," Dogar shook his head. "But we'll correct that, too. Now, before training, I will conduct a brief inspection of our camp. As my assistant, you have to figure out the what, where and how of all the things that need to be done."

"Yes, sir."

"Leave that toothpick behind. My aide shouldn't go around with a sword that I can bend with just two of my fingers."

And, to demonstrate that he wasn't exaggerating, Dogar really did pick up and fold the sword over using only two of his fingers. It was a good, solid sword, not an artifact, mind you, but suitable for battle. It was possible to strike armor with it without the blade getting any notches on it. And Dogar had bent it, just like that...

Hadjar was inspired. He understood that it was pointless to argue, not that he wanted to do so, and followed Dogar.

They came out of the empty medical tent and... Hadjar didn't see anyone.

Walking between the tents, Hadjar could hear snoring or sniffing from time to time. As far as he knew, the soldiers wouldn't get up at the crack of dawn, and would instead start the day when the wake-up call was sounded, two hours after dawn

Consequently, a senior officer would be in charge of rousing them.

"What do you know about the army, Hadjar?"

Dogar walked in front, with his arms crossed behind his back. It looked as if a giant from legend was striding among mere mortals. He suppressed the will of all around him with just his appearance and even silenced the dogs tied to pegs around the camp. They lay down on their bellies and covered their ears with their paws, assuming the most submissive poses they could manage.

"In the army, they feed us several times a day and give us an opportunity to become stronger."

The giant grunted.

"You're right. By the way, hold on to this." Dogar took out a locket on a leather strap from his pocket and threw it over his shoulder. Hadjar caught it deftly.

"It's the army seal. The number on it will change after each of your achievements."

On the front side of the medallion, in addition to the designation of their army, was a metallic character indicating 'zero' in that world. I wonder how a metal engraving can even change...

Damn it! Hadjar was still annoyed that the diary of South Wind had been ruined. He still didn't know anything about spells, although he had seen them used several times before.

They were somewhat disturbing and fascinating at the same time.

"What do these numbers track, sir?"

"Usually it just how many enemies you've killed in battle. For more, they show how much of a reward you've earned, but only the General can bestow it. And only with the approval of the War Council. So, rewards are rare around here. Well, if we raid the monsters in the woods, we can get a reward for slaying them, too."

"Do you often go raiding around here, sir?"

Dogar turned back to look at Hadjar over his shoulder.

"Do you always ask so many questions?"

As soon as Hadjar began apologizing, the Bear laughed.

"It's a good trait in an assistant. My last assistant was so afraid of me that he was ready to swallow his own tongue as soon as I glanced at him. He was stronger than you and was at the first stage of the Bodily Rivers, but I like you more."

Dogar was a surprisingly straightforward person, considering his rank.

"When there is no war on—there are raids. When there are no raids going on—there are exercises. You can also get Honor points during the exercises. That's what they're called, by the way. But I personally don't find anything especially honorable in them, so I just call them 'figures'."

"I understand, sir. Can I ask you one more question?"

"As many as you want, deputy. Your secondary task, after training, is to ask me as many questions as you can think of."

Hadjar looked at the camp and at the carts and wagons already moving through the gates of Spring Town. He looked at the carts laden with countless bundles of spears, arrows, bows, and swords that could be seen in the southern part of the camp. Others were fully loaded with all sorts of provisions.

"Nomads or neighbors?"

Dogar laughed.

"You're smart. However, what else can I expect from an 'One with the Sword' practitioner... Yes, they're for the nomads. Last week, the War Council and the General decided that we would move north exactly one month from today."

Dogar spoke in a rather odd way, but Hadjar had quickly gotten used to it.

So, a month from now, they would hit the road and be on their way to fight the nomads. It was earlier than Hadjar had anticipated, but it was still within reason. He should have a chance to carry out his plan.

He had to advance to at least the fifth or the sixth stage of the

Bodily Rivers during this month. Otherwise, he would most likely end up killed and never get the chance to attend a Royal reception at the Palace.

Elaine...

Hadjar shrugged off the unwelcome thoughts. He needed to focus on the here and now if he hoped to have any success in the future.

"Now, Hadjar, if you don't want to get stabbed, don't make any unnecessary movements."

They approached a distant, but enormous tent. It was much larger and more luxurious than the one where the General lived.

At the entrance stood...Imperial Legionnaires. They were soldiers clad in green armor. Hadjar felt the aura of the Transformation stage emanating from them. What sub-level? There were no sub-levels.

Unlike the Bodily Rivers and the Bodily Nodes stages, the stages that came after them had no divisions within themselves. But Hadjar knew almost nothing about them. South Wind hadn't had the time to tell him the details.

"Senior officer Dogar," the Bear introduced himself. "My new personal assistant, officer Hadjar, is with me."

Full names were rarely used around here, almost never, in fact.

"Go on in," one of the Legionnaires moved aside the curtain covering the entrance.

Dogar entered first and Hadjar followed after him. Only after he'd entered the spacious, bright rooms did he understand why the Imperials were here.

Many officers and even some ordinary soldiers sat inside, among the wooden shelves filled with a variety of scrolls. An old man was pacing in front of them, one whose type of aura Hadjar would never fail to recognize.

He was in the presence of a Heaven Soldier once again. A creature that could destroy almost half of Dogar's group with only one movement of his hand. But what was he doing here?!

"Senior officer Dogar," the old man greeted him, extending his hand.

The Bear shook it, simultaneously nodding his head slightly. Apparently, this would do in place of a bow.

"Is this your assistant? I seem to recall that the previous ones never received such an honor."

Before today, Hadjar had seen only two true cultivators in his life—Primus and the Governor. That's why his impression of them, in general, wasn't very nice. But this old man, with his long, gray beard and warm eyes, seemed to be quite pleasant. Hadjar just hoped it wouldn't turn out to be a ruse.

"I have a good feeling about this one."

"Well," the old man approached Hadjar. "Officer Hadjar, would you mind if I checked you?

"In what way?" He'd spoken without thinking. He immediately bowed. "I beg your pardon, venerable adept."

"I'm just a librarian," the old man smiled. "And nothing more. I lost my opportunity to move forward on the path of cultivation long ago, so now I live among the various works and books you see here. Maybe a young man like you wouldn't consider it the most pleasant fate, but I'm not complaining. So, now that you know me better, will you let me know more about you? Otherwise, how can we find the right Technique for you?"

Hadjar looked at the interior of the tent once more. There were many officers and privates sitting at the tables. Sometimes they got distracted from reading the scrolls lying in front of them and would look in Hadjar's direction, obviously curious.

"These are all. ..."

"Techniques," the old man nodded. "I presume officer Dogar has told you about the Honor points?"

"Yes, honorable adept."

Hadjar could not call a Heaven Soldier something as mundane as 'librarian.'

"In here, you can find all four types of Techniques," the old man looked at his possessions almost lovingly. "From Techniques involving weapons to the Techniques of external energy."

Techniques of external energy? Even South Wind hadn't heard about those!

"Most of them are simple. But there are Mortal ones among them, and, in order to motivate you, I'll tell you that there are several Techniques of the Spirit in here as well."

Techniques of the Spirit?! Hadjar felt like he was going to faint, but he came to his senses in time. In the past, people from the Kingdom of Lidus could not have even dreamed about learning Techniques of the Spirit.

"If you want to study those, you'll need at least ten thousand points."

"For killing a beast at the Leader stage, ten points are given," Dogar whispered into his ear. "For killing an enemy during a war—only one point is given."

Hadjar was absolutely shocked. These Techniques had surely been sent here just to show that they existed in principle.

"Let me explain. You weren't brought here to be taunted by things you can't have. A senior officer has the right to bring their assistant here and they'll be given a free Technique of the Mortal level to study." The old man smiled kindly at Hadjar.

"Otherwise, what's the use of an assistant?" Dogar added. "If they just get killed in their first real fight."

Hadjar nodded. So, the General wasn't trying to 'punish' me. She was humiliating Colin by almost publicly rewarding the commoner who'd dared to raise his hand against her adjutant.

"Now, if you just allow me to check you and find out your strengths and weaknesses... This is a completely painless procedure. I'll just put a little bit of my energy into yours for a moment, and then I'll take it away."

Hadjar looked at the numerous scrolls and then at the old man. Damn it! Damn it! Should I risk it?

He wasn't sure that a Heaven Soldier, with the help of his mystical crap, wouldn't be able to detect the heart of a dragon. And something told Hadjar that any cultivator could probably find a thousand and one ways to use such an ingredient in his own cultivation. It was just too dangerous.

Even if this old man had talked about his inability to progress...

Things got tense. The pause had gone on for too long.

Chapter 38

Hadjar fell to his knees once again and pressed his forehead to the ground. Perhaps I should start wearing something over my forehead, to avoid injuring it when I do this sort of thing in the future.

"I beg your pardon, honorable adept," Hadjar said, voice full of regret. "The spiritual patron of our village doesn't allow us to use someone else's energy."

"I'm not going to let you use it," it seemed like the cultivator was a little taken aback by this.

"Please forgive me, venerable adept," Hadjar was banging his head on the ground now, ignoring all the older man's arguments. "If I let you do this, I won't be allowed to go back to my village!"

Dogar and the old librarian looked at each other.

"He's from a remote village full of superstitions."

"Get up, officer," the librarian sighed and continued talking only after Hadjar had risen to his feet. "We won't deprive you of your peace of mind. But you have to choose the Technique by yourself, in that case."

"I would advise taking something that strengthens the body," Dogar added. "You're too frail."

"You have ten minutes, officer," the cultivator walked over to a table that had an hourglass on it and flipped it over. "Please don't think that this rule is one I see much point in, but... rules are rules."

Hadjar, wiping away imaginary sweat from his brow, began

perusing the rows of scrolls. He immediately passed by the section that contained the regular Techniques. The Steps and the Sword were enough for him. He wasn't interested in something like a 'steel jacket'.

These Techniques required long-term training and would eventually become unnecessary at the stage of Transformation. Hadjar planned to go far beyond the Transformation stage.

He immediately went to the section of Mortal Techniques. There were fewer scrolls here than in the previous section. The reason why was clear. Just eleven years ago, there had only been a few such scrolls in the entire Kingdom. Hadjar found himself in front of a treasure trove of knowledge.

"Why are there two price tags everywhere?" He asked without turning around.

"The first one is for taking a scroll out for an hour," the librarian explained. "And the second one is for buying the full copy. To answer the question you no doubt wish to ask, you'll get to keep your own copy after we mobilize."

It was both an inspiring and depressing prospect. It was unlikely that the Empire had sent the really good Techniques they had if they were being allowed to spread throughout the Lidus Kingdom. But, alas, Hadjar didn't know which Techniques were 'useful' and which weren't. So, he just walked along the rows and waited for some sort of insight.

'Seven steps of emptiness' (Analysis... Structuring and general data... Entering it into the evaluation system... Cost: 0.15 points of Energy/sec)—bodily Technique that allows the wielder to move at the speed of a deer at the Leader Stage. A copy cost five hundred points, and renting it cost exactly ten times less—only fifty points.

Hadjar smiled inwardly but had a brooding and indecisive facial expression outwardly.

How many men in the army have a photographic memory? Maybe ten or twenty in every two million do. The army will obviously lose out on a lot due to these people. After all, they just need to read the scroll and don't need to buy it.

Hadjar didn't have such a talent. But he still had the neuronet. He would never have to buy a full copy while he had it. For the price someone would pay to learn one scroll, he could go through ten.

'Misty hammer' (Analysis... Structuring and general data... Entering it into the evaluation system... Cost: 0,23 Energy Points/Use) — a weapon Technique that increases the strength of a hammer blow twofold.

The other Techniques were even more impressive: Techniques that made the body as light as a feather. Techniques that improved one's vision. Techniques for archers which could turn one arrow into several midflight.

But these were mere Mortal Techniques. They didn't belong in the category of 'multi-volume'. One of the best examples of 'multi-volume'

Techniques had been the 'Fried Sparrow', which the Master and Colin had used.

The problem was that the scrolls laid out on the shelves in this library were all one-volume. They were only valuable to the practitioners below the stage of Transformation.

Hadjar just looked at them as he passed by.

Finally, he was at the end of the hall. There were exactly 47 scrolls here, divided into five sections. One of the scrolls had been set apart in the last, fifth section.

[Analysis... Impossible to analyze. Error 12@#$47]

"Meditation Technique?" Hadjar read, clearly surprised. Spiritual Level. Twelve thousand points. But... what is this Technique of meditation?

"I'm not surprised you don't know about it," the old man sighed, leaning heavily on the table. "When I first came here, most of your best cultivators knew nothing about meditation Techniques. That's one of the reasons why you didn't have Heaven Soldiers before."

Hadjar looked at the other price tag. You had to pay three thousand points to rent it. Three thousand points, just to read this scroll for an hour!

"What do you cultivate before the stage of Formation, officer?"

"The body," Hadjar replied.

"And before the Transformation?"

"The capability of the body to create and... store energy," Hadjar decided not to use words like 'generation' and 'accumulation'.

It would look very suspicious considering his supposedly rural background.

"And how is the transition from the Transformation Stage to the path of the true cultivators carried out? I mean the first, truly 'real' stage of the Heaven Soldier."

Hadjar gazed hungrily at the scroll, literally feeling its significance and value as a tangible aura around it.

"If only I knew…"

"The answers to these questions are in this scroll, officer," the old man took a covert look at the clock and the sand in the hourglass slowed down slightly. Dogar pretended that he hadn't noticed anything.

"The Meditation Technique lying in front of you will reveal the secrets of this cultivation. In other words—it describes how to absorb the energy of the world, how to properly circulate it, how to use and store it. Different meditation Techniques have different depths of knowledge and comprehension of this truth," the librarian continued. "A Technique of the Spiritual Level, like the one lying in front of you, is able to guide you on the path to becoming a Heaven Soldier."

Here it is! That's what Hadjar had been looking for—a way to get to the level of a true cultivator!

"And, of course, I can't choose it."

"That would be too easy. But now you know exactly what to strive for."

Hadjar reluctantly walked away from the meditation scroll and began to examine the remaining four sections. As expected, there were plenty of volumes there—one for each type of Technique.

Alas, he couldn't find a weapon Technique for swordsmen here. Only spear Techniques were present. This fact, by the way, explained the General's skill with that type of weapon.

"Can I take one of these?" Hadjar asked.

Each tome of a multi-volume book was estimated at a thousand points. The cost to rent them was exactly a hundred points.

"Only a copy of the first volume," the old man nodded. "This is, of course, not the best version of the Technique. The last, tenth volume will be useful to you only at the Superior Stage of a Heaven Soldier."

"Do the stages after Transformation have subdivisions?" Hadjar was surprised to hear this. Meanwhile, the old man made a copy of the first volume for the 'Mount' Technique. A Technique that made the body as strong as a rock.

Judging by the description attached to the scroll, it was necessary to rub a hundred different powders made from thousands of different herbs into the body to cultivate it. And in order to fulfill the requirements of the first volume, which could only slightly increase the strength of his skin, Hadjar would either have to spend all his wages at the scientists' shops or run around the woods like a hare.

"They do, but it is not as complicated as with the early stages," the old man laid out the Technique scroll, along with a blank one, on the table in front of him.

He took out a yellow talisman from his pocket, squeezed it between his index and middle finger, and said something. A gold seal, made up of many different characters, began spinning in the air immediately. The text from one scroll was slowly printed onto the other.

"Could you, venerable adept, tell me about it?"

"There's nothing to tell," the old man tied a red ribbon around the copy and put a simple wax seal on it. "Each level after Transformation is divided into four stages: the Initial Stage, the Average Stage, the Advanced Stage, and the Superior Stage. And, I have to add, the difference between a newly advanced Heaven Soldier and one who has a lot of experience at this level is simply enormous."

The last grain of sand fell and the old man nodded his head in the direction of the empty clock. Dogar and Hadjar, who was carefully holding a copy of the scroll, bowed. They turned around almost simultaneously and walked out.

While leaving the tent, Hadjar noticed something reflected in the hourglass. Something that, for a moment, had flashed in the librarian's previously calm gaze.

I doubt he's lost the will to develop his power! That old fox...

Hadjar thought he should be wary of the old man from now on. He stared at them as they left with far too much interest. It was easy to guess what would've happened if the cultivator had found out what Hadjar had in his chest.

The heart of a dragon... not only cultivators but whole countries would fight for it!

"We chose a Technique for you, now we must pick your weapon," Dogar went ahead again.

He moved through the crowd of soldiers like they weren't even there. The soldiers were hurrying to get to the cauldrons full of porridge.

A quarter of an hour later, they reached another tent. It was even bigger than the library had been.

Chapter 39

 Ordinary legionnaires guarded the Armory. It was obvious why no elites had been posted here as well. No one would allow ordinary soldiers and officers access to artifact weapons. The Techniques were much more valuable than the weapons. But the scrolls that the old librarian had kept before the Empire provided new ones had been worthless, not even worth a bowl of food, by Empire standards. Even a mere mortal weapon was thousands of times more valuable in comparison to them.

And so, Hadjar just chose the sturdiest classic (by native standards) blade from the collection presented to him. Ordinary soldiers couldn't choose anything, they just used the weapons they were given.

"Good choice," Dogar nodded after they returned to the camp. "A sword of good quality and a Technique suitable for your needs. Now, go to our doctor and tell him that I sent you. Maybe he has some of the herbs from the librarian's list."

Hadjar used the neuronet and a thousand different names of herbs appeared in front of his eyes. Damn it, even if they all grew in the same field, it would take at least a day to collect them!

And it's necessary to grind them into powder, in order to not lose the desired properties... I still need to find them, I can worry about processing them later.

The sword in Hadjar's hand was different from the sword the

Master had given him for training. It was solidly made, but not from the best materials. An artisan, not an apprentice, had forged it, but it was still a mass-produced weapon. At the same time, this one had been forged, hundreds of the same exact blades had also been made; so the quality was worse because of the limits of the local technology.

"Well, are you ready to train, deputy?" Dogar's smile was almost bloodthirsty as they passed by the camp and stopped in the clearing where the parade ground was.

The parade ground looked like a field specifically set aside for the purpose of torturing people. At least that's what Hadjar's initial impression was. A thousand warriors were busy with their daily exercises. A hundred of them were running around the oval parade ground with huge logs on their shoulders. Another hundred were trying to avoid getting hit by the spinning dummies on the obstacle course.

Fifty people were trying to avoid the stones being thrown at them by the dummies and simultaneously trying to hit the target located about a hundred steps away from them. At the same time, there were multiple pairs of people sparring in the center of the parade ground.

They were fighting not with blunted training weapons, but with real ones. Therefore, the sand under their feet had turned red.

"Everyone!" Dogar roared out, and Hadjar clutched his ears, realizing that all this time, the huge man had been communicating in a whisper.

"Senior officer!" A thousand people greeted him in the chorus.

"The daily routine is as follows," Dogar whispered again, hurrying over to the pyramid of logs twenty-three feet in length and with a diameter of eight inches. He sat down and, using some belts, hoisted five of the logs onto his shoulders.

"First, two hours of running with logs on your back. Followed by five minutes of rest, so you can drink the poison of the healer."

Hadjar looked to the side. A scientist with a scroll in his hands was sitting in the shadows. There was a barrel of malodorous brew next to him.

"It will restore your power and treat your wounds a bit," Dogar tested the weight of the logs, sat down, and added another log. "After that, two hours on the obstacle course. Five minutes of rest. Two hours of sparring. Five minutes of rest, and, as a light finale, fifteen minutes of running with a log. Five more minutes of rest, and then the healthiest among you will carry the injured back to the healer."

Dogar got up. He looked like Atlas holding up the sky. And the soldiers definitely respected him. After all, he was going to train right alongside his subordinates, carrying a lot more weight on his back than them, thereby motivating them and setting an example for them to strive toward.

Dogar was a proper senior officer, deserving of his rank.

Hadjar sat down next to the pyramid of logs. He covered his neck and back with the specially prepared rollers, then grabbed the belts and threw the logs onto his shoulders, all in one motion. When Hadjar began to rise, he heard a rather ominous warning.

"If you ever try to weasel out of doing your fair share of training, assistant, I'll ban you from drinking the medicinal brew. For your first time, since you're such a squishy, delicate thing, I'll take pity on you. You'll need to get used to the idea of carrying twice or even three times that weight soon enough, however. And now, pick up the pace, keep your back straight, focus on your breathing!"

The last orders were addressed to the soldiers. Their faces grew more severe at once, and they ran around the parade ground behind Dogar, who, for his part, was running as casually as if he weren't carrying nearly a ton of logs on his shoulders.

Hadjar, sweating heavily, jogged at the back of the group. It was very difficult for him to run every lap; his heart was racing and the veins in his temples were throbbing. But he kept running, in spite of his fatigue.

It seemed to him like this running would never end. It was useless to try and count the laps. And so, in order to add to his training, he tried to keep track of the movements of each of the dummies on the obstacle course. Sweat and pain prevented him from doing the exercises properly. But Hadjar was ready to train not just twice as hard, but three times as hard, if it meant he'd grow stronger.

He knew that only an iron will and constant, impossibly difficult training would help him defeat his foes.

Therefore, when, two hours later, the soldiers who were sparring and the 'loggers' exchanged places, he still kept dragging the logs around.

While all the soldiers were consuming the healing brew, he continued to carry the logs on his shoulders.

At some point, only he and Dogar were still running. The senior officer looked as fresh as he had in the morning, while Hadjar could feel the blood streaming down his back.

Finally, he dropped the logs and started greedily gulping down the nauseating brew with the thirst of a Bedouin that had found a life-saving oasis. After the first cup, Hadjar began to feel his pain and fatigue melt away.

The soldiers, watching Dogar's new assistant drinking the poison avidly, turned away. They weren't very good at hiding their urge to vomit at the sight.

"Good," Dogar nodded, throwing off the logs as well. He washed his face with the brew, almost causing people to faint. It should be noted that this disgusted everyone, even the doctor.

Hadjar, who saw it happen through the misty veil of his fatigue, appreciated the act of his superior and also decided to take a risk. He was unspeakably amazed when, after washing himself with the brew, he felt normal again and was even able to see without the whitish shroud and red circles floating everywhere in his vision.

"Now, everyone moves on to the obstacle course, forward march! And if one of you lets a dummy break something, I'll do the same on the other side as well, for symmetry. And don't even think about going to the doctor to have a nice nap!"

Hadjar nodded and began staggering toward the dummies when a mighty paw fell on his shoulder.

"Wait, assistant." Dogar walked around the pyramid of logs and brought out two clinking pairs of overalls. Judging by their numerous, bulging pockets, they had been stuffed with weights.

"They're made of bluestone," the senior officer handed one of them to Hadjar proudly.

He sighed and took the overall with both hands, as he was too afraid to try and hold it with just one hand. Bluestone was a fairly dense material. One blue stone, the size of a teenager's palm, could weigh up to 88 pounds.

It was a very heavy substance.

The pockets of his overall had been stuffed full of blue stone. Hadjar didn't know how the fabric could withstand such a weight. The silver sparks appearing on the cloth were definitely being caused by the blue stone.

"Put it on," Dogar was already dressed in his own overall. It looked like it weighed several times more than Hadjar's. "While you were sleeping, I measured you and sewed it overnight. I hope it fits."

Hadjar imagined this bear using a needle and thread and smiled.

The overall, surprisingly, fit him. Hadjar almost sat down on the ground, he was so shocked.

"Let's run."

And they did. They ran the obstacle course, over and over. For four hours. Without any rest.

Hadjar endured when the dummies struck his legs. He pushed through it when they beat his back with clubs. He even managed to keep going when he took a wrong step and was hit in the groin. Fortunately, he wasn't hit too hard, because a steel bar had been sewn onto this area of the overall. But when four dummies struck him all at once, Hadjar couldn't keep going. He unsheathed the blade tied to his back (he'd tied it there so it wouldn't get stuck on his belt) and began to run through the obstacle course with a sword in his hands.

No, he wasn't going to cut the dummies. He just felt like he was in a real fight when he held a blade and it was easier to concentrate.

The neuronet had already offered to show him the best route available. Twenty times. But he wouldn't have been Hadjar if he'd decided to use an 'outside' force. The neuronet was just a small, helpful device and nothing more. He had to grow stronger and stop relying on it.

Four hours later, Hadjar, quite literally, crawled over to the barrel of the brew. Only he and Dogar were still on the parade ground. The rest of the warriors, supporting each other, had trudged back toward the camp. Or, if they hadn't been clever and strong enough, had been sent to the healer on a stretcher. Among the thousands of warriors, there were several monsters, who, after asking for permission, had gone into the forest.

They'd looked tired but unharmed. That's why Hadjar hadn't been that surprised when he'd seen about two dozen people rushing into the thickets to hunt. After all, they could exchange the creatures' energy Cores for Honor points.

"Now, sparring."

Dogar wore fighting gloves and stood in the center of the parade ground.

Hadjar took the sword in his trembling hands. It seemed even heavier than when he'd roamed the world in the guise of a cripple. But he was far more alarmed at the fact that no one except Dogar was standing on the sand.

"Against you?"

"Do you see anyone else?" Dogar replied with a question. "Hurry up, I just got warmed up."

The senior officer jumped around to stay warmed up, his landings causing something like an earthquake. Hadjar was praying to the heavens to spare him, but it was unlikely that the native gods knew or would acknowledge 'The Lord's Prayer'.

Hadjar staggered, stumbled over to the sand and 'stood' in front of Dogar. And the battle started... Well, something started. Considering that Hadjar couldn't even raise his sword properly, then... well, it was mostly a beating. In general, Hadjar ate a lot of sand that evening.

Hadjar did not give up on training even at the healer's tent, while everyone else was lying around and moaning. He closed his eyes (although, admittedly, he couldn't have opened them even if he'd wanted to), assumed a lotus position, and began to absorb the energy of the world, pushing through the infernal pain, trying to open new channels inside his body.

Hadjar didn't see it, but Dogar looked into the tent for a second. He looked at his assistant appraisingly and nodded his approval.

Three weeks passed like this.

Chapter 40

Status, Hadjar ordered after washing up.

The sun had not yet painted the sky a vibrant red, but Hadjar was already hurrying to get to the parade ground. Dogar, putting on his pants as he went, ran behind him, cursing. He couldn't allow his subordinate to come to training before him.

He always started first and left last. Otherwise, what kind of commander would he be?

Name	Hadjar
Level of cultivation	Bodily Rivers (5)
Strength	1,6
Dexterity	1,95
Physique	1,55
Energy Points	2,3

If someone found out that he'd progressed five levels in a mere three weeks... they wouldn't have believed him. And if they did believe it, they would have dissected him at once.

"Senior officer," Hadjar smiled, putting the fourth log onto his shoulders.

"Admit it, Hadjar," Dogar puffed, affixing six logs to his own back. "Your grandmother sinned with the Iron Bars, didn't she?"

"And did your granny sin with the Six-Legged Bear?"

While people, reluctantly, trudged on toward the parade ground to suffer, Dogar and Hadjar arranged to race each other. They'd started this fun tradition a week ago. They ran for four hours and then compared who had run more laps. Dogar ran with weights slowing him down, but that didn't spoil their fun.

Hadjar was worried because he'd noticed that his results didn't reflect his actual characteristics.

People with more stat points than him couldn't stand for even an hour with two logs on their backs.

The day started and continued on as usual. Hadjar was very glad about his body's reaction to the Herculean workout. After each of these 'workouts', it became extremely easy to absorb energy and create new channels in his body. Endless sparring with various opponents also allowed him to advance along the path of the sword wielder.

He'd managed to earn either the respect or the recognition of everyone in Dogar's group in just three weeks. Nowadays, no one doubted that the seemingly frail Hadjar was worthy of his position and title.

To gain this recognition, he had had to defeat almost four dozen people in the sparring area. And he'd been fighting three opponents at once in the last few battles.

"Senior officer Dogar!" A cry came from the edge of the parade ground.

"Keep counting!" Dogar shouted.

"I don't want you to just give me the victory."

"Officer, you've already lost six barrels of beer. And you don't even have enough money left to buy one cup!"

"It doesn't matter, commander."

Dogar let out an odd laugh that sounded like a grunt as well and went over to the person who had called for him. Hadjar kept running, turning his face toward the wind. His legs were stiff, his back was bleeding, but he could feel how his soul and body were getting stronger. He wasn't the same as he had been just three weeks ago.

Admittedly, nothing about him had changed, at least outwardly. This unusual elegance and almost inhuman refinement caused people to shake their heads in disbelief. Hadjar hadn't added a single gram of muscle. He still looked like the well-groomed son of a nobleman who had never picked up a sword in his life.

"Officer Hadjar!" The bear's roar resounded.

Hadjar was surprised, but, after turning around, he immediately rushed over to his superior. As much as it was possible to rush with four logs on his back, anyway.

The senior officer who had administered his exam was standing next to Dogar. He still wore a fur cloak around his shoulders, as if he weren't affected by the summer heat.

Next to him, a guy in shackles was standing on his knees...

"Nero?" Hadjar asked, clearly shocked.

"Oh, Hadj, hello," Nero smiled as if nothing had happened, and waved his hand. "I mean, that is, officer Hadjar."

"He said he knew your assistant, Dogar," the senior officer continued the conversation. "So either take him into your group or send him to a penal battalion."

"And what did this private do?"

The senior officer looked at his now former subordinate.

"He wounded his fellow soldiers while on leave. Six people were sent to the healer because of him."

"I wish to say, in my defense, that they had molested a maid in a very unpleasant way."

"She was the employee of a brothel!"

"It doesn't change the fact that they hadn't been planning to pay her."

Hadjar sighed. He didn't know Nero that well, but judging by their conversation, the woman was the guy's personal religion.

"What do you say, Hadjar?" Dogar asked, straightening up and strapping a log that was about to slide off firmly back into place.

"Are you having a bonfire?" Nero asked, observing the officers curiously.

Because of the bushes in the way and his own posture, he couldn't see the parade ground.

"Were they even armed, Nero?"

"Don't insult me, Hadj. I mean... you've insulted me, officer Hadjar. Of course, they were armed! I even have a few scars to prove it."

Six privates... Nero is literate, too. I wonder why he didn't take the officer's exam.

"He'll be my responsibility, commander."

Dogar sighed and motioned for the key to the shackles. Naturally, the shackles weren't ordinary ones, and a stone seal served as the key.

"If I were you, I would..." The departing senior officer grumbled. "Get rid of him."

"He's your headache now, Hadjar. I'll be waiting for you at the training area."

Dogar turned and ran toward the parade ground.

"Forty-three!" He shouted pointedly, his voice loud and clear, showing that he had continued to count the laps.

Hadjar only cursed. He figured that he would owe the man another keg of beer by the end of the day.

"Have you eaten?" Hadjar asked Nero, who was rubbing his wrists.

"I'm not completely well-fed. Military prisoners, you know, aren't fed very well."

"Have you slept?"

"I slept alone, which was very sad. If it hadn't been for the city guards, I would've clearly been able to salvage that night and spend it enjoying myself."

"Well then..." Hadjar nodded and brought Nero over to the border of the parade ground.

He examined everything carefully and turned to Hadjar.

"Listen, have you already thrown the key away? Why don't we just lock me back up again and send me to a penal battalion? I don't mind at all."

"Take a log and make sure to keep up," Hadjar laughed.

"Hey! I'm serious!" He shouted from behind Hadjar.

After ten minutes, Nero was puffing along somewhere at the back of the column, and Hadjar was thinking about how great it would be when he visited the forest today. For the past week, he had had enough strength to hunt after training.

In addition, he had been able to master the first volume of the 'Mountain' Technique. He'd spent all of his salaries on herbs (luckily, they were paid every week), and the camp healer had helped a little. Now, Hadjar's skin was much stronger. Although, for some reason, he felt that it was getting stronger with each new level of the Bodily Rivers, without any Techniques being needed.

In a week, he had managed to save up half of the required sum by hunting beasts at the 'Awakening of the Mind' stage. 47 Honor points showed on his medallion, and a hundred points were needed to rent the second volume. It would be the second volume that would make Hadjar's body as strong as a tree.

That evening, after dragging the groaning Nero on a stretcher to the healer's tent (and in fact, just recently, he had been the one getting dragged there), Hadjar asked for permission to go hunting.

"No training tomorrow morning," Dogar, who had assumed the meditation pose, announced suddenly.

"War Council?"

"That's it." The senior officer nodded. "We will be marching in a week. The intelligence reports say that the nomads have come to the borders. I'll take you with me; you'll observe, listen, and learn."

"Yes, sir."

Hadjar turned around and went into the forest.

Thanks to the teachings of Robin, an old hunter from a village in the Valley of Streams, he moved through the forest as silently as a leopard, avoiding noisy twigs, passing by nesting birds soundlessly. His loose clothing also didn't make a single sound and the sword strapped to his back did not rattle.

It was easier to run this way, but it was harder to unsheathe his sword.

Hadjar got lucky, finding something promising in just an hour. He was on the trail of the Black Wolf. It was a beast at the 'Awakening of the Mind' stage. A large predator, it was almost five feet at the withers and about eight feet from the mouth to the tail.

Hadjar touched the tracks. The ground was loose, damp and still slightly warm.

The beast was no more than a quarter of an hour's walk to the north.

Taking out his blade, Hadjar followed the trail. As night fell in the forest, the twilight shadows began their crazy dance. They turned everything around Hadjar into a theater of confusion. Big creatures looked like small ones and the small ones had seemingly disappeared from the earth.

The shadows hid those who sought their protection and exposed those who were too stupid to recognize their usefulness and thus ignored them.

Hadjar respected the shadows and they reciprocated. He managed to approach the beast covered in black fur without being noticed. The wolf, immersed in its own hunting, had hidden in the shadows, not knowing that he'd become the prey long ago.

The beast had known no worthy opponents in the forest, but suddenly, he felt the gaze of something terrifying upon him. He'd felt the attention of a being whose mere presence could've stopped his heart.

Terrified, the wolf, looking like a black lightning bolt, rushed into the bushes.

Hadjar didn't chase after him. He didn't swing his sword, launching a ghostly strike from it.

Three people had blocked his path. Two of them had axes and one was armed with a sword. They didn't look like simple bandits. Despite their cheap, tattered clothes, their gazes were similar to those of the soldiers in the army camp.

Without a doubt, these were soldiers standing in front of him.

"I hope you have a good reason for interrupting my hunt," Hadjar said quietly.

"Yes, officer. Adjutant Colin asked us to convey his regards to you."

Chapter 41

Hadjar didn't need the help of the neural network to determine the levels of cultivation of these so-called "messengers". All three were at the eighth level of the Bodily Rivers. For a simple practitioner, it would be almost impossible to defeat an opponent a step above them. Let alone three.

But Hadjar didn't even try to retreat.

He swung his sword and began walking in a spiral.

The soldiers smiled greedily, and with slight laziness, looking at their defenseless, at least in their eyes, victim. They did not care at all about the fact that Hadjar had defeated Colin in a fair fight less than a month ago. They, after all, knew that, at the end of the fight, the General had interfered and the adjutant hadn't actually been defeated. Besides, there were three of them.

Numerical superiority always made even cowards braver. It made them feel stronger. Being part of a herd gave them confidence.

But they made a mistake.

They decided to attack one by one.

The most impatient of the soldiers rushed forward, swinging a double-headed battle ax. His level of cultivation allowed him to cut through the trunk of a century-old tree with ease.

Hadjar certainly didn't want to try his luck. He stepped back smoothly, like a morning breeze. It was as if an invisible force had lifted him off the ground and dragged him about three feet through the air. Then Hadjar extended the hand his sword was in and lunged forward, the tip of the sword flashing as it caught a moon ray.

The blue, sharp sword tip plunged into the soldier's stomach. Scarlet sparks flared up and the soldier's chain mail proved to be too fragile to stop the strike.

The soldier shuddered violently. He saw a gray shadow.

Hadjar, after moving a step back, slid forward once again, creating a small tornado of leaves in his wake.

He moved to the side, flicked his wrist, and swung the blade upward. The two halves of a once whole and foolish soldier fell to the ground, watering it with his blood.

The two remaining soldiers took hold of their weapons' handles more tightly and began to surround Hadjar from different sides. All of this happened in absolute silence.

Hadjar, standing between them, didn't pay any attention to the bloody rain drenching his face and hands. He turned toward the swordsman, turning his back to the ax-wielding soldier.

He gave in to the temptation.

Ready to cut Hadjar down, he took a step forward. And that was the last step he ever took.

Hadjar turned and, arching his back as he did so, swung his sword.

The ax whistled past, over his head, colliding with and deflecting the enemy's blade. A ghostly slash flew out from Hadjar's sword.

The soldier couldn't comprehend why his feet seemed like they'd been covered in boiling water, and he suddenly became somewhat shorter.

Lowering his gaze, he saw his feet lying off to the side, then he fell onto his back.

He died quickly after the second strike pierced his chest and tore through his heart.

Hadjar and the swordsman were left alone.

Thrown back by his ally's vicious attack, the soldier hit a tree, which was the only thing that saved him from falling. He immediately put up his sword defensively in front of himself, waiting for the retaliatory attack from Hadjar. But he was just twirling his blade in order to cleanse it of blood. Then, once again, he began to whirl around in a spiral. Like a hungry predator toying with defenseless prey.

Sweating, the soldier cursed the night he'd agreed to carry out this mission for the General's son, for a few measly gold coins, at that.

'He's a simple hillbilly...' 'Just a sucker with a sword...' Colin had claimed.

And what did the soldier see in front of him right now?

Eyes that were blue, clear, and full of rage, staring at him intently. He saw something terrifying that looked like it would devour his very soul, not a mere man!

Swinging his sword, he launched a mad attack comparable in its desperation to the last leap of a hunted tiger.

Hadjar held his breath and assumed a low stance. He swung the blade five times but did it so quickly that few would have seen anything more than a blurry shadow and a blade glistening in the light of the full moon.

Five ghostly, almost ethereal slashes broke through his opponent's guard... And then broke his opponent.

The soldier hadn't been able to reach his target. At first, he squinted and began to fall toward the left. Then he saw his own hand flying off in front of him, clutching his sword. The last scene his eyes witnessed was the body lying on the ground. His body. Which he'd seen from above.

Hadjar cleared the blood off the blade with another wave, and the next moment, the head of the dismembered soldier fell to the ground.

It may have taken a while to describe, but the tornado of leaves hadn't even fallen yet by the time Hadjar was putting his blade back in its sheath.

He'd moved as smoothly as a swan rising into the sky and faster than a predatory cat when it pounced on prey.

He came over to the first of the defeated enemies and sat back on his heels. He examined the body (or rather, its remaining halves) and found a miraculously intact coin pouch. Untying the ribbon holding it closed, Hadjar found two gold and several silver coins. He found approximately the same amount in the pouches of the other attackers as well.

Now, taking into account the officer's pay he also received regularly, he had almost ten gold coins at his disposal. That would be enough to buy a house in a village, along with a sizeable, arable field.

"Now I'll be able to master the second volume much faster," Hadjar muttered to himself, calculating how much money would be left after he bought all the necessary ingredients.

It turned out that the coins he'd taken off his slain foes weren't going to be enough for his needs. Hadjar, to get everything required to use the second volume of the 'Mountain,' would need about... the same amount of money he had available. Maybe even more than that. And he couldn't even get a loan if he did need more.

He sighed heavily and shook his head. Even such simple resources, in this world, were much more expensive and rarer than gold.

"I wonder... How did you find me?"

Hadjar examined the bodies once more but found nothing on them. They only had ragged, clearly taken from someone else, clothes, along with the standard army weapons, and... Nothing else.

Suddenly, Hadjar understood. He had nothing much on him, either. Cheap, worn robes, a piece of rope instead of a belt, and sandals tied with a cheap cloth. He looked just like the day he'd come to enlist. Except for one thing. The medallion that now hung around his neck.

Hadjar removed the trinket. It showed that he had a little less than fifty Honor points.

The answer had been in front of him the whole time.

How had the senior officer known where Nero had been and how had the city guard found him? It was unlikely that the guy had been running around the brothel and shouting that he'd hurt his fellow soldiers. Not a single messenger would have had enough time to get back to camp. Well, one would assume that they would've had to run back to the camps, but even then, they would've needed a direct command...

"Ah, so that's why you need the locket?" Hadjar smiled, placing the trinket back around his neck.

All this time, he hadn't just been wearing an "achievement counter", but also a "beacon" of sorts. It was a magical device intended for tracking. Local officials were craftier than he'd given them credit for - it was quite a convenient system. It probably decreased the number of deserters in the army as well.

After a few weeks of wearing it, Hadjar had, for the most part, forgotten about the medallion. The people who had been serving for more than one year had probably already gotten used to it. Why had the soldiers taken off their lockets, going into the woods? They had obviously been forced to do so.

And who better than an adjutant to know all about the various properties of these trinkets? An adjutant probably also had access to a tracking device for the lockets, whatever that may be.

"So, Colin, you most likely already know about this incident..." Hadjar mulled things over.

The adjutant had certainly already run to the General and was dragging her over to see Dogar. What a war crime. Killing fellow soldiers. Hadjar wasn't going to be shackled as Nero had. No, he'd be sold into slavery at best. And the money would be given to... well, ideally, to the families of the dead men. In reality, the greedy hands of the bureaucrats would take 90% of it for themselves.

"So, you set a trap for me and I got caught in it?"

Hadjar chuckled.

Trying to trap a former circus freak and brothel worker? Ha! Hadjar knew tricks that Colin hadn't even heard of!

And yet, Hadjar had been right about one thing. The adjutant, General, and a few soldiers in armor were already heading toward Dogar's camp.

Chapter 42

"Senior officer Dogar!"

The General entered the tent. She looked the same as when Hadjar had seen her that first time. Her tight braid was as thick as Dogar's wrist. She was dressed in half-armor—an iron skirt and gloves. Except for this time she hadn't brought a spear.

But, given the late hour, it became clear that the General hadn't yet gone to bed. Apparently, she had been preparing for the War Council or had been engaged in something equally important.

"Dogar!" Colin entered the tent behind her, the warriors trailing after him.

He looked sleek and polished, wearing white robes belted with a wide, silk ribbon. He looked like one of those rich men who spend all of their evenings in the best taverns and restaurants in the city. Not like a soldier or a warrior of the army.

The armored warriors following the General looked completely different.

Still, Hadjar was glad to see Colin's smile wither. The "armored lady" seemed to stumble over her words. Well, who could blame them?

Who knew what they'd expected to see, but it clearly hadn't been the scene in front of them right now.

In addition to Dogar and Hadjar, the twenty best warriors from the group were also in the tent. Each of them, without any exaggeration, was worth a dozen ordinary soldiers. And, apparently, they looked so intimidating that the General's bodyguards began to unsheathe their swords.

"Stop," the lady said quietly, and the soldiers immediately returned their blades to their sheaths.

She looked at Dogar. The General looked like Thumbelina compared to the bear of a man. Fragile and defenseless. But the mighty Dogar wilted slightly under her gaze. A fierce determination and great power radiated from it.

"My General," the senior officer knelt and punched his chest with a meaty fist, saluting her.

The rest of the people did the same. Well, except for the three dissected corpses on the floor who couldn't really salute their General. Admittedly, they weren't able to do anything right now.

Being dead usually had that effect on people.

"What is the meaning of this, Dogar?" the General asked, allowing everyone to get back up.

"General, my assistant, officer Hadjar, stumbled upon a group of nomad scouts while hunting in the woods."

Colin, who had already begun to say something, decided to remain silent.

The General walked over to the bodies. She calmly bent over the corpses and inspected their faces and bodies. It looked strange to Hadjar since various images from the past world were still fresh in his memory.

"They don't look like nomads…" the General stood up and looked at Hadjar.

The young officer withstood her gaze, despite the power behind it. His father had used to look at him the same way, many years ago, when he was being too naughty. And the power of the King had been enough to make stone statues kneel in front of him.

"Officer Hadjar!"

Only after being directly addressed did Hadjar fall to one knee and put his fist to his heart.

"My General," he responded, with genuine respect.

"Tell me what happened."

"Yes, General."

Hadjar straightened up and told her everything. Down to the smallest detail.

He had gone to the forest to hunt. Then he'd followed the trail of the Black Wolf. He'd thought luck was on his side. The wind was blowing in his face, and the beast itself was engaged in the pursuit of game. Hadjar had followed the trail, but three men blocked his path. Two with an ax. One with a sword. All of them had been at the level of the Bodily Rivers, no less than the eighth or seventh stage.

"You managed to beat three warriors at the eighth stage of the Bodily Rivers by yourself?" Colin snorted. "I remember you were only in the first stage three weeks ago."

"Adjutant," the General cut in, the warning clear in her tone.

"But…"

"Adjutant!"

Colin sighed and raised his hands in a gesture of surrender. He wasn't going to argue with the commander. While he didn't think that the crazy girl was worth scraping off the sole of his boot, it was still too early for him to make his move. No one knew what could happen during their battle with the nomads… Generals often died in battle and new, stronger, more determined and decent people would then take their place.

His father had taught him that.

"Go on, officer Hadjar."

"Yes, General."

First, he killed the lanky guy who'd wielded an ax. Hadjar pointed at the two halves of his body. He demonstrated the deadly attack for everyone. However, he had to restrain his ghost blade so it wouldn't ruin the tent, which was now fairly crowded. There were a lot more people stuffed inside it than had originally been planned for.

Then there were two more men left. He killed them. It ended quickly.

As soon as Hadjar had cleared the blood off his blade, he immediately tied a rope around the bodies and carried them over.

He showed the General the bloodstained rope.

"And we were about to come to see you, my General," Hadjar continued. "When you yourself came to us. Have you already been told about the nomad scouts?"

The General shifted her gaze from Hadjar to his sword, and then to the corpses.

"Dogar," she said.

"Yes, General."

"Let your people go and get some sleep. I've seen your training, they're gonna need a lot of strength tomorrow."

The Bear turned to his subordinates. They were staring at the soldiers behind the petite lady. Yes, she was their General. Yes, they respected her immensely and would die on the battlefield for her if she demanded it of them. She'd led them through such terrible victories and battles that many couldn't even comprehend it.

But who'd made them strong and powerful? They were feared and respected by the entire army. Who had made that happen?

Dogar.

He stood a step above the General, and even the King, in the eyes of these warriors.

"You heard your General! Go to bed! Double training tomorrow!"

"Yes, sir!" the warriors thundered and, marching in unison, shaking the very earth, exited the tent.

Each of them shot an unambiguous glance at the General's bodyguards before disappearing into the night.

There was more space in the tent, but Hadjar still didn't dare to breathe in deeply. He could smell the armored soldiers. They had been sweating far too much as the two dozen elite heroes walked past them.

"It would seem that a bandit gang had appeared in our forests." The General said, adjusting her gorgeous hair. "Adjutant Colin."

"Yes... my General."

"I want you to form a team and scour the southern edge of the forest. Move out tomorrow after the War Council and come back the day before the march."

"But this... officer," Colin literally spat out the last word, "killed the bandits in the north!"

The silence hung heavy in the tent.

"With all due respect, General," Hadjar bowed. "I didn't mention that I'd encountered them up north."

"Thank you, officer," the General nodded. "I don't remember that either. You're leaving tomorrow, adjutant. That is my direct order."

Colin stared blankly at the commander for a second, then let out a loud snarl. If he'd had the chance, he would've slammed the door behind him. But there were no doors on the tent, so he just waved his hands around so hard that he ripped off one of the canopies.

Hadjar mentally showed the adjutant one of his most rude gestures. Well, he could've shown it for real, as well, because no one would've known what it meant. But that would've been rude to do in front of a lady.

"Three of them..." the General sighed sadly. "Did they have any money on them, officer?"

Hadjar handed her the three bags of gold and silver coins silently.

"I expect these coin pouches to be handed over to their families," the lady said suddenly.

Dogar and Hadjar looked at each other.

"They don't look like bandits at all. They look like my soldiers."

"My General!" Dogar and Hadjar immediately collapsed to their knees.

Who would've thought that she was so insightful?

"Stand up, officers," the fatigue was plain in the lady's voice. "I hope that after the battle against the nomads, my adjutant will be promoted and become the General of another Royal army."

Well, there were several such armies and generals in the country. Hadjar served in the Northern, and there were also the Southern, Eastern, Western, Central and numerous Fort garrisons, which were all ruled by generals.

"Good night, officers. I'll be waiting for you at the War Council tomorrow, Dogar."

"My General," the senior officer bowed. "Let me bring my assistant along."

The General looked at Hadjar.

"It's up to you," she said, leaving the tent, then paused for a moment. "Twenty Honor points, officer Hadjar, that's all I can do for you. A soldier in his own camp should feel safe and it is the General's task to ensure he does... Twenty points…"

Then she left.

Hadjar handed Dogar the bags of money. He put them in a trunk and promised to personally make sure their families received them.

He and Hadjar were decent people.

They weren't like the greedy officials. Children could end up starving because of Colin's and the soldiers' stupidity. No one wished to subject them to such a fate.

Hadjar left his superior's tent and went over to his own. Along the way, he saw the General, standing by herself in the camp. She was looking up at the sky and thinking about something.

Oh, God. She was so beautiful.

But neither lust nor other, more tender feelings were evident in Hadjar's gaze. Only immense respect. He now understood why two million soldiers revered her so much. She was a real General. And soon enough, he would have the opportunity to see her in battle.

Chapter 43

The entire camp knew that a War Council was going on in the General's marquee. Therefore, the situation was extremely tense. There was almost no conversation or laughter. No one sang or danced around the fires.

People walked around with grim expressions on their faces. Many of the soldiers were cleaning their armor or sharpening their weapons with abandon. Someone tried to forget about it by distracting themselves with training or, if they were at a high stage of cultivation, by immersing themselves in meditation.

Hadjar, after adjusting his sword, came up to the huge marquee. It was decorated richly, with an enormous entrance that fueled one's imagination.

"Be quick," Dogar told his assistant cheerfully, going inside.

Hadjar hurried into the marquee after him.

The inside looked as lavish as the outside had. There were no floors in all the other tents. At best, there were mats that had been placed on the ground. But in here, Hadjar had to climb some steps to get to the wooden deck of the General's marquee.

Several chests filled with scrolls stood along the walls. A long, rectangular table with carved chairs was in the center of the marquee. In the distance, a bed was visible behind a luxurious curtain. It wasn't like the bed where Hadjar slept (though his bed was still better than what he'd had for the last ten years). It was a really spacious double bed with a woolen blanket, a comfortable, thick mattress, and pillows stuffed full of feathers.

Yes, the generals lived well... and no one could say that it was undeserved. Well, at least in this particular case.

A map made from animal skin had been stretched out across on the table. Various flags, stone turrets, soldiers, miniature cavalry, etc. had been placed on its surface. There were also long sticks with coloring at the top. These were the pointers.

Various senior officers had come to attend the Council. Hadjar had already seen some of them. He noticed a tall, leggy woman with a scar across her face. She commanded the archers. All of the army's archers!

He also spotted the tall man with tanned skin and a slightly cocky gait. The locals believed they were gods of war. The cavalry was nearly worshipped.

In addition to them, Hadjar noticed a few other familiar faces in passing. There were about twenty senior officers and only three assistants present for the Council.

The always arrogant and sleek Colin was also present, of course. He looked at Hadjar like he was horse excrement.

"Senior officer Dogar," the General nodded. "Please join us. We were just getting started."

"My General." Bear greeted her respectfully.

The situation was businesslike, without any excess formality.

"Tim," the General addressed a short man who looked to be about thirty.

The spymaster took a pointer in his hand.

"The military intelligence reports that the nomads are currently moving to take Zagr Fort. It should take them two weeks to arrive on horseback."

The officer moved three horsemen figurines...

"Right now, they are at the Blue Wind ridge. They're stocking up on provisions for their horses and preparing arrows. As you probably know, the greatest threat is their horse archers."

The three cavalrymen figurines were left standing on the seam of the map, which marked the mountain ridge. The General nodded and turned to the other woman in the tent.

"Lian, what do you have to say?"

The archer thought about it for a bit, and then also picked up a pointer.

"I can post my archers here, here, and here." She put three archer figurines atop the sides of the Fort. "If they decide to try and take this Fort by encircling it, then let them get washed away by the rain of arrows."

"What if they hit us from the front?"

"Then it will only take me half an hour to move my forces to the front."

"They will get at least the first seven groups of horse archers through in half an hour," the cavalryman shook his head. "We'll have a massacre fight on our hands, up close, and your archers will be useless as usual. My guys can go around them and launch arrows into their unprotected back."

"Your guys can't even get it into a woman who is in their bed, and here it will be necessary to get an arrow into the enemy at a distance of seven hundred steps."

"Come with your ladies to my camp tonight and we'll show you our skills."

"Who would ever want to see your-"

"Officers!" The General raised her voice slightly, but it was enough to end the argument.

Everyone was on edge, which meant that these kinds of arguments weren't all that surprising.

"Lian, send two teams to the flanks. The third group will be with the main forces."

"Yes, my General," Lian nodded, rearranging the toy archers.

On the map, these movements looked simple, but in reality... Well, thanks to South Wind and the Master, Hadjar had received an excellent education. Including a military one.

The young officer was well versed in military affairs, tactics, and strategy. He wasn't a military genius, but he'd earned Haver's approval in the past.

"Tuur, any suggestions?"

A man with what looked like glasses on his face took a pointer. He looked like an ordinary scientist, though he wore a dagger on his belt.

"We'll set traps in the north and northwest. That way, we get rid of the danger of being attacked by their reinforcements. This will help us concentrate our troops in the east," the scientist pointed to a hillock on the map. "The nomads will probably try to take that hill, and we won't be able to do anything about it. It's simply too far from the Fort."

"What if you were to arrange your artifacts around it in advance?"

"They'd need to be brought in, powered up, hidden... even if my entire corps had started doing that a week ago, we wouldn't have had enough time."

The General shook her head.

"It's not a good time for us," she said. "The east wind is blowing. It'll start raining soon. The nomads feel at home in such conditions, but it will be hard for our soldiers to adapt to them. Helion, what's your opinion?"

"I suggest we surprise them with a preemptive strike," the cavalryman moved the toy riders forward. "I, along with half of my squad, will break through their defenses and Lian's archers will support us."

"I support that suggestion," the archer agreed, despite the fact she'd been arguing with the cavalryman not ten minutes ago. "When Helion breaks through their lines, my people will arrange for nightfall. The whole sky will be full of arrows."

"How many of our own soldiers will fall due to such an attack?"

"Less than if we were to let the nomads come closer," the adjutant spoke up for the first time. "I support Helion's plan. Maybe we should send Dogar's squad in with them. They're always on the front lines anyway. In any case, they'll bear the brunt of it."

Everyone in the tent was silent. No one loved Colin, but right now he was making sense. A bloody sort of sense. It sounded like a sacrifice. But it made sense.

If the horse archers of the nomads' forces approached the Fort and encircled their army, the meat grinder would begin and hundreds of thousands of soldiers would fall.

"Dogar?" The General raised her head slowly.

She knew that she was sending one of her best officers to his death. And yet, it was the best possible option.

"My people will obey your every order, my General. We will smash the enemy to pieces."

Bear was a simple man. He saw the enemy. He beat the enemy. That's how his brain worked.

However, Hadjar saw a more elegant solution on this map. Perhaps it hadn't been noticed by the others because they did not have a neural network. As soon as Hadjar had entered the tent, he'd ordered the analytical module to begin calculating the optimal solution for the situation, based on the data presented to them.

The current power of the neural network was enough to highlight the most logical plans to implement.

"My general," Hadjar addressed the commander. "May I speak?"

Now the people around the table were really silent. It was so quiet inside the tent that one could've heard a feather hit the ground.

"A peasant speaking during the War Council..." Colin snorted. "What utter nonsense..."

"Adjutant," that time, to everyone's surprise, Colin had been interrupted by Hadjar himself. "You and I have the same officer rank. The fact that you are serving directly beneath the general doesn't make your rank any higher than mine. And, by calling me a peasant, you call yourself one as well."

Colin blinked several times and grabbed the hilt of his sword.

"How dare you!"

"If you have any complaints against me, then, according to the officers' regulations, we can resolve them with a duel."

No one intervened. Everyone wanted to watch the show for a while and relax a little. Even the general remained silent. Hadjar saw a gleam of support in her gaze. She could turn a blind eye to many things and tolerate quite a lot from the entitled brat. But she could never forgive the fact that three soldiers had died because of him.

She valued the life of every soldier in her army.

"Do you think I'll stoop so low as to cross swords with a commoner?"

"It seems to me like..." Hadjar pretended to think. "The general saved you last time."

"She saved you, you foul smelling peasant! Or do you think I'll really fight at only half my power again?"

"You can even bring your friends along to help you, adjutant. In a week, just before the march, when you come back from chasing the bandits around, I'll be ready to fight you."

Silence descended on the tent once again. Many had heard of that very fight. Many knew about Hadjar's talent in the path of the sword. But they also knew that he was only at the first level of the Bodily Rivers, while Colin had the power of the Transformation stage.

The difference was almost two whole stages! That was a difference that only geniuses could overcome. Well, Hadjar was talented, but he wasn't one of those young monsters being hunted by the clans, sects, and Academies of the Empire itself.

"I'll cut off your tongue right now, bastard!"

"Adjutant!" the general was still calm and poised. "If you draw your sword, you will find yourself without your hands. Without your legs. Without your heart. And I'll mount your head on my own spear, right in the center of the camp. And when your father comes here, then ..."

No one ever heard what came after that 'then,' but judging from the General's look, nothing good would've followed the word.

"In a week, peasant," Colin snarled through his teeth. "Please forgive me... my general," the adjutant almost spat again. "But I have no time for this farce. The bandits can't wait."

Sliding the blade back into its sheath with a loud screech, he left.

"Speak, officer. We will hear your ideas."

Hadjar cleared his throat and gave a mental order to the neural network.

[I am processing your request... The request has been processed. I am creating an optimal plan for solving the problem given to me... A plan has been drawn up. I am initiating the projection ...]

"The east winds will bring rain. But the nomads will strike from the east first. The roads on the ridge will have been washed away and we'll return from the route almost a week earlier than the nomads will come down from the mountain."

"That time is not enough to set traps," Tuur said thoughtfully. "But…"

"But, please, let me finish," Hadjar spoke as politely as possible. "Yes, we will not have time to set up magical traps."

"Trenches!" the scholar exclaimed. "We can dig trenches and put light infantry there. They will quickly occupy the hill during the battle and prevent the nomads from going forward. Plus, they can finish off two thousand horsemen."

"And there is a forest in the southwest," Lian pointed out immediately. "If we cut down enough trees to make several archery towers, then I can cover the perimeter with one group and free up two more to support the army."

"We can place a detachment of cavalry at the bend of the river," Hadjar moved one of the equestrian figurines. "Well, this isn't a hill, but the distance is enough to allow you to accelerate to a gallop. The heavy cavalry will crush the western flank of the horse archers and open a passage for the infantry."

"And then we can surround them," the general finished. "I'm surprised none of us noticed that the east wind could give us a week to prepare…"

"I'm from a mountain village," Hadjar came up with something to say immediately. "The rains often blocked our roads and we played soldiers out of boredom."

"Here's another thing," Lian continued...

As a result, the council lasted until late into the evening. The Prince didn't need to say anything else because the neural network's prompts were enough for the experienced officers to get the most out of the situation.

Hadjar, absently following what was happening, only thought about one thing - how to survive before the start of the battle. How could he become stronger during the week and prevent Colin from killing him? Because Hadjar had no doubt that the fight would be to the death.

Chapter 44

"May I ask you a question?" Nero, chewing a blade of grass, was lying on the pyramid of logs.

They were the only people on the parade ground at this late hour. The lazy son of a minor official who liked chatting about women and their charms, and Hadjar himself. He, breathing heavily under the weight of the five "shells" on his shoulders, was running laps around the training ground.

Nero, looking at how his friend was torturing himself, mentally thanked fate for the fact that he hadn't been the one who had challenged the adjutant to a duel. For the sixth day in a row, Hadjar was doing nothing but training from sunrise to late at night. Actually, he didn't rest at night, either, since he was constantly meditating.

"Feel free to ask away," Hadjar exhaled and kept running.

"Well, I know there are many strange things under the endless sky, but you, my friend, are something amazing. Why did you challenge Colin to a duel? He's several times stronger than you."

Hadjar, after looking at the shadow which a pillar in the center of the parade ground was casting, threw the logs off of his shoulders. He'd been running for five hours. That should have been enough to warm up the last day before the fight.

He had very different plans for tomorrow, so he would not be able to train. The adjutant would be returning from his fruitless search the next day. Hadjar was convinced that as soon as Colin set foot in the camp, he'd immediately call for their duel to commence.

"To become stronger," Hadjar responded, sipping the doctor's potion.

Nero turned away and almost stuck out his tongue in disgust. The taste of that "medicine" was so loathsome that it could poison a well or turn a lake into a swamp. But the officer gulped it down like it was fine wine. Although, something told Nero that Hadjar had never tried anything stronger than water.

He was damn right about that.

"Stronger? Maybe you meant to say - deader?"

Hadjar still had four minutes of rest left, so he leaned his back against the log pyramid. He put a blade of grass in his mouth, following the example of Nero, and raised his gaze toward the sky. There, in the endless, blue expanse of it, huge, fluffy clouds were floating. Serene, gigantic, they haughtily gazed at the earth, shielding people from the sun that was already well beyond the horizon.

They bathed in the scarlet and gold colors, turning from white giants into bloody titans.

"Now I only have two choices," Hadjar said slowly. "Either I'll become stronger, or he'll kill me."

Nero turned and looked down at Hadjar. His friend was standing calmly, even serenely. Just like those clouds in the sky.

"Are you using this situation to motivate yourself?"

"I like to push myself."

"Gods and demons, Hadj," Nero stretched out, turning back to the sky. "I'd thought Dogar was crazy, but it turned out I was sleeping near a real psycho all this time. Just one tent away"

"I have a marquee," Hadjar remarked and, smiling slightly, added: "Only privates live in tents."

"It doesn't matter."

The Prince had at least two more minutes of rest left, so he decided to continue the conversation. Recently, he'd become very close to Nero. Well, they couldn't exactly be called friends (that didn't prevent Nero from using that term), but it was pleasant to talk to him.

"Why didn't you take the officer exam?"

"I am too modest for all the luxury being one entails, Mr. Officer."

Hadjar laughed. Nero smiled. It was a slightly tense and nervous expression.

"In our squad, you show the best results in all areas. Well, after me, of course."

"Of course," Nero mocked Hadjar. "It's just that I'm not crazy enough to train for twelve hours a day, and then spend eight more in the woods. When do you even have time to sleep?"

"I get a special potion from the doctor."

"Demon!" Nero exclaimed.

They were silent for a bit.

"My father," his voice suddenly sounded from the top of the pyramid. "He was an officer, too. A long time ago. I was quite small then. I don't remember much, but... In general, I don't want that life. I'll serve my five years and return home. With money. And, I promise you, Hadjar, I'm going to have a great feast. And not only a feast - all the families of Spring Town will have to hide their daughters from me for a whole week!"

"I think they're hiding them already."

"Sure," Nero nodded. "But I'm not a sucker, either. I'm gonna go through the gardens, then up to the roofs, and climb in through the windows. Every girl will be happy to spread her legs…"

"No more details, please."

They were silent again. The shadow cast by the post almost

reached the mark showing nine o'clock in the evening. Hadjar had never understood why there were 24 hours in a day. Maybe the multiple suns and moons followed each other closely on this planet (if it even was a planet)?

That sounded crazy, though.

"Do you understand that if you kill Colin, his father will get you?"

Well, Hadjar couldn't argue with that. Of course, he'd had a great plan for how to get justice for Stefa's restless soul and not follow the girl in death. But everything, as usual, had gone slightly wrong.

The march had started too soon. Colin had reacted to Hadjar's attempt to speak during the council too sharply. And if the Prince hadn't spoken, then he would have obviously fallen into the meat grinder along with Dogar's squad. And if Hadjar hadn't silenced Colin, he would not have had the opportunity to speak.

Everything had deviated from what he'd initially planned, but still... Even now, he could get out of it.

He hadn't been a circus freak for anything. And they were capable of all sorts of tricks and deceptions. Life had forced them to learn.

"He will not get to me during the march. And while the war with the nomads rages on, he will have an even harder time getting to me. Then, after that, no one knows where our army will be sent. The power of the General of Spring does not extend beyond Spring Town itself."

"You forgot the Ax clan."

The Ax clan... It was something like a horror story that scared nobles, not children. This was one example of a mafia family becoming an organization. It had acquired disciples, its own territories, and even a school for the arts. Martial arts, of course. They even had their own cities from which they received taxes.

The Axes were known to carry out any mission they'd been hired for. From protecting a trade caravan to killing someone. In general, they were like some kind of mixture between mercenaries and assassins.

"That just means I will need to become even stronger, strong enough to not fear even them."

"Damn crazy," Nero repeated and jumped down from the top of the pyramid.

He pulled his heavy, two-handed sword out of its scabbard. Despite its size, Nero was far from slow and clumsy with his weapon. Hadjar had seen what had happened to the last fool who'd thought so. He'd been halfway chopped into sushi during sparring, and not even particularly appetizing sushi.

Nero handled his blade only slightly worse than Hadjar did. But this "slightly" had allowed one of them to become 'One with the Sword', and the other to just avoid becoming a laughing stock.

"What do you think," Nero asked while they sparred, like they had all the previous evenings. "Will it be scary?"

"What?"

"Fighting in a battle... my father never told me anything about war."

Hadjar had wanted to answer "me too," but stopped himself on time. After all, he was from a mountain village that had never produced even a single soldier. Hadjar was supposedly the only person in the whole village talented enough that he'd been allowed to descend into the valley and explore the wide world.

"I don't know. Probably."

Each of them assumed a fighting stance. Nero held his sword with both hands, the handle positioned slightly over his right shoulder. Hadjar angled his blade in front of him, raising his left hand, which served both as sight and a way to balance himself, above his head.

"Do you remember our agreement?"

Hadjar sighed.

"I remember."

"If you end up having fewer honor points than me," Nero smiled broadly, "Then I take you with me to the fun house."

"Call a spade a spade, you're gonna take me to a brothel."

And then the swords struck against each other which caused barely noticeable waves to ripple through the sand at the force behind their blows.

A heavy, almost metallic atmosphere thickened over the camp. Only a few days remained before the march.

Chapter 45

"Status," Hadjar ordered.

The neural network responded immediately and appeared in front of Hadjar's eyes. It was like he was wearing augmented reality glasses. But, alas, local scientists could hardly have created something like that.

However, they still had plenty of mysterious spells which the Prince still hadn't learned or seen.

Name	Hadjar
Level of Cultivation	Bodily Rivers (11)
Strength	1.8
Dexterity	2.1

Physique	1.85
Energy Points	2.9

Yes, thanks to the help of the doctor and Dogar, Hadjar had once again been able to achieve an awesome result with his training. After three weeks of training, he had been able to advance by four levels, then, in just one week - by as many as six.

It had been possible only because Dogar and the doctor had almost opened a line of credit for him. He'd borrowed so many different potions, powders, and herbs from them... Most likely, he would end up having to spend his whole "premium" after the battle with the nomads to pay off the debts. And even then- it'd probably not be enough.

Well, something told Hadjar that the heart beating in his chest was also somehow involved in this rapid progress. It was a pretty weird heart. Too weird.

Hadjar didn't feel much difference between when he'd been a six-year-old boy and the present, almost twenty-year-old young man he was today. Although, according to the neural network, he was no older than three months. That was the time that had passed since Traves had died, breathing new life into a little man.

At the same time, such stats should never have been able to allow Hadjar to shoulder the seventh log. And that was what he had, secretly, in order to make sure, done that morning.

Even Dogar, with his advanced Formation stage and insanely muscular and strong body, could not have carried more than six logs. And even then, the sixth log would've left him breathless and without any energy at the end of the day.

"Data analysis," Hadjar ordered.

But, the same as with all his past attempts, the neural network simply responded with this:

[Data analyzed. System failures - 0. Errors in calculations - 0.]

"Useless thing," Hadjar said.

He still couldn't understand how the heart of the dragon affected him. Why the numbers said one thing, but in reality, everything was completely different.

"To hell with it," Hadjar waved the matter away.

He put on his patched and threadbare clothing and, placing the sword behind his back (to make running easier), left the tent. He was probably the only officer who looked even poorer than the brand-new privates.

All of his salary was being spent on the purchase of various drugs, without which he couldn't have achieved such rapid progress. No, it was possible to manage with the bare minimum. But then the eleventh, penultimate step of the Bodily Rivers would've been achieved in a year. And Hadjar had no extra days, let alone an extra year to grow stronger.

And it was during those days that he had to accomplish the impossible - break through to the level of the Formation stage. Only by doing that could he defeat Colin and prove his potential.

After that, even if the adjutant's father wanted revenge, nothing would help him except the Axes. Hadjar was hoping to achieve a high status earned by his own handiwork. Especially if the neural network had been right about how the rains would affect the future battlefield.

Then, when the soldiers found out whom they had to thank for not being sent into a monstrous meat grinder ... Well, one didn't need to be a genius to understand what'd happen.

"Senior officer! Sir!" Hadjar called out to Dogar, standing by the marquee of his superior.

Obviously stifled moans were coming from behind the not very dense fabric. Hadjar heard curses and, finally, Dogar's red, perspiration-covered head popped out from behind the canopy.

"What do you want, assistant?"

"Let me go hunting."

Dogar cursed again.

"Today's the last day and night before the march. All the other officers and privates have long been indulging in carnal pleasures. Are you really going to go into the forest, even now?"

"Yes. Do I have your permission?"

"Go, Officer Hadjar... to the forest."

Dogar had obviously wanted to say something different, but he stopped himself on time. Without delay, he returned to the tent from where sweet moans could once again be heard.

Passing by Nero's tent, Hadjar prudently put his hands over his ears. Unlike the marquees, there was too little space in these tents. So, even though Hadjar didn't hear anything, he saw the silhouettes of at least three people. Well, besides seeing the tent itself shaking quite noticeably.

Hadjar probably wouldn't have minded a chance to go to the center of the camp and choose one of the newly arrived priestesses of love. They were doing brisk business today. Most of the soldiers, married or not, always brought workers from brothels into their tents before heading out to battle.

For some... for many, it was the last time they'd get a chance to do so. So they did not hesitate to spend their coin and "worked out" as if they would never touch the female body again.

From the girls' whispers back at 'Innocent Meadow', Hadjar knew that the prostitutes themselves had been waiting for this day eagerly. They said that no man loved them as much as a soldier leaving for battle.

But Hadjar had a completely different adventure planned that day. He needed to get 30 more points to finally have a hundred Honor points. He'd be able to copy a meditation scroll into the neural network's database using those hundred points. It'd allow Hadjar to break through to the next stage in a short amount of time.

So, Hadjar was going to have a proper hunt in the forest. And if he got lucky, he would even find a way to kill a weak Alpha.

He could earn ten points at once for that.

True, it might be an impossible task. At least...

"Hadj! Wait a minute!" Nero was running after him, fastening his sash and putting his boots on as he went.

... By himself.

Hadjar turned around and looked at his friend in surprise. At that moment, two pretty, but upset, female faces looked out of the man's tent.

"Listen, I have a lot to do..." Hadjar looked at the sun. It was already starting to rise. There was very little time left. And, of course, he didn't have enough time for group sex...

"I'll go with you," Nero interrupted him, smoothing down his hair and straightening his sword.

Hadjar was really surprised to hear that. Genuinely surprised.

"You're not obliged to do that at all, besides..."

"In addition," Nero again interrupted him. "There're as many girls in this world as grains of sand on a beach, but I have only one friend like you. I do not want any other soldier to cover my back in battle, only a sword that I can trust."

Nero extended his hand. Hadjar hesitated for a moment and then shook it.

"Well, you're almost not a virgin anymore."

"Why?"

Nero moved his eyebrows funnily.

"If you only knew what I've recently been doing with these palms and fingers of mine..."

Hadjar sighed and, pulling his hand back, turned to the forest. He'd managed to read not just disappointment, but also real thirst in the girls' eyes. Apparently, his friend was good at more than just gabbing. However, perhaps that was what had inspired those ladies...

Shaking his head in an attempt to rid himself of unnecessary thoughts, Hadjar entered the forest first.

He would have time to spend with women. But only later. When he survived.

"If we hurry, we will have time to get back to the ladies..." Nero muttered.

Hadjar immediately regretted taking the talkative man along with him.

However, he was glad that someone would be watching his back. For the first time in his life, he wouldn't have to look back every few steps. It was a strange, but very... warm feeling.

"What have we come to hunt for, my friend?"

The early morning forest, full of moisture and almost lazy shadows, looked calm and peaceful. It was difficult to imagine that beasts could even live in it. It was difficult to imagine that any living creature could live here, disturbing the serenity.

"For beasts at the stage of the 'Awakening of the Mind'..."

"Not as bad as I'd thought. We can handle one together if we find an old and weak one."

"And for Alphas," Hadjar finished.

Nero swore loudly.

"Have I told you that you're crazy?"

But Nero didn't suggest they go home. He followed Hadjar calmly. A nice feeling indeed...

"Keep up with me," Hadjar whispered and ran.

Chapter 46

Over the past few hours, fortune favored the hunters several times. They managed to catch and defeat five weak and sick animals at the stage of the 'Awakening of Power'. Their five cores would bring in about ten points, but that was already a third of the required amount.

At first, Hadjar had insisted that Nero take half of the money, but his friend refused, saying it was a contribution to the future and that there would be no sense in him helping Hadjar if he died in a fight with Colin. It was probably just an excuse, but Hadjar made a mental note—one day, he would pay his friend back for this.

During the time they spent hunting, Nero learned some of the hunting signs. Now he could understand Hadjar, but couldn't answer him. So, all of their 'dialogues' turned into 'monologues'. Nero simply nodded when he understood the sign and shook his head if he hadn't.

At the moment, they were crawling along the ground, hiding under the branches of bushes hanging from above. It was a very dirty job, causing Hadjar to roll his eyes mentally. For a city boy, Nero had mastered hunting quite well (even if he didn't have a neural network giving him hints), but his clothes... In his leather jacket, pants, and boots, he looked like an everyday, urban guy. A normal, very dirty, slightly tired guy.

Hadjar raised his fist and they stopped.

In a clearing lay a huge wolf, hidden from the sun by the thick crowns of the trees. It was so big that if you were to put a horse next to it, they would be the same height at the withers. And from the muzzle to its tail... well, it was about three and a half yards long, not an inch less.

The beast's main feature wasn't its gigantic size, nor its frightening fangs the size of a man's palm, not even the tight, corded muscles visible under its 'fur'.

No.

The danger came from the fact that, instead of fur, he was covered in thin, emerald threads. They emitted a smooth, green glow and rang slightly in the wind. Their ringing caused small emerald spikes to shoot up from the ground. They would briefly dispel the darkness, then turn into dust, blown away by the wind.

It was an Emerald Wolf, a beast at the Alpha stage.

"Alpha. Wolf. Emerald." Hadjar signaled to Nero, who couldn't see the clearing.

Nero shook his head. Then again. Then slammed his fist against his palm.

Emerald wolves were considered to be one of the most dangerous animals at the Alpha stage. Comparable to a man at the stage of a 'Heaven Soldier'.

"Plan. Trust. We can. Hunting".

Nero sighed heavily and, with his glance, made it clear that if they died, he would get Hadjar in the next world.

Hadjar smiled and nodded.

Yes, while such a beast was comparable in strength to a real cultivator, it still lagged behind in terms of smarts. And Hadjar was going to use that difference.

Like any other creature, an Emerald Wolf had its failing—light. That's why it lay in the shade of thick foliage. If the sun's rays touched the emerald threads on its skin, they heated up so much that the beast would burn alive.

It took ten minutes to explain the plan using the hand signs. After that, Hadjar rose from the ground and unsheathed his sword.

As soon as he came out of the bushes and into the clearing, the Wolf opened its eyes. Its pupils weren't black, but green and the iris glowed slightly.

Without rising up, it roared. This roar made emerald spikes pop out of the ground. They were sharp, thin, and could easily pierce steel armor. And, of course, Hadjar's simple, damned useless clothes.

The beast didn't want to fight. It wanted to sleep. Last night, it had

had an unsuccessful hunt and it was tired. More tired than hungry. In addition, the two-legged held a glowing stinger in its strange paws. The light caused it discomfort. It wanted the two-legged to leave. So, it warned him away.

Hadjar sighed. What had this beautiful beast done to him?

Nothing.

But that was how the world worked. Hadjar and the beast both understood that.

They hunted and fought to survive and become stronger. The difference was that, right now, the hunter wasn't the wolf, but the man.

The beast understood that as well and jumped to its feet.

It howled and snarled.

Hadjar pushed off the ground easily and soared into the air. He managed to do so a second before an emerald spike shot out of the ground in the spot where he had been standing. It didn't hurt him when Hadjar stepped on it. His bast shoes, woven from the bark of a special tree, were stronger than any armor.

Thanks to Robin and the mysterious village of the Valley of Streams...

Hadjar swung his blade, slashing toward the wolf. But it didn't reach the beast, crashing into the emerald 'wall'. From behind it, the wolf pounced like green lightning.

Its long claws stretched out like sharp daggers, ready to pierce Hadjar's chest. At the last second, the young man managed to step aside. He moved as gracefully as a swan taking flight, and as fast as a falcon swooping down to catch its prey.

However, that wasn't enough to beat a predator at the Alpha stage in terms of speed.

When Hadjar descended back to the ground, blood flowed from a wound along his leg, where his flesh had been torn away, but he didn't pay any attention to it. He had to soar into the air again to avoid being pierced with a spike.

From behind another wall, the green lightning appeared. This was the beast's tactic. It forced its victim to rise into the air, where it would be left defenseless in front of its rapid strikes.

Hadjar managed to dodge again, but he hadn't been fast enough. Now his left shoulder was covered in blood. The pain was so intense it felt as if his body had been submerged in boiling water.

"Do you want to play?" Hadjar growled.

When the spikes shot up from the ground again, he rose into the air and waited for the green lightning. And it appeared. The beast had created a 'wall' in front of it, and then jumped out from behind of it.

It was ferocious and grinning. Fast and strong. It wasn't used to feeling like a victim in this forest, where the Alpha beasts were the Lords of everything and everyone. No one could challenge their power here.

This two-legged bug shouldn't have even thought about hunting it!

This time, Hadjar didn't dodge the strike. He had been waiting for it. He met it fearlessly, but his efforts looked almost laughably pointless. It was like a small fishing boat had been thrown into the thick of a storm at sea.

When the beast was close enough to him, Hadjar swung his blade. His sword turned into three, and three ghostly slashes struck out from each of these blades as well. They intertwined into a fishing net.

The beast, due to leaping forward, was in the air as well. It turned out its attack was a double-edged sword, with which the one who had used it could cut themselves.

The wolf got entangled in the net and fell to the ground. But the strikes hadn't left even a cut on its skin. All of them had been powerless against its emerald fur. It only rang out like a spring stream and... That was it.

The wounded, bloody Hadjar descended a few meters away, in front of the grinning snout of the unharmed beast.

This battle had already been lost...

The beast jumped forward, full of rage and excitement.

"Now!" Hadjar shouted, preparing to strike.

... By the Emerald Wolf.Nero, who had been hiding somewhere all this time, cut down the branches with just a few movements. The branches came down with a loud crash and a lot of noise, letting the rays of the midday, summer sunshine on the clearing.

The wolf howled and groaned when its fur flared up with green fire. It collapsed on the ground, never reaching its victim.

For the first time, Hadjar took the handle of his sword in both hands. Using his full strength, he slashed downward. The roar of a dragon sounded out. It was barely audible, almost indistinguishable through the whistling of steel and the noise of the foliage, but it was there.

A dragon would take the beast's life.

Not a bad death...

It closed its eyes, awaiting its final moment.

For a second, the sun burned the wolf's fur and Hadjar's sword, shrouded in ghostly blue light, pierced the Alpha's heart.

It died instantly. Twitched a couple of times in the aftermath and then froze.

Hadjar collapsed next to it. Breathing heavily, he sat on the cold ground. The battle had taken only a few minutes, but they had been the longest and most terrible minutes of his life.

But—he had defeated an Alpha!

"It's a pity that the skin has been damaged," Nero muttered, coming down from the tree. "We could've gotten a lot of money for it. And now we only have the claws."

He handed some medicine-soaked bandages to Hadjar. While he was treating his wounds, Nero managed to cut out the core, and also get the claws and the fangs.

The core looked like a large agate, but the claws and fangs... Well, emeralds the size of a person's palm could never look bad or unappealing. Nero had to focus in order to wrap them in fabric and leather and not cut

off his fingers in the process.

"Take the claws and fangs," Hadjar said, rising to his feet.

His body ached, but the blood had coagulated quickly, and the medicine would gradually lessen the pain.

"I won't say no to that. You look horrible, Hadj. Let's get out of here."

"No, I need ten more points. Without them, Colin won't just 'beat me down', but outright kill me. I'll have time to recover a little during the night."

"Then let's lower the difficulty—we can just get five more beasts at the 'Awakening of Power' stage."

Hadjar agreed and was surprised at how easy it sounded. Six months ago, the creatures at this stage had inspired awe in him, but now, they were like rabbits that he was going to catch and have for dinner.

It was easy because of the fact that the forest around Spring Town was wild. People never went too deep into the forest—there weren't many cultivators around that were strong enough to survive or hunt there.

As for the army, there were few soldiers willing to risk their lives for the sake of such small gains. So, this hunt was more like a walk through the zoo than the dangerous adventure the one back in the Valley of Streams had been.

Two hours later, after they'd gotten two more cores, Nero showed his talent. He hadn't noticed a slope hidden behind the bushes and ended up tumbling down. Hadjar followed him. When they'd come to their senses, they found themselves in a spacious ravine, hidden by the foliage. And the creature in this ravine could've normally killed them with barely more than a thought. But, right now, it wasn't even able to move.

In the foliage, bleeding profusely, lay an old tiger.

A horned tiger that was as big as a house.

A beast whose aura exceeded that of the Alpha stage several times over.

[Analyzing... The analysis is not possible. Level of danger to the host (according to existing data): extreme. The probability of the host's death: 99,9999%]

"An ancient beast," Nero whispered. "Damn it. We are dead. We're dead, Hadj. This tiger is at the Ancient stage!"

Hadjar, even if he'd known what the 'Ancient stage' was, couldn't have responded to Nero.

He could only stare intently into the tiger's bottomless eyes. He heard a wheezing, feminine voice in his head.

"Greetings, Lord of the Heavens in a two-legged body."

"Fuuuuuuuuck! I haven't even slept with those twins," the pale Nero lamented. "I'll die without fulfilling my dream…"

Chapter 47

"Greetings, Honorable Tiger," Hadjar didn't even know what this creature was. But the fact it was able to speak already said a lot.

This 30 feet long, dying tiger was clearly much more powerful than a Heaven Soldier. It could probably slap a Spirit Knight around like a simple bug.

What was such a beast doing in this backwater? And why was it hurt?

"Apparently, Fate itself has brought us together, Lord of the Heavens," the voice in his head sounded again.

And yet, the tiger was much weaker than the dead Traves had been since he'd still been capable of speaking out loud. Wait, did it just (the voice sounded feminine) call him the Lord of the Heavens? Only dragons would have such a title. Actually, this is one of the old names for their race.

Damn, how old it is...

Its mighty chest heaved and the ground trembled slightly from each breath, while the leaves flew away. The wound on the tiger's body, left by some powerful claws, looked neither fresh nor old. The beast had most likely been wounded no more than a month ago.

He wondered who was capable of fighting such a creature.

Damn, this world was truly huge and Hadjar was small and inconsequential. And he was supposedly going to overcome this difference in strength one day? It wasn't surprising that Nero considered him a psycho!

But being aware of this fact didn't stop Hadjar. The iron will that shone in his clear, blue eyes could still bend the sky itself to his desires.

"You have a good look about you, two-legged with the heart of the Lord of the Heavens."

The tiger roared slightly and made the blood freeze in their veins.

"Please, forgive me for the deception, Honorable Tiger," Hadjar apologized immediately.

He had no doubts that even in this state it could flatten them faster than they could even think about unsheathing their blades.

"Don't apologize, two-legged. I deceived myself. I'm getting weak. My sight is getting blurry. My power is leaving me." The tiger, or rather, the tigress, sighed again, causing its blood to pump out more quickly. "The wound, inflicted by the serpent, is poisoned and I have almost no time left."

"I'll immediately go get you some medicine, Honorable Tiger,"

Hadjar bowed as low as he could, considering that he was still lying there.

The main thing was to get away from the ravine. Later, after the war, he and Nero would be able to return here and take the tigress' body. But for now, the crucial thing was to find any excuse to escape.

"You are cunning, two-legged. Not like the Lords of the Heavens. They are... simple, like a young tree."

Damn it! It had seen through him easily!

The tigress kept breathing, but with difficulty. Every movement caused its unbearable pain. And yet, it continued to cling to life.

"Fate..." It whispered mentally. "It's cruel and fierce, like the best of tigers. I was born a simple kitten, and after millennia, became a tiger."

Is a simple kitten able to become a tiger in this world? Hadjar hadn't expected that.

"But my dream was to become a human."

A scene appeared in Hadjar's thoughts —a small, richly dressed girl was caressing a kitten. Holding the animal in her arms, she danced among the painted walls and hundreds of different nobles on the amber floor.

Hadjar didn't recognize their clothes or the architecture of the hall. It wasn't the Kingdom of Lidus or the Empire of Darnassus. For the first time, Hadjar was seeing a new, distant country.

The kitten was happy. Its emotions overwhelmed Hadjar. But suddenly, the scene changed.

The girl hid her beloved friend in a deep vase. The kitten didn't see anything, but it smelled blood and heard screams. It got out after a long time had passed, but instead of the beautiful floor, it saw only rivers of blood, and instead of the people— only dismembered bodies.

And its mistress...

Hadjar had seen many terrible things in this life, but they didn't disturb his dreams. However, he had no doubt that the sight of what had happened to the kitten's mistress... Damn, it would surely haunt him for several years, in the most terrible of nightmares.

The tigress sighed. The horns growing from its shoulders and decorated with blue threads, cracked. The blue patterns on its golden fur faded. It wasn't red with black stripes. No, it was golden with wide, luminous blue stripes.

Hadjar was sucked into the whirlpool of its memories again.

The kitten was on the streets. Completely alone. It didn't know anything. It couldn't do anything. It was starving and freezing, but soon, the scene changed.

The now adult cat was hunting mice and even rats. It fought for food with dogs and other cats. Sometimes, it made its way into the Scholar's shop, where it managed to gnaw a hole in a small chest, tearing the skin on its muzzle and breaking its fangs.

From there, it took some bitter grass. It didn't know why. It just felt that it would become stronger. And it did.

The ordinary cat became a big cat. It no longer hunted rats. Deer were its prey. Then it began to fight other beasts. For food, territory, water, and power. Many centuries passed.

The cat became a tiger. A fierce, formidable, lonely predator. It lived in its cave by the stream and didn't want to see anyone. At night, it would think back on the times when the little girl had carried it in her arms. It had had a funny name—'Princess'. That was what the other two-legged creature had called her.

It lived without a purpose, just delaying the moment when it would be old and its attacks would no longer be dangerous or cause fear. The moment when, in a fight with another, younger and more ferocious beast, it would lose its life.

But then some humans came to its stream. At first, it had wanted to drive them away. Its sensitive ears were disturbed by the swimmers' laughter and splashing around.

But then it sniffed. It recognized the smell.

It tracked them.

They lived in a large stone cave. It had already seen such things on the 'pictures', as the little girl had called them. She had said they were 'castles.'

Now it had a goal. A purpose.

It kept getting more powerful. Decade after decade, century after century, until, at last, it razed this cave to the ground. For many long nights, it enjoyed the cries of the humans who had taken Princess away from it.

But then…

"I feel the same thirst in you, a man with the heart of the Lord of the Heavens," the voice in his head proclaimed, and Hadjar felt emptiness.

A pervasive, terrible emptiness. It sucked him out of the tigress' memories. He, like it, had once wanted to howl and beat his head against the walls of his cave. Because of that same empty feeling. Because he'd lost his purpose in life.

It had killed by avenging its beloved little girl and killing those two-legged. What did it have to live for, now? What would stave off the emptiness?

It stayed empty, until one spring, it felt a new life flare up inside its body. It cared for this life and the emptiness disappeared. A new goal had replaced it.

It didn't want this life to spend its years just like it had—in an eternal struggle to survive. It wanted this life to live calmly and quietly.

That's why the tigress hadn't allowed this life to come into the world. It hadn't wanted to give birth to a tiger. It had wanted to give life to a human. And to do that, the tigress had to become a human itself.

"I didn't manage it, two-legged. The Serpent was stronger than me."

The tigress raised its paw. Beneath it, curled up, a little white kitten slept. Compared to its mother, the kitten looked like a defenseless, miniature pearl. It could've fit on Hadjar's palm easily.

"Gods curse me," Nero breathed. "Is that a cub?"

"Swear to me, two-legged, that you'll make my daughter a human. Swear it, or I'll kill you on the spot and satisfy my thirst with your blood before I die."

The tigress snarled and thousands of birds soared into the sky, while the mountains began to tremble somewhere in the distance. Or so it seemed to Hadjar. However, there was no fear in his eyes. Just sheer willpower and determination.

"Sorry, Honorable Tiger, but you'll have to kill me. If I take your daughter with me, then thousands of fights and a road full of hardships will await her."

The beast fell silent. Suddenly, it got up, shaking. It was majestic and proud. The size of a two-story house. Its fangs were like swords, and its claws were like spears.

"You are as sly as a two-legged. You are as honest as a Lord of the Heavens. You are as weak as a newborn kitten. But…" Two sky blue eyes looked into eyes that were almost the same color. The only difference between them was in the shape of the pupils. "… Your will is strong and boundless, like the black sky that appears at night."

It gently pushed the kitten toward Hadjar.

"If you had made such an oath, I would've killed you on the spot. However, you aren't like the other two-legged. You are like my cub. Like my Princess."

Again, Hadjar saw the face of the little girl, dancing with the kitten in her arms.

"I'm leaving, a human who isn't a human. Take care of my daughter. Be with my daughter. I ask only this of you. Will you be with her?"

Ignoring Nero's attempts to lower him back to the ground, Hadjar rose. Compared to the tigress, he looked like a bug.

But the beast thought that he was a fierce and fearless bug, like the best of tigers…

"For as long as my heart beats within my chest!" Hadjar saluted the dying beast with the same respect he would've given a general standing in front of him.

"Then I'm leaving, human. Take the heart of my power—it'll help you to become stronger. Take my claws and fangs—you'll make a new, better stinger out of them. Take my skin—it's stronger than the iron that you're wearing. But please, leave your flame with me. I've shown you what it did to me. How it nearly took my soul."

Instead of answering, determination shone even more fiercely in Hadjar's eyes.

"I see that you can't part with it... May Heaven help those against whom you wield it. And may it save you when you are consumed by it. I'm leaving."

The beast looked at the sleeping cub for the last time and took its final breath. In this breath, Hadjar heard: "Her name is Azrea."

Hadjar knelt and pressed his head to the ground. Nero did the same.

Together, they honored the kitten who'd become a tiger.

It towered over them like a mountain. It was as proud and noble as ever. It met its death the same way it had lived its life.

"Well, you may be a psycho, but, damn, you're a very lucky one," Nero laughed hysterically.

However, like Hadjar, he wiped away a tear that was running down his cheek. Nero had also seen the scenes from the tigress' life.

Blinking away the uninvited tears, Hadjar picked up the white kitten. She was no bigger than his palm. Small, fluffy and warm.

"Azrea," the Prince said, and the kitten meowed, then yawned.

Chapter 48

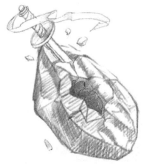

"Can you at least wait for me to take her cub away?" Hadjar asked, outraged when Nero began climbing the tigress, armed with a sword.

"But it asked you to take..." Nero looked around the gigantic carcass. "Its skin, core, and the other stuff."

"But not in front of Azrea!"

"You're behaving like a young mother!" Nero huffed while doing very dirty work. "Listen, she's sleeping. Put her away in your clothes and help me. Without your ghostly strikes, I won't be finished with this for at least for a month!"

"Look, we can't even scratch its skin."

"We couldn't normally," Nero cleaned the blood off his face. It wasn't his blood. "But before it died, it did something to its defenses. Now even my knife will cut through."

Hadjar sighed. He wasn't greedy, but he respected the creature's last wish. The creature who could've killed him easily. Besides, it had done it not for him, but for its cub.

Although, to be honest, Hadjar would be glad to have blades made from its claws and armor made from its skin. These things would be artifacts, very high-level ones at that. Heaven Soldiers would've probably torn out each other's throats to get even one such artifact.

"Just wait a bit."

"Don't take too long. I really need help!"

Hadjar wandered through the ravine until he came across the grass he had been looking for. It was normally an ordinary weed, but if a little energy was added to its juice, it would become a decent enough sleep medicine. Thieves usually drugged watchdogs with it.

He'd learned a lot while wandering the world with the circus.

Making sure that the kitten wouldn't be waking up for the next few hours, Hadjar put her against his bosom. She curled up tightly and Hadjar's chest immediately became warmer. Azrea was a good source of warmth...

"God forgive me," Hadjar sighed.

This work made him sick, deep in his heart.

Together, they managed to finish it by late in the evening. It wasn't easy to carve through the carcass of the creature at the Ancient Stage. While they worked, Nero explained to Hadjar that after the Alpha stage there was the King of Beasts stage. A beast at this stage was equal in strength to a Spirit Knight. But this wasn't the end or the pinnacle in beastly cultivation. After the King of Beasts stage came the Ancient Stage.

And an Ancient beast was equal to the Lord stage of humans. Nero said that he'd never believed in the existence of such creatures or Lord-level humans. He'd considered it an absurdity from children's tales and legends.

But the things he'd seen today had changed his view of the world significantly. Now Nero felt like a little frog which had considered it well to be the whole universe. Then, suddenly, it had been thrown into an open ocean and it realized how naive it had been before.

Traves had been much stronger than the tigress. At what stage had the dragon been, then? How far from Hadjar was the peak of the cultivation of martial arts?

By the time the shadows, playing with the moonlight, woke up within the forest, they had finally finished. Covered in blood, reeking to high heaven, they sat on the edge of the ravine and looked down. They watched as a flame flared up.

They weren't afraid of starting a forest fire—they had dug a trench around the ravine and cut off the nearby branches. But they'd decided to get rid of the tigress' remains in a fire, just in case.

Next to them, the tigress' fangs lay—the strongest, sharpest, and largest fangs either of them had ever seen. The twenty claws that were more akin to spears had been the hardest part of the work. Even touching them proved tricky. Despite their owner's death, the predatory aura was still around them. If an ordinary person had approached them, not a practitioner at the stage of the Bodily Rivers, they would've cut them down at a distance of ten steps.

Fortunately, Nero and Hadjar were at sufficiently high enough stages of cultivation to avoid dying so foolishly.

This made Hadjar suspect some things and even tempted him.

He had never scanned Nero. Previously, there had been no reason to do it, but after all the things his friend had done for him... It would've been too dishonorable, almost dastardly. And Hadjar wasn't a scoundrel. Especially with those who had done right by him.

His simple code of ethics was—pay back both the good and bad a hundredfold.

He couldn't permit himself to scan his friend. But, Gods, how great his suspicions were, and how great the temptation.

"Don't look at me like that! I won't marry you!"

"Who'd want you, a womanizer?" Hadjar laughed, trying to clear his hands of blood.

"Why are you staring at me, then?"

"Because I can't understand what stage you're on."

Nero looked at his comrade, then at the claws, and sighed. Only now he realized how stupid he had been.

"You know, I trust you, officer. But I'll warn you, I don't know how to be friends. I've never had any."

Suddenly, Nero spat on his palm and offered his hand to Hadjar.

"What are you doing?" The Prince asked. "Why would I need your saliva?"

"Where do you come from, Hadj? Is there really no such custom in your village?"

"The custom to spit on your hand? No, our people are clean. Or do you want to kiss me indirectly?"

Nero grimaced, "Even the mere thought of it might put me off from being in bed with someone for the next week. And you know that, to me, it's torture to spend even a single night without a woman."

"Well, wipe your hand then. I don't want to touch your saliva."

"Why do you keep misunderstanding me, Hadj?" Nero said in a frustrated, plaintive voice. "This is a custom here."

"Where?"

"All over Lidus! And in the Empire, I guess. In general, brotherhood is sealed with blood. And friendship is sealed with saliva. If your intentions are serious, of course."

"If your intentions are serious..." Hadjar repeated. "Are you sure you aren't proposing to me?"

"No, I'm not. And if you continue to play the fool, I'll hit you so hard that no one ever will."

Hadjar laughed. He spat on his own palm and they shook hands.

Nero had just become his first friend ever, even counting his past two lives. It was a damn good feeling.

"Formation," Nero said in a low voice as if he were afraid of being heard. "The Seed Stage."

"For fuck's sake... Have I been hitting you so hard in our fights that your brain's been scrambled or what?"

"No!" Nero lightly hit the ground with his fist. "This is really starting to annoy me. Come on, friend, have you always been this dense? What have you been eating? While you are 'One with the sword', I have twice the energy capacity you do!"

Hadjar looked at the moon that was rising into the sky. It was beautiful.

A white muzzle popped out from under his clothes and yawned.

Damn! The kitten needed to be fed something! What did a young tiger at the Ancient stage usually eat?

"My blood is not entirely human," Hadjar answered.

"Is it heritable?"

"What?"

"Bumpkin." Nero sighed. "In short, according to some legends—and I believe they're true after tonight—once upon a time, strong beasts would take on the appearances of people and walk among us. Well, of course, they'd spend their nights in people's beds, not alone. Then, people with 'not entirely human blood' would be born. The first of these people with the beasts' blood became legendary heroes of old. They had a lot of power and they jumped through the stages of cultivation like children going up the stairs."

Well, Hadjar didn't know what percentage of the dragon's blood was currently circulating through his veins.

"Then, of course," Nero continued. "The strength of that inheritance waned. After thousands of years, it came to naught. But sometimes, it awakens in their descendants. Like in you, for example. By the way, whose inheritance do you have?"

"Grandma said that it was a dragon's."

Nero slapped himself a couple of times and then cursed foully.

"I swear to you, Hadjar, that I'll never tell anyone about this," Nero said quite seriously. Lending severity to his words, he waved a knife over his palm and blood appeared, flashing with a golden glow. He'd made an oath on his very blood, and now, if he broke it, he would burn in the same flame. "But, demons and gods, never tell anyone else about this. Unless you want to become a heap of ingredients."

"Of course not! I'm not going to run around and shout about it in each square."

"That's good!"

They fell silent. The kitten meowed louder. Hadjar took a piece of dried meat out of his pocket.

"Kittens need..." Nero looked on incredulously as the kitten grabbed the meat and dived back into Hadjar's clothes. "...Milk..."

"Yeah," Hadjar said. "We must return to the camp. I have to catch up to you and be at the same stage by the end of tonight."

"And how are you going to accomplish this?"

"Well, we'll share the spoils. Take all the cores for yourself, but I'll get the tigress' one, please, forgive me. Not for personal use. Maybe Azrea will need it later. I'll buy it from you..."

"You don't even have enough money to buy beer with," Nero reminded him.

"Ok, I'll borrow the money, if I have to," Hadjar said. "One core of the Alpha. I'll give the army a claw from my share. That'll get me no less than fifty points. Then, with the help of the core, I'll break through to the Formation stage during the night."

Nero nodded his head, then slapped himself in the face and sighed heavily.

"I know a great Scholar in Spring Town. He treats people who have mental illnesses. I can tell you his address."

"What do you dislike about my plan?"

"To begin with, the whole plan," Nero inhaled slowly. "To begin with, you don't need to buy anything from me. We're friends! And you have to go with me to see some girls after the battle. I don't want my friend to be a virgin. It shames me as well as you!"

Hadjar grumbled but agreed.

"Now, on to the main point. Why would we show our spoils to the army? It'll be taken away! Even if they're not, where are we going to hide them? We're leaving tomorrow! How are you going to learn the meditation scroll in an hour?!"

Now it was Hadjar's turn to inhale slowly.

"We aren't going to show our spoils. Only two of the claws. You'll bring one, I'll bring the other. Let's say that we found them in the forest during the hunt. The rest of the spoils we'll keep at Dogar's."

"Do you trust him?"

"Absolutely," Hadjar nodded. During his life as a freak, he'd developed a good sense for discerning people's nature. It had never failed him. "Bear is our best bet. Of course, we'll have to give him a share, but he won't take too much or betray us."

It was evident that Nero didn't really agree, but he also didn't argue with Hadjar. He didn't know the giant, as well as his new friend, did.

"As for the scroll... I've got a good memory."

Nero swore again.

"I don't understand if you're the unluckiest person I've ever met or the luckiest."

Hadjar shrugged.

"Okay," Nero sighed and rose to his feet. "And now for the most important question—how are we going to carry it all back?"

"That, my friend, is the right question."

And both of them started huffing and rubbing their chins, trying to think of a way to carry it all to the camp. Finally, Nero had an idea. From then on, Hadjar would be wary of any of his friend's ideas and suggestions.

Nevertheless, they managed to lug their trophies back. Then Hadjar went to get the most important thing—the meditation scrolls that would ensure his breakthrough to the next stage.

Chapter 49

"The Transformation Stage... Tell me everything again, and this time in more detail," Dogar asked.

They were sitting in the senior officer's tent. Dogar didn't look very happy. He kept adjusting the animal skins that served as his blankets. They slipped off all the time. With them, he'd covered the part of his body that neither Nero nor Hadjar wanted to 'admire'. Judging by the commander's overall size, they might end up traumatized and with an inferiority complex.

Autumn was coming and the nights were getting colder. Perhaps that's why Dogar had been so angry that he'd had to drive a pretty, slim lady out of his tent. She'd left, taking her money.

"We found a battlefield in the forest," Nero repeated once more. "A tiger was in a deep ravine. The size of...like that" he demonstrated with his hands the beast's size. "Well, we managed to carve it up. We've taken everything—the claws, fangs, even the pelt. But we didn't find the core of its power. Apparently, someone else had already managed to take it."

"And then?"

"Then we burnt everything to the abyss," Hadjar finished.

Dogar sighed and rubbed his nose. He wasn't wearing anything except for the animal skins. Anyone could see his black tattoos, bronze skin, and long, pink scars. There were far more scars than tattoos.

"Why, for demons and gods, did you burn it?"

"Commander, what else were we supposed to do?" Hadjar spread his hands. "We were in the forest, in a ravine forgotten by the gods. There was a beast at an unknown power level there. We'd carved it up, left only the skeleton and the meat behind. What if someone had found us? If the beast which had killed the tiger had appeared? So, we set it on fire."

"You set it on fire... What if a forest fire erupts tonight?"

"We dug up a trench," Nero said immediately. "And chopped off all the nearby branches. Even if a strong wind comes in, it'll rain soon."

Dogar sighed.

"And what is this?" He shouted so loudly that the tent almost flew off into the sky.

Because of this cry, Azrea, who had been chewing on the senior officer's stocks peacefully, jumped up and meowed menacingly. She showed the giant her sharp fangs and claws.

"Is this ball of fur eating my meat and hissing at me?"

"She has a difficult temper," Hadjar nodded.

"Why do you need her, Hadjar? Do you think there will be no food on the march and you've prepared some supplies?"

"You're so mean, senior officer," Nero said. Hadjar didn't even get a chance to answer. "Don't you know about Hadjar's problem?"

"What problem?" Dogar was surprised.

Realizing what his friend was talking about, the Prince picked up the kitten and put it back under his clothes. Azrea yawned immediately and fell asleep again. Maybe she was still affected by sleep medicine, but, most likely, she just loved taking naps.

Hadjar was happy she did. He didn't want to think about what would happen when the kitten realized that her mother was gone. He only hoped that Azrea didn't remember the tigress at all... It would be easier that way.

"His bed has never been warmed by a woman."

Dogar glanced at Hadjar.

"I understand... That's why you're a little strange, assistant. So... nervous."

"I agree completely, Senior Officer Dogar," Nero nodded.

Hadjar pretended to hear nothing and continued to sharpen his sword menacingly.

"Okay, damn it," the commander sighed. "What do you want from me?"

"We want you to help us with the items we've collected," Hadjar said quietly.

"How, officer?"

"Well," Hadjar raised his head and looked into Dogar's eyes. "If we were to carry all of this to the General right now, we'd get several points..."

"A thousand points," Dogar corrected. "Maybe even ten thousand. Maybe, for such a treasure, you'll be granted medals. Maybe even higher rank."

"But we'll get neither the claws nor the skin."

Dogar sighed again.

"So, you are talking about doing that, Hadjar..."

"We'll share with the army. Two claws will be enough for them."

The giant adjusted his blankets again. He was thinking, and as he did so, he assumed the position of Rodin's 'The Thinker'. He looked quite stern and menacing. Nero and Hadjar had to wait for his decision.

"The General doesn't deserve to be deceived in such a way," Dogar said finally. "We'll give her the pelt and fifteen of the claws. Leave the rest for yourselves. I'll take only one claw, no more."

"But, Senior Officer Dog-"

"Shut up, soldier," Dogar interrupted calmly, but Nero bowed his head immediately. "We're going to war. Not chasing skirts in the city, Nero. And not participating in a village brawl, Hadjar. Hundreds of thousands of lives are at stake and, instead of thinking about yourselves, you'd better start thinking about the families of those who won't return. About their mothers, sons, wives."

Hadjar looked down in shame. The wealth had clouded his mind completely. He could see the bigger picture now. If they found the right use for them, these claws and the skin could save the lives of many soldiers. The soldiers of his kingdom. Lidus, the kingdom his father had been prepared to die for.

"I beg your pardon, Senior Officer!" Hadjar lowered his forehead to the ground.

Nero followed his example.

"Stand up," Dogar waved his hand. "I understand you—such a fortune would make anyone greedy. But, nevertheless, you risked a great deal to get these trophies, so you deserve a part of the spoils, not just Honor points."

Nero and Hadjar looked at each other again. They looked at the items. Dogar had set aside a portion that would've normally cost as much as a noble rank, or a castle with its surrounding lands, or hundreds of servants. But... they would not be able to sleep easily if they took it.

They could sleep on a water mattress, but not on a mattress filled with the blood of those who would be standing shoulder to shoulder with them. Who wouldn't flinch and would fight the enemy without sparing themselves.

"We'll take two fangs," Nero said. "Hadjar and I only need two for swords."

"And as for money..." Hadjar said. "Money will come in time."

"Good," Dogar nodded. "And now..."

The senior officer began to rise, dropping the blankets to the ground. Fortunately, Nero and Hadjar had managed to leave the tent before their male confidence was inflicted with a strong blow to its very core.

Soon, after hiding their share in the senior officer's chests, they wrapped most of the booty in the skins and took it to the General. She wasn't sleeping and, unlike most of the soldiers and officers, was completely alone. She was sitting at the table, observing the map and moving the figures around, coming up with alternate plans and strategies.

When Dogar, his adjutant, and the soldier came in with their 'gifts', she didn't believe her eyes at first. Then, after listening to their story several times, she sent for the chief engineer.

He was overjoyed. He said that using this treasure, he could reduce the number of nomads dramatically and would surely find a use for the huge pelt as well.

After him, the main blacksmith ran in, as the tiger's claws weren't made of bones, but from an unknown metal.

The blacksmith was delighted too but didn't touch the materials. He said that they needed an artifactor, because he, an ordinary craftsman, would only ruin everything.

As a result, the General asked the librarian to come in as well. He appeared almost instantly, and Hadjar noticed a greedy gleam in his eyes.

"I'll send a message to the Palace immediately," the librarian said with a slight bow. "Perhaps they'll manage to send an artifactor to the fort."

"I would be very grateful to you, Honorable Adept," the General also bowed slightly.

Hadjar couldn't understand how the old man could 'send a message to the Palace'. The capital was very far away, as far as London is from Beijing. The Internet or even the phone hadn't yet been invented here.

He probably meant to do it with some mystical spells.

"General Leen," the librarian said, "to give the artifactor an idea of what he will be working with, I need... three claws..."

Three claws out of twelve... He was an old, cunning, greedy fox!

Despite having come to the same conclusion as Hadjar, the General still replied courteously. "Of course. Thank you for your help."

The dried up, old man carried the claws on his shoulder easily. They didn't leave a cut on his skin and couldn't even rip his clothes. Damn adepts...

Finally, when everyone left, the General turned to the hunters.

"I'll gather the War Council in the morning and it'll approve your reward. Now, go to the librarian and tell him that you'll surely be given a thousand Honor Points."

Nero and Hadjar pressed their fists to their chests and bowed. "You can go. And you, Senior Officer Dogar, I ask that you stay behind."

Dogar nodded.

As Nero and Hadjar were leaving the tent, Nero suggested they stay behind and eavesdrop. He was sure that General Leen had asked their commander to remain in her tent due to 'a very important reason'—to take the edge off. If he made a hole in the tent, he could see the General naked...

Hadjar warned his friend that if the General found out, she would put his head on a spear. Besides, Hadjar had something more important to do. And he wasn't a pervert.

So, they parted. Nero stayed to risk his life, and Hadjar went... to do the same. Which of them would prove to be the better 'psychic' was the question.

Ten minutes later, Hadjar was already at the 'doorstep' of the library. As always, it was being guarded by two soldiers in green armor.

"Officer Hadjar," they suddenly greeted him.

"Legionnaires," Hadjar nodded and went inside.

As always, several soldiers were sitting inside and studying the scrolls. After all, Hadjar wasn't the only one who wanted to become stronger—there were tens of thousands of soldiers and officers who desired that exact same thing as well.

"I'd figured you would be coming by, Hadjar," the librarian smiled, having already hidden the claws somewhere.

"Good evening, Honorable Adept," the Prince bowed. The presence of the old man annoyed him, but Hadjar could do nothing about it. "I'd like to rent the scroll with the Meditation Technique. The Honor points on my medallion are not enough, but the General asked me to tell you that my award will be approved in the morning."

"Well, then you should come back in the morning. You'll have enough time before the march begins."

"I beg your pardon, Honorable Adept, but I need the scroll right now."

The old man, dressed in amber robes, leaned on the edge of the table.

"Do you think this will help you in your fight against the adjutant?"

Hadjar just nodded.

"Youth," the old man sighed, and, with a wave of his hand, the necessary scroll levitated onto the table. "Hot blood, sharper blades. You know, sometimes I miss the old days, back when I was the same."

He put the hourglass next to the scroll and turned it over.

"You have an hour." With these words, the librarian went back to the shelves.

After some time, Hadjar left the tent. A detailed copy of the scroll was now stored in his neural network, and all he had to do was wish for it to appear before his eyes and it would immediately do so.

Its contents... They've really opened up new horizons for me. Who would have thought that energy could be absorbed in more ways than just sucking it in like a cocktail through a straw? It can be absorbed in various ways, circulated at different rates, concentrated at different speeds...

All of this had been described in the scroll in great detail, accompanied by diagrams and drawings.

If he'd had such knowledge before, he could've been at the early stages of the Transformation level by now!

But, alas, history wasn't compatible with the subjunctive mood, so he had to work with what he had.

When Hadjar returned to his tent, Nero was waiting for him at the entrance. He was sitting on a bench, holding his two-handed sword in his lap.

"What are you doing here?" Hadjar asked.

"Saving your life," Nero answered seriously. "I'm sure the adjutant will send someone after you tonight. While you are busy with your cultivation, you'll hardly be able to ensure that someone won't pull your tongue out of your throat."

Hadjar froze in place. He didn't know what to say, therefore, he just quietly said, "Thanks."

"You're welcome," Nero nodded. "But... are you sure you want to form your Heart of Power with the help of the animal's? The pain will be awful."

Hadjar just smiled at that.

"That's one thing I'm definitely not afraid of. Pain," he said, and entered the tent.

Assuming the lotus position, he placed the core, or as it was also called, the Heart of Power, of the Emerald Wolf in front of him.

Closing his eyes, Hadjar began to circulate the energy as it had been described in the scroll. With every breath, he plunged deeper and deeper inside the essence of his being, his mind, and soul.

It was dark in there. Warm, but dark. The endless darkness would only occasionally be disturbed by eleven blue lines. They flowed through this bottomless darkness like the streams in the valley where Hadjar had relearned how to walk.

Like thin, almost wispy, but still swift and mighty streams.

Hadjar reached for them.

At first, they slipped out from under his finger, but then they succumbed.

According to the scroll, in order to advance to the next stage, Hadjar had to catch them all. After catching them, he had to 'decant' the energy from them, which would give him the ability to form the 'Seed' of his future Heart of Power.

As soon as he touched the first stream, he had to 'close his eyes' because of the bright, white light.

When Hadjar could 'open' his eyes again, he was in a beautiful Palace instead of the previous emptiness. Minstrels could've sung songs and bards could've made up stories about such a Palace for a thousand years.

There was a man standing in the center of the Palace. He was as proud and majestic as the sky in the afternoon.

Golden hair fell past his shoulders, over black silk robes adorned with gold patterns. The presence of the horns on his head and the spirals in his pupils indicated that he wasn't a human.

"Hello, Prince Hadjar Duran," a familiar voice said.

"Greetings, Lord of the Heavens Traves," Hadjar bowed.

It was the dragon.

Chapter 50

"Is this a dream?" Hadjar asked, looking around.

The ceiling of the Palace was so far away that it looked more like the sky. All the walls and pillars had been carved and decorated with amazing craftsmanship. The scenes captured on them seemed to come to life easily and the great warriors and battles depicted almost flooded the hall. The marble floor was covered with patterns of unprecedented beauty.

Such a Palace couldn't have been built by ordinary masters.

Hadjar noticed... mysteries in every stone, every pattern, and carving. Mysteries that were unattainable to him, with his limited knowledge of the world.

Hadjar didn't know it, but even the librarian couldn't have comprehended the secrets and knowledge hidden in the Palace. They were beyond the understanding of an ordinary Heaven Soldier.

Let alone the Prince, who was still looking for the true path of cultivation.

"Yes and no," Traves answered evasively.

In the guise of a human, he looked like a young man of about twenty-seven. Without the horns, he would have looked like one of those handsome men whom young ladies dream of.

"Then why and, most importantly, how are you here, talking to me?"

Traves was standing in the center of the hall. His long sleeves were almost dragging across the floor. A wide belt with the emblem of a dragon on the buckle cinched his robes.

"I put my heart in you, Hadjar," Traves' voice was thick, entrancing, like the sound of the wind blowing through the treetops. "Not the whole heart, of course, only a tiny fraction of my blood, from which I created a small heart."

Hadjar 'touched' his chest involuntarily and started. He was in a world of illusions, but it had felt just like a real heart. Hadjar had felt his own touch.

He squatted down and touched the floor.

It was cold.

It was stone.

"How is this... pos... sible...?" Hadjar said, stumbling over the words.

"Even if I tried to explain it to you, you wouldn't understand. Simply put..." Traves came closer. His every step was immensely powerful like a mountain was approaching. "You received a fraction... a billionth of my power, Hadjar. And with it, you also got a bit of my mind."

Hadjar rose and looked at the creature that had given him a new life.

"So, you are actually dead?"

"I am," the dragon nodded. "What you see is just my shadow. My last bit of will, left behind to help you find your justice and my revenge."

"Why have you come now?"

"So, you want to know about the 'why'..." Traves looked around. He looked at the Palace with a touch of sadness and inexhaustible pride. "You don't even realize what's in front of you and where you're standing."

"I think I'm in a Palace. A very strange Palace."

"A Palace," Traves repeated. "You could call it that, I suppose. We have little time, so I'll speak plainly—I shouldn't have appeared to you."

Hadjar looked into the dragon's eyes. The same amber colored and bright eyes that he'd had during their last meeting.

"Then why did you?"

"To stop you from making a stupid mistake, Hadjar. The scroll you're about to use is a trap."

"I don't understand..."

"If you advance to the Formation stage using the methods described here, then your best will always be the initial stage of the Heaven Soldier. You'll never be able to go above that, no matter the circumstances. This kind of Technique is called a 'slave' Technique, and they were created specifically to make a lot of slave adepts. They live longer than ordinary ones. Are stronger than ordinary ones. And they can be used for many different purposes."

Hadjar flinched.

Everything made sense now. Why should the Empire create strong kingdoms around itself? Why would it need extra organizations, ones that could have cultivators at the Heaven Soldier level, or even higher than that? It's constantly rocked by internal conflicts. Sects fighting against sects. Clan intrigues aimed at ruining other clans. Kingdoms trying to steal land from their neighbors...

And this library... is just a front. On the one hand, the opportunity to become stronger lends credibility to Primus, as well as the Governor, who represents the Empire in Lidus.

On the other hand, even if there are geniuses capable of getting enough Honor Points to acquire a Meditation scroll, these geniuses... They'll never become a threat to the Empire. It'll stop them and weaken them while they are in their most vulnerable phase.

"Damn, that's clever," Hadjar cursed, acknowledging the imperial officials' cunning scheme.

They would kill not just two birds with one stone, but entire generations.

"I've already begun forming my Heart of Power with the help of this accursed scroll!"

"But you haven't finished yet," Traves reminded him. "You have the whole night ahead of you to correct your mistake."

"One night," Hadjar said. "And tomorrow morning, I'll have to fight."

"Is your enemy strong?"

"He's probably at the Awakening of the Soul stage, at least."

The 'Transformation' level, which came after the 'Formation' one, was divided into three stages: The 'Mortal form'—the stage where a practitioner cleansed their body. They would get rid of all filth, diseases, and other dead weight acquired during their life.

'Awakening of the Soul'—the stage where the energy in the body changed its quality. It became denser, stronger, and visible.

And the 'New Soul', which was the most mystical of the stages. Few people understood its essence, but they said that, at this stage, the practitioner's soul would be strengthened. Whatever that meant...

Because of these three stages, it was believed that the 'Transformation' level was the transitional period between being a simple practitioner and a true cultivator, a Heaven Soldier.

However, stepping over the threshold that separated the 'Transformation' from the 'Heaven Soldier'... Well, only one out of ten thousand people were capable of it.

"So, he is much stronger than you... Well, that's good. It's only in the face of a deadly threat when you need to do the impossible, that you can really progress down the path of cultivation. This is the only way to reach the top, to gain power over your destiny, and then true freedom."

"That's great and your speech is really inspiring, but..." Hadjar shook his head. "I don't have another scroll."

"Are you giving up?" Traves asked.

In response to his question, Hadjar's eyes filled with that same indomitable will that had once impressed him so much. The will that would one day be able to break the heavens themselves.

"I thought as much," Traves turned to one of the columns.

A horde of all kinds of monsters, numbering in the thousands, were depicted on it, and all of them, hungry for blood, were descending on one figure. And this figure, standing proudly and bravely in the middle of a sea of enemies, was crushing them one by one.

"I shouldn't have appeared before you reached the stage of the 'Heaven Soldier'. My knowledge, the legacy which I bequeathed to you... only a true cultivator could begin to comprehend it."

"I'm sorry I inconvenienced you."

"This isn't your fault." Apparently, the shadow of Traves' consciousness didn't really understand the concept of sarcasm. "I'm only going to teach you the Techniques I personally created. I can't give you the ones that were taught to me by great masters, even after my death. Not because I don't want to, but because I am bound by oaths."

Great masters! Traves had actually referred to them as great masters? Damn it! A thousand times damn it! Even now, Hadjar didn't feel like he had made even the first step along the long road of cultivation.

"Nevertheless, I can give you one Technique right now. A Technique that is used by dragons, for our meditation."

"Sorry, but I do seem to be a human, don't I?"

"Precisely. 'Seem' is a strong and meaningful word, Hadjar. Haven't you noticed the various transformations brought on by my heart?"

It was true. In the last few months, he had been plagued by one simple question—why were the indicators shown by the neuronet so different from reality?

"Are you turning me into a dragon?"

Traves smiled for the first time.

"No, you won't become a Lord of the Heavens, but later, maybe in a hundred thousand years, or even a million years later, if you survive, you'll cease to be a human. But you won't turn into a dragon. My heart is changing your blood slowly, drop by drop, and no one knows what will come of it. It's unprecedented. Your very heart and soul have been interwoven with my hearts' blood."

Suddenly, Hadjar understood.

"Neuronet, show me the measurement system!"

[Measurement System: Unknown.]

"And now show me the scanning system."

[Scanning system: Human]

Hadjar read the messages again and swore.

"Perfect. When it scans people, everything works fine. When it scans its host… it's like I'm asking it to 'calculate something' in a totally unknown system."

That's why the data was so wildly inaccurate. The heart had transformed him, and the neural network didn't understand how, why, and what data to operate on now. And it had gone crazy as a result.

Apparently, in order to provide the database with all the necessary information, Hadjar would have to dissect a dragon. Yeah… dissect. A dragon.

Totally possible.

"Damn it," Hadjar growled, angered by yet another failure.

"The Technique which I'll give you will allow you to advance your cultivation up to the level of a Spirit Knight."

"And then?"

"Then? Then you'll have to look for a stronger meditation Technique. The one I used is sealed because of my oaths and I can't share it with you."

It had been foolish of Hadjar to think that, at least once in his life, he would get something 'for free'. Even the heart had been granted to him under the condition that he fulfill the dragon's last wish. Which he, admittedly, had yet to learn.

"But, of course, you won't just give it to me, will you?"

"Anything that isn't won through a struggle, earned with blood and sweat, is the same as a fine summer's day. Easy come easy go. Only the things you acquire through your own effort are important in this world. This is a true cultivators' way."

Traves put his hand on one of the columns and everything was suddenly bathed in white light.

When Hadjar opened his eyes, he found himself standing in the middle of an endless body of water.

He looked up and saw that the sky was full of thick, dark clouds. The sun's rays penetrated them, creating the illusion of golden pillars that were holding up the firmament which had been placed on the water.

"I warn you, Hadjar Duran!" The dragon's voice thundered. "This world isn't the fruit of any delusions on your part, it's real. If you die here, your body will die in the world outside, as well."

The distant horizon, which seemed like it was merging with the water, suddenly became a clearly visible black stripe.

"Win the right to be my disciple, Prince. Or die! A weakling won't be able to get justice for himself, nor revenge for me!"

Accompanied by loud cries, the cracking of various weapons and rattling of armor, monsters rushed at him. They had huge fangs, were covered with fur… In a word, nightmarish.

Hadjar assumed a fighting stance.

"Scorched Falcon!" He shouted, and the sword in his hands flared with light.

He'd practiced the Fire Techniques poorly. Every time he'd trained and used it in secret, he'd heard an offended howl coming from the wind.

It had called to him, promising to give him more power than the fire ever could.

Alas, Hadjar didn't know any Technique for the sword that harnessed the wind. He didn't know anything except for the 'Fired Sparrow'.

The enemy horde was approaching. There were so many of them that they had completely surrounded him, taking up all the available space. They were all a different height, had different physiques, wielding different weapons, but they were similar in one respect. Each of them was at the third stage of the 'Bodily Rivers'.

"I'd love to have some music right about now," Hadjar sighed, adjusting the strap that kept his long, black hair tidy and out of the way.

The unstoppable avalanche of monsters seemed to fill the world as far as the eye could see. The sky was no longer reflected in the water, it wasn't even visible because of the thousands of bloodthirsty foes.

[Does the host require a soundtrack?]

Damn, of course! If the neural network could reproduce text-based information from the database, then why not information based on sound, as well?

"How many tracks do you have in your memory?"

[Number of audio files: 17200]

It was so simple... In fact, a person would never forget anything either, they just couldn't use the stored information immediately.

The neuronet didn't actually have a 'database', only access to Hadjar's memory.

The monsters approached.

Hadjar could hear the slaps of their legs repeatedly hitting the water and the clanging of their armor.

A list of different songs from many time periods and peoples popped up before his eyes.

An involuntary smile appeared on his face.

Well, it'd be rather ironic.

He chose the song 'Fortunate Son' by 'Creedence Clearwater Revival'.

Hadjar heard this once foreign language in his head. Gods, he wasn't aware that he'd missed it so much.

He swung his blazing blade and met the incoming swarm of enemies with a roar that shook the sky.

Chapter 51

"Are you sure you used the potion correctly?" A quiet voice coming from the foliage said.

"Yes, I'm sure!" A second voice answered.

"Then why is this... 'Knocked out guy' still awake?"

The man pointed at Nero, who was still sitting near Hadjar's tent with his sword in his lap. He kept staring straight ahead, sometimes changing his posture and stretching his arms to stay awake.

"I have no idea," the second voice snapped in response. "Could Colin have given us the wrong potion?"

"But everyone else has fallen asleep," the first voice pointed out.

"What are we going to do?"

Silence. Apparently, the man who'd spoken first was thinking hard. On the one hand, the tent he needed to get into was being guarded by someone, on the other... The adjutant had promised to pay them a huge sum. The gods would've been angry at him and taken his good luck away forever if he'd refused such a chance.

They would be paid a dozen gold coins for the life of an officer who was only at the level of the 'Bodily Rivers'.

For a practitioner at their level, it wasn't that easy of a task, but still doable. Especially if they worked in pairs.

"He's just a soldier," the first one said finally. "We'll kill him and ask Colin to pay us more."

Silence again. They were probably nodding at each other in agreement.

Nero had suspected something was wrong from the very moment the moans around him had subsided. It would've been normal for the carnal pleasures to come to an end in a couple of the tents at the same time. But in a hundred... There was clearly something wrong here.

His suspicions were confirmed when two men came out of the darkness. Wrapped up in black cloth, they kind of looked like mummies. The visitors were silent, almost invisible. Nero saw only the white squirrels which were reflecting the torchlight.

Soon, the torches went out as well.

As if a strong wind had come through and extinguished the flames immediately.

Night fell onto the clearing, but before that happened, Nero had managed to see an emblem on the cloth of the two people. Crossed axes. This meant that the members of the Ax Clan had infiltrated Dogar's camp. Assassins. It had probably worked in their favor that this particular camp was so far away from the others.

"You should think three times before taking the next step," Nero said calmly, not even getting up from his chair.

"Get out of here, soldier," a voice hissed in the darkness. "Or we'll take your life."

The clan members weren't idiots. Nobody had promised that the slippery adjutant would pay for this soldier's life as well. And the Axes never killed for free. They took only those lives which they'd been paid to take. But in this case, they would make an exception.

There was an obstacle on the path to their goal. The obstacle was stupid enough not to heed their sound advice.

"The only ones who will lose their lives here are those who dare to touch this tent," Nero set his aura free. The two Axes were struck by the power of a practitioner at the 'Formation' level.

Nero had never had friends... All his life, he had watched others laugh, play, go everywhere together, get into trouble, get out of it, freak out, and then discuss their adventures afterward.

He had always been alone.

When he grew up, he was able to brighten up the crushing emptiness of his everyday life with the help of women. He loved women. He loved their bodies, their souls. He loved them deeply and with true warmth. But he didn't have anyone to discuss his triumphs with or even just joke around with.

He had no one he could rely on in case of trouble. There was no stalwart person in his life. Someone he could trust the same as he would himself.

He got used to it.

He convinced himself...

That women were all he needed to give his life meaning.

But now he had a friend. He was as reliable as a rock. Nero had probably looked for a friend all his life, but he could never have imagined that he would find one in the army.

That's why, even if the whole of the Ax clan came, or even one of the gods personally came down from Heaven, they would all still have to fight Nero.

Because Nero didn't doubt that Hadjar would have done the same for him. That if Nero had been in trouble, Hadjar would've fought against the whole world.

"Go away or I'll send you to your ancestors."

The Axes simply unsheathed their narrow, long blades in response...

Nero rose and gripped the handle of his sword with both hands. A bloodthirsty grin appeared on his face. He'd been waiting for a fight for a long time.

***

All of Hadjar's attacks made a tongue of flame shoot out of his blade. He stood on a hill of bloody, dismembered corpses. Hundreds of butchered monsters lay under his feet. Thousands more were still climbing up to try and end his life.

Their black blood had long since defiled the clear water. The phantom world gradually plunged into darkness. The small sparks of light that sometimes happened as his blade struck against armor or other weapons seemed as bright as the stars.

Another enemy got close. Hadjar still didn't use the Technique. He didn't send out the 'Fired Sparrow'. He used only the flame itself and the fact that he was 'One with the Sword'. He chopped, sliced, slashed and stabbed...

His blade struck true, adding a new body to the growing mound of corpses, even as he broke the enemy's sickles, spears, swords, and other weapons as they attacked him.

Hadjar dodged the inept spear thrust of a pig-like demon easily. With a single swing of his blade, he cut off its head and turned around, breaking three more enemy blades with a follow-up slash.

He spun tirelessly, moving smoothly and quickly. His sword multiplied, creating illusions. Hadjar seemed like he wasn't using just one fire blade, but several of them at once.

The monsters didn't stop their assault. Many of them died, but the rest continued to climb up over the bodies of their brethren.

Hadjar didn't know how long he could hold out. But he knew that he would die standing on a mountain made up of thousands of his enemies' dead bodies.

A bloodthirsty grin was on his face, reflecting the fiery flashes of light.

***

A faint shadow flashed through the darkness. Nero casually swung his blade, which seemed to ignite some sparks. The dagger he'd blocked fell to the grass and the sparks ignited the nearest torch.

The two assassins were circling Nero like hungry dogs. But he didn't take even a step away from the tent. He clutched his sword tightly, confronting his opponents fearlessly.

They struck simultaneously. They were experienced killers,

accustomed to working in pairs.

One of them aimed for Nero's femoral artery with his dagger, and the second one—for his central vertebra.

Nero was ready.

With surprising ease, considering his build and weapon, he... soared into the air. It was almost like what Hadjar had done during the battle with the Emerald Wolf.

While in the air, he swung his blade overhead. A blue glow appeared around it. Then Nero cried out: "The Giant's Hand!" The sword descended sharply and a ghostly, giant hand came out of its blade. Instead of fingers, it had five sharp blades.

It nailed one of the attackers to the ground, plunging him to the bottom of a pit that was at least a yard deep.

Nero landed on his feet easily, then turned to break the enemy's dagger that had been aimed at his belly, but...

He heard only gurgling and wheezing. Looking around, he saw the second killer's body. He was twitching, having terrible convulsions, and clutching at something around his neck.

The white kitten jumped off the dead body silently. But now she was white and scarlet.

Azrea's paws and mouth were stained with blood.

She hissed in the direction of the enemy she'd defeated and sat down next to Nero. She looked at him, meowed, and extended her paw.

"Oh, no," Nero grunted, dropping back into his chair. "I'm not Hadjar, and I won't coddle you. You stained your paws, so you'll wash them yourself."

Azrea mewled indignantly and began to rub her paws on the grass.

Nero sighed wearily. He hoped that there would be no more killers coming for Hadjar tonight. However, these assassins hadn't been a real threat, only being at the third stage of the 'Rivers'. Apparently, Colin hadn't sent them to kill Hadjar. He'd just wanted to make his enemy a nervous wreck before the fight.

Nero had spent a quarter of his power to execute his Technique.

"Hurry up, my friend," he said, seemingly addressing the tent, and began to clean and sharpen his sword.

***

The mound of bodies had doubled in size by now, but the enemies kept coming. Hadjar was bruised from head to toe. He was breathing heavily and could barely see anything. His vision was covered with a purple shroud and his legs kept slipping on his own and the monster's blood.

He lowered the flaming sword. He didn't know how much longer he could hold out. How many swings could he manage? Five? Six? Obviously no more than ten.

But there were still lots of monsters left, far more than he could handle.

It had been foolish to think that he could complete the Heaven Soldier's test while still being a practitioner at the 'Bodily Rivers' level.

Another pig-demon climbed the mountain. Hadjar could barely muster the energy to swing his blade and cut off the monster's head. When it came off, Hadjar snarled in pain and anger.

His back felt like it had been burned with a branding iron.

He could only turn around to see a giggling pig shoving a spear into his side.

With an animal roar, Hadjar grabbed the spear, and at the same time, felt more burning pain. Another monster had landed a hit with its spear. Then another one, followed by one more spear, then a second one...

Hadjar stood there, with five spears sticking out of him, and dozens of demons already climbing up the hill manically, thirsting for his blood.

"I'm not going out alone!" Hadjar growled.

There wasn't even a shadow of doubt or fear in his gaze. Only inflexible determination and will.

"The Scorched Falcon!" He shouted.

With a loud 'Hah' a bird the size of a sparrow shot out of his blade. But it was bright and hot enough to scorch the battlefield. It devastated a whole section of the sea of demons. But it was only a small part, which was immediately filled in by the oncoming horde.

Hadjar stood ramrod straight, clutching his sword.

As the enemy blades struck him, he was no longer breathing.

He died on his feet.

***

"Frankly, I'm surprised."

Hadjar opened his eyes and sat down abruptly. He didn't feel any pain. He wasn't dead.

He was still in the center of the magnificent Palace. Traves was standing in front of him.

"Have I failed?"

"Why would you think that?" Traves looked at him differently now. With respect. "That test wasn't meant to check your strength. The demons would have never stopped. It's just like fighting against a waterfall—you can't beat it. Only overpower it for a moment, but no more."

"Then what was the point? You said I would die if I lost."

"And you haven't lost," the dragon shrugged exactly as a human would. "Do you know what the most important thing for a cultivator is?"

He pointed at his heart. "This."

Then he raised his hand, pointing at his head.

"And this." He turned to the column that had the image of the horde of monsters on it. Hadjar could now discern that the figure depicted on it was actually him. He was the one standing on the hill of bodies. "If you had retreated, begged for mercy, tried to escape… I would have known that your spirit is weak. That you aren't worthy of my heart. Then I would have let you die. But you didn't give up. Didn't retreat. Even when you died, you did it on your feet, without releasing your sword. Your heart is strong, and that is the most important thing. Everything else—your body, Techniques, knowledge—can be learned and refined. But the heart... The heart is almost impossible to strengthen. Either a person has it, or they don't."

Traves waved his hand and dozens of shelves, each holding a variety of scrolls, appeared in the hall.

"These are all my Techniques. There are exactly 600 of them here."

"And..." Hadjar prompted him.

"You passed the test, so I'll let you choose any two scrolls you want to use. Considering that you have to take the scroll for 'The Path among Clouds' meditation Technique, you can only have one more."

"I feel like this is a trap."

Hadjar rose to his feet and shook himself off, even though he looked very fresh and unharmed.

"You'll see me three more times. If you pass the test each time, I'll give you three more of my Techniques."

"Only five? Out of six hundred! How should I choose? I'll need to spend at least a week reading the descriptions. And a week more choosing…"

"The knowledge of what is in here will be with you at all times," the dragon answered, turning away from Hadjar. He went to the shelves and took out one scroll. "Today you can pick up 'The Path among Clouds' and, to help you with your choice, I'll give you what I think will best suit you. This isn't my best Technique. I have never been strong with a sword, but a true cultivator should know a little about everything. And so, while meditating over the path of the sword in the Mountains of Eternal Wind, I got this."

He held out a scroll titled 'The Sword of the Light Breeze'.

"It's too pathetic," Hadjar muttered, but still took the scroll with a low bow.

Despite his grumbling, he was happy. After passing the dragon's test, he was now one step closer to his goal. He'd get the chance to become a little stronger.

"The Sky Level!" Hadjar cried out in astonishment.

"Yeah. The Techniques at the Sky level will be useful to you until you become a Spirit Knight."

"Thanks," Hadjar bowed even lower.

The Palace began to flicker and disappear slowly.

Hadjar was waking up. But before awakening, he heard a distant voice.

"I fell for the trap you found me in because all my life I'd relied on someone else's power, Prince. Think about that."

The voice disappeared. Hadjar opened his eyes.

It was still nighttime, which meant he had enough time to learn the Techniques he'd obtained.

Hadjar assumed the lotus position and continued his meditation. The night would be long and, in the morning...

Before plunging into his inner world, he remembered dear Eina.

Soon, she would rest in peace. He would make sure she finally got her long-awaited justice.

Chapter 52

That morning, two million soldiers gathered in the wastelands near the camp. They hadn't come to see the duel between the officer and the adjutant. No. This sea of red standards, banners, shields, spears, and helmets was preparing for a march.

The cavalry columns were at the front; the archers were located in the center of the formation; behind them was the light infantry, and the wagons were at the back of the procession.

They stood in absolute silence. Only the wind, ruffling the fabric of their banners, made any noise.

They were waiting for General Leen's orders. She stood in the center of this ocean of soldiers. The soldiers had formed a circle which was big enough for two practitioners to fight in without harming anyone else.

Dogar was also there. Dressed in his leather armor and with a crumpled steel helmet on his head, he looked even fiercer than usual.

All the senior commanders had gathered there as well. They were curious about whether Hadjar would be able to actually follow through with what he'd said he would do to Colin, back at the War Council.

Next to them, Nero stood, holding the sleeping white kitten. Wearing heavy armor and with a massive sword attached to his belt, he watched an inconspicuous old man. Who lets him enter the camp? But, apparently, the personal servant of the General of the Spring Town garrison had his ways.

The old man in black clothes kept his eyes on the improvised arena. Sometimes he would look over at Colin proudly.

The adjutant, who was also wearing armor, was warming up with the blade. He made rapid attacks, cutting through the air furiously, all the while moving on the sand more easily than a swan through the water. His feet didn't even leave marks on the sand, just kicked up dust into the air.

"He's late," Dogar said, watching the shadow of a spear stuck in the ground.

The duel had been scheduled for noon. However, a quarter of an hour had already gone by past the designated time.

"He'll come," Nero replied confidently, continuing to stroke the white kitten. "No doubt about it."

But Hadjar didn't come to the parade ground even after they all waited another ten minutes.

"Where is the bastard?" Colin laughed, continuing to swing his blade gracefully.

His sword tip intercepted a sunbeam that had penetrated through the clouds and caught the reflection of a figure descending from a hill.

"I told you," Nero smiled.

Holding a sheath that had been fastened with a rope to his belt, Hadjar walked calmly, as if he were out taking a stroll, rather than approaching a mortal enemy. He passed through the ranks of the army as easily as an arrow through a sheet of paper.

The soldiers parted in front of him, doing it without any conscious thought. Something in this new Hadjar made them do so. Something in his walk. In his gaze. Something... annoying. Something bestial.

They felt like dogs that had seen a wolf. They were afraid of it, wary of it.

Hadjar wasn't a wolf. He walked on two legs and wore clothes, albeit torn and frayed ones. And yet, when someone gazed at this handsome young man, a disquieting feeling would arise in their soul. An annoying desire to check the condition of their weapon, armor, and then run away.

"You're late, Officer Hadjar," the General said in a stern tone.

"Please forgive me, my General," Hadjar bowed. "I was wrong about the time it would take me to break through to the 'Formation' stage."

The General tilted her head to the side. The wind ruffled her golden hair, which had been tightened into a bun. She held a very inelegant, absolutely masculine helmet in her hands. Hadjar didn't doubt that, even while wearing it, she would still be enchantingly beautiful.

"It's impossible for a mere village bumpkin to completely overcome all the stages of the Bodily Rivers in just a month," Colin snorted. "These are just the pathetic excuses of a farm boy. Don't listen to him, Gene-"

Hadjar's aura, which had suddenly been unleashed, didn't allow the aide to finish his mocking diatribe. Circles similar to ones formed when a stone is thrown into calm waters spread across the sand around his feet.

The wind was turning into a whirlwind and it seemed like the air had gotten a bit heavy.

The soldiers standing nearby that had a lower level of cultivation began to breathe harder.

"Excellent, officer Hadjar." the General nodded. "And yet, that does not give you the right to violate the rules of the duel."

"I beg your pardon, my General," Hadjar repeated.

Leen thought for a second.

"According to the rules of the duel, you'll fight until one of you surrenders or until one of you is seriously injured. The adjutant may attack three times without Hadjar retaliating. That is the punishment for your lateness, officer Hadjar."

"Three attacks?" Colin chuckled mockingly. "One is enough. But, my General, may I say something before we begin?"

Leen just waved her hand and Colin continued, "Every time I see this officer, he's disrespecting the Royal army and the nobles. This behavior is unacceptable! He is nothing more than a weed, a weed stealing the sun destined to go to more deserving flowers! Such behavior... no, such weeds must be eradicated immediately!"

"What do you mean, adjutant?" Leen asked, adjusting her creaking saddle.

Her horse snorted and wagged its tail, chasing away the bugs that had been attracted to its heat and sweat.

"I'm asking you to let us fight to the death!" Colin said, looking like a triumphant and glorious warlord.

He straightened his back and lifted his chin toward the sky, frozen in the pose of a man who had just defeated an army of demons.

"Have you gone insane, Colin?" Dogar shouted.

The old man in black immediately became furious, "How dare you call the young master something so demeaning, you worm?" Nobody paid any attention to him.

"Commander," Hadjar bowed to his senior officer. "Let me accept this challenge."

The General turned to the most devoted of her commanders. Dogar had never let her down, so she completely trusted him. Perhaps that was the reason why Leen had sent the guy whom she considered to be promising to the 'Bear's' camp. And maybe her instincts had been right.

Someone of her rank had to make the decision regarding whether to allow a duel to the death, according to the military laws. So, Leen had to decide what to do here. She would most likely not be in any danger from Colin's father, whatever she decided.

She wasn't the owner of a brothel, after all...

The whole town knew that Larvie's family had burned 'Innocent Meadow' down. People said that the fire happened because the hostess had

had some information concerning the patriarch of the family—the General. But that was just a rumor. No one knew what had really happened.

"Hadjar, are you sure?"

"Yes, commander."

Dogar looked into the eyes of his assistant. As usual, he saw nothing but immense willpower and an unshakable determination within them.

"You have my permission."

Hadjar nodded gratefully and turned to face his opponent.

"General?" Colin turned to Leen once again.

"You have my permission," the General nodded without hesitation.

The smile on the adjutant's face was almost painfully wide. He took his favorite stance, reminiscent of a scorpion with its stinger raised above its head before it attacked. Wearing his high-quality armor and steel boots, he looked much more impressive than his counterpart.

The east wind was blowing through Hadjar's clothes. Torn and old, they inspired nothing but skepticism and a bit of pity.

"Seconds," the General commanded.

The old man walked up to Colin. He whispered something to his 'young master' and took the army medallion from him.

It was impossible to wear the medallions during a duel. The army had to be consolidated and indestructible, not torn apart by internal conflicts. That was the reason why officers could fight in duels as ordinary people, but not as soldiers. The laws were quite contradictory.

"You were late on purpose, right?" Nero asked as he approached Hadjar.

"I did it so it would be easier to provoke him into a fight on my terms: 'To the death'. He is not walking away from this."

Hadjar stroked the yawning Azrea. It was hard for him to believe in his friend's story. This cute, fluffy, warm lump the size of his palm surely hadn't torn a practitioner apart. Even if he had only been at the seventh stage of the Bodily Rivers...

However, the offspring of a tiger could never be just a normal kitten. Hadjar should not have forgotten what fate had placed under his care.

What did Colin do to you?"

"He killed a good friend of mine," Hadjar removed the medallion from his neck. "She'd been so kind, naïve, and trusting. Fatally so."

"A girl," Nero's entire countenance darkened.

He had a thing about females being harmed...

"He raped her in front of her mother, slit her throat, and then burned her while she was dying," Hadjar finished explaining.

Nero didn't say anything else. He only moved to his 'designated' place, looking very gloomy. He clutched the military locket with such force that his fist turned white.

"Are you ready to die, loser?" Colin laughed, circling his opponent.

Hadjar did not reply.

He only looked up at the boundless, blue sky.

Was she looking at him right now? Were Senta and Eina waiting for their justice? Were they there at all, among the clouds in the azure sky?

Hadjar wanted to believe that they were.

He unsheathed his blade.

"Begin!" The General ordered.

Chapter 53

 Colin didn't even intend to lunge forward. He let loose so the people around him could feel his power. It was the power of a practitioner of the Transformation stage of mortal form. The force of it was enough not only to create waves in the sand but also to scatter it as well, exposing the ground and rocks beneath.

Some of the weaker soldiers staggered back. Many of them clutched their blades and began to desperately gasp for air.

Hadjar met the wave of wind and sand with the calm of a mountain before the storm.

It didn't even reach his body as it flew in different directions, dispersing once it met the barrier that was the power of the commanders.

Colin wasn't embarrassed at all. He'd have been very disappointed if the jerk he was going to humiliate had died from just being exposed to his power. No, he would kill him slowly. He would demonstrate all his skill so that, next time, no one would dare to get in his way. And then they would have a second General in their family.

Father would be pleased, and Colin would finally get revenge on Leen for all the years of humiliation.

She would scream and moan when he did everything he had dreamed of for so long…

Colin rushed in swiftly. His level allowed him to move at the speed of a young cheetah. He had been standing ten yards away from Hadjar only a moment ago, and then he was suddenly within range, using his blade to attack him.

Shrouded in black light, the sword turned into a Scorpion sting for a second. It was not as ghostly and ephemeral as last time. This time, it was clearly visible and could almost be felt.

And yet, Hadjar tried not to block it, but to dodge it.

He moved his left shoulder to the side, avoiding the sword point, but... It had been stupid to expect that he would be able to fully evade the strike of a practitioner at the Transformation level's mortal form.

It seemed like the sword hadn't touched Hadjar. But then he felt a scorpion sting penetrating his chest.

The strike was so strong that Hadjar was thrown into the air, flipped over several times, and then hit the shields of the soldiers standing around the fight.

He rolled on the sand after bouncing off their shields.

Colin, defiantly, moved the blade to his side and stopped, waiting for his enemy to recover.

Hadjar was slowly getting back to his feet. For some reason, he remembered the lessons of South Wind.

"Everyone fights in this world, my Prince. The fisherman fights the fish and the ocean, a blacksmith fights the fire and iron, the farmer fights the weather and the earth, but only the adepts fight their own destinies."

Hadjar stood up.

"You forgot to take out your sword, peasant," Colin chuckled.

He didn't even think about defending himself. Anyone observing would be able to see so many mistakes in his stance that even a young man with a kitchen knife in his hand could've fought him.

Hadjar took hold of his sword but did not even untie the ribbons from the crossguard, leaving it sheathed.

"Are you afraid of cutting yourself, yokel?"

Colin rushed in to resume the attack. The ghostly sting became even clearer and even manifested away from the blade this time. Now it was flying ahead of it, at a distance of a few palms.

Hadjar saw all of it and realized what was going on, but for most of the other people observing the scene, what happened next consisted of only a few fragments of obscure images. At first, there was Colin, looking like a bolt of black, steel lightning, and then...

Hadjar swung the blade hidden in his scabbard. The spectators made a slight noise for a second, then Colin slammed into the shields.

"What the..." the adjutant was spitting up blood.

He'd managed to spot a ghostly blue light and nothing more. It looked as if Hadjar had used his Oneness with the sword, but... had added something new to it. Something relating to the wind that was now blowing across the sand.

But Colin's servant and the others were much more concerned about the fact that Hadjar still hadn't taken out his blade.

"I'll kill you, freak," Colin cried out, his eyes were crazy.

A ring of black flames swirled around his legs. The Scorpion sting descended from the tip of the blade, across the hilt, and flicked against the adjutant's hands.

This time, his lunge was faster than the previous one. Only a shadow flashed across the sand, and then there was a burst of fire, as Colin pressed his enemy back.

Hadjar could only defend himself with quick strikes, each time moving a few steps back. It looked as if a dog had angered a bull and the bull had moved to crush the dog like a simple bug.

At that moment, the spectators considered Dogar's assistant dead and buried.

They still thought so even after Hadjar, having found an opening in Colin's relentless barrage of attacks, was able to move his body to the side and lightly chop Colin's knee with the scabbard. Colin was about to fall down, his pace slowed, and Hadjar, forgetting that he was a swordsman, punched the adjutant in the face.

Colin stepped aside and, unbelievingly, spat out blood and a piece of his now broken tooth.

How could this peasant worm of the Formation stage hurt his body at the Transformation stage? Had this worthless yokel found a mystical artifact in the woods? Well, then it would be a trophy for Colin! An added reward for his victory!

The adjutant assumed a new stance: his sword was in front of him and his feet were spread shoulder-width apart. He still resembled a scorpion, but now he mostly looked like a swordsman. Due to this, Hadjar realized that his opponent knew many stances of this Technique.

His level allowed him to use more sophisticated Techniques as well.

"Scorpion's venom!" the adjutant shouted as he swung his sword.

This time, it was Colin, not Hadjar, who sent out the illusion of a strike. It was not a slash, but a stinging thrust. Its black flame changed to green.

At first, Hadjar had wanted to block it, but a sense of danger howled like a siren in his mind and he dodged aside as swiftly as he could. As he was rolling away, he managed to spot the flames as they hit the shields of the soldiers and... Began to eat away holes in them.

The warriors panicked, but they calmed down when General Leen waved her hand to extinguish the poisonous fire.

But her power didn't affect the rags which had been serving as boots for Hadjar and were currently covered in green fire.

Azrea meowed loudly but didn't wake up.

Demonstrating a high degree of self-control, Hadjar took a handful of sand, imbued it with his force, and threw it into the flame. One of his legs had been burnt so badly that green blood vessels and veins had appeared on it.

The shoe from his wounded leg fell to the sand. Hadjar put the other one next to it.

Barefoot and dressed in cheap clothes, Hadjar stood in front of Colin, who was wearing armor that was light but still offered great protection.

"Draw your sword," the adjutant growled.

Instead of answering, Hadjar attacked first. His movements were slower than Colin's, however, they were... not only smoother but also more 'correct.' Where Colin had to make two steps, Hadjar made do with one.

Where Colin invested too much power in every attack, Hadjar only used as much as he needed to.

His prowess was made evident with every swing of his sword and scabbard. And despite the fact that the blade enveloped in green flames could easily overpower his strikes, the audience saw who the real swordsman was.

The approving whispers irritated Colin. He'd imagined this fight going differently. How is this bug still fighting me? Why wasn't it defeated after the first strike? This isn't how things were supposed to go!

He was Colin Larvie, the son of General Larvie! The whole world was his to do with as he pleased. He was a king. He was a swordsman!

The adjutant growled. He fought off another one of Hadjar's strikes and pushed him in the chest to create some distance between them.

He turned around sharply and swung his blade in a wide arc, sending out three green stingers. Two of the stingers plunged into the sand, and the third one was stuck in Hadjar's chest.

The audience held their breath.

Nero sniffed nervously.

Dogar closed his eyes.

But…

Nothing happened. There was no blood, no pained groans, and no smell of burning flesh.

Hadjar, even after taking a dozen steps back, was still upright. His injured leg seemed to be bothering him a bit, and the cuts on his hands and shoulders were bleeding. Otherwise, he seemed to be unharmed.

He held his sword in front of his chest. It wasn't shining or glowing, but its blade had protected Hadjar from the stinger.

Hadjar waved his hand and the green petals of flame fell to the sand with a hiss.

His scabbard fell to the sand as well, almost inaudibly.

Suddenly, the banners and tents started to flutter in the wind. This new wind was blowing through the General's hair, and the spectators had to hold onto their coats which seemed like they'd come alive.

"The first stance… The Wind Rises," Hadjar said, and his blade pierced through the space between him and his foe.

[Host is using... an offensive energy structure. The power level is 2.1 Energy Points]

Chapter 54

There were seven stances in Traves' 'Sword of the Light Breeze' Technique. The first of them, the 'Rising Wind', demanded that Hadjar apply all he knew about the sword and all the skills that he had picked up over the years. It was their quintessence and demanded only his honing of the skills that he already had available to him.

The second stance was so mystical, ephemeral, and fickle that Hadjar couldn't even understand its foundations. He'd managed to improve his skill with the first stance over the course of last night and he could now use it twice.

He had neither the strength nor the energy to use it more than two times. Despite the fact that his ability to use the first stance had grown and changed for the better, it was still insufficient for anything more than that.

After Hadjar swung his blade, a vortex rushed toward Colin. If a simple swordsman who had been lucky enough to learn Traves' Technique had used it, the vortex would have remained as just a razor-sharp wind...

The adjutant had to protect himself not only from the wind, which was able to cut through stone but also from the ghostly blades hidden within it.

The audience witnessed something incredible—a practitioner at the Formation level was making a man who stood a whole level above him fall back and desperately scramble to protect himself. It was as if Hadjar was a hero from the old legends and not an ordinary officer.

Colin, even if he had been thrown five steps back, was still able to dispel the Technique he'd been struck by. His face was covered in bleeding cuts, his hands were a scarlet mess, and his whole body had been badly wounded.

He shouted something, but Hadjar didn't pay it any mind.

He rushed in once again. He could probably avoid the green sting but Hadjar wasn't sure that he would be able to repel it a second time, which meant the fight needed to end. Besides, Hadjar had only one minute of energy left, if not less.

Colin most likely had enough to keep fighting for much longer than that.

Hadjar slashed at Colin's wrist. Colin blocked and the sound rang out as he deflected the blade, almost making Hadjar drop it. Using the inertia of the block, Hadjar whirled like a dervish and crouched down, going for Colin's feet.

Colin jumped into the air and launched a 'Scorpion sting' from above. It was immediately bisected by a ghostly strike that was now a little more distinct than it had been before.

Their fight resembled a chess game.

Each strike was met with a strike in turn. Every move was countered.

Sparks flew as the blades crashed against each other dozens of times within the span of a few seconds. The bodies of both fighters were covered in wounds, and the splashes of blood glittered like rubies as they filled the air.

Sometimes, the 'fragments' of their Techniques and the sheer force of their sword strikes would ripple out. They tore into the banners and even struck the soldiers' shields.

Hadjar went for the throat, and then, the very next moment, he was forced to dodge a strike aimed at his stomach.

Colin tried to hook Hadjar's shoulder but was forced to scramble back to avoid the slash that had been aimed at his face.

They were fencing at the speed of a mongoose chasing a snake. Their blades fluttered gracefully but with a lethal swiftness. They moved smoothly but with deadly and cold brutality behind every action.

Many of the ordinary soldiers did not dare to even blink, lest they miss a single moment of the fight. Thanks to this amazing duel, they would be able to learn something new and get inspired, maybe even move forward to the next stage of their cultivation.

Still, Colin kept pressing Hadjar. Hadjar slammed into the soldiers' shields after each new collision, with each new spark or drop of blood.

The adjutant felt the excitement and the fire of self-confidence flare up inside him. He had long since forgotten that he was fighting a 'peasant at the Transformation level.' On the contrary, he was facing an opponent that he had to defeat in order to become stronger and survive.

He wasted a little more energy with each new strike. He became more and more entangled in Hadjar's web of careful deceit every time he felt that his enemy was weakening, with each new movement that was just a bit more wasteful than the previous one had been.

And when Colin finally made a mistake, Hadjar took a low stance once again.

His palm lay over the blade, and his legs were slightly bent at the knees. He looked like a bird getting ready to swoop down on its hapless prey.

"Rising Wind!"

A whirlwind of swords overwhelmed Colin as he was about to attack. The whirlwind lifted Colin, who was unable to defend himself, into the air, spun him around, and then threw him to the ground.

Colin suddenly found himself in a position that was much worse than his opponent's: he was bloodied and wounded. Hadjar was breathing heavily and limping on his burned leg, wiping blood and sweat off his face.

Colin had been beaten black and blue. This time, Hadjar's strikes had damaged him severely.

"Filthy, filthy peasant," Colin whispered, suddenly 'remembering' who his enemy was. "Damn you! Bastard! You're nothing but the son of slaves! How dare you...How dare you even breathe in my presence!"

"Young master," the old servant whispered. "What are you doing, young master?"

Colin took something out of his pocket. Something red, glowing, about the size of a nut.

"Stop, adjutant!" The General cried out suddenly, but it was too late.

Colin roared, but the tone of it was strange. His body throbbed with agony as he screamed and his veins reddened. It was like he was getting bigger. His armor creaked under the pressure of his swelling muscles. The handle of his sword cracked under the force of the black claws that were replacing the previously normal nails.

"No... Young master." The old man put his hands over his mouth, horrified.

"Spear!" The General held out her hand, but...

Colin was turning into a red-skinned, inhuman creature. It happened surprisingly fast and was seemingly a simple process. There was a bang and a small pit formed where he was standing. Colin rose up, roared, opened his maw, and started to attack Hadjar from above.

The strike looked like it could destroy the city wall, let alone some old clothing and flesh.

Hadjar managed to block the strike with his blade and felt as if a truck had run him over. Colin's hit forced all the air out of his lungs and tossed Hadjar a good ten yards into the air.

A new bang was heard and the red creature, which had been Colin until recently, was once more next to Hadjar.

It was hard to say whether they were falling or flying. The only obvious thing was that the blade, held by a clawed paw, was coming down, toward Hadjar.

Hadjar didn't have any time to react. He wouldn't have been able to block it anyway, but he didn't even see the strike as it landed.

Hadjar could only look at a sparrow flying through the air. The sparrow was small, defenseless, but proud and fast. It mocked the ground every time it flapped its wings. It was conquering heaven with every second it remained in the sky.

Everyone fights in this world, my Prince... His mentor's voice sounded in his head. The fisherman fights the fish and the ocean, a blacksmith fights the fire and iron, the farmer fights the weather and earth, but only the adepts fight their own destinies.

Time slowed down. Hadjar suddenly understood what had been eluding him all this time.

While fighting the enemy, he'd forgotten the most important thing. His feet still tread along the ground, fighting its power. His blade cut through the air, trying to overcome its resistance. The steel in his hands warmed with each strike. His blood covered the grass.

He'd been fighting the enemy while somehow forgetting about the outside world. It had struggled against him too, since the day of his birth, from his very first breath. The crying newborn was rushing to make a long jump toward the grave. A jump filled with endless struggle.

But why? Why did his sword fight against the whole world, when he had only one enemy? Why couldn't he direct the world to his advantage? What was stopping him?

The answer was a little sparrow, piercing through an inaccessible sky.

Nothing.

The General, after getting her spear, did not rush in to intervene.

All the soldiers, looking up at where the fight was still raging, couldn't believe their eyes.

The creature's sword fell toward Hadjar's head, and he... seemed to have changed a little. It was as if his blade had merged with the wind, parrying the strike easily. Although... 'parrying' wasn't quite the right word. He'd flung the creature aside as easily as a lion kicking away a naughty kitten.

The creature fell from the sky with a roar, and when it got out of the ravine it had made upon impact, it saw Hadjar waiting for it, his back straight.

He seemed to have merged with the outside world. He wasn't fighting it anymore, instead, he was cooperating with it.

"One with the World," the audience whispered.

"He became 'One with the World' during a battle."

"Is he a genius?"

"No..."

"He's a monster."

Well, they were... somewhat wrong. Hadjar still hadn't reached the level of 'One with the World', but he was close to it. As close as he'd ever been. But even this amount of progress was enough for his strike, which had previously only had a range of five steps, to now be able to reach as far as seventeen steps.

The attack launched from his blade was no longer ghostly or shimmering. It was a transparent strike of the sword, clearly visible even to a mere mortal.

Hadjar's attack, which was ten feet long and ten inches wide, easily split Colin's blade.

The creature howled when Hadjar's strike also tore through the thick, red crust that had replaced its skin.

A blue light flashed and a pale, emaciated, and even aged Colin lay on the ground. He prostrated himself and began muttering something. Miserable and broken, all he could do was endlessly repeat: "Have mercy, have mercy."

Hadjar hobbled in his direction with the relentlessness of a servant of the God of death. He was leaning on his sword, blood had covered his eyes, but he kept walking forward, getting closer to his goal, to Eina's peace.

He finally reached the adjutant. He stood above him and raised his sword above his head.

"Stop!" A voice thundered.

Almost the whole army turned toward the thundering cry. A tall man with a scarred face and an inhumanly cruel and ferocious look stood on a hill, wearing crimson, almost bloody armor.

"Sir," the old servant fell to his knees.

"Do you know who you're fighting, peasant?" General Larvie bellowed. "He is my son! Stop, or you will suffer such a terrible fate that children will be scared by the tale of it for a thousand years!"

"Do I know who I'm fighting?" Hadjar spoke through busted, bleeding lips. "A coward. A rapist. A killer."

His sword whizzed through the air.

As his head rolled away, Colin didn't have time to say one last, "Have mercy."

The General on the hill growled like a wounded beast and picked up his war hammer.

Hadjar didn't see anything else. He collapsed, falling asleep as blissfully and calmly as he had in the Palace, all those years ago.

His heart had finally calmed a bit. At least he'd managed to get justice for someone.

Now Eina could finally rest peacefully…

Chapter 55

 He was having an amazing dream. He was dressed in fine silk clothes and sitting in his room in the 'Innocent Meadow'. A pipe full of fragrant tobacco lay on a small table in front of him. Water was boiling in a pot somewhere nearby, spreading a

sweet tea aroma around the room.

A girl with multicolored eyes and hair that had been kissed by fire was sitting in front of him and smiling.

"Play some more." She requested, looking at him fondly.

"As you say."

And Hadjar played his best song for his best friend. He played like he had never played before and would never play again. He played only for her, for the girl he hadn't loved because he couldn't love. For a girl, he would never get to love because she was already dead.

"You're a liar, Hadjar," Eina spoke at last.

"Why?"

"You once said you would never turn into a handsome man. That you would always be a monster."

They were sitting so close together that he could feel her breath on his face.

Turn into a handsome man?

The young man raised a hand before his face. It was no longer covered in ulcers, scabs, and warts. No, it was normal, tanned skin, maybe just slightly rough on the palms.

"What?" Hadjar couldn't understand what had happened to him until fragments of obscure memories began to emerge in his mind.

Cave. Dragon. Army. Adjutant.

"Eina," Hadjar said.

"I'll miss you, Hadjar," the girl smiled, tears rolling down her cheeks.

"Eina..."

He tried to grab her hand, but his fingers caught only elusive fog. The room melted away and the entire scene disappeared.

Hadjar fell into the void. He shouted, trying to grab onto anything he could, but only ended up falling faster into the dark abyss.

Suddenly, bright, white light flooded in, illuminating everything around him, and he heard: "Thank you, Hadjar. Thank you, and goodbye."

***

"Hey, hey! Calm down, calm down, I said!"

Strong hands pressed Hadjar's head into a pillow.

"It's me, Hadj. It's Nero. Everything's ok. It's all right, buddy."

Hadjar opened his eyes. The sun's rays made their way through the cracks of the boards that served as the ceiling. The creaking of heavy wheels, the neighing of horses, and the clanging of metal—those were all the sounds he could hear. Well, Nero's voice was another sound, but Hadjar had already gotten used to it.

The room Hadjar was in swayed from side to side. Some ropes

hung on the walls, all the way down to the floor, and the bed had been built out of bales of hay. The wounded Prince had been placed on it and covered with a patchy blanket. That was a good sign.

"What happened with the General?" Hadjar croaked out.

His throat felt like a desert. He coughed and gratefully took a bowl of fragrant, apparently healing liquid from Nero and greedily sipped from it, but that only made things worse. The desert had been replaced by the pain of a blacksmith's hammer striking his throat repeatedly...

He only quenched his thirst on the third attempt, with Nero's help. He held both the bowl and his friend's head up, letting Hadjar drink properly.

"What General?"

"General Larvie," Hadjar said. "Or have we already been captured and are currently being dragged to his dungeons?"

Nero grinned and moved the always sleeping Azrea from a bale over to Hadjar's chest. The kitten stretched, yawned, meowed, and then curled into a tight ball.

She's so warm...

"No, buddy, we're marching, moving toward the border Fort."

Well, yes. That makes sense. This explained both the sounds and the cart, which was serving as Hadjar's refuge.

Judging by the flashing lights alone, the cart was moving at the speed of a train, if not faster.

Honestly, there's no other way for the army to travel so far...

The common soldiers probably have it especially hard—they have to not just 'march', but... run. Each world has its own quirks, I suppose.

"And this... Larvie," Nero was clearly finding it unpleasant to remember the General of Spring Town. "You should have seen how furious he'd been. He was out of his mind with how badly he wanted to end your life. He decided to kill you on the spot. And you were so injured that if it hadn't been for the healers, you'd be dead."

"Thank you."

"No need to thank me," Nero coughed bashfully. "Well...he charged at you, and then General Leen appeared with her spear. I swear to you, if I had ever thought of choosing a wife, it would've been Leen."

"But being limited to just one woman...."

"Isn't for me." The ladies' man known all over the prefecture agreed. "She stood in front of him, solid as stone, and shouted to the army: "Get ready". Two million soldiers hit their shields with their swords all at once. The bang was as loud as if the universe were crashing down. I'd never heard or seen anything like it."

Hadjar imagined it and regretted that he had lost consciousness too early.

"Well, Larvie raged and promised terrible retribution, hinted at Ax clan assassins and so on, but the General just ordered the army to, "Prepare for action!". And the bang of swords on shields rang out again and people began to line up in attack formation. I'd never thought such a fragile girl could give orders so loudly."

"It's probably some kind of Technique that lets her be heard across the whole battlefield."

"Well, maybe. But I was almost deafened by it."

It was an interesting thing to consider. How was the communication between different divisions in the army carried out? Hadjar wasn't particularly well versed in medieval technology, and it was unlikely that they used the sort of tech his world had used. After all, they had some kind of magic at their disposal here.

"He finally went away, cursing. However, he was allowed to carry the body of his son with him. He carried Colin's head away, and the old servant carried the rest of the carcass."

Despite the fact that the scene Nero had just described was somewhat sentimental, Hadjar... did not feel any remorse. They'd all deserved their fate.

The question was whether karma had carried out its will using Hadjar's hand or had Hadjar carried out the karma on his own? And was there a difference between the former and the latter?

It was a foolish thought, but something made it very important to Hadjar.

"Why were you yelling like that?" Nero sat down on a nearby bale.

He took an apple from his pocket, cleaned it on his pants, and took a bite, licking the greenish juice from it.

"I'd imagined how I would have to listen to your chewing all the way to the camp and cried."

They looked at each other and laughed. Hadjar felt like the laughter was hurting him. His whole body ached. Azrea, after waking up, snorted, clearly dissatisfied, and got under the 'blanket' to be closer to Hadjar. Sticking out only her face, she curled up once again and fall asleep peacefully.

"If only I could do that," Nero sighed, "Just sleep the whole day away with somebody at my side, warming me up."

"I knew it," Hadjar exclaimed. "You still have feelings for me!"

"Go to... sir officer... go in a well-known direction. You'd better tell me how it was to make up for being so cruel."

"What are you talking about?" Hadjar didn't take the hint.

"Well," Nero waved his hand somewhat vaguely. "How was it, being 'One with the World'? There are fewer than a thousand soldiers in the army with such abilities and all of them belong to the elite. They're way out of our reach."

Oh, right. The level that he'd demonstrated through the

enlightenment he'd gained really had resembled 'One with the World', but it only resembled it. Uncountable hours of training, endless sparring, battles with monsters, and other adventures had been enough to simulate it in a moment insight, but nothing more.

Hadjar felt that he had still not reached the second stage of sword mastery. But still, he was already close to it.

He explained this to his friend.

"Really? What a pity! You really looked as impressive as a master at some of the tournaments in the Empire. They can do such unbelievable things!" Nero never took a bite of the apple. He blinked a couple of times and smiled. "My father took me with him once, when he went on business with the merchant fleet. It was the thrill of a lifetime for me."

The Empire...

"What's it like?" Hadjar asked.

"How do I even begin to answer you? I can't describe it in two words."

"We've got a whole week."

"Four days," Nero corrected. "You've been sleeping here for three days and I'm mentally exhausted, you know. I can't run with my fellow soldiers because I'm lying in a damned cart with a friend. I also had to endure the humiliation when officer Dogar sent me here."

The joker and womanizer managed to utter all of this in a pathetic, miserable tone of voice.

"Tell me about the Empire and its tournaments already."

"Well, okay, listen up," Nero made himself comfortable. "Everyone is obsessed with their cultivation in the Empire."

"So are we."

"If you're going to interrupt me, you may as well tell the story yourself."

"Excuse me."

"Now, they are so fanatical about it that the parents try to send their five-year-old children somewhere, depending on their abilities and income. Usually, children are sent to the sects or to the Academy. People who aren't relatives won't be accepted into the clans, except maybe as servants. But no one wants such a fate for their child. Tournaments are often organized there—something like competitions between different art schools, let's say. The winners get the honor, praise, and various prizes, sometimes even a personal apprenticeship from some famous master."

"And the winners' organizations become well-known and have a great influx of new students."

"What did I say about interrupting me?"

Hadjar only muttered something inaudible in response.

"I was at a local tournament in a border town. But the performance was amazing. Especially in the final match, where two girls faced off. One was from the Moonlight clan, and another was from the Military Academy. I can't forget their breasts and thighs. You can't even imagine how supple they were. Well, also, both were already at the stage of Transformation of mortal form at fifteen."

Hadjar was so astonished that he almost choked on air.

"Fifteen?"

"Yeah," Nero nodded a little sadly. "It's no wonder they consider us to be savages. And this was only a local tournament. There is also the main one. It's held every twenty years. It's called 'The Tournament of Thirteen Branches.' Even the Imperial Palace takes part in it; it's something akin to an unofficial, fourteenth branch. And every year, the top ten contenders at this tournament are given prizes so valuable that by selling one of them you could buy our entire Kingdom, and you'd still have enough money left to purchase a neighboring kingdom as well."

"And what is their level?"

"I don't know much regarding their levels, but last time, a guy won. He was eighteen years old and was at the initial stage of the Spirit Knight."

Now Hadjar really was choking on air.

"I had the same reaction," Nero nodded. "Humans don't live there, man. Only monsters."

Was Hadjar really going to seek out such monsters? He wasn't just an 'ordinary' practitioner when compared to them, he was an untalented pig.

"How huge this world is…" Hadjar sighed.

"You're right about that, my friend."

They rode on in absolute silence until nightfall. The creaking of the wheels and the planks, as well as the clanging of metal, were the only sounds that accompanied the march of the huge army. A war was coming.

Chapter 56

Hadjar was able to get back on his feet, but it took two more days. All that time Azrea and Nero were with him in the wagon. It seemed like the latter had decided to compensate for the fact that the kitten was always sleeping. When Azrea had been driven away from her bale, she, scratching herself, angrily climbed up to Hadjar's hair and fell asleep there.

Hadjar didn't want to try and take the kitten off his head, worrying about the safety of his scalp.

"Assistant," someone knocked on the wagon from outside.

Hadjar leaned on his crutch and climbed out. Only a few tents had been set up in the boundless prairie. The soldiers were so tired from a whole day of continuous running that they'd fallen asleep directly on the grass. Some of them had put sleeping bags on the ground, but the majority had just thrown bales on top of their removed armor and used that as a makeshift bed.

It was mostly the cavalrymen that had set up tents. Perhaps that was why they weren't all that loved and were also envied at the same time.

A large, full moon was in the sky—a silver disc, bathing the ground in white light.

"Commander, sir," Hadjar greeted his superior.

Dogar, even while exhausted, could still stand on his feet. Recently, Hadjar had begun to suspect that the soldiers at a certain level of cultivation were recruited into the army not because of their strength, but because of their endurance and speed when running.

Was there another way to transport an army numbering two million someplace that was more than 6213 miles away?

The sight of two million people running anywhere was somewhat absurd, but only to the conceptions of an Earthling. Hadjar could hardly remember his home world anymore and didn't consider this to be something surreal.

"I want to talk," Dogar sat down wearily.

"About Larvie?"

Dogar nodded. He leaned against the cold planks and looked up at the sky. His breathing was already evener.

"You killed his son, Hadjar."

"In a fair fight, according to army law, there's nothing to prosecute me for."

"I doubt any of them," Dogar emphasized the last word, "Is interested in the law. King Primus and his Palace are far away, and we are so close. Larvie has destroyed other people's lives for less grievous sins. I heard his dog once bit the son of some merchant during a walk. So, he publicly skinned the merchant, and then cut off his son's…"

Dogar flinched and winced.

Hadjar felt somewhat uncomfortable.

"Do you think the royal investigators came after him? Not even close. I don't think he even had to pay a fine. They simply paid no attention to it."

"I'm an army officer," Hadjar reminded him.

"One of ten thousand. Do you think General Leen will always be there to protect you? I assure you, she didn't let Larvie kill you simply because she could have lost her credibility." Dogar took a piece of dried meat from his pocket and offered it to Hadjar. He refused. "He won't let you rest, Hadjar. He won't stop until he's tortured you in his dungeons and driven you completely insane…"

Hadjar also looked up at the sky.

Distant, indifferent stars shone there.

"What are you trying to say, commander?"

Dogar turned to his assistant. A heavy hand fell on Hadjar's shoulder.

"I know a merchant in the Fort," the huge man handed him a small, iron seal that had the image of a camel on it. "He will surely leave with the caravan on an expedition before the siege starts."

"I don't know what you're talking about…"

"You're a good guy, Hadjar," Bear smiled. "One of the best I've met in my life. My old friend always needs reliable people to guard his deeds. He will take you with him. Go with the caravan, Hadjar. You can see the world, make some money, maybe you'll find a place where you want to stay or you will find another merchant later, one of those that cross the Sea of Sand to get to the Empire…"

Is he telling me to take a trip around the world?

Sometimes, Hadjar had dreamed about doing just that while sitting in his room in the Palace. The windows had faced a huge garden and lake with a mountain behind it. His father had told him that there was a family castle on that mountain and that he would take him there one day.

Everyone's probably dreamed about that—traveling around the boundless world full of amazing and beautiful places, seeing all that it had to offer…

"I cannot desert the army, commander," Hadjar shook his head, pushing the medallion aside.

"What are you risking your life for, Hadjar?" Dogar asked suddenly. "I understand most of the other soldiers. They want money, power… Well, the illusion of power anyway, and women, of course. But what do you want?"

What did Hadjar want?

Not much— to find his sister and chop off Primus' head.

"Let's go to sleep, sir," Hadjar got up and stroked the sleeping Azrea. "Will we get to the Fort soon?"

Dogar straightened too. He was enormous, unapproachable, but looked as if he'd aged a bit just now.

"I respect you, officer Hadjar. Even though you are a fool, I respect you," he held out a hand. Hadjar shook his head ruefully as they clasped hands.

When he got back to the cart, he noticed Nero staring at him while also dozing on his bales.

"I agree with him," his friend said. "You're a fool."

"In my village, they say that it's better to be a dead lion than alive but a jackal."

"That's a beautiful sentiment," Nero nodded and turned around. "But it's stupid. A jackal that stays alive could turn into an Azure Wolf one day. But the dead lion could turn into nothing except fertilizer for the trees."

Hadjar lay back and wrapped himself in a blanket. Azrea squeaked, got off the bale she'd been napping on and went straight to Hadjar. She climbed up on his cheek and curled up. Her hair tickled Hadjar's nostrils slightly, but not enough to keep him awake.

"Would you run?" Hadjar asked.

"No," Nero answered. "I must be a fool, too."

Everyone pretended to fall asleep, but for a long time, they looked at the distant sky through the holes in the roof.

All sorts of unwelcome thoughts and memories assaulted Hadjar. He didn't know what Nero was thinking. He recalled how his mother had brushed his long hair with a comb in the evenings. She would sing to him and smile as she did it, and sometimes his father would be there as well. He'd seemed large and invulnerable back then, just like the mountain that Hadjar had seen from his window while waiting for the army to return from the war.

War... he'd never thought that he would get to fight in one, but now... With each new dawn, he literally heard the approaching war drums of the nomads, the clang of steel, the screams of the crows and the groans of the dying people.

When Hadjar went outside to talk to Dogar, he saw an ocean of sleeping soldiers. In fact, most of them were lying there, just like he had been. They looked at the faceless stars and remembered their homes, their mothers and fathers, the people they wanted to be with when they got back...

How many of them won't come back? And even among the ones that do, how many won't want to have their own children? And those who already have them are probably praying that this will be the last war. Though they know that wars will never stop and never change, they desperately want to live in a world where their children don't have to take up arms.

Perhaps, at that moment, Hadjar finally began to understand the last words of his mother.

"Sorry," Hadjar whispered to the distant star that Queen Elizabeth had used to tell him stories about. "I can't. Forgive me..."

He slept firmly that night, without any dreams.

In the morning, feeling the cart begin to move again, he began to meditate. He needed to strengthen the foundation of his future path of cultivation as soon as possible.

The neuronet responded quickly and showed his statistics,

Name	Hadjar
Level of Cultivation	Formation stage (Seed)
Strength	2
Dexterity	2.3
Physique	2.05
Energy points	3.8

After he'd transitioned to a new level of cultivation, all his parameters had increased greatly. Not as much as the parameters of talented people would have, but enough to feel it even without confirmation from the system.

Most importantly, his energy had changed. The figures were, of course, good, but they didn't reflect the main change— the quality of it. His energy had increased in quality with each new level, with each new leap up the ladder toward the pinnacle of cultivation.

Hadjar mentally probed 'inside' himself.

If he'd previously had to draw energy from the 'nodes', then from the 'rivers', everything had changed now. Now, the power that he received from the outside world came into his nodes first, then spread through the meridians, nourishing and strengthening his body, and then accumulated in the center located somewhere in his abdomen.

There, within the endless darkness, a small crystal was now burning. Its size was no greater than a grain of wheat, however, it was much brighter than the nodes and meridians.

It was the 'Seed' of his power. The seed that he had to break into a few pieces. Only by doing so would it be possible to move on to the 'Fragment stage'.

Those who could break it, but failed to stabilize it, lost the opportunity to move to the next stage forever. And, if his Master had been right, only one out of forty thousand people would be able to break the 'Grain' and create 'Fragments.'

"It's the Fort!" The cries of the soldiers who were traveling ahead spread among the other warriors...

Nero and Hadjar leaned out of the cart.

A real fortress city towered above the sea of grass in front of them. It was no surprise that a fort with a garrison of 170,000 soldiers was enormous.

It looked like a small, circularly built town, and was situated on a hill. It was a town with high walls surrounding the central castle like two rings. The tiled roofs of all the houses, the trees in the gardens, as well as the massive divider walls connected the first and second ring of the fortress walls and formed something like sections.

If the nomads were to break through, they would get caught up in the close range fighting in the streets, where even a tenth of General Leen's soldiers could make bloody mincemeat out of them.

So why had a two million strong army arrived at such a well-fortified city? The reason was that the nomads could just go around the Fort. And if the garrison had tried to hit them with a rear assault, the horsemen would've turned the infantry into minced meat on the prairie.

The Kingdom of Lidus had no choice but to defend this Fort. The nomads had no choice but to besiege the city so as not to be surrounded during some other battle, down the line.

War wasn't such a complicated thing when soldiers forgot about the existence of the word 'choice' and realized that there was only 'must'.

"It begins," Nero said, unwittingly checking the sword in his scabbard.

Black clouds of smoke rose above the city—the cannonballs were brought out. They were being taken out and placed on the walls. The engineers reinforced the gate with iron sheets. A combustible mixture was poured into the moat. The archers were practicing, shooting arrows into the sky.

Hadjar smelled fire, iron, and fear.

These were the smells of war.

Chapter 57

It was better than settling on the borders of the Kingdom, where thieves or groups of nomads often raided. Even so, such villages still existed.

Their inhabitants either negotiated with the enemy or survived as they could because it was difficult for them to move somewhere else... Hadjar figured that the peasants simply refused to leave the habitable and cultivated land.

They set up their camp near the central gate. The Fort couldn't accommodate two million people.

The senior officers had been given permission to live within the walls of the Fort, but they had refused. They had to monitor the army and direct it. Allowing the lower-ranking officers to control the army would mean it would be less disciplined. Nobody wanted it to come to that right before the big fight.

And so, the soldiers set up their tents, following the example of General Leen.

Tired from the week-long march, the exhausted soldiers could hardly wait to reach their beds. But the officers and commanders had to go to the War Council. This time, the messenger who came to Dogar's distant camp unexpectedly invited both the senior officer and his assistant.

Hadjar barely had time to put on his impractical, bulky armor and clothes before he had to follow Dogar. Dogar had asked him to wear the armor, but Hadjar felt it was pointless. After all, the armor wouldn't protect him from a serious attack, same as how regular chainmail and leather armor wouldn't have been able to protect him. So Hadjar didn't see the point.

A lot of people had gathered in the tent, except for the people whom he'd met at the last meeting, and an outsider was there as well—the head of the Fort. He was a general too, but his status was below that of the army's own general.

He looked a little pathetic.... He didn't have the appearance of a general, as he was short, dressed in silk robes, pointy suede shoes, and had quite a prodigious gut. He looked more like an official that had been stationed in the Northern fleet for a few decades.

"Do you know lady Leen?" He asked in a mocking voice.

"General Leen," a serious, golden-haired female warrior in armor corrected him.

Several soldiers stood behind the head of the Fort. At first, Hadjar didn't understand what it was about their armor that troubled him so much and then he realized that... They were wearing new armor that glittered in the light of the torches and lamps, and had a polished, shining surface. This kind of armor was good for a parade or celebration, but not for war.

Damn it, how many years has it been since the nomads last came to the north? And why did they suddenly decide to show up now? It's clear that the south is an almost lifeless desert. All the people have been forced into the mine. And even those who weren't forced into slave labor have barely enough to survive on. They have nothing that can be robbed.

But why are they attacking us now—before the rainy season? After all, the nomads tended to invade in the early summer, when their horses could graze freely, and the ground was quite hard.

"We can position 120 of your guns here," the General moved the toy gun closer to the hill. "They will not be visible from behind the hill and we can fire two or three volleys before the battle starts."

"For the sake of two or three volleys," the head of the Fort was clearly mockingly parodying Leen's voice. Some of the senior officers took up arms. Including Dogar.

But the head of the Fort merely shook his head, "I won't even give you ten guns for that. They will remain on the walls, I won't give them to your soldiers."

"I wish to remind you, esteemed head of the Fort, that I have a direct order from the Generals. You and your entire garrison are at my complete disposal. So, my making it a request was merely a platitude." The General frowned, and it was a clear warning sign. "In reality, it's an order."

"Oh, well, if it's an order..." The general of the Fort smiled condescendingly. "Luka, tell me, what is the status of the guns?"

A man that was more reminiscent of a rat than a human came out of the shadows of the tent. He was hunched over, wearing large, expensive, and oversized clothes. One of those poor people who'd acquired money and power, but no dignity to go along with them.

"The mandatory minimum prescribed by the Generals is up on the walls. Six hundred, twenty-four guns."

He couldn't even pronounce numbers properly.

"Can we remove them?" The head of the Fort asked smugly, already knowing the answer.

"No, General," the rat-man bowed.

"It turns out we can't do it," the Fort's commander repeated, turning to Leen.

"I don't want your primary weapons," the General, despite the fact that she had obviously been made fun of, did not lose her temper. She was apparently used to being in similar situations. "You must keep at least four hundred spare units of the weapons in reserve, according to the law, in case your primary weapons get destroyed. You'll give me a hundred and twenty of them. That is a direct order."

"A direct order," the official sighed sadly. "Luka, let's help this beautiful lady out. Give her one hundred and twenty cannons from our stock."

"I beg your pardon, General," the servant, or maybe even the lover of the fort commander, bent his back again as he bowed low. "But according to our recent estimates, there are only... four spare cannons in our inventory."

General Leen exhaled and clenched her fist.

"Where are your weapons, Fort commander?" She snarled.

"Oh, well, I don't even know," the fat man leaned on the table where the map had been laid out and started to drum his fingers against it. They were topped with gold rings that had expensive, precious stones in them. There were bracelets on his wrists that were even more expensive and conspicuous. "Where are our cannons? What a nuisance. Maybe someone has sold them!"

The senior officers looked at each other and each of them was ready to gut this boar. He was mocking them! Without any fear at all, he was actually mocking them—the commanders of an army that had two million soldiers. He must have felt he was untouchable, to allow himself to ridicule such powerful people.

"We have had no war for a hundred years, General Leen," the official blew on his nails and then wiped them on his gold and brocade clothes. "The royal treasury probably allocated insufficient funds to our Fort, so the weapons fell into disrepair. I ask them to increase our allowance every month. Awful. It's truly awful, General Leen. But, as you can plainly see, I can't give you any cannons. However official and direct your order might be."

General Leen banged her fist on the table.

"Are you out of your mind, Sirius?" Her gaze made even Hadjar feel uneasy. "Have you truly grown so insolent? I'll put you on trial."

"Of course you will," the official nodded. "But before you do that, you'll be fighting against the nomads for a couple of months, sitting under my walls, eating my food, and under the protection of my people. Then you'll judge me. But think twice about that... There might be no provisions for you in my stocks. Or arrows, medicine, or anything else, really."

"Are you threatening me, Sirius? Shall I grab my spear?"

"Of course, my dear Leen. Don't delay at all, take up your famous Moonbeam and stick my head on it, then put it in the center of your camp, as you love to do. Then you yourself will have to explain to the tribunal why, during a time of war, you murdered a fellow general."

Despite his pitiful appearance, during this diatribe, the fat man's gaze was full of steel and self-confidence. Maybe, long ago, he'd led hundreds of thousands of soldiers, but during the years he'd spent in warmth and comfort, he'd gotten fat and insolent.

"Mark my words, Sirius, —I won't forget this."

"Will the Moon General herself remember me and even think about me? Gods, I haven't wasted my life."

"Get out."

"My respects," the official bowed.

Before leaving the tent, he turned and smiled.

"These walls are impregnable, my dear. For thousands of years, no enemy has breached them. What can these savages do? Nothing! You'd better come visit us—we'll be having a feast soon. It's for my birthday party. I'm inviting you and all of your soldiers! The more the merrier. Besides, we've recently built a new brothel..."

"I thought I ordered you to get out. Or are you challenging my direct order?"

"No, my General," the official said. "I just suggested that we might want to have a good time and relax—the nomads won't be coming here. By the way, a circus has just arrived. They have such funny freaks there."

Giggling, General Sirius left the tent. The garrison soldiers, urged on by Dogar's menacing gaze, followed after him.

The General slapped the table and sank heavily into her chair.

"Without the cannons, our plan with the hill is doomed to failure," the chief engineer removed the toy cannon from the map. "We must invent something new. Perhaps we'll be able to take some gunpowder from them..."

"You still don't understand, Commander Tuur," the General smoothed her hair and pulled herself together. "That idiot has sold everything he could. There are no stocks left in the Fort. And I can't take even an arrowhead from his own inventory. The charter doesn't allow it, and he knows that. He's using it to thwart us."

"Damned politics," Lian, the commander of the archers, cursed.

"Damned greed," Helion corrected her.

"And yet, Sirius' words have a grain of reason to them," the General said, leaning above the map. "There has been no war in the north for thousands of years. Why are the nomads coming now and why are they coming here? Tim, what do your scouts report?"

"The squads I've sent out along the border are sending regular reports," the spymaster said. "As for the scouts that I sent to the rear... No one has returned or sent any messages yet."

Everyone in the tent became gloomy. That was bad news. Very bad news.

"There are mountains there, my General," Tuur explained, moving the pointer. "My people don't know that area very well. In addition, there are many nomad patrols, and the wind and rain have ruined all the roads. I'm afraid my scouts are useless there. It's a waste of forces and resources. We'll have to act at random."

"At random, you say," the General repeated, casting a meaningful look around at everyone present, settling her gaze on...

"Officer Hadjar!"

"Yes, my General!" Hadjar punched his chest and bowed.

"You said that you lived in a mountain village and it rained a lot."

"Yes, my General."

"And that you lived in the north..."

"Yes, my General."

Leen sighed and pointed to the Blue Wind ridge.

"Do you know that territory?"

Hadjar looked at the map and requested a detailed description of the ridge and its terrain from the neuronet database. Fortunately, there had been enough scrolls with information about the area in the Palace. And Hadjar had managed to see most of them, which was quite enough for the neural network.

"Yes, my General," he answered again.

"Then, Senior Officer Dogar, allow me to use your assistant."

"Yes, sir," Dogar saluted immediately.

"Officer," the General turned back to Hadjar. "How many people will you need?"

"Only one."

"One?!" The spymaster snorted. "A lot of my people are dying there, and you want us to send only two of you to the ridge?"

"With all due respect, Senior Officer, they are dying because there are too many of them. In the mountains, people are strangers. Out there, even one man can be easily seen, not to mention a whole detachment. Two men have more of a chance than twenty men."

"Okay," the General nodded and raised her hand, interrupting Commander Tim. "Take as much food as you need and hit the road."

"When do we leave, my General?"

"Right now, Officer Hadjar. We're pressed for time. As far as I can see, your wounds have already healed."

Hadjar nodded.

"This is your mission, Officer," the General took the pointer. "You'll go along the ridge and find the nomads' camp. We need information about their overall numbers, readiness for battle, how many riders and infantry they have. We also need an estimate on the approximate stages of their Commanders as well as any elite units you might encounter. Artifacts as well, if you see any. In general, we need all the information about the enemy you can get us."

"I understand, my General. May I leave?"

"You may."

Hadjar turned on his heels and walked out.

General Leen shouted: "Good luck, Officer Hadjar! We're counting on you!"

We're counting on you...

Nero is unlikely to be delighted with this... 'We're counting on you '.

Chapter 58

"Let's go to a brothel, Nero. Let's have fun with a couple of girls, Nero. Let's get drunk, Nero. Let's go to the freak show, Nero. No! Damn it! He's cuddling up to me and saying—let's go toward the enemy, Nero. Fuck you, Hadj. I'll be dying soon, and I've never slept with twins yet!"

Nero kept grumbling but still carried the bag

that had the supplies they'd obtained and a communication artifact inside it. It looked like a raven figurine, covered in mystical runes and drawings. Hadjar couldn't understand the secrets that those symbols held, but, on the other hand, he now knew how to send messages over long distances.

The wooden 'raven' artifact worked like a walkie-talkie.

Object	A communication artifact
Range	~ 120km

"You wanted adventure, didn't you?" Hadjar shrugged.

They were walking out of the camp and toward the forest, so there was no need for secrecy. When they were outside the perimeter, at the border, then they would have to be alert. Who knew how many scouts the nomads had already sent out? They might have been scouring the woods at that exact moment, doing exactly the same kind of work that Hadjar was doing.

"Adventure, even a demon spawn is fine, but not a trip to my own execution!"

"Everything will be fine, Nero."

"Of course, I don't even doubt it!" The guy snapped, adjusting his bale. "I'm unhappy because I've found out which brothels have twins in them and you've taken me away from those."

"Well, maybe you'll end up liking a nomad girl."

"A savage?" Suddenly, Nero stopped and thought about it, remembering something. "Demons and gods, I've never been with a savage!"

He overtook Hadjar and shouted over his shoulder, "Hurry up, Hadj!"

Hadjar smiled. Nero could complain as much as he wanted, but in fact, he was glad to be doing the investigation. He was just 'grumbling' for decency's sake. But in reality, both of them, like madmen, had greeted the new adventure with smiles.

As they walked toward the forest, they discussed the advantages of the savage girls and their trained bodies over soft, untrained bodies. Nero came to the conclusion that he had to bring Hadjar to a brothel. His friend just shrugged, adjusting his bag.

Back at the 'warehouse', they'd taken enough food for a week. Thanks to Nero's impudence and talkativeness, they'd also gotten several explosive shells, some combustible mixture, and some other things as well. As a result, they looked more like saboteurs than scouts. Even if they were both more or less ordinary foot soldiers, just part of Dogar's elite unit.

When they reached the forest, they tied down and adjusted their bales so that they were like backpacks. They smeared themselves with clay, trying to get rid of the smell of sweat and smoke that had gotten stuck to them back in the camp.

Like Hadjar, Nero had replaced his boots with knitted bast shoes. They wrapped them in a cloth, smeared them with the same clay and immediately shook them vigorously. This was enough to tone down the smell and not cover the 'shoes' with a crust that would crack and rustle as they walked.

Then the friends firmly strapped down anything that could make any sounds and, making sure both of them could understand each other's signals, moved into the forest.

It met them with the cries of birds, the rustling of leaves, and the distant noises of various animals. The forest had dense foliage and was very dark as a result. It was also larger than the one near Spring Town.

Who in their right mind, except for them, would even go into the border forest? Any visitors would probably be killed by an animal, a nomad, or a bandit.

The tree crowns were not as thick as they'd expected, letting in enough light to keep their eyes from straining. Pillars of light caressed the huge tree trunks, making them shine with an almost coppery sheen.

Their feet would sink into the soft, wet moss slightly as they walked as if they were walking across an expensive carpet, and not on the ground.

The smell of the swamp that was coming from the west was slightly unnerving, but they got used to it quickly.

"Watch. Two eyes. Four sides." Hadjar signaled, warning his comrade to be careful.

"Prey. Alive." Nero signaled.

Hadjar thought. Did they need a so-called 'tongue', a person who would tell them something about the nomads? Hadjar didn't know the savage language, and he doubted that Nero knew it.

It was worth checking to make sure.

He realized that he didn't know the right sign. The sign language of Robin and the other hunters from the Valley of Stream village was suitable for the pursuit of an animal, but not a human. This language had no signs necessary for explaining things in such a situation.

After thinking about it, Hadjar showed his tongue hanging out and pointed at Nero.

It took Nero only a few seconds to understand what his friend was asking him about.

He showed him the sign for "No."

As expected, Nero also didn't know the savage language. They didn't even have just one, but a hundred different dialects. There were so many tribes in the southeastern steppes that it would've been easier to hang themselves than to try and count them all. For example, there was the D'Zah'nura-Fura-Lura-Gura-Zumra tribe...

Something like that.

The names tended to be a real tongue twister.

"Prey. Dead." Hadjar signaled.

For the next ten hours, they moved through the forest quietly. Every time they saw an animal, even if it was weak and old, clearly easy prey, they didn't hunt it.

This time, they'd come to the forest seeking other prey. The beasts' paths were just a signal that they needed to change direction. Alas, even after spending so long searching, they didn't find a single hint of other people in the forest.

By evening, they'd managed to cover quite a decent distance. Before they tied themselves to the upper branches of a tree, they climbed to the top to assess the situation.

The sun was already moving to the west, trying to disappear into the Sea of Dreams. This sea was larger than the total size of all the oceans back on Earth, according to the map South Wind had shown him. One of those big organizations that controlled several empires was beyond it.

But who was controlling Darnassus?

Such thoughts disappeared from his mind as soon as Hadjar spotted the mountain range. He looked like a captive beast beneath the scarlet gold sky, ready to rise above the ground and tear the heavens apart at any moment.

The mountains seemed so close that one could think that they were only a day's ride away.

Hadjar knew that they had to keep going for at least two more days. It was just an optical illusion. The bigger the mountain was, the closer it seemed, no matter how odd that sounded.

They fell asleep quickly, having tied themselves to some branches for the night. They didn't need to set up a watch rotation. Their senses were so developed at the Formation stage that they would wake up if someone else was nearby.

In the morning, they had to cover themselves with dirt again. It couldn't serve as a substitute for a shower, as the amount of dirt on their bodies only increased, but at least the smell of sweat gradually disappeared.

Hiding among the elusive shadows for four hours, they moved through the woods. A normal scout most likely only moved at night, but Hadjar didn't want to risk it. There were too many predators prowling in the night, both bipeds and quadrupeds, that could jeopardize the mission.

Their goal wasn't to catch a 'spy' (whom they would not even have been able to deliver back to the camp), but to count the enemy troops.

Man plans and the gods laugh.

They noticed a group of nomads at the foot of the mountains by the end of the second day, around sunset. It was difficult to determine whether they were lookouts or 'partners of fate', as they themselves were.

Hadjar saw real savages for the first time in his life. They looked like ordinary, heavily tanned, black-haired people. They were tall men with flat noses and massive lower jaws. Their hair had been tied into several braids decorated with colorful beads. The color and number of the beads varied depending on their rank.

Their women were petite, coming up to just above Hadjar's lower ribs. They were all dressed in makeshift jackets and pants made from the hides and skins of animals. The savages had slanted eyes, high foreheads, and bronze skin, probably because it had been exposed to the sun of the steppes a lot.

"Loot", Hadjar gave the signal to Nero and began sneaking to get into position.

They immediately hid in the nearest ditch. Nero pulled out his pocket spyglass, covered the lens with his palm (to avoid any reflected sunlight possibly giving them away), and stared.

"They are weak," he signaled after a while. "Perhaps at the level of 'Awakening of Power'. It was a good idea to equate human stages to animal stages. At least now the language of the hunters could help them out a little.

'Awakening of Power' was equal to the human level of the 'Bodily Nodes'. What did nine practitioners of the 'Bodily Nodes' level mean to two people at the 'Formation' level? It was akin to a handful of ants getting in their way.

"Hunt", Hadjar showed.

"Why?"

"We're going back. Our house. Way. Prey is coming. It's bad."

Nero thought on those signals for a moment and then nodded. It was best not to leave any enemy forces behind them, even weak ones such as this.

"We're surrounding," Hadjar gestured. "On my signal. Bird's cry"

They went in different directions. Hiding in the bushes like predators, they circled around the enemy squad. When the moment was right, Hadjar imitated a bird call, drew his blade, and rushed in to attack.

Chapter 59

Hadjar had decided to go around the nomads and attack them only after making sure the wind would be blowing toward him. He did this out of habit, not because he was afraid that the barbarians had a sense of smell as good as animals'. All professional hunters used the wind to cover up their scent because then the prey was less likely to escape.

Admittedly, practitioners at the 'Bodily Nodes' level hardly had any chance to begin with.

Hadjar quickly and silently dealt with the man walking at the back of their camp. He came out of the bushes as gracefully and silently as an owl hunting for a vole. Hadjar gripped the nomad's mouth and nose and slashed his knife across the man's throat, immediately tilting his head forward and slightly lowering the body.

The nomad didn't get a chance to cry out or make any noise at all. The Prince had made sure to not let the body fall or any blood gush out and alert the others.

Hadjar had cut through the man's aorta, muscles, and the vertebrae. It was as easy as a knife going through butter with his strength.

Gently placing the body down on the ground, Hadjar drew out his sword. He was sneaking up to the girl with the whip. A steel string had been inserted into the handle of the branching whip. It certainly wasn't used to herd cattle. It would be possible to remove several layers of skin with just one its strikes.

Hadjar knew this weapon well— he'd been beaten with such a whip a couple of times in the dungeon. The scars left by those lashes were so deep that, even after his rebirth, they could still be seen on his back.

Hadjar moved noiselessly, almost like a shadow, as he moved away from the cover of the tree. But, alas, bad luck can counter even the greatest skill.

The nomad turned around.

Maybe she'd felt something or she'd wanted to check and make sure there was a fellow nomad warrior at her back. Maybe... maybe she'd just turned around.

Her amazing, black eyes met the clear and blue eyes of Hadjar.

She was beautiful enough to make a man's heart beat faster, but not enough to delay Hadjar's sword. His attack was swift and brutal.

As she fell, she couldn't understand what had happened, and then the darkness swept over her...

Hadjar didn't stop. He'd killed the nomad messily, making a lot of noise in the process, and the remaining seven turned toward the sound. They drew their curved swords as they walked, but it was too late. Their opponent already had his sword out. Even if the weapon had still been in its scabbard, they still wouldn't have had a chance.

Hadjar moved quickly. He seemed like a blur to his foes who were only at the Bodily Rivers. They barely noticed the flashes of metal and the two blue eyes peeking out of the darkness.

Hadjar swung his blade, slicing a nomad's hand off, and immediately jumped to the side. Two arrows pierced through the spot where Hadjar had been standing moments ago. But since he was now gone, the arrows flew further until they hit the nomad who was screaming in pain. Still holding his bleeding stump, he fell to the ground. Twitching and choking on his blood, he couldn't decide what he should grab first—the arrows or the stump.

Hadjar took in this scene only out of the corner of his eye.

His sword continued its bloody dance.

Moving almost like a child trying to spin around to get a rush, Hadjar blocked two arrows and then plunged the blade into the belly of his enemy. He could no longer make out any faces or the gender of their prey. Right now, everything was simple in his world—he had an enemy in front of him and he had his sword: either he would kill them all or he would be killed.

Turning his blade, Hadjar pushed the body it had been stuck in away with his foot. The nomad waved his hands as he fell, trying to somehow keep his entrails from falling out. He failed.

Only six enemies were left. Two archers that had moved back a little and four swordfighters. Their short, curved swords were shining with a predatory glow. But they all paled in comparison to the majestic radiance of Hadjar's sword.

While the sword wielders tried to surround Hadjar, the archers were already pulling the strings on their bows back. They felt the wind and the rustle of the grass and aimed without looking. Hadjar was moving so quickly that it was almost impossible to see him. So, they were going to shoot not where their opponent was, but where he seemed like he was going to be.

The sound of the bowstring was heard and four arrows... Flew into the bushes.

Hadjar didn't even flinch, but two of the nomads were already collapsing, dropping their swords as the life left their eyes.

A ghostly strike produced by his blade had cut through his opponents. They couldn't believe what had happened—they had been at a distance of twelve steps from the enemy! Despite that, his attack had still reached them.

Their numb legs remained standing. The rest of their bodies slid to the ground with horrific slowness. They didn't die immediately and still had time to experience horror and panic. They didn't feel pain. Their lives ended too quickly to feel any.

Hadjar turned his back to the archers. They couldn't believe their luck as they pulled back the bowstrings once again.

In the next moment, they fell to the ground in chunks, as if torn apart by a bear that had been forcibly woken up during winter. Nero, holding his massive, five-foot sword, came out from behind the bushes. He looked like a bloody beast while in battle, the hunger for slaughter clear in his gaze.

"They're mine," he said as he approached his friend.

"As you wish," Hadjar shrugged.

He cleaned all the blood on his sword with a single movement and sheathed it once again.

With only one slash, Nero sent two nomads to the vast prairie of their ancestors, where the eternal feast and hunt awaited them. The rest of their group were already there, ready to meet them.

The fight hadn't taken ten seconds. Everything ended almost silently and almost too quickly. Only some birds made noise, leaving their trees and flying away from the danger.

"You know, back when you talked about the savages, I'd thought you were hinting at taking them to bed," Nero sighed, cleaning his sword and putting it back into its scabbard.

Ten bodies lay among the trees. The blood flowing downhill merged into a thin stream. Hadjar stared at them and rubbed the bridge of his nose. He'd already killed women before. They had been attacking his mother. And these women...

Hadjar looked at them.

How many mothers and children would've been killed by these women if they had managed to go through the Fort and into the country? There is no difference between the genders in this world if one disregards what's in people's pants.

"What took you so long?" Hadjar asked as he leaned over the first victim.

He grabbed the man's pack and dumped the contents on the ground.

"I was trying to come up with a way to capture those female archers."

"Why, we still don't know the language, right?"

"I wasn't going to talk to them," Nero shrugged. "Oh, fine, stop looking at me like that. I just figured that, if you and I could do some pantomime, we could communicate with them. I don't know, they could've drawn something on the ground for us."

Hadjar thought about it and decided that his companion was right, they'd rushed things a bit. Considering the fact that they were not very experienced in intelligence gathering, it was understandable. It was difficult to think about every contingency and to predict everything without any prior training.

It's too late to implement his good idea now. The savages have been killed. If we meet anyone else, we'll try to interrogate them.

Suddenly, Hadjar staggered back as if a snake had bit him. Although, if there had been any ordinary snakes around here, they would've fled from a practitioner of the Formation Stage.

"What's up?" Nero walked over. He hadn't found anything unusual in the packs he'd inspected. Two metal collars with mystical inscriptions were lying on the ground in front of Hadjar. He'd already seen these kinds of collars before. He hadn't only seen them, but had worn one for five years.

"Damn it," he said. "They're not scouts."

"Definitely a strange decoration… Would people even buy this sort of thing?" Nero picked up one of the items from the ground.

"It's not an ornament," Hadjar shook his head. "It's a slave collar. It completely cuts off all the energy in a person's body and makes a mere mortal out of even the strongest practitioner."

"Demons and gods!" Nero dropped the 'decoration' as if he'd been holding burning hot metal.

Such devices were one of the worst nightmares of any practitioner. They took away their two most important possessions—their freedom and strength.

"Why do the nomad scouts need these…" Nero carefully put the collars back into the pack. "Artifacts?"

"They must've been capturing prisoners from the nearest villages."

"Do you think so? There should be some patrols from the garrison walking around. It's unlikely that even a hundred savages would be able to defeat one such patrol."

"You haven't met the head of the Fort. I'm sure there are no patrols. Anyway, I seriously doubt that the garrison mentioned in the documents exists. There's probably less than half that number stationed in the Fort."

"Do you think they share the salaries of the non-existent soldiers?"

"I'm sure of it," Hadjar nodded.

"Damn officials," Nero cursed. "My father always said that they cause more harm than good."

Hadjar considered the situation.

Why do the nomads need slaves? It would be understandable if the scouts were trying to capture other scouts or soldiers. But they're clearly killing them instead, on the spot... None ever get taken back to camp.

It turns out that the savages are hunting ordinary people and, at the same time, avoiding the notice of the Lidus army. Only people who are up to something and trying to conceal it would behave like that. But what could ordinary, seasonal bandits be hiding, even if they're wandering around in large groups?

"I don't like this at all."

"Me neither," Nero pulled out a leather pouch he'd found.

He untied the ribbons holding it closed and pulled out a few beautiful coins made from a green metal. They had interesting patterns on them and a square hole in the middle.

"The nomads have no currency," Hadjar said thoughtfully, examining the coins. "Especially such deftly forged coinage."

"Take into account the fact that this is money from the Lascan Empire," Nero supplied. "My father showed it to me once".

Hadjar and Nero looked at each other. Where had the simple savages found coins from a country that was at war with the Darnassus Empire?

"Damn it!" They said in chorus.

"We've got to hurry, buddy. Something tells me you and I are in a bit of trouble." Nero added

"We're in big trouble," Hadjar nodded.

They threw the bodies into a ditch, covered them with branches, took the green coins, and then went into the mountains.

Something felt off about this situation; the first peals of thunder were heard from the east. The seasonal rains had begun.

Chapter 60

Two days later, fighting against the wind that kept growing stronger, Hadjar and Nero were climbing up a cliff. The wind tried to tear off their cloaks. They looked like tiny bugs crawling across an endless, gray space.

There was a deep abyss underneath them. It was covered with a carpet of green treetops.

Lightning flashed. There was a crash that sounded like the very sky was being rent apart. Hadjar clung to the cliff and held his breath. A huge cobblestone tumbled down and passed near him.

Avoiding the mountain paths, he and Nero had decided to climb up a precipice. For an ordinary person, this might've been an impossible task, but it wasn't difficult for them. Their fingers easily found even the thinnest cracks and clung to them like a steel vise.

In just three hours, despite the rainstorm, among the flashes of draconic shapes made up of white lightning, they managed to climb almost three miles— which was a monstrous distance for a mortal's standards, but an ordinary, everyday bit of exercise for practitioners at the 'Formation' level. Their bodies were mighty and their energy was strong.

After climbing up the cliff, they threw their hoods over their heads. Not because of the rain, but in order to blend in with the cliff's surface.

The top of the cliff was twelve miles away, but the nomads would hardly have climbed all the way up there. They were most likely on the plateau—an oasis in the country of solid stone.

The two men crawled there silently. A few hours later, they reached the slopes. On the way to the plateau, they'd noticed several large nomad outposts. Too large.

When they reached one of the ridge peaks, near the plateau, they saw a huge plain covered with grass and a few low trees. It was difficult to understand what was going on below them because of the noise the rain and storm were making.

Fortunately, they'd brought some useful things with them from the camp.

Nero took out a telescope from his pocket and, covering it with a hand, studied everything intently. After a flash of lightning illuminated everything, he whispered, cursing in surprise. "Demons and gods… What the hell?"

Nero handed the telescope to his friend.

Hadjar pressed it to his right eye and peered through the dull, cracked glass.

Lightning flashed and Hadjar cursed as well.

There, on the plateau, among the fires, was not only a sea of grass but also of herds, horses, and tents. Hundreds, thousands, probably a hundred thousand!

"How many nomads are they expecting?" Nero asked, taking the telescope back and inspecting the darkness.

"Three hundred thousand. Maybe even half a million."

Nero swore.

"I wonder what they'll say about the five fucking million down below."

Right now, on the plateau, according to their most modest estimates, there was an army of at least four and a half million people. And at least one-tenth of them were horse archers.

Damn it. Damn it.

He decided to use the neuronet:

Analysis of the structure underway...	The calculation in progress... The calculation is finished...
The total number, with a margin of error at 0.05%	4,127,203 objects are present which are comparable to the host in their structure

Never before had isolated nomadic tribes gathered into such an enormous horde. They'd usually sent around two hundred thousand at most, rarely more. Lidus had always sent a numerically superior army in response, inflicting a crushing defeat on the enemy and making them hesitate to come back for at least five years.

But now... More than four million nomad fighters were there. With four hundred thousand horse archers. They'd surely sweep away the army of General Leen as an avalanche sweeps away a young tree!

"We have to report this right away!"

Hadjar got the communication artifact—a wooden raven—out of his pack. He took hold of it, closed his eyes, and then began activating the figurine with his thoughts and power. It felt like a bundle of energy from which a ghostly thread was stretching out and into the distance. Hadjar had almost activated the artifact when Nero snatched it from his hands.

"Look over there," he gave Hadjar the telescope and indicated where he should look.

Hadjar peered into the darkness. There was a meeting going on near the biggest tent. Judging by the number of beads everyone had and their colors, the tribal leaders had gathered there. About twenty of them were present, maybe a few more. His friend had been right, the armies of the whole steppe had been brought here.

The most amazing thing was that the leaders were sitting on stones and smoking pipes while listening to a person. He was a tall man with a short, gray beard, dressed not in leather armor, but in simple, black robes that had been fastened with a silk belt. He looked calm and confident and was speaking a language that Hadjar was unfamiliar with.

Alas, the neuronet couldn't translate it, because no information about this language had been stored in the database.

The oddity wasn't so much in the man's clothes as it was in his aura that Hadjar could feel even at such a great distance.

"He's clearly stronger than a Heaven Soldier," Hadjar whispered, fearing that, even while being a few kilometers away, this cultivator could still hear him.

"A Spirit Knight," Nero slid down the stone on which they were lying. "An accursed Spirit Knight. Of all the rotten luck..."

After taking another look, Hadjar noticed a medallion on the cultivator's chest. It was made of jade and amber and had the same patterns on it as the coins had.

"Look. Behind their tent."

Hadjar looked closely and his mouth opened in surprise. Among the hastily constructed enclosures he saw... Thousands of trebuchets, hundreds of cannons, several siege towers and... Some monsters that had been trapped in cages. Monsters whose power was clearly not inferior to an Emerald Wolf's.

Analysis of the object is underway...	The object is of an unknown structure
The average indicators	
Level of cultivation	Awakening of the Mind (8th step)
Strength	2
Dexterity	3
Physique	2.8
Energy points	1.5

"This isn't a nomad raid..." Following the example of his friend, Hadjar also slid down the stone.

They lay in a small niche, hidden from everyone's gaze. Only the indifferent heavens, which were black, turbulent, and full of fire dragons could see them now. With a roar, the fire dragons dived down toward the ground but melted halfway.

"Darnassus and Lascan are at war," Nero took the telescope back and put it in his pocket. "The Solar Ore in our mines isn't such a special material by Imperial standards. To us, its value is enormous, but to them, it's the same as iron is to the smaller kingdoms. A good but quite ordinary ore."

"But in any war," Hadjar said, "victory consists of many small details, not just one big battle."

They looked at each other and nodded—they'd come to the same, simplest, and most logical conclusion.

The Lascanians had united the nomads. Maybe they'd bribed them, threatened them, promised them new lands, or something else. It didn't matter how they'd done it. The fact they were going to bring this horde to the land of Lidus was the important thing. They wanted to cut off the supply of Solar Ore to the Empire.

"How long would it take the legion to come here?" Nero asked.

"It won't," Hadjar shook his head. "If Lascan had wanted to, they could've already sent their army here. But they won't do that because it'll cause a chain reaction which will lead to a decisive battle. How long have they been fighting for?"

"About half a century."

"Exactly. And in all that time, they've only had small, by their standards, clashes, and sieges. There's been no large scale battle. And no one will initiate one without being completely confident in their total victory."

"I understand," Nero nodded. "If one of them loses such a battle, they'll lose the whole country. So, they want to weaken their enemy by any means. Alas, those same means will be the ruin of our kingdom."

Hadjar sighed. Nero was right, Lascan was going to crush Lidus. What is a small kingdom to one of the empires? No more than a provincial village. And when one such village suddenly began mining the Solar Ore which their opponent could use in battle…

"That's why all the scouts have been slaughtered. And that's why they've settled here on the ridge—it's almost impossible to find them here."

"Yeah. If it hadn't been for you, Hadj, no one could've ever located them."

And it was only thanks to the neural network that it had been possible to map out a route by which they were able to sneak onto the plateau unnoticed.

"Well, let's sum up," Hadjar began to tick off on his fingers. "There are four or five million savages armed to the teeth on this plateau—they have guns, trebuchets, and even some monsters."

"But they would need to know how to use the cannons and trebuchets. The savages have never had such weapons…"

"I'm sure you aren't the only one who thought about this," Hadjar interrupted his friend. "The Lascanians must have trained the nomads. Look at this horde—they've been gathering it together for many years."

Nero swore. He pulled out the telescope and crawled up the stone again.

"What kind of monsters are there?" He asked.

"I have no idea," Hadjar bent another finger. "We can't send a message to the camp—the Spirit Knight will surely feel it."

"Yeah. That's probably how they found the previous scouts. By tracking the damn signal."

It was like a magical radar built into the enemy cultivator's head.

Hadjar continued, "So, they have almost double our numbers. Their cavalry is six times more numerous than ours."

"And their archers are both better and more numerous," Nero

reminded him. "The nomad children are born with bows in their hands."

"And with a saddle between their legs," Hadjar agreed.

"You didn't give me a chance to see what was between their legs."

The friends smiled rather nervously at each other.

"Are you thinking the same thing I am, Hadj?"

"I'm afraid so, yes," Hadjar sighed, also climbing onto the rock. "We'll most likely die in the process."

"Well, we'll certainly die if this mob attacks the fort and we're there."

They looked at each other, then turned toward their packs that had been filled with explosives.

Lightning flashed and outlined the silhouettes of two bugs crawling onto the plateau. These bugs were preparing to try and stop a few million opponents.

Chapter 61

 Shrouded in shadows, the two infantrymen who had at first become scouts, and were now saboteurs, crawled around the camp. Every now and then, they would freeze in the tall grass, waiting for the flashes of lightning. The period of illumination they provided was enough for them to study the nomads in detail.

They were relaxed and half-drunk. Some were shouting and some were laughing. In the glow of the fires, silhouettes of men and women merged in ecstasy could be seen. The savages were celebrating the upcoming battle and death.

They passed around skins filled with strong koumiss. The women rode the men wildly. The men caressed the women's small, firm breasts. The camp looked more like an orgy than a military fortification. But such was these people's tradition and Hadjar didn't condemn them for it. Regardless of their debauchery, they were worthy warriors and, in the upcoming battle, they would surely be fierce opponents.

Judging by the expression on Nero's face, he wanted to join the fun.

"Be careful," Hadjar signaled quickly.

And immediately received an answer. "I know."

Reluctantly tearing their eyes off of one of the fires, where the people were lying on the ground in a tightly packed group, looking like a coiled snake, they moved on.

Because the mighty foreigner was there, as well as a large number of guard posts, the nomads had lost all of their vigilance. Wine had intoxicated them and lust had rendered them unable to reason. They greeted every lightning bolt with loud shouts, and it responded with a thunderous roar.

In the rain and mud, Nero and Hadjar crawled toward the trebuchets and cannons.

They were especially careful when skirting the central tent. It was almost half a kilometer away from them, but who knew what the Spirit Knight was capable of. They certainly didn't want to find out.

A few hours later, they were near the pens. The horses were grazing peacefully. A few nomads hurried to cover stacks of mowed grass with some cloth. They didn't want the future food of their horses to get wet and rotten. The rains would really delay them, but not for long. It wouldn't be nearly enough time for the army to get ready for their arrival.

"Food." Nero pointed at the haystacks.

Hadjar didn't understand at first, but then smiled murderously. They could remove the tarp. It wouldn't do much harm since there were thousands of haystacks there. But at least they could inconvenience the enemy.

Coming up to the nearest stack, Hadjar was about to slit a working nomad's throat when Nero stopped him.

He pointed toward the central tent and signaled quickly. "The strong beast."

Hadjar nodded and stowed the dagger. Could the Spirit Knight feel someone's death? He didn't want to risk it.

Waiting until the nomad left, they removed the tarp. The ten-foot stack was now exposed to the rain, so they went further into the darkness. They moved slowly as they were removing the tarps and, after the tenth stack was uncovered, both of them came to the conclusion that this was a useless exercise.

"Too long. Complicated. No time." Nero showed.

"Another way. Trap."

Hadjar pointed at the explosives, then the gunpowder, and finally at the rain which seemed to be drenching everything. Gunpowder meant combustible mixtures. Such substances burnt even in water. They'd cover water with a thin pellicle and would burn so hot that a man's skin would melt right off.

Hadjar and Nero were faced with a choice—to burn a certain part of the haystacks or to undermine most of the cannons.

While hiding in the ravine, they thought over the situation.

The cannons could shoot at a long distance and every shot that hit the ranks of their soldiers would end hundreds of lives. But, on the other hand, they were absolutely useless in a melee, unlike the horse riders, who were able to spend hours circling around the flank, showering enemy fighters with well-aimed arrows.

Exchanging glances, they nodded and went toward the cannons, which were a little further away and were being guarded quite vigilantly.

Pointing to a part of the cliff, Nero 'walked' with his fingers. He was suggesting they climb up and skirt the guards on the mountain. This way, they would remain unnoticed and wouldn't have to cut the nomads' throats. They had to keep the Lascanian and his power in mind, after all.

Hadjar nodded. They began to climb the cliff again. But this time, the task was more complicated. If they had been crawling vertically before, now they were moving horizontally.

They had to drag themselves along like snails. It turned out to be much harder to pull off.

Perhaps that's why Hadjar nearly fell when he heard a female voice from below. "Hey! Help me!"

The voice spoke Lidish without a single trace of a savage accent.

Hadjar looked down, and, during the next flash of lightning, saw hundreds of crowded cages. The wet, weakened people stood there, leaning against each other and shivering from the cold.

Damn, there was probably at least ten thousand of them in those cages!

What was even stranger was that the cage from which the female voice had come stood close to the rock and about thirty meters away from the others. There was only one girl in it.

Isolated, lonely...

Hadjar swore, noticing that Nero was already going down. His friend couldn't leave a lady in trouble. The sun was more likely to rise in the west, rivers to flow backward, or cherries to blossom in winter.

Nero sometimes demonstrated the qualities of an absolute imbecile.

Hadjar hurried after him and soon they were back on the ground.

"Are you crazy?" Hadjar hissed.

"I won't leave a lady to the mercy of these savages."

Nero went to the cage and, taking something out of his pocket, began to pick the lock.

"Hurry up," the voice urged. "The patrol will pass by here soon."

After a few moments, there was a muffled click, the cage opened, and the girl came out. Lightning flashed and they managed to see her appearance. She was short, had an hourglass figure with a very thin waist, beautiful legs, a high forehead, thick, black hair, and dark, olive skin.

Name	???
Level of cultivation	Formation (Seed)
Strength	1.6
Dexterity	1.7
Physique	1,3
Energy Points	7.2

Wait, she has how many energy points? What!

Hadjar grabbed for his dagger, but Nero had already brought his blade down to the girl's throat.

"Make a sound, savage," he hissed through his teeth, "and I'll send you to the endless steppe."

"It's a plain, ignoramus," the girl replied calmly. "They believe in the endless plain, not a steppe. Which one of us is the savage, I wonder..."

"It's a trap, Nero," Hadjar hissed. "Knock her out and let's go."

"Gods, you are both idiots!" She rolled her eyes and looked far too calm, as if a sharp blade wasn't pressed against her delicate neck. "I'm not a nomad."

"You sure seem to be one," Nero looked at her pointedly.

"I'm from Underworld City."

"Never heard of it."

"It's in the Sea of Sands."

"What nonsense," Nero snorted, and had already raised his fist, but then Hadjar stopped him.

"Wait," he whispered and took the seal out of his pocket. The one that South Wind had left him before his death.

Lightning flashed again and the girl showed emotion for the first time. She jerked back and gasped.

"Where did you get the Master's seal?"

Hadjar cursed foully and put the seal back.

"Put the dagger away, Nero."

"Maybe it would be better to..."

"Put it away, I said," Hadjar closed the cage carefully and the three of them dove into darkness.

Hiding under a rock canopy, Nero untied the rope binding the girl's hands and reached for her neck.

The girl recoiled.

"The collar has been fastened to my neck with the Lascanian's power. If you take it off, we're all dead. He'll know about it immediately."

Nero shrugged and went over to Hadjar, who was on watch, peering into the boundless darkness. How many prisoners were gathered here? Fifty, maybe up to seventy thousand? Why were there so many of them?

"What is Underworld City? There are only Bedouins in the desert."

"I'll tell you later," Hadjar said. "Why do they need so many slaves? I haven't seen any construction work going on."

"Maybe they're going to use them like meat shields? You know, I've heard some generals actually do that. They put prisoners in front of their army to decrease the opponent's morale. Thus, they deprive the opponent of their will to fight because they have to kill their own relatives."

"Maybe..."

"Maybe you are both idiots," the girl came up, rubbing her wrists. "These captives are here because they feed them to their monsters."

Hadjar looked at her. She looked painfully emaciated, was wearing ragged clothes, and was covered in blood and bruises. But she was still beautiful. In general, most practitioners were. The body changed during cultivation, acquiring the features so many men and women enjoyed.

"How long have you been here?"

"A month," the girl answered. "Maybe less, maybe more. I don't know."

"How did you end up here?" Nero asked.

She just rolled her eyes again.

"Do we plan to sit here discussing that or do you want to go and set fire to their haystacks and get off the plateau?"

"How did you know our plan?" Nero nearly shouted in alarm and grabbed his dagger again.

"You're definitely a couple of idiots. I've been here for a month, boys," she'd said 'boys' with a particularly potent loathing. "I've come up with a hundred and one plans for how to get revenge on them. And setting fire to the haystacks is number one on the list."

Hadjar and Nero exchanged glances. Judging by how heavy and complex the collar was, the girl clearly wasn't at the first levels of cultivation. Perhaps she was even stronger than either of them. Maybe even both of them combined. But only when not wearing her slave decoration. With it, a mere mortal could've beaten her.

"If you end up slowing us down, we'll leave you here."

And then three silhouettes dived into the downpour and darkness.

Chapter 62

"Water," Nero signaled. Hadjar nodded.

Armed with his dagger, Hadjar went in the direction of the barrels and boxes. He left Nero and the strange lady to deal with the explosives. He didn't trust the former prisoner, but he could fully rely on Nero.

Underneath a canopy of coarse cloth, there were boxes of gunpowder, piled high on top of each other. Hadjar didn't touch them. He was much more interested in the barrels full of the combustible mixture. The nomads were probably going to cover the stones intended for the trebuchets with it.

What could be better than a huge boulder that could break through walls? Setting that huge boulder on fire.

Bypassing the first post, which stood guard over the gunpowder, Hadjar moved on.

What were the chances of him meeting a person from the city where South Wind had lived for some time? Less than the probability of winning the lottery jackpot twice a week. And yet, Fate had clearly disagreed.

Hadjar crept up to one of the guards without the aid of a flash of lightning.

He abruptly struck the broad-shouldered nomad in the temple with the hilt of his dagger. The strike was strong enough to stun the guard but too weak to send him to his ancestors.

Picking up the man's unconscious body, he carefully lowered him to the ground. A second later, he snuck out of the darkness and knocked the second watchman out in exactly the same way.

It was easy, not only because Hadjar had the power of the Formation Stage, but also because they were relaxed, had drunk two wineskins of strong koumiss, and the sense of security that they had due to the presence of the Lascanian.

In the eyes of the nomads, the Spirit Knight was a mythical hero or a demigod, and the inhabitants of Lidus would've been just as awed. Who could remain vigilant on such an evening, when everybody knew that it would be impossible to enter the camp unnoticed? This 'knowledge' was dangerous because it was more deceptive than any mirage.

Hadjar began to carefully but quickly uncork the barrels, pulling out the plugs and allowing the smelly, black liquid to mix with the downpour. They flowed down simultaneously, like small streams, toward the pastures and the haystacks covered with fabric.

At this point, Hadjar regretted that they hadn't managed to remove some of the covers. They, despite the rain, would've burned much better than wet grass.

After uncorking all the barrels he could, Hadjar tied up the unconscious guards and gagged them with rags, covered their eyes with dirt and plugged their ears with grass. That way, even when they woke up, they wouldn't be able to understand what was happening.

It's pretty hard to wake up from such a 'sleep' and not be disoriented, even without being deprived of your senses. Hadjar knew this better than anyone.

Getting back to their designated meeting spot, he waited for Nero and the girl.

Smeared in mud and clay, they looked more like cave trolls or something along those lines, but definitely not normal people.

"We must wait," Hadjar ordered through hand signals. "Water flows. We are waiting for when... There should be enough water."

If they detonated the explosives right now, the fire wouldn't have time to burn down even a tenth of the pasture. Moreover, the horses burning in the fire would start to neigh, and the whole tribe would run to them. A horse was more important to the nomads than their mother, father, and bow combined. And these three things were sacred to any savage.

"Do you have any talismans?" The girl asked.

She had started to say something else, but Nero put his hand over her mouth. He put a finger to his lips, his entire appearance showing her that it was necessary to stay silent.

She just moved his palm aside.

"Nobody can hear us, you damn idiots. There's the rain, all the thunder, and even the noise of a lot of drunken and mating savages."

"I have some," Hadjar replied in a whisper, figuring she was right.

He took the talismans that the Master had given him from his pocket. They were strips of yellow paper with red letters inscribed on them.

"Do you always carry these with you?" The girl took a few of the 'pieces of paper' from him so carefully it looked like she was touching a bomb. "These spells... I recognize this style. They were made personally by the Master. Where did you get them?"

"A good man gave them to me. He was your Master's apprentice."

"Really? Maybe I know his name and-"

"Perhaps we could discuss this later?" Nero interrupted. "Why do you need the talismans? You're still wearing your collar, and it's not like I could've taken it off earlier. I don't have the seal. I just wanted to take a look."

"A key-seal isn't needed," the lady shook her head. "You could just destroy it. Otherwise, the savages would have pestered the Lascanian endlessly."

"Let her keep them," Hadjar said firmly. "When we burn down everything, it'll be useless to try and hide. The Knight will find us wherever we go. We'll tear off her collar and run away."

"I'm very experienced when it comes to the art of escaping," Nero smiled, trying to defuse the situation.

He failed.

"Let me ask you this, most esteemed master of running away" the girl said dryly. "How are we going to get away? If you're planning to steal some horses, we won't be able to even get past the first slope before we're killed."

"Actually, we had another plan."

Hadjar and Nero didn't waste time. They took some rope and tied it to the girl's waist. She winced from the unpleasant feeling of the wet rope touching her skin and frowned, but remained silent.

Perhaps she had once worn pretty nice clothes, but now, her slender legs were being shown off beneath a tattered, green skirt. It was obvious that some jewelry had been torn off her waist, neck, and wrists. Her skin was slightly paler in those places.

Round, shapely mounds protruded from underneath the scraps of fabric that had once been a white blouse. Nero and Hadjar tried not to look. Not because it was an unappealing sight or uninteresting, but because the time and place weren't very suitable for such things.

They began to climb up the cliff. It was much harder than they'd expected it to be.

The girl couldn't help them and just hung there like a weight. She couldn't even cling to the rock without her practitioner strength, let alone climb up it. Therefore, the ascent, which would've normally taken about fifteen minutes, lasted more than half an hour.

Hadjar was waiting for his death to arrive with every passing minute, with every new flash of lightning and thunder.

He didn't know when the unconscious sentries would wake up, how soon they would raise the alarm, or whether the Spirit Knight would kill them the very next moment, or maybe a second later.

It was difficult to plan their next steps while distracted by all these concerns, so when the edge of the cliff became visible, Hadjar sighed with relief. They didn't untie the lady when they finished climbing. Instead, they just made sure the knots were still tied firmly and looked down. There was a huge abyss below them, the bottom of which was still covered by a massive forest.

"Are you ready?" Nero asked him.

He took out a small artifact that looked like a detonator.

"Let's go," Hadjar whispered in response.

Nero blinked for a moment and then there was an explosion so loud it could've competed even with the noise of the heavenly thunder. A huge flash lit up almost the entire camp and the desperate neighing of burning horses filled the air.

Smashing through the pens, they rushed through the camp, setting fire to tents and trampling people. People starting crying out in dismay and confusion and the plateau was plunged into chaos.

"Go!" Hadjar shouted, feeling like something was coming toward them.

Nero tore the girl's collar off immediately. The aura of the Transformation Stage washed over both men.

The lady immediately grabbed one of the talismans, squeezed it between her fingers, and whispered a few words. The paper turned into ashes and then various symbols appeared, spinning over their heads. They merged together in a mad dance, forming something resembling a dome.

Right after that, a gigantic flame sword struck the dome! Hadjar couldn't believe his eyes. The symbols cracked and distorted under the force of the sword which was the size of a whole tree. The damn blade was at least fifty feet long, and as thick as two grown men!

Blood started leaking from the girl's nose.

"Hurry," she croaked.

Nero and Hadjar turned and ran toward the cliff. They were running without even seeing where they were going, like the horses that were burning the camp down below, on the plateau. But while the horses had encountered no obstacles, they were less fortunate. The gigantic, fiery blade flashed and the symbols faded away in a couple of seconds. Their death was imminent and they all knew it.

The girl screamed and fell to her knees. Nero and Hadjar caught her by the arms as they ran, trying to get away.

They came to the cliff.

"We need to jump," Hadjar said.

[The probability of the host surviving such a scenario: <23%]

Hadjar just shrugged off the message.

"Are you crazy?" His friend shouted.

"Are there any other options?"

And then it became difficult, almost impossible, to breathe. Both of them felt it. Hadjar barely managed to turn around. A silhouette was floating in the distance, about a hundred yards away, without the assistance of wings or any other device. He just slowly descended from a great height.

It's the Spirit Knight. Damn that Lascanian!

He only touched the handle of his sword and the wave produced by the aura of his blade rushed toward Hadjar. It was a simple aura, the mere desire to draw a blade, but it was enough to cut through rocks like they were plain paper, even at a hundred yards.

Hadjar's instincts began blaring like a siren.

He knew that, once the aura touched them, only three red smears would be left behind.

Drawing his blade, Hadjar assumed the 'Strong Wind' stance. He slashed with his sword, unleashing all of his strength and putting all the skill he could muster into the strike.

Astonishment was plainly evident on the cultivator's face. Why is this ant of the Formation Stage still alive?

A whirlwind of razor-sharp wind, within which ghostly blades danced, emerged from Hadjar's sword. The attack collided with the aura and... Could only delay it for a couple of seconds.

The Spirit Knight had been able to unravel Hadjar's Technique with only a simple touch against his sword hilt.

But that couple of seconds had been enough for the talisman in the lady's hands to burn up.

The cry of a crane rang out in the sky and Nero and Hadjar jumped off the cliff.

The cultivator roared with rage. Stones crumbled from the force of it as the trio flew away on a ghostly crane that had been created from the same hieroglyphs as the recently employed shield.

"We have to get back to camp as quickly as possible," Nero said, holding the bloody and pale girl in his lap.

"I hope this bird knows where to go," Hadjar muttered, staring at the shape of the mountain range disappearing off in the distance.

He knew that the cultivator wouldn't follow them. If he got too close to the camp, the Librarian would feel it. And such a meeting would immediately lead to a chain reaction that none of the parties involved in the conflict wanted yet.

"At least we're still alive."

I made it...

Chapter 63

General Leen's tent was once again crowded because of the numerous people that had gathered inside. On top of that, she had ordered that Sirius, the head of the Fort, attend the meeting as well, which everyone else disapproved of.

He appeared to be arrogant and confident, just like last time, wearing gold jewelry, precious stones, silks, and brocade. The only thing that made him a general was his title and the insignia that went along with it. The valuable badge of office hadn't been stolen purely because thieves avoided targets who were too important.

"Do you believe these soldiers?" Sirius pointed his thick finger at Nero, Hadjar, and Serra.

That was the name of the girl they'd saved, Serra. She now looked a little better than she had a couple of hours earlier. Dogar's healer had treated her wounds, given her his brew, and even some clothes. The brown leather jacket and high boots suited her, emphasizing her shapely figure.

"I swear on my power and blood..." Hadjar slashed his knife across his palm and his blood burned. "I'm telling the truth."

For a couple of seconds, people just stared at him, but Hadjar didn't catch fire like any person that had violated a blood oath would have.

"You see, Sirius, he's telling the truth."

"Or he thinks he's telling the truth," the official replied immediately. "You never know what he might've imagined seeing in the storm."

And as if in confirmation of the official's words, lightning struck and the thunder rumbled so loudly that the figures on the table shook.

"That's nothing, Sirius," the General suddenly stepped around the desk and approached the paunchy man. The petite girl still looked like an enormous tiger stepping on a mouse's tail. "Where are your patrols, Sirius?"

The official turned paler and sweatier with every step Leen took. He turned to his soldiers, but they weren't eager to draw their weapons. Several senior officers were also in the tent, so any move would've been truly suicidal.

"The patrols are patrolling," the head of the Fort shrugged nervously.

"Really? That's a surprise, Sirius. Then why didn't you tell me then that the nomads were capturing the people of our Kingdom?"

"Well, they looted a couple of villages..." Sirius' adjusted his collar nervously. He couldn't breathe. "Should I send the garrison out every time someone burns down a village on the border?"

"A couple of villages? What villages are you even talking about, when they've captured a quarter of a million people? Something tells me, Sirius, that they've sacked not just a couple, but a couple hundred villages! Where are the patrols?"

"Yes, well, I..."

"Where are the patrols, you fat bastard?"

The General grabbed Sirius's shirt and easily lifted him off the floor. The fort soldiers took up arms, but Dogar silently came up behind them and laid his huge paws on their shoulders. He pushed them down so hard that their armor cracked and began to fall apart. He kneaded the metal just like baker's dough.

Rat-man, the official's ever-present companion, looked around hastily. Apparently, he would be the first to abandon the sinking ship.

"No patrols!" The tubby 'general' screamed hysterically, his legs dangling in the air. "No guns, no patrols, no garrison!"

Leen loosened her fingers and Sirius fell to the floor like a sack of potatoes. Tears were streaming down his red, sweaty face, washing away the paint he had coated it in.

"What do you mean by that?"

"There are a total of forty guns on the walls," the official muttered. "We haven't sent out any patrols for almost ten years. Only twenty-seven thousand soldiers are left in the entire Fort."

"Where are the others, Sirius? Where?"

Leen's palm lit up with a steel light and she swung it down.

The official curled up and raised his hands above his head. He looked so pathetic that many became uncomfortable with not only having to look at him but even having to be around this miserable waste of flesh.

"There are no other soldiers! Some of them were dismissed, some became mercenaries …"

"Really now!" She swung again.

"The mine! I sold them to the mine!"

The tent was silent.

Forty guns and twenty-seven thousand soldiers... that meant they couldn't count on the Fort's support. General Leen's army was alone, facing a horde of nomads that had been trained and equipped by the Lascanians.

"I saw many people in the Fort, far more than twenty-seven thousand."

"They are simple civilians," the once-celebrated general whined.

High positions disfigured people. South Wind had said that it was very rare for a high-ranking official to remain a good person and not become the embodiment of greed and weakness. On the outside, they looked important and unapproachable, like a mountain, but inside, everything had long since rotted away.

"That is treason, Sirius," the General sighed, leaning heavily against the edge of the table. "It's high treason."

"I wanted to build a city, Leen. A real city. I had such plans…"

"What plans? Plans on how to decorate yourself with gold and how to make your own palace by taking from the fortress? I've seen it—you have stained glass in your bathrooms, Sirius. Gods damned stained glass!"

"Do you think it's easy?" The official shrieked suddenly. "Do you think it's easy to live for forty years in a military fortification, to always be around sweaty and smelly soldiers? There are no streets, no squares—only the parade grounds and training. I could smell the stink of gunpowder in my dreams at night... I wanted to live, Leen. Live! Not simply exist."

"Everyone wants that."

"Everyone does, and I had the opportunity to make it a reality. And I did! Or do you think I have a bad life? It's great! We have a bustling industry, we paved the streets, built houses, built the Central Square. We built taverns, schools, and pubs. Circuses come to our town! Or do you think the soldier's families can have a lot of fun in the garrison? They lose their children when they're still young, sending them to study in the city, knowing that they would never come back."

Some of the people, feeling disgusted, turned their backs to Sirius.

"Yeah, I got my share of the profits," the official continued. "But who didn't get a share? Everybody did! Even the king, I'm sure, has appropriated a portion of the proceeds! That's life. If you want to do something good for people, you have to sacrifice something."

"And you sacrificed your soul."

"My soul?" Sirius got up and straightened his back. He wiped his face and smoothed out his clothes. For a moment, looking at this hog, Hadjar caught a glimpse of the general that had earned an award the King had presented him with personally.

"You're a fool, Leen. And all of you are fools if you think you can stand up to this horde! You have to negotiate! Maybe you'll give them a part of your army. Maybe it'll be something else…"

"You're crazy."

"They're just puppets," the official laughed hysterically, "If you die, the army won't exist. You are senior officers. A simple soldier can always be replaced."

Hadjar looked at the General. He met her steely, grey gaze. She nodded slowly.

"This is treason, Sirius," she repeated. "Burn in the abyss."

"You're a foo-"

Before the pompous fool could finish his sentence, his head fell from his shoulders and rolled across the boards.

Hadjar placed the sword of the soldier who was being held by Dogar back into its scabbard. He had no intention of staining his own blade with such blood.

"Now… As for you," Leen said slowly, turning to the human rat.

"Ye-ye-yes, my General," he fell to his knees and began beating his head against the floor.

"You're the new garrison commander. I don't care how you do it, I don't care where you find them, but in two weeks, there better be a hundred guns on the walls. Do you understand me?"

The rat kept banging his head against the floor.

"Do you understand me?" She roared.

"Yes, my General," he wailed. "That's how it will be, my General."

"Get out."

He literally ran out of the tent, stumbling and getting tangled up in his expensive clothes. The limping soldiers, whose collarbones had seemingly been broken by Dogar, followed after him.

"Are these meetings always so much fun?" Nero whispered in Hadjar's ear.

"You have no idea," Hadjar nodded.

Chapter 64

"It's rather strange..." Tim, the spymaster, gestured to the ridge with a pointer. "Why is everything so complicated? If a Spirit Knight is really there, he could've just used a protective spell and we would have never found them at all."

"Don't you believe my people, Tim?" Dogar could hardly keep from growling.

"I do believe them, it's just..."

"Simply put, if he had used such a spell," the tent flaps moved aside and the old librarian entered the War Council. "I would've sensed them. I would have had to make a report to the Empire and then..."

"And then something that neither of the Empires wants would've happened," Leen concluded.

The librarian nodded.

"Tell me, venerable adept," the General squeezed her pointer and turned slightly pale. "Will he intervene in our battle?"

"Probably not," the Darnassian shook his head. "We, the cultivators, are prohibited from participating in the wars of mortals. We can fight only in the general, large scale battles of the Empires, but such battles are not very similar to what you are doing here."

"I've heard that..." The commander of the archers suddenly spoke. "Heaven Soldiers are killed by the hundreds of thousands during battles between Empires..."

The librarian smiled.

"That's right, my dear. We Heaven Soldiers are just pawns in the wars of the Empires."

Everyone fell silent. Any cultivator was almost like an inhabitant of the heavens compared to them.

"Besides, taking into account the report of officer Hadjar, I can assume that a Spirit Knight of only the initial stage is helping the nomads. He's much stronger than me, but far weaker than most of the officers in the Empire's army."

Hadjar imagined an officer corps consisting of ten thousand cultivators who were stronger than the flying man. It would be interesting to see what a battle of their armies would look like if that flying man had almost destroyed part of the mountain by just touching the grip of his sword.

"And why have you come here, venerable adept?" The General squinted at him.

"I think you already know why, General Leen."

The General nodded.

"You've already sent your report and received a reply. If the Lascanian cultivator helps the nomads, then you were asked to help us."

"They didn't ask me to do so, they ordered it. That means I'm yours to command. I will help however I can."

"And what can a single cultivator do to help us?" Tuur asked.

"I can do a few things," the old man responded vaguely. "But I see you have a scholar and magic caster now."

Everyone turned to Serra. She was not a citizen of Lidus and was not obliged to risk her life.

"Lady Serra, I understand this will be a very brazen request, but…"

"They killed my teacher and my fellow students," the girl almost hissed. "I'm with you, General, and I'll do everything I can."

"Thank you." Leen said sincerely.

"Then let me take this lovely lady with me. We have something to discuss."

And the librarian took her out of the tent. Nero watched them go with longing.

"I think I'm in love," he whispered.

"You'll forget her in two days," Hadjar assured him.

"No, my friend," Nero sighed sorrowfully. "This time, it's serious…"

They all stared at the map silently for a while, looking for a solution. Hadjar tried to use the neuronet at full power, but it could not find an optimal solution in which the life of the host wouldn't be in great danger.

Each of the proposed options had a red threat level. Such a color meant that the probability of Hadjar's death was more than fifty percent.

"We need to send for reinforcements," Helion, the commander of the cavalry, broke the silence. "We can't do it alone."

Leen listened to his words and then turned in the opposite direction.

"How long will the rain delay them for, Officer Hadjar?" the General asked.

"Two weeks. Maybe a little more. Maybe a little less."

"Plus, taking into account your success with the sabotage, alongside private Nero..." the chief engineer, Tuur, mumbled pensively. "It's unlikely that you've burned down a significant part of their horses and provisions, but the total damage should still delay them."

"Overall, we have two weeks," Leen finished. "We'll proceed with that figure as a baseline. We'll immediately send a report to the General Staff, but..."

"But the nearest army will have to travel for at least a month to get to us," Tim finished the sentence for the General.

"If we bog them down in protracted battles," Lian suggested, "then we can buy enough time for the reinforcements to arrive."

"There'll be no protracted battles," the general pushed all the figurines from the ridge over to the plain. "They know that we know the state of affairs. Moreover, a Lascanian Spirit Knight is with them. He wouldn't risk a chance to interrupt the supply of Solar Ore. They will hit us right away. No probing battles and minor hassles. A decisive battle. Everything'll be decided in one day."

"That damn coward was right," the cavalryman hit the table angrily. "We won't be able to fight them. They have five million people. Cannons. Horse archers. Trebuchets and even monsters that we don't know anything about."

"Are you suggesting we retreat?"

"No, my general," Helion snarled. "I propose we figure out how we can sell our lives at a higher price so that these creatures don't break through to the interior of the country."

The General looked around sternly. No one faltered under her gaze and not a single person flinched. Nobody mentioned running or trying to negotiate. Each of the people standing at that table loved their homeland. Somewhere out there, among the meadows and fields, their families were waiting for them. Yes, they might never see them again, but the sky itself would collapse before they allowed a horde of savages to ruin their land. To kill their children and spouses.

As long as they drew breath, they would fight for their homeland. Not for the king, officials, or because of orders, but so their loved ones could sleep peacefully and not have to take up arms.

"Alright. Let's think about how we can do the most damage to the horde."

The discussion continued for six long hours. Contrary to the statute, the right to speak was given to anyone who wanted to do so. Nero spoke a couple of times. He suggested simple, but very sensible ideas. For example, digging trenches and filling them with fuel in order to divide the opponents' flanks.

Hadjar didn't lag behind either. Even without the neural network's prompting, he remembered the anti-tank barriers that had been used to stop tanks in his old world. There were no tanks here, but no one had said that such barriers couldn't be utilized to prevent the enemy cavalry from destroying the infantry with its famous wedge formation.

For the most part, however, the senior officers were the ones who spoke. Their extensive knowledge and, most importantly, their experience with military affairs, helped them. In the end, they even managed to briefly discuss a plan that would allow them to defeat a foe that had more than twice their numbers.

The plan was stupid and defiant, almost childishly stubborn, but even stranger things sometimes happened. A person faced with their inevitable death was ready to resort to any kind of madness, if only to put off the hour when they had to plunge into the abyss and go on to their rebirth.

In this world, people sincerely believed that a person would be born again after their death. They'd have a new destiny, and a new body, but without their old memories. No matter how silly it sounded, Hadjar could believe in such a circle of reincarnation. After all, he himself was a kind of living proof of such a faith having merit. However, by some miracle, he'd retained all of his memories.

After the Council ended, they went back to their camps and units. After they had a good, long rest, accompanied by the rain drumming against the tents' fabric, lots of hard work awaited them. They all had their own tasks and assignments.

Nero and Hadjar, who had both also received several orders, were now sitting on the hill near which the bloody battle would soon be fought.

They smoked pipes, breathing out rings of smoke and looked into the distance.

"Well, she sure is beautiful, huh?"

"Who?"

"Serra," a dreamy smile appeared on Nero's face. "Brave and beautiful."

Hadjar looked at his friend's glittering eyes and listened to his pent-up sighs.

"You've fallen in love," Hadjar stated.

"I already told you that."

A white, fluffy muzzle poked out from under Hadjar's clothes. The kitten yawned, then she meowed, demanding some food. Hadjar offered a piece of dried meat to his "pet". Azrea grabbed it with her teeth and ducked back into the warmth and comfort beneath Hadjar's clothes. She soon fell asleep again.

"What about your love of twins?" Hadjar asked. "Or is that in the past now?"

"Well, what if Serra has a sister?" Nero shrugged.

They were silent for a moment and then broke out into laughter, which soon gave way to the oppressive silence from before.

"We'll survive, Hadj. We'll survive for sure."

"We'll get medals."

"And all the girls will be ours."

"I seem to recall you saying you were in love."

"Well, okay, all the girls will be yours."

Nero gave his friend's shoulder a nudge and they continued to smoke.

Despite the upcoming battle, their souls were at peace.

Chapter 65

Standing in the pouring rain, Hadjar trained.

A week had already passed since the most idiotic and therefore the most viable plan had been approved by the War Council. Every soldier had been given a specific task. Hadjar had also been given an assignment, but his commanding officer had freed him from that dull obligation and had ordered him to train instead.

Because, according to Dogar, if he were to become 'One with the World', he would be worth hundreds of nomads in the upcoming battle. And they could not afford to lose such an advantage.

And so, Hadjar trained. Every day, he fenced with the wind, rain, earth, and fire. He tried to recapture the feeling that he'd had during his fight with Colin. That same moment of enlightenment, when it had seemed like he had touched on some mystery of the world. When he'd seen the edge of the true essence, which was usually safely hidden from the eyes of mere mortals.

And yet, he was missing something. Something elusive, ghostly, ephemeral, but still incredibly important.

Hadjar could still feel the earth and how it gave strength to his steps. He felt the wind, whose currents directed his blade. He felt the fire from which his sword had been born and felt the water pouring from the heavens. But it wasn't enough.

He was still missing something.

His sword strikes were quick and smooth. He moved in the rain, battling with hundreds of invisible foes. He did it so gracefully it was beautiful to behold. So elegantly that, had there been an artist around, he would have surely been inspired and produced a masterpiece.

But Hadjar fought alone in the rain.

His every attack was filled with energy and always found its goal. The strikes cut through the thousands of drops falling from the sky. Drenched in sweat and rain, Hadjar was able to cut through at least ten drops every time. He didn't just batter them, but cut them so quickly and neatly that one drop would turn into two.

As he trained, concentrating on his battle with the rain, Hadjar recalled the 'Light Breeze' scroll. The first of its stances, the Strong Wind, was like a storm descending into a calm valley from atop the high mountains.

Hadjar made a particularly sharp attack with his sword and the rain cut through the wind.

The stance was just as wild, savage, and fierce as a storm in the darkened sky.

The second stance was too mystical and Hadjar couldn't understand it. He lacked the skills and knowledge required, both in the path of the sword and in the elements of the wind, in order to comprehend the secrets of the 'Calm Wind', the second stance of the Technique Traves had left him.

Unable to grasp the secrets of the Technique, nor the secrets of 'One with the World', Hadjar continued his senseless and endless battle with the rain.

Raindrops that had been cut in half were falling to the ground. But each of those drops was quickly replaced by a myriad of others.

It was said that a practitioner shouldn't meditate and study all the time. They also had to participate in life and interact with the outside world. Travel. Fight. Live.

Only then would they be able to acquire knowledge, which would coalesce in a rush of insight when the moment came and the cultivator would be able to comprehend something new. A deeper, more mystical secret.

Hadjar, after his 'fight' with the Spirit Knight, the Emerald Wolf, and Colin, felt that he was close to comprehending some profound truth, but couldn't understand what it was. Enlightenment kept evading his grasp.

The battles had hardened his hands, strengthened his will, and presented him with knowledge. But he couldn't merge them together.

The raindrops continued to strike the blade.

Hadjar was fighting the rain, but couldn't win.

"It's very beautiful," a voice sounded.

Hadjar flinched and lost his rhythm. His sword missed its 'target' and the Prince almost lost his balance.

A girl with red hair and a tenacious gaze stood behind him, wrapped in a cloak.

"Stepha?"

Hadjar thought he was seeing a mirage. No, it couldn't have been

Stepha, he'd left her behind. Somewhere far back on the road of his life. Almost seven years had passed since he'd last seen her. Hundreds of thousands of miles separated them now.

"Did you remember my name after the performance?" The girl was surprised.

Suddenly, Hadjar recalled what Nero and Sirius had said.

"By the way, a circus has just arrived. They have such funny freaks there." Hadjar remembered the words of the official he'd executed.

"Let's go look at the circus freaks..." Nero had suggested.

"Yes, my lady," Hadjar bowed slightly, suddenly having to deal with an uninvited lump in his throat.

"Lady..." Stepha repeated. She was as beautiful and passionate as he remembered her being. "No one has ever called me that. Although, there was one man... but he died a long time ago."

What were the chances that a circus in which Hadjar had spent five years of his life would arrive to this remote Fort? Approximately as infinitesimal as the chances that he would meet a thread leading to Underworld City in the mountains, among the horde's prisoners. To a place where he could unlock the secrets of spells.

For a moment, it seemed to Hadjar like all the roads of his life had been woven into a single thread that was tied around that Fort and the upcoming battle. As if fate itself had led him here, as well as the people who'd helped that fate come to pass.

"What are you doing in this downpour?" Hadjar asked after sheathing his sword. He picked his cloak up off the ground and covered Stepha's shoulders with it.

Once upon a time, she had been taller than him. Now she barely came up to his chest.

"We put on a show at your camp," she didn't doubt for a second that the man in front of her was from the military.

The swordsman's gaze, his posture, his walk, and his self-confidence all signaled that he was a soldier. And yet, Stepha had never seen such an interesting man in her life. Despite the fact that he looked like the well-groomed son of a nobleman, his strength and power could be felt a mile away. It was almost like the aura of a wild beast...

"Then you should go back," Hadjar pointed to the Fort. "Better yet, go west. It'll be dangerous if you stay here."

"Yes," Stepha nodded. "We're leaving tomorrow."

Tomorrow... For some reason, Hadjar knew that he'd never see this girl again. Tomorrow, their paths, which had miraculously come together on the great journey of life, would once again diverge, and this time, it would be forever.

She was standing very close to him and her scent was the same as always. She smelled like a bonfire, grass, and some sweet flower.

"You have very beautiful eyes, soldier."

Her thin, worn fingers touched his cheek.

Suddenly, she asked, "Have we met before?"

Her fingers ran a little lower, entangling themselves in Hadjar's hair and then went further down, to his clavicle. She pulled him even closer. So close that he got goosebumps from her hot breath tickling his skin.

"What's your name, soldier?"

Hadjar looked into her eyes. They held neither fear nor sorrow, only a thirst for life. They were bright and free.

Instead of answering, he hugged her tightly, pressing himself against her. He removed the hood and buried his face in Stepha's hair. Wet, but so fragrant.

She hugged him back, feeling as if she were clinging to a ferocious predator. It was a frightening and therefore intoxicating feeling.

They loved each right there, throwing the cloak onto the cold ground and ignoring the ceaseless rain. Hadjar took her fiercely, then gently, and she gave herself to him passionately and ardently.

Hadjar didn't know how long it had lasted, but when he opened his eyes, he found himself alone on his cloak.

Stepha never stayed with a man. She never stayed in one place. She was as free as the wind blowing across an endless valley. Even when she was with other people, she was also always alone with the whole world.

Hadjar sighed and looked west.

He said goodbye to Stepha and let his past drift away. Hadjar released that dark clot that had been hovering around his heart. The year he'd spent in prison, full of torture and pain. Those five years of being a worthless slave. The years he'd spent with Eina and her mother, as a musician in the brothel.

He got rid of all of it. Banished the pain and sadness, leaving only the rare moments of joy behind. And it all went away.

Suddenly, Hadjar rose and picked up his sword.

The rain was still coming down, it didn't care who was drenched in the life-giving moisture. Demons and gods, heroes or villains, all were equal in its eyes.

Hadjar started his battle with the rain again, but this time, his sword didn't cut through even a single drop. No, it seemingly kept finding a gap between the raindrops every time and going around them. Each time, it would find the practically nonexistent moment when a passage opened up between the millions of drops.

Hadjar had once again made a small step toward reaching the top. He now knew a secret about the world. He didn't have to fight it. Struggling was useless, the young man had to take it into himself, instead.

He had to take the whole world in.

"Calm Wind," Hadjar said, assuming the second stance of Traves' Technique.

The raindrops kept falling. Only now they weren't touching Hadjar, or his sword, which was dancing through the air. They flowed around the warrior, as if coming across an invisible barrier.

If 'Strong wind' was an attack stance, then 'Calm wind' was a stance focused on the wielder's protection.

Hadjar swung his blade and the ghostly strike flew as far as nineteen steps before it disappeared into the darkness.

He'd almost reached the second stage of blade mastery. He'd almost become 'One with the World'.

"Well, that's enough for now," Hadjar sheathed the blade and picked up his discarded clothes.

He looked west again. Yes, the second stance was called 'Calm Wind', but he would forever associate it with one name: Stepha.

Hadjar returned to the camp. He'd reached the absolute peak of his capabilities. He had no way left to grow stronger before the battle.

There was only one thing left to do - wait for the war to begin.

Chapter 66

Hadjar looked toward the horizon. The sun was rising. The endless rain had subsided for a while and the sky had brightened only to turn into the bloody veil of a new day in the very next moment.

Two million warriors stood behind Hadjar. Some wore light armor, others had armor so heavy it was a miracle they could move.

Dogar's detachment was always in the front rows and held the center. That was why some people believed that it was almost impossible to survive even one battle in that detachment.

Dogar himself didn't look like a bear anymore, but like a giant from old legends. He was wearing leather armor, a close helmet, and his fighting gauntlets. He was a terrifying sight. He had a bandolier full of daggers across his chest, and a long, wide knife was attached to his left shoulder. They all looked like gnarled animal fangs, ready to dig into the enemy's throat.

To his right, Nero was letting out slightly nervous breaths. Before the fight, he'd dyed his hair white. Hadjar didn't know why, but judging by Serra's angry look, it was somehow related to the fact that Nero had gotten drunk and then slid into her tent. Not quite passionate shouts followed, accompanied by the flashes and noise that usually came with spells being cast.

He had already been like this when he'd left her tent—white haired and covered in numerous bruises. But he'd also been sober.

Now, clutching a heavy sword in his hands, he was flaunting a rather strange armor. His torso and legs were fully enclosed in it, but his shoulders and forearms weren't even covered in chain mail. Also, steel plate armor protected his wrists but everything else was exposed. Perhaps this armor was appropriate for the requirements of Nero's technique... or he'd simply lost part of his armor.

Hadjar himself looked the same as always—wearing chain mail over leather armor, and with ordinary clothes over both. This time, they were a dark red color so that the enemy wouldn't see his blood...

Hadjar checked whether the leather strap holding his long hair out of the way was still whole.

The crows were already circling above them, in the sky. They cawed as if urging people to begin the battle.

Suddenly, the line of the horizon turned black. It was as if an artist had smeared paint on it and decided to leave it, without finishing their newly begun work.

The soldiers became anxious. The creaking of armor and clanging of weapons filled the air.

The valley ahead was slowly covered in a golden veil which was emerging from the previously dark horizon. Hundreds of thousands of horsemen, clad in armor, were riding toward the battlefield.

Suddenly, six horsemen rode forward, and the most powerful of them rode at the head. He was wearing gold armor and a lightweight helmet. The sun shone on his chest, and his horse was so mighty it kicked up chunks of earth as it galloped.

General Leen and the senior officers moved to meet him. They met somewhere in the middle, descended from their horses, and sat down opposite each other at a table covered with a white tablecloth.

"What do you think they're discussing?" Nero whispered, adjusting the helmet on his head.

"They're trying to frighten each other," Hadjar guessed.

The generals of both armies had been discussing something for about fifteen minutes. Then they drank something and went their separate ways. Judging by the joyful cries of the savages and the annoyed growls of their general, they hadn't been able to come to a consensus.

Leen paused after she was once again standing in front of her people. Her hair had been pulled into a tight bun, and she wore full, heavy armor. The wind ruffled her blue, woolen cape, and her personal contingent of giant warriors standing behind her glittered in the sun because their armor was so polished.

A general probably had to give a speech to inspire people at moments like this. The General, however, was only looking at her army in silence. At the faces of the young men and women whose eyes were full of fear and uncertainty.

How many of them had only recently held on to the hem of their mother's skirt or had been frightened by their father's belt.

And now they were standing at the front of an army. An army facing a whole horde of nomads.

What was she supposed to say?

Behind her, in the distance, the enemy general, pacing energetically in front of the ranks of the savages, was giving an inspiring speech. The echoes of his thundering voice reached all the way to their own ranks.

Leen was silent.

Suddenly, she raised her spear and struck the ground with its shaft. At the same moment, a roar rose up, so powerful that it was like a mountain had collapsed or the ground had split open somewhere, so deafening was her strike.

She raised her spear once more and then struck the ground. The earth shook under Hadjar's feet, and he himself seemed to calm down slightly. As if his frantically beating heart had begun to accept the beat of the spear instead.

Soon, one of the soldiers bared his mace and hit it against his shield. Then another comrade joined him, and after they started it, more and more took up the rhythm.

In absolute silence, without uttering a word, two million soldiers began to beat their weapons against their shields or their spears against the ground. The cavalrymen struck the ground with the hooves of their horses, and the archers struck the drums with their open palms.

They went faster and faster, louder and louder, until the frightened neighing of the enemy's horses could be heard from the other side of the valley.

Then the soldiers, all together, like the awakening of a mighty beast, roared and charged the foe. General Leen, now wearing a helmet, was at the forefront.

Hadjar ran silently, only tightening his grip on the blade. Nero, who was shoulder to shoulder with him, was straining his throat enough for both of them. The enemy army, driven by their general, rushed to meet them in battle. A whole sea of hooting horsemen and neighing horses barreled toward them.

Two oceans of steel, flesh, fear, and sweat were about to collide.

"Turn!" Dogar's voice boomed out when just a few yards remained before the collision.

The first ranks of the infantry immediately stopped. Hundreds of thousands of warriors turned to the right in sync, letting the forward troops of heavy spearmen through. They plunged their special, spiked shields into the ground, then put their long spears into special hollows. The second row of infantry put their shields on top of theirs, the third row did the same, and so on and so forth, until the first rows were completely covered by the shield formation.

A moment later, it was as if a ram had hit the shield wall, but the shield spikes the spearmen had dug into the ground held fast. The spearmen grunted with the strain, but held the line, sometimes lunging forward with their spears, and then the army would be greeted by the welcome cry of a dying enemy.

Suddenly, a buzzing rang out. It sounded like thousands of mosquitoes had risen into the air at once. There were so many of them that they blocked out the sun.

Hadjar looked at the sky but saw nothing except for the swarm of arrows the archers had loosed. They covered the azure sky with a black curtain, and then the battlefield was flooded with the sounds of arrows hitting flesh, armor, and people's cries.

The rain of arrows both sides had launched collided with one another. The arrows met in the air and fell, but some still found their mark.

A soldier standing next to Hadjar clutched at his throat and, choking on his own blood, fell to the ground. He tried to gasp when Hadjar thrust his sword into the man's skull. The body of a seriously wounded soldier, writhing in agony, would only hinder them in the battle to come...

Other warriors did the same if a dying comrade fell close to them. One such body could lead to the death of ten strong warriors. The healers never appeared at the beginning of a battle, it would be useless.

"Hold!" Dogar shouted as the cannons slammed against the other side of the wall of shields.

This time, the whistle could be heard only at the last moment, when the cannonball was already so close that it would be impossible to dodge it.

Hadjar could hear heart-rending cries behind him. The smell of burning flesh filled the air and a severed hand landed right next to Hadjar.

"Damn it," Nero hissed, throwing the grotesque bundles of flesh to the side.

Some of the very young soldiers vomited. Right into their helmets.

"Hold!" Dogar shouted, helping the spearmen hold the wall of shields.

Hadjar saw their foes rushing in, trying to find gaps between the shields. They beat against the shield wall with their maces, trying to break through it.

Not a moment too soon, explosions could be heard from their side of the barrier. The Fort had launched its first salvo, and while they had half as many cannons as the nomads did, their cannonballs flew much farther.

Suddenly, a loud whistle assaulted their ears.

Hadjar managed to notice Dogar's look of stunned horror, and then everything was plunged into chaos.

A shell, tearing through the flesh of the horses and horsemen alike, slammed into the wall of shields. Great chunks of earth, destroyed iron, and people flew into the air. The enemy immediately flooded through the newly-formed gap.

"Stop them!" Dogar cried out, wiping other people's flesh and blood off his helmet.

Some infantry immediately moved toward the new center of the battle.

"Hadjar!" Nero cried out as he was being carried by the general stream of soldiers toward the battle with the cavalry.

"Damn it," the young officer swore.

His line was holding the shields. But he couldn't abandon a friend, nor could he break through dozens of firmly entrenched soldiers.

Using someone's thigh as a step, Hadjar climbed onto the shoulder of a warrior next to him, and then stepped out onto the edge of the wall of shields.

With his sword drawn, he towered above the front line, which stretched out for many miles.

The arrows buzzed through the sky and the cannonballs whistled. From somewhere in the west, huge trebuchets were being pulled closer to the battlefield and high siege towers were getting closer to the Fort. The battle was already bloody and had been costly for both sides. It looked like things would only get worse.

The fiercest battle was being waged on the hill, where thousands of people had already died.

Both the Fort's and the enemy's artillery were constantly firing, as evidenced by the smoke clouds rising above them.

The screams of soldiers dying in agony resonated with the vicious cawing of the crows that had risen high above the field of battle. They were circling over it like sharks, waiting for the beginning of their feast.

Just a couple of minutes had passed since the battle had started.

Hadjar, after locating Nero, ran over to help his friend, deflecting arrows along the way.

Chapter 67

"Nero!" he shouted and jumped off the 'wall' directly onto a horse.

He cut the rider's throat and then threw him off the horse, after which the rider was quickly slaughtered by the infantry's hooks. Each of the front rank soldiers had been given a hook—the soldiers would slam these hooks into the cavalrymen's hips and pull them down from their horses, turning the enemy into helpless, easy prey.

Nero was fighting five savages at the same time. Their light sabers caused sparks as they struck his heavy blade, but after each of these sparks, someone's severed leg or hand would quickly follow.

"Forward!" Hadjar hit the horse's sides and it neighed and rushed into the thick of battle.

Horses, people, blood, steel—everything was mixing into one boiling brew of fear and pain. And only because of that same pain and fear, the people, despite the hail of arrows coming down repeatedly and the whistling of cannonballs overhead, fought as if they'd been born only yesterday and never intended to die.

Hadjar slammed into the enemy ranks from behind. Holding the reins with his left hand, he delivered swift and brutal sword slashes with his right. A rider fell to the ground after each strike.

Hadjar's sword easily cut through even the strongest armor, not to mention pliable flesh and bones. Part of the savages died immediately, and those who'd gotten away with only a wound were trampled to death either by the enemy or their own allies.

"Hadj!" Nero, after decapitating one more opponent, stretched out his blood covered hand.

Hadjar, bending down, grabbed his comrade's forearm and pulled hard. Nero jumped up onto the back of the horse at once.

"You came just in time," he patted Hadjar on the shoulder, and a moment later, ran an approaching enemy horseman through with his blade.

Pushing the dying savage off the horse, Nero climbed onto it.

Emergency message!	If the enemy's artillery threat is not neutralized, then the host's probability of survival will decrease to a critical value: <5%

"Cannons!" Hadjar shouted, cutting off someone's hand, and then stabbing them through the throat. "We need to destroy the cannons! They'll crush our entire flank if we don't!"

And then another volley rumbled overhead as if to confirm Hadjar's words. A cannonball swept through the crowd of nomads with a whistle, killing them on the spot. The savages did not spare their own soldiers if they saw an opportunity to weaken the enemy.

Human bodies and shattered shields soared into the sky along with the dead horses.

"Infantry!" Nero shouted, raising his sword into the air. "Attack!"

Hadjar and Nero, urging their horses forward, rushed into the battle, pushing the enemy away from the ever-increasing gap in the wall, and the infantrymen raced after them, shouting wildly. They struck the enemy with spears and swords, leaving the ground covered in blood, and the dying groaning in agony under their feet.

Hadjar swung his sword tirelessly on either side of him. He wasn't a cavalryman, and therefore his strikes were much weaker than usual. But they were still strong enough to end a life every time he struck.

They were going through the enemy's flank like a thin nail through a heavy board. It was difficult and slow-going, but with each new hammer strike, it went in just a bit deeper and deeper.

A savage infantryman tried to stab Hadjar's side with a spear. The Prince released the reins and, clutching the metal weapon under the deadly tip, pulled hard. The man flew up into the sky, and then his body, which had been split in half, splattered on the riders hurrying to organize a counter-attack.

Nero once again swung his sword, cutting off the head of an enemy's horse with one strike. It fell, burying the screaming savage beneath it. The infantry coming up behind them finished him off right then and there.

Thanking his friend with a nod, Hadjar put the spear on his shoulder and threw it with all the force he could muster. It pierced through a galloping horseman, then crashed into a second one behind him, knocked him off his horse, and stopped only after ending a third soldier. All three died together, killed by the same spear.

Losing themselves in cutting their way through the enemy riders, Nero and Hadjar didn't know how long they'd been wading through the hordes of enemies to get to their nearest cannons. But, judging by the number of volleys they'd heard, they hadn't taken long to get there. The nomads were numerous, but they were poorly organized and not very well trained. They had been hardened by endless raids, but nothing more.

Most of them couldn't do anything to stop two practitioners of the Formation level. And therefore, they'd probably channeled their energy and hatred toward the infantry following after the two cultivators. When Nero and Hadjar saw the cannons in front of them, which the gunners were dousing in water carefully so that they'd cool down, but not crack, then...

"Damn it!" Nero swore when, after turning around, he saw nothing but a bloody battle in the distance.

They were alone in the midst of enemy troops.

A moment later, Hadjar's horse whinnied and began to roll over onto its side. The Prince managed to pull his leg out of the stirrup and jump down. As he did so, he noticed numerous wounds on the body of the animal.

"Get up!" Nero extended his hand to Hadjar, but as he did so, an enemy spear slammed into his horse.

He barely managed to jump out of the saddle and avoid being buried under the carcass of the dying animal.

They stood back to back. A bloodthirsty grin danced on Nero's face, which was covered in his own and other people's blood. Hadjar was calm and concentrated. His clothes had turned from red to purple.

Dozens of opponents surrounded them. They were wearing light armor, armed with short sabers, axes, or maces. With their painted faces, they resembled fiends from the abyss, hungry for the flesh and blood of outsiders. They were going to tear apart the two brave souls that had dared to try and seize their cannons.

"Whoever gets to a hundred first," Nero growled. "Is buying the wine."

"Ok," Hadjar nodded.

They didn't move except to circle in place, keeping their backs to each other. The nomads didn't wait long. They saw only two opponents in front of them, while there were dozens of them.

A young man couldn't wait any longer and attacked first. Armed with a saber and a small shield, he rushed at the enemies. He managed to lift his saber, but in the next instant, his body had already been reduced to bloody chunks. A fountain of blood shot into the sky and its scarlet drops hadn't even fallen to the ground yet when Hadjar sent a second savage to a better world as well.

Due to standing back to back with him, he could feel Nero was wielding his blade, and thanks to that comforting feeling, his heart grew stronger, and a sense of confidence arose from the depths of his soul.

And so they stood, unyielding. Two warriors against hundreds of savages. They kept fighting. They blocked attacks, chopped limbs off and impaled foes. Scarlet blood soared into the sky. The severed arms and legs fell to the ground.

Someone tried to stab Hadjar with a spear - but the officer cut it off with a flick of his sword, and then sent the severed tip forward with a sweep of his hand. It pierced through the larynx of one nomad and got stuck in the eye of a second. Two cries of agony merged into one. The savages fell to the ground, but their comrades walked over their bodies, overcome with bloodlust.

A mace whistled on his left and Hadjar grabbed it at the base and, pulling on it to force the enemy forward, rammed his sword through the savage's gut. Pushing the body aside and into the path of other foes charging at him, he struck down with the mace, toward his right, striking the head of another enemy. It broke like a rotten watermelon. Scarlet liquid and gray matter painted Hadjar's chest, and he immediately threw the mace. It knocked down at least four of the savages, and they choked on blood, feeling the fragments of their ribs piercing their insides.

"Break through!" Nero shouted and they abandoned their previous position.

Nero managed to carve a hole in the ring their opponents had made around them, and they rushed through together. Shoulder to shoulder, they were sending the enemy fighters to meet their forefathers. Their swords, the cries of the dying, and splashes of blood—that was their entire world in those moments.

They covered every inch of the ground separating them from the cannons with the bodies of dead and dying enemies. Hadjar didn't even immediately notice that someone's severed hand was slowing his pace. It was gripping his ankle tightly.

He swung his blade, sending the stump into the air. It crashed into the face of another savage, obscuring her view for a moment. Actually, that stump was the last thing that the savage saw in her life. Soon, her head fell to the ground, and Hadjar threw her body at the opponents chasing them. They fell to the ground after another attack, and remained there forever – Nero had used his 'Giant' technique.

A giant palm made of energy, with swords instead of fingers, had nailed at least a dozen savages to the ground at once.

"Save your energy!" Hadjar ordered while dismembering a foe.

"I know, I know," Nero growled.

They couldn't constantly use their Techniques and were therefore forced to save energy so they could strengthen their own bodies.

Finally, they reached the cannons. The savages, upon seeing the two demons of the underworld burst through the ranks of the cannons' defenders with ease, abandoned their posts and fled in terror.

Fifteen cannons had been left without any protection or gunners.

"Blow them up!" Nero cried out, holding back the enemy's onslaught alone.

The cannons had been positioned on a small hill that had only one path leading up to it. The only other approaches were covered in grass made slick with blood, rendering it impassable, and so Nero was holding almost a couple of hundred opponents back quite successfully. They were forced to line up and could not attack him in groups of more than two or three people at a time.

Hadjar looked to the west. The high siege towers were already moving forward, threatening the walls of the fort.

The hill for which the bloodiest battle was being fought had been ruined. One of the traps the engineers had set up had worked as it should have, sending several thousand savages to the plain. Alas, hundreds of defenders had joined them in death.

The 'Fire water' was burning, forcing the enemy riders to separate into smaller groups. Helion's cavalry was fighting them with all their might.

The cannons thundered from atop the walls of the Fort, their flashes blooming like crimson flowers in the night. Because of the flames, soot, and constant cannon fire, the sky was covered with black clouds. The part of the valley where the sunlight might have come through had already been enveloped by nightfall.

It was only the second hour of the battle.

"Keep them back!" Hadjar cried out.

He sheathed his sword and, gasping for air, turned each of the cannons toward the west. As he loaded the cannonballs, he watched Nero, who didn't seem to be encountering much resistance from the enemy. Practitioners at the Bodily Nodes level, and especially at the initial stages, posed as much of a threat to them as mosquitoes did. They were annoying, they could bite them, but they weren't actually dangerous.

Ten minutes later, fifteen cannons fired. Fifteen cannonballs flew across the sky and struck the other gunnery hill. It was torn apart, chunks of earth flying into the air, and the metallic debris of the blown up cannons rained down on the fleeing crews.

Filling 'his' cannons with gunpowder, Hadjar ignited the wicks on the demolition charges.

He joined Nero and they rushed into the enemy ranks. Two minutes later, after exchanging tired glances, they collapsed to the ground, hiding underneath the corpses of their enemies and the bodies of those who were already bleeding to death.

Protected by this improvised shield, they waited for the explosion. The cries of the wounded and those who had been burned alive filled the air around them.

Getting out from under the bodies, they looked around. The battle had moved farther west, to where the siege towers had already been deployed.

General Leen's army had diminished noticeably, but the horde of nomads was still spread out over almost the entire visible space.

"Damn it…"

Nero pulled off his helmet, which was a clear sign of how disturbed he was.

Winged, humanoid creatures were flying up from the hills. They were clutching spears and flammable barrels in their hands and paws, their slave collars plainly visible. Some savages flew by them, riding some winged raptors.

"That's why they needed those creatures," Hadjar exhaled, wiping his own and other people's blood off his face.

"Damn Lascanian," Nero took hold of his sword with his other hand and turned to Hadjar. "Are you thinking what I'm thinking?"

There, in the east, monsters had joined the savages' ranks. The monsters that were in the sky attacked the army with 'bombs' and killed the gunners and archers at the walls of the Fort with spears. But there were other monsters - huge creatures, crawling on the ground. Something like small catapults had been hoisted on their backs. Encased in armor, they were easily trampling General Leen's army. And giants with faces akin to sea creatures followed after them.

They were also wearing armor, their giant fangs bared. They could send several soldiers to the other world with just one sweep of their paws. Streams of water burst from their mouths with a roar and cut through people as if they were sharp blades.

"As always, buddy," Hadjar nodded. "As always."

They ran, and, pushing off the pile of bodies, soared into the air. Clinging to the paws of the monster flying over them, they jumped on its back.

Both Nero and Hadjar raised their swords over the nomad who was guiding the beast. They beheaded him so swiftly it seemed like he hadn't noticed a thing.

"How do we control this creature?" Nero yelled while grabbing the reins of the flying raptor.

Chapter 68

In the end, directing the monster was a process similar to 'steering a horse'. Nero commanded the creature, and Hadjar operated some kind of a huge, automatic crossbow. It had about a hundred short bolts in its 'cassette'. By turning the wooden handle, Hadjar launched one dart after another.

Together, they flew over the battlefield, soaring through the sky. Every one of Hadjar's shots found its target. He was not a prodigy marksman, and indeed - he looked more like a drunken jester than a warrior with a bow in his hands. But with the help of the neural network, which told him when and how to shoot, he was a real sniper of the skies.

Each dart would send the other winged creatures crashing down.

"Great shot, Hadj!" Nero tried to shout out, despite the roaring wind.

The winged humanoid hadn't had time to drop the barrel full of the combustible mixture. Rather, the creature and the barrel both fell right into the midst of the savages' horse archers. Hadjar and Nero cheered triumphantly, but their reign over the heavens couldn't last for long.

After a couple of minutes, two reptiles were on their tail. Darts whistled past their heads. And even if Hadjar wasn't a natural born marksman, Nero seemed like he'd been a pilot in his past life in Hadjar's old world.

"Hold on," he shouted to his friend and began to perform a sharp turn.

They weaved through the sky, dodging the projectiles fired by their pursuers. Explosive barrels hit the ground repeatedly. Too many creatures with bombs were still in the sky.

As they made a sharp turn, Hadjar managed to spot Lian, the head of the archers. She was bloodied and barely standing on the wall. Actually, she'd braced two short spears on the parapet floor and was leaning on their handles to stay upright.

She gave an order and a cloud of arrows flew into the sky. They mostly struck warriors. The savages or the Lidish – that distinction wasn't very important right now. The archers fired indiscriminately. But some of them also managed to bring down the winged creatures in the sky.

"We won't last much longer!" Nero shouted when two more nomads on winged reptiles joined their pursuers.

"Fly down!"

"Down where? Only the devil knows what's going on around here!"

Hadjar crawled over to his friend and pointed at one of the monsters. It was swinging its scaly paws. The claws, which were covered in thick, sturdy membranes, gutted horses and people alike. The streams of water escaping from its mouth left deep grooves in the ground as they sliced through everything.

"Over there," Hadjar said.

"You're crazy," Nero said, but still slapped the reptile's head with the reins.

He went into a steep dive. Their pursuers sped up behind them. They probably thought that the reptile they were pursuing would come out of its vertical fall at the last moment. That's what they believed would happen and so they waited for it. But the reptile crashed into the monster's back head on, and two silhouettes jumped off at the very last moment.

The savages failed to react quickly enough and all the four-winged monsters slammed into the nomadic cavalry.

"It's so nice to be back on the ground," Nero exhaled, holding his sword casually as he relished the feeling.

"There's the second one!" Hadjar shouted.

And so they rushed toward the nearest monster. It was about ten yards away. They once again cut their way through the enemy. But this time, they were on foot, fighting through the ranks of the cavalry, which was engaged in battle. The hooves of horses struck out like hammers, passing mere inches in front of their faces, and the spears and long broadswords fell like guillotine blades all around them.

Hadjar pulled someone off their horse, but instead of climbing on it, he only chopped off its legs and then pushed it with all his strength. And he was a lot stronger than he looked. With a wild neigh, the horse flew forward and collapsed on top of several horsemen. They stumbled and fell, buried under a pile of bodies.

The nomads that had been galloping behind them couldn't jump over the barrier and ended up stuck in the general heap. Hadjar and Nero used the piled up bodies to once again jump up. Nero mounted a horse and began cutting his way through. Hadjar, however...

As if he weighed less than a feather, he kept jumping from one horse to the next. The riders were all clustered tightly together, making it easier for him. With every leap, Hadjar brought his sword down on someone's neck, head, or torso.

The spurts of blood and the cries of the dying followed him. But Hadjar had gotten used to them. On the contrary, he now welcomed them. They were the harbingers of the ghost of a victory that might be snatched from this hell full of scarlet and orange. An inferno of blood and fire.

At some point, after forcefully pushing off from yet another rider, Hadjar landed behind Nero, who was swinging his heavy blade around like a child would a toy. Each of his blows found a new target.

Nero spurred the horse on and it jumped over another hill of bodies. On the other side of the mass of corpses, the battle with the monster and the savages was already underway. The infantry and horsemen were all trying to overwhelm the creature and bring it down. But it only growled as one 'bug' after another tried to penetrate its armor.

The monster was no less than twenty feet tall and crushed its enemies like ants. Its water attacks only made the situation worse.

"You're on top, I'm on the bottom!" Nero shouted.

"You're nasty," Hadjar smiled and pushed off the horse.

He soared into the air, aiming for the monster's muzzle. Hadjar, swinging his blade through the air, used the first stance of the 'Light Breeze' Technique while still airborne. A whirlwind consisting of cutting wind and blades was launched from the sword and crashed into the creature's paws.

The wind shredded the armor, and the blades destroyed its scales and spilled its blue blood on the ground.

The monster growled in pain, but the attack hadn't been enough to bring him down. Thankfully, Nero was already standing at the beast's feet. He swung his sword and a gigantic palm with knives instead of fingers grabbed hold of the creature's right leg. When the fist opened, the leg was gone.

The monster fell and Hadjar landed on his chest. He took a single, floating step and thrust his blade into the monster's throat.

"Lidish," Hadjar heard a low, menacing voice with a strong accent.

A giant, worthy of doing battle with Dogar, stepped forward out of the infantry ranks of the savages. Six and a half feet tall, two feet at the shoulders, holding a huge hammer in his hands.

"Cover me," Hadjar asked his friend and jumped down.

The soldiers of both armies formed a circle around them. Sometimes, someone too hotheaded would break the temporary 'truce' during this separate phase of the battle.

The would-be troublemaker was soothed by Nero's sword right away. The young warrior had Hadjar's back and would not allow anyone to interfere in the fierce battle.

The giant was circling Hadjar and displaying his tan muscles, which were covered only by the skins of various animals. He wore no armor. At all. Only skins, leather pants, and boots. Apparently, a single hammer was enough for him. Somebody's remains dripped down from it, but Hadjar believed that it would also be quite easy to break through the walls with such a weapon.

The savages greeted their illustrious warrior general with shouts of joy. He walked in circles, shaking his gigantic hammer. He growled like a wild beast and his red hair, tied into braids, sparkled, decorated both with beads and the teeth of his defeated enemies.

He was strong and powerful and saw only a little man with a pitiful sword in front of him. What could a sword do against his omnipotent hammer! He'd squashed dozens of swordsmen with his weapon, he'd forced hundreds of people to cry in terror and beg for their mothers. He was one of the most ferocious generals in the savages' army. He'd won his way to fame and fortune. He was powerful and strong. He would be the master of this battle!

Snarling like a mountain lion, he rushed in with a surprisingly fast jump. Bringing the hammer up over his head, he brought it down with such force that the ground around Hadjar sank slightly. But none of the warriors could understand what happened next.

The red-robed swordsman assumed a light, smooth stance. He slightly moved his blade and the hammer capable of crushing town walls didn't touch a hair on his head. It, as if directed by an invisible stream of wind, had twisted around Hadjar and hit the ground a yard from him. Many soldiers felt their bodies shaking from the strike and almost lost their balance, and in the place where the hammer had struck, a hole nearly three feet in diameter had formed.

The barbarian general was unable to raise his mighty weapon once more. He didn't even get a chance to growl one final time or comprehend his own death.

Steel whistled, the blade flashed, and his head rolled off his shoulders.

The savages howled with rage and rushed in to attack, but immediately ran into the infantry and cavalry of Lidus that had come to the rescue.

Suddenly, two lightning bolts flashed in the sky above the Fort, and then a rain of white lightning dragons struck the ground.

"The signal!" The officers of Lidus shouted and sent their troops toward the Fort to reinforce it.

To a casual observer, it might've looked like the army of General Leen had faltered and began to retreat. The savages roared in anticipation of a quick victory and charged in to pursue the Lidus army.

Hadjar and Nero ran to the Fort as well. But they chose a difficult path. Instead of running toward the gate that had been broken by the ram, they rushed in the direction of one of the savages' siege towers.

It was the fourth hour of the battle.

Chapter 69

Nero and Hadjar cut their way through to the siege tower. It was a huge construction made up of logs and covered with sheets of iron and shields from the outside. Inside, hundreds of savages were climbing the stairs. They would walk up in a continuous line until they were at the bridge.

Said bridge was a kind of 'tongue' that came out of the siege tower. It was positioned above and behind the battlements on the wall and had been fastened there with several hooks that were so heavy that they could not be easily removed.

Hadjar and Nero climbed the logs which had been drenched in blood. Arrows sometimes found a gap in the outer wall of the tower and then found the bodies of the besiegers. Any corpses were dropped straight down, and that is why there was no wall or any other kind of barrier on the back of the tower. Otherwise, within ten minutes of the attack, the stairs would've been clogged with dead bodies.

Slaughtering their enemy from behind, Hadjar and Nero kept climbing higher and higher. After they'd gotten past the first flight of stairs, someone had noticed that they were being pushed not by their allies, but by two warriors with bloodied faces and blades. Their eyes burned like the gems of the abyss, and not a single part of their bodies or armor was clean.

The battle inside the tower began. But despite the fact that Hadjar and Nero had already started breathing heavily, and were wielding their blades slower with each passing second as fatigue caught up to them, the savages still didn't have a chance. They were killed by the dozen, and their bodies were thrown down, filling the entrance to the tower, hindering the infantrymen hurrying to their comrades' rescue.

Hadjar swung his blade and then snatched an enemy's sword from his cut off hands. He nailed one of the savages to the wall with that sword, and, quickly turning around, kicked the falling body of the first enemy down the stairs. Waving his bleeding stumps, the savage fell on his back and rolled down, knocking over the fighters that had been able to get past the barrier of corpses.

The barbarian that had been nailed to a log with a sword croaked something, but Nero jabbed his pommel in the guy's face as he was passing by. The savage's skull crumpled like a cardboard box and he quieted down.

Nero's sword was too long for close quarters fighting, so he walked behind and slightly to the right of Hadjar. That way, he could cover Hadjar's side and prevent particularly zealous opponents from getting a hit on him with a saber or even a short spear.

Hadjar cut off a tall man's leg and threw him down. He screamed, and then a gentle thud was heard. It wasn't far to the ground, after all.

A woman with a saber stepped forward, but she didn't manage to reach Hadjar's right side, as she was impaled on Nero's long sword as soon as she tried. Her body tumbled down as well, following the previous one.

Setting a fast pace and carving a path through their foes, Hadjar and Nero quickly reached the bridge. There, covered by shields, the archers were on their knees. They were launching arrows at the parapet so that the defenders could not get to the hooks and get rid of them.

Nero and Hadjar finished off the archers with just two slashes and threw the shields at the savages running toward them.

Jumping onto the wall, they, without saying a single word to each other, immediately ran to opposite sides of the bridge. The hooks had been fastened with special chisels, and when they pried them out, the defenders of the Fort came just in time to push the bridge down.

Someone also brought a canvas bag and then threw it into the open 'mouth' of the tower. An archer, after dipping an arrow into some flammable liquid, shot at the bag. The bowstring sang and a powerful explosion rang out. Burning logs fell on the savages rushing in to attack and they screamed as they burned and died.

The arrows flew into the sky from down below and Hadjar and Nero, like the other defenders, immediately crouched, hiding behind the protection of the wall.

"Officers," one of the defenders crawled over to Nero. "Thank you. We've been fighting to get rid of this tower for half an hour."

"What's the situation, soldier?" Hadjar asked.

He looked out over the wall. Endless streams of enemies were flocking to the Fort. On horseback, on foot, some were even on monsters, and all of them were hurrying to trample and slaughter the last of the Lidus army.

"The gate was blown up about an hour and a half ago. There's fighting in the streets," the soldier spoke hurriedly, sometimes pausing in order to hide from the next cloud of arrows.

"Where's the senior officer in charge of this section of the wall?"

"He's dead," the soldier reported immediately. "As well as the mid-level officer. I've been commanding this sector for nearly three hours already."

It turned out he'd been in charge almost since the beginning of the battle...

"You've held on well, soldier. Keep up the-"

An arrow whistled and the man with whom Hadjar had just been talking fell onto his side. The arrow had pierced his helmet and then his head. It had flown through his right temple and the tip had exited from the left one.

The soldier's eyes rolled back and he began to fall on Hadjar, who immediately pushed the body aside, throwing it off the wall. The savages already had ladders up against the walls.

"We need to get out of here, Hadj," Nero said. "We'll have to exit the Fort on the other side."

"Let's go along the wall," Hadjar suggested after orienting himself.

But, unfortunately, there was an explosion and the neighboring section of the wall was blown to pieces like a demolished house of cards. The stones fell on the savages and the defenders found themselves plummeting. Screaming in terror, they tried to grab on to something but failed. They fell and met their death.

"You might want to stop talking," Nero suggested.

They turned in the other direction and saw that the bridge of a new siege tower had already been attached to the battlements on the wall. Dozens of savages were already rushing to the parapet.

"What was that you said about me not speaking?"

"Jump!"

Hadjar didn't have time to understand why Nero had dragged him down. They tumbled from the wall. Hadjar fell with his face turned up, so he didn't see where they landed. The only thing that he'd felt before landing was a terrible stench.

They found themselves in a seat that resembled a huge saddle for at least five people. Actually, Nero had already killed those five people by the time Hadjar had come to his senses and gotten back up.

"Go!" Nero yelled and cracked the reins.

A gigantic beast, resembling both an armadillo and an elephant simultaneously, went through the gap that had formed in the enemy ranks. There were usually five savages riding these monsters. Four archers and one 'driver'.

Nero and Hadjar, sticking to the tried and true methods, had once again captured an enemy transport.

"Hold the reins!" Nero threw two leather ropes to Hadjar.

He caught them on the fly and immediately stood on the edge of the seat. He directed the monster further into the fort, trampling and crushing the savages that had flooded the streets.

Nero, taking advantage of his long blade, was attacking the nomads who were trying to get on the monster and throw off the invaders. Every slash of his sword cut off arms or heads.

"Go south!"

"I know!" Hadjar snapped.

He pulled the reins to the side, guiding the beast out from under the rubble of a collapsing building. The monster wasn't very fast, but it ran with the weight and inevitability of a steamroller. Hadjar looked around. Rivers of blood were flowing through the channels along the streets. Hundreds, no, thousands of corpses had piled up all around them. Broken barricades and the cries of the dying helped paint a grim picture. Lots of fellow soldiers tried to get to Hadjar and Nero.

Many of them were killed by spears or arrows along the way. Some of them managed to reach the monster, but Nero and Hadjar couldn't take them 'aboard'. They would only turn away from them, continuing on their way, deep into the city.

As soon as they slowed down, even for a second, in order to take on a passenger, they would've immediately been riddled with arrows.

"Damn it!" Hadjar cried out, spotting something gravely dangerous.

This time, it was his turn to grab Nero and jump down. A painted savage, covered in small bags with burning wicks, had run out of a half-ruined building.

Roaring madly, the savage ran at the beast, and then there was an explosion.

A wave of hot air threw Nero and Hadjar aside and launched them about a dozen yards down the street.

Getting back up and shaking off the fetid entrails of the monster, they found themselves in the middle of a wide avenue. A horde of enemies was running toward them from the direction of the blown up gate, and a barricade of bales and carts piled up in a mass was blocking the street to the south.

"Over here! Quickly!" The people behind the barricade shouted.

"Gods," Nero wiped his face and tore off some blood that had gotten crusty on his eyelids. He almost tore out all of his eyelashes as well. "Will this day ever end?"

And so they ran to the barricade, deflecting arrows as they did.

Chapter 70

"Where's that damn second signal?!" the officer behind the barricade shouted.

Nero and Hadjar took the bows of the dead Fort defenders. In total, there were about forty people behind the barricade. Each soldier fired at the attackers as best they could. Huge waves of nomads flooded the streets and rooftops.

Whether they were on their monsters and horses or on foot, they were rushing toward the city. Some immediately started looting while others attacked the barricades or got bogged down in battles on the streets.

Hadjar pulled back the bowstring and fired. The arrow flew forward and then went almost a yard over the enemy's heads.

"Give that to me!" Nero roared, taking the quiver away from his friend. "You'll only waste arrows!"

Nero fired three arrows in quick succession. Each of them sent a savage to the next world.

"Where-"

The officer didn't have time to finish his question before pillars of white light struck the battlefield once more. The lightning bolts descended like angry dragons from the black skies to tear through everything and everyone.

"Pull back!" the soldiers screamed immediately.

Discarding their bows, arrows, and even part of their ammunition, the defenders jumped off the barricades and rushed toward the southern gate. They ran so fast that the steel soles of their shoes produced sparks when striking the stone of the streets.

Passing by the flashes of explosions and dodging buzzing arrows, they rushed to get to the southern gate. All the defenders and the army of General Leen were already gathered there.

They merged into a single, dense stream, trying to push through the narrow gate. The people shouted, pushing others aside. Someone fell and was immediately trampled underfoot, which turned the paving stones into a bloody mess.

Steel was creaking, the people were shouting and arguing, and the savages were riding their monsters, getting closer by the second.

"Not even a tenth of our people have left the Fort yet," Nero said.

He was breathing heavily, streams of sweat that mixed with blood and dust flowing down his red face.

"How much time do we have?"

Hadjar didn't look any better. He licked his dry lips from time to time and always spit it out right away – he'd tasted stone chips and someone else's blood. He had long since gotten accustomed to the taste of his own blood, but, surprisingly, the blood of a stranger had a different flavor.

"About ten minutes."

Hadjar looked at the horde charging toward them and then at the mass of soldiers rendered useless by fear. After all, they weren't even thinking about using all the space they had available or organizing in order to escape more quickly.

A frightened crowd behaved in much the same way a frightened beast would - always rushing forward, driven by their horror, ignoring all common sense.

"Again?" Nero sighed, realizing what was about to happen.

Taking a firm hold of his blade, he stood shoulder to shoulder with Hadjar.

A rather narrow street led to the gate. It had absorbed all the other streets so that there was only one way out of the city. The army had taken care to ensure it and had closed all the other approaches over the past month.

"They mustn't get by us," Hadjar grumbled, taking a fighting stance.

And once again, they were standing together against a whole army. Their swords gleamed and war cries erupted from their throats.

Hadjar caught an arrow as he fought and thrust it into the eye socket of a very young savage. He was fifteen winters old at most, maybe even younger. Hadjar threw his body toward the other attackers.

Nero did the same.

Less than a minute later, a 'barricade' had formed, made up of the bodies of their enemies. The incoming foes had to climb over it, and sharp swords awaited them on the other side.

Hadjar literally split a savage falling from the barrier in half, right down the middle. The young officer threw the two halves of the body at the foundation of the 'barricade', strengthening the 'wall'. Both Hadjar and Nero slashed, chopped and hacked relentlessly. They took someone's life with every swing.

The wall of bodies was growing and getting stronger, but there was no end in sight to the attackers' forces.

At some point, Hadjar felt the earth shaking.

He and Nero only had time to glance at each other, and the very next second a huge, armored beast broke through the barrier.

"Damn it!" Nero cried out.

The beast easily scattered the bodies and kept going forward. The jubilant horde was gleefully hooting behind it, hoping for an easy victory and a rich harvest. They could already see themselves riding their dashing horses across the expanses of peasant fields. See themselves burning villages, raping, killing. Taking the enemy's goods, stealing their money, and then bringing hundreds of thousands of beautiful women and handsome men back with them to be their slaves...

Hadjar stood in the way of the oncoming beast. Archers sat on its back, in a huge saddle. They launched dozens of arrows and darts at him, but they were all diverted thanks to the prince's blade.

"Calm Wind," Hadjar said dispassionately and assumed the second stance of the 'Light Breeze' Technique.

He waved his sword so smoothly and effortlessly it was as if he were checking its balance or just having some fun. And yet, the beast, even going all out, crashed not into Hadjar, but into the barrier of wind that had arisen.

The creature's speed had been so great, and the resistance so tough that its head immediately plowed into the ground. Its neck broke with a loud bang, and its hind legs flopped upward, nearly rolling over its own head.

The savages fell from the saddle and Nero's sword was already waiting for them. He killed them all and threw them under the feet of the charging horde. This made them freeze up slightly. The nomads were not particularly bold and when they saw that a situation was not going their way, they usually fled.

And they'd just witnessed a thin soldier in torn, red robes overcoming a gigantic beast with just one slash of his sword.

Suddenly, white lightning flashed in the sky for the third time.

"Demons!" Nero and Hadjar breathed out in unison.

They turned to look at the only way out of the city. There were already far fewer people there, but the crowd was still trying to squeeze through the arch. And after the third signal, they were doing it in a far more insane and desperate manner.

There wasn't a single chance that they would be able to break through to the outside. Neither of them had what it took to carve a path through their own comrades.

"I have an idea!"

Nero cut the creature's armored belly open with one slash and pointed at it. Hadjar nodded and sent a whirlwind of cutting wind and blades toward the horde. It turned about a dozen nomads into something resembling minced meat.

After buying themselves some time, they pulled out the monster's insides and... holding their breath, crawled inside. It was ugly and hot in there, but safe.

And after a few heartbeats, everything around them shook. It didn't simply 'shake', either. It was as if the sky, earth, and the universe itself had all collapsed simultaneously.

The carcass of the monster, in which the two madmen had hid, was lifted like a light feather and then dragged ten yards across the ground.

Nero and Hadjar got out, groaning in pain as they did so.

One of them pressed his hand to his side. Something white protruded from his bleeding forearm. It seemed Nero had an open fracture.

Hadjar tried to put some dirt on the hissing fluid which had coated his right thigh. Alas, it didn't help much, and the monster's boiling gastric juice still scalded his leg severely. Not to the bone, but enough that his flesh and muscles were visible.

"In any case, we're better off than the rest," Nero nodded toward the Fort.

Or rather, where the fort had once been. There wasn't even a single pair of stones left. Only a black ravine. Blood rained down and charred pieces of bodies, tiles, stones, and iron joined it, making for a truly macabre downpour.

Nero and Hadjar had been thrown far enough back to avoid the danger of being 'killed by the sky'. And, smiling widely, they watched the horde scamper back toward the forest.

Leaving behind their weapons and wounded soldiers alike, the savages ran away from the battlefield, screaming in horror all the while.

"It seems like the General's plan worked," Nero sat on the grass.

Hadjar, hissing in pain, collapsed nearby.

"Did you doubt it would?"

"That we can lure the horde into the fort, and then blow it up? No, I didn't doubt that for a second."

"What, then?"

Nero looked at the sky. Among other things, large flakes of black ash were falling from it. Stone dust mixed with flesh.

"The fact that you and I would survive."

Hadjar laughed.

Nero joined him.

And so they lay, sprawled out on the grass and laughing, and then they wept from the pain wracking their entire bodies. And even parts they could've sworn hadn't existed before today. In any case, Hadjar had never thought that even his hair could ache. He'd been proven wrong.

And yet, they were glad that they'd lived to see the end of the war.

"I wonder where our camp is now…"

"What?" Hadjar asked.

"I mean… Where do we go?"

Hadjar thought about it for a while and then swore.

Chapter 71

As it turned out, the camp wasn't that far from where the animal carcass had recently landed. The doctors had noticed the anomaly flying through the air and had hurried over to inspect it.

They hadn't been planning to try and save the creature and hadn't known that it might have soldiers inside it... they'd just hoped to get some meat from it. Because what the wounded soldiers needed most was food. And the army didn't have much left, to say the least.

Alas, along with the carcass, they ended up having to drag two more soldiers over to the new camp. The soldiers were either crying or laughing hysterically - it was hard to tell.

Hadjar and Nero were literally thrown on some mats spread on the ground. The young men were smeared with something fragrant, drank something smelly, and were then wrapped in bandages, covered with white blankets, and left for the gods to pass judgment on. If they survived, that would be good. If they didn't - it'd be very bad, but nothing could be done about it.

Soon, thousands of gravely wounded soldiers and tens of thousands that had sustained minor injuries were brought to the camp. The biggest problem was all the burns. People with those kinds of injuries were the most prevalent.

Soon enough, there was no place left in the meadow where they could lay down a new mat, which meant the 'healthiest' had to be asked to 'give up their mat for comrades in need'. Hadjar and Nero were also asked to leave the meadow at some point.

Nero's protruding bone had been set, he'd been given a few pills, and then put in a shoddy splint. He and Hadjar had to redo the splint. Fortunately, they were able to find a few of the more high-quality, metallic splints that the local orderlies used to fix a broken arm and had replaced the first splint with those.

Hadjar's burn had been slathered in ointment and then bandaged. Trying to help his recovery along, he found a doctor from Dogar's detachment and took some of the famous potion from him. The wound could at least heal a little faster with the help of that medicine, even if it wouldn't completely erase it.

Hadjar and Nero also heard some not exactly cheerful news from the doctor.

Dogar's detachment no longer existed. According to initial

information, only the two of them had survived. And whether that was true could easily be checked with the help of the medallions that they wore around their necks. The devices didn't just watch their actions and award them points accordingly, but also determined whether they were alive or were already dead.

Yes, the information might've been inaccurate. The medallion could've come off, been lost in the heat of battle or something else, but still...

"The commander?" Hadjar asked while fixing the bandage on his leg.

The healer shook his head sadly.

"Damn it!" Nero kicked the ground.

Hadjar sighed and looked at the sky that had begun to brighten.

The mighty Bear Dogar had been a warrior among warriors. The person who'd made him, Hadjar, much stronger, and not just physically. Dogar had strengthened his will, his heart... the commander had taught him to truly take responsibility for himself and his actions.

And now that man was gone.

Hadjar touched his heart and saluted.

"Live free," he repeated Dogar's favorite saying. "Die worthy."

Nero kicked the ground once again and then calmed down.

"Hey, you two," one of the passing orderlies cried out. "Do you have any strength left?"

"A little!"

"Then follow us – we need help getting the wounded soldiers back from the field."

Despite their wounds, and the day full of fighting, and the fact that they had barely enough strength left to breathe, Nero and Hadjar followed after the healers.

Passing through the camp, they looked around. There were mats with moaning, crying and screaming soldiers lying on them everywhere. Many of them clutched at stumps that had once been legs or arms. The orderlies, right there on the ground, would insert sticks into the soldiers' mouths and amputate their limbs.

Despite their victory, the camp looked like a small subsection of hell where the demons had already begun to torment poor, damned souls.

The new army camp, or what was left of it, was behind a small copse. Passing through it, Hadjar and Nero froze for a moment.

"Finish off the enemy," the commander of the medicinal corps ordered. "As for our soldiers, the ones who can't be carried back to camp or... won't survive even if we carry them back... should also be given mercy."

The orderly he was talking to turned away too abruptly and went to the field.

Hadjar could not take a single step further. The whole area, as far as the eye could see, was littered with bodies.

Dead, moaning, wounded, dying, impaled on a spear, torn to pieces, burned, broken people... were everywhere.

The once beautiful plain was covered in bodies, all the way to the horizon.

Hadjar looked at his feet - they were buried in blood up to the ankle.

"Damn it," Nero hissed. "Damn it... Damn it!"

"Let's go," Hadjar said softly.

Overcoming their fatigue, they kept dragging the bodies back to camp until nightfall. Only when they themselves had almost collapsed on the battlefield from exhaustion were they replaced by the lightly wounded soldiers. As well as by those warriors who'd come out of this monstrous meat grinder with no more than a couple of cuts or bruises. Those people must have been cared for by God since their birth.

The hard, brutal days stretched on.

Hadjar and Nero set up their tents a small distance away from the general camp out of habit. But no one else was there with them, at the site Dogar's detachment had used to occupy. Only Healer. But after a couple of days, even he withdrew from the spot and went to stay where his fellow doctors were encamped.

And so, they stayed together.

Serra came one night. Not to Hadjar - but to Nero.

Hadjar figured that it would be good to take a walk around the camp. After all, he wouldn't be falling asleep any time soon, not with the throaty groans of those two filling the night air.

He wandered through the camp. But there was no dancing, no guilt, only sad, old songs. The soldiers sang them around the fires, peering into the flames as if they were looking for answers.

"Officer Hadjar," one of the soldiers saluted.

Hadjar was surprised, but nodded in reply.

"Officer," came from the other side.

"Officer Hadjar."

"Officer!"

The words were said by many soldiers, officers, and even senior officers. They saluted him, and Hadjar was surprised at the fact they knew his name.

Why was he walking around the camp? It looked more like a graveyard, only filled with the living dead. Expressionless faces, dead eyes, nothing more...

Maybe he'd hoped that he would find a familiar face among the soldiers. The indestructible giant would get up, stretch out his hand and say,

"That was a glorious battle, assistant... Be ready for training tomorrow!"

But there was only wind, blowing through the treetops, instead. It produced a sad, hopeless rustling of leaves.

"Officer Hadjar," a young soldier saluted him. "Join us."

Several dozen officers, soldiers, and even commanders were huddled together on some fallen logs by a small fire. Hadjar nodded a greeting to Helion, who was pressing a hand against the bandage that covered his left eye.

After a battle, every warrior, regardless of rank, would try to find comfort in their comrades. That way, they could believe that they were alive, and the reality surrounding them wasn't simply their last dream.

Hadjar nodded and sat down beside the young soldier.

He leaned on someone as well, seeking support.

His soul calmed.

Grabbing an old lute, one of the soldiers began to sing. He was shortly joined by the rest of the warriors sitting by the fire. A light tune caressed the flames and fields stretching out all around them.

> I bravely fell in that last fight,
> In battle I proved my might!
> Now take a step toward the light,
> Life is no longer your plight.

Each and every soldier put on their armor on the third day. Some were groaning in pain and others were gritting their teeth. But everyone who could stand on their feet, even if only with someone's support, put on their armor.

They stood around the huge funeral pyres in orderly rows.

Less than three hundred thousand had survived of the two million that had gone into battle.

> I will lie beneath the wall,
> I will lie beneath the sod,
> Please, come visit, by God...

General Leen stood among the warriors. She was barely managing to stay upright, leaning on a wooden crutch, and the sleeve of her simple, canvas clothes dangled in the wind instead of her left hand. She was pale and looked aged, but she'd also come to pay her respects to the soldiers who'd died in the fight.

Nero was standing next to Hadjar. Serra was somewhere nearby.

They peered into the huge bonfires. Perhaps they would see their commander's face somewhere in the depths of the orange flashes.

That morning, I held on like a fool,
I kissed your lips, I stroked your hair,
Your name repeated like a prayer -
Losing you was my nightmare...
But the reality is far more cruel...

The general, whose beautiful face now had several terrible scars, lifted her spear. She hit it hard against the ground and the soldiers once again felt the earth shake under their feet.

They grabbed their weapons and struck them against their shields and armor.

I lie beneath the stone.
I lie beneath the glade.
The path to me is overgrown,
Covered with rust my blade.

They all continued to tirelessly make noise, trying to drown out the crackle of the fires. They said farewell to their fellows, their commanders, their friends... who were now on their last journey. They said farewell to the warriors who'd shed their last drop of blood for their native land. Those who'd died so that other people might live.

They said farewell to the heroes. They sent them off with war cries and the sound of weapons striking armor.

I don't know what to say,
My Mom and Dad...
Both still wait up and pray...

Well, there'd always be new battles, new deaths, and the ash and smoke of funeral pyres would once more fly into the night sky. But people would continue to sing songs about the Moon General and the Battle at the Blue Wind Ridge for hundreds of years to come.

Songs about how two million people had destroyed five million savages. Of how'd they fought against the flying creatures, of how they'd blown up the Fort. Of how they'd done everything in their power to preserve their homeland.

They continued to beat their weapons against anything they could, and the general steadfastly continued to slam her spear against the ground.

Their friends were leaving.

I am...
Beneath the wall.

Love me,
Forget me,
I'm not with you now
My love…

Chapter 72

The army of the Moon General Leen had been stationed at Spring Town for three months now. It was licking its wounds and recruiting new privates and officers. Hadjar had been in charge of the exam a couple of times. Alas, it had always ended badly. For some reason, when he was the examiner, he would often get swarmed by the women.

"It's all because a lot of people know about you and me," Nero said, placing one more dummy on their parade ground.

The place where about a thousand trainees had once used to suffer and train now belonged to the two friends. A feeling of loneliness sometimes came over them because of that fact, but more often than not, they were calmed by it.

And they'd had to cut some new logs. The old pieces of wood had gotten covered in grass during their absence.

"How could they know?" Hadjar waved his friend's words away.

He was carrying something like a huge plow on his back. Only instead of digging up the ground, this tool was used to remove the soil altogether. They would then have to bring some sand in and make a completely new training ground.

"What about all the songs praising our deeds in battle? Do you know how many songs there are about us?"

"Nope."

"I don't know either, but it's a lot. Especially considering that you and I covered the withdrawal of the army from the Fort."

"Yeah, we sure did," Hadjar smiled wryly. "You and I were saving our own asses and weren't covering the retreat of the army at all."

"Well, the bards aren't very interested in those details," Nero shrugged. He fanned himself with a towel and leaned on the dummy he'd been working on. "In addition, we blew up forty cannons, flew across the sky on a reptile, burned down a siege tower, killed two monsters, and you also sent the nomad general to the endless prairies."

"Plains," Hadjar corrected.

"Same difference. Let's rest a bit."

Hadjar agreed. They hadn't yet recovered their strength enough after such an exhausting battle, and they often needed smoke breaks. Quite literal ones, in fact. After getting back to the city, they'd bought some medicinal tobacco from the healers and now filled their pipes with it often.

It was tasty and healthy.

Sitting on a pyramid of logs, they each lit a cigarette.

Someone meowed. Hadjar stretched out his palm and Azrea jumped on it immediately. She grabbed a piece of dried meat out of habit and climbed into her customary spot against Hadjar's bosom.

"Do you think she's gotten bigger?" Nero asked, blowing a ring of smoke into the sky.

"Of course she has," Hadjar replied.

Azrea had used to fit on his palm with room to spare. Nowadays, while she could still fit, it was getting a bit too small for her.

"I can't wait for our weapons to be forged."

After returning to Spring Town, Hadjar and Nero had brought the fangs of the Ancient Tiger to the artifactor who'd come from the Empire. He'd taken too long to get there and Hadjar suspected that it was somehow related to the librarian. But only demons knew the true reason. He was more worried about forging his new sword, which had already taken three months by now.

"Have you been arguing with Serra again?"

"What makes you say that?"

Hadjar smiled. His friend was quite predictable.

"When you two quarrel, not only does your tent start to burn, but you also begin to talk about weapons all the time."

Nero grunted, and then sighed sadly.

"It's just that... When we're together, we argue constantly. And yet, when we're apart... I immediately feel awful."

"That's love... I guess."

"You should also find someone, Hadjar. Oh, right, I forgot you don't have to look for a woman, you just need to crook your finger and half of Spring Town will come to you."

Hadjar smiled.

"I only need him," the Prince pointed at the messenger hurrying toward the parade ground.

"You have bad taste," Nero commented, grinning at his friend.

"Go to hell, officer Nero."

By that time, the general's messenger had already reached the pyramid of logs.

"Senior officer Hadjar," he saluted. "You and your assistant are being summoned to the War Council."

"Thanks. You're free to go."

The messenger saluted once again and rushed off in the opposite direction.

"You could have made someone else your assistant," Nero jumped off the pyramid. "Senior officer Hadjar."

"Don't be cranky, officer Nero."

They exchanged playful strikes (which could've sent any practitioner below the level of the Bodily Rivers to their forefathers) and went to the General's tent.

Along the way, Hadjar nodded at numerous greetings and salutes. He had to admit, he'd probably become at least somewhat famous after the battle.

And yet, no matter how paradoxical it may have seemed, he'd also become stronger. After such an exhausting battle, one that had pushed him to the limit of his abilities, Hadjar realized that he had touched on certain truths. They were still mystical and mysterious truths, but now they were somewhat closer to him.

He hadn't managed to become 'One with the World', but the Honor Points he'd received had been enough to buy numerous ingredients. Thanks to them, Hadjar made relatively easy progress to the next stage of the 'Formation'.

Last night, he'd been able to break his Seed into Fragments. And he'd not only broken the Seed, but, more importantly, kept the Fragments from falling apart.

Status, Hadjar ordered mentally, nodding at a man passing by.

Name	Hadjar
Level of cultivation	Formation (Fragment Stage)
Strength	2.2
Dexterity	2.56
Physique	2.16
Energy points	4.2

Of course, the numbers were important, but not exactly very accurate. In fact, Hadjar could now pick up six logs and run with them on his back for almost four hours. And when sparring, he had to fight against at least five practitioners at the last stages of the Bodily Rivers at once to get any effect.

He and Nero often sparred, but their fights looked more like chess games these days. They knew each other's tactics too well.

Finding other practitioners in the camp who were at the Formation Stage wasn't a trivial task.

They approached the General's tent. The guards at the entrance immediately hit their iron gloves against their breastplates.

"Senior officer Hadjar," they greeted. "Officer Nero."

"At ease," Hadjar nodded and went inside.

All the commanders of the army had already gathered in here. Astonished, Hadjar had recently discovered that he was now one of them. He'd learned about it after the General had handed him the medallion of a Senior Officer.

"Commander Hadjar," the Moon General nodded. "We've been waiting for you. Now we can begin."

Hadjar felt a bit of déjà vu. He remembered how, until quite recently, she would greet Dogar like this... May he rest in peace.

Several people had already gathered at the table. Helion, the commander of the cavalry, looked more serious... without an eye. The beautiful Lian, the head of the archers, stood next to him. She had a broken leg, but that wasn't much of a problem for the strong practitioner.

Tim, the spymaster, was... dead. Instead of him, a tall, lean, middle-aged man was attending the meeting. He didn't have a sword or saber, but two curved, long daggers. He looked at people a little strangely, as if he saw not the people themselves, but through them. It was the look of a professional killer.

And rather creepy.

Hadjar greeted the new spymaster with a nod.

Simon was a good man with a difficult past. He and Hadjar often chatted.

Tuur, the chief engineer, now walked with a crutch. His leg had been cut off by a healer. However, the most important thing for the chief engineer was that he'd kept his brain, as he could work even while missing a leg.

"I want all of you to listen to the report from the Generals."

The General, who was now covered with scars, pointed at a figure hidden in the shadows with the wooden prosthesis that had replaced her left hand. The woman she'd gestured toward looked like a shitty person at first glance.

Wearing a light leather jacket and high-heeled boots, she stood ramrod straight and constantly adjusted her brown hair.

"By the order of the Highest Generals, the army of the Moon General Leen must be at the border with the Kingdom of Balium in two months."

The commanders looked at each other. Damn it! Why were they being sent to the cursed north again? To the border they shared with a kingdom Lidus had never fought against before. What could Balium, the birthplace of 'The Black Gates' sect, ever need from such a backwater as Lidus?

And now the situation had been turned completely around. What did Lidus, aided by the knowledge and resources of the Empire, need from such a 'beggar' as Balium?

"You'll camp there and wait for further instructions from the Generals."

Helion suddenly banged his fist on the table.

"Fuck you with your 'wait for further instructions'. You're sending us to war!"

"I hasten to remind you, Senior officer, that you are a subject of the King. As the King decrees, so it shall be. The orders of the Generals are the King's orders."

"Does the King know that we have less than half a million soldiers?" Hadjar asked. "More than a hundred thousand of them are untrained recruits. We don't even have enough ammunition, or supplies, or even carts to load it all on!"

The messenger of the General Headquarters turned around and gave him an icy look.

"You're Senior officer Hadjar, if I'm not mistaken. Is the medal you received for your actions at the battle of Blue Wind Ridge too heavy for you?"

"I'll have to sell this medal to buy food and armor for my soldiers!"

"Then do it," the messenger answered calmly. "Orders aren't up for debate, Senior officer. I'm surprised I need to remind you of that."

Immediately, all the commanders started shouting at once. They suggested the messenger do several... Highly uncomfortable things.

"Easy!" Leen said, and they all fell silent.

The General turned toward the unpleasant woman, who shuddered slightly in response. The Moon General, even after losing a hand, was feared and respected by all. And as for the few who didn't respect or fear her—they were either dead or a fool. The latter meant being dangerously close to becoming the former.

"Does the King know about our poor condition? How drastically we suffered in that battle? Or did you just give him some papers and tell him some stories?"

The messenger twitched as if she'd been slapped, then snorted again and threw several scrolls on the table.

"Here is the order. On the first day of the third month, you must be encamped near the border with Balium, otherwise… It'll be treason."

Looking at them haughtily, she left the tent.

"Bloody officials!" Helion struck the table again. "This is suicide!"

"No, it's an order, Helion," Leen took the scrolls and handed them to the others. "We're once again going to war."

Chapter 73

Hadjar and Nero came out of the tent. They saw hundreds of young, carefree men and women walking through the camp. The fresh recruits were trying on armor and testing the balance of their weapons. They looked like kids who'd decided to play 'knights and demons', running around, laughing and without a care in the world.

They didn't look like soldiers. They weren't ready to die.

"Senior officer Hadjar," everyone around them said reverentially.

He was saluted and people bowed to him. Hadjar tried not to look into their eyes—he didn't want to remember those who would soon be taken by the grim reaper.

Going past the general camp, Hadjar and Nero returned to their own camp. Where there'd once been a thousand tents, not to mention Dogar's own marquee, now only two tents remained. The larger tent belonged to the senior officer, the other, more colorful tent belonged to his assistant.

Hadjar moved the tent flap aside and went in. Unlike the General's tent, the ground in his dwelling was covered with old, shabby mats, and not with planks. He'd inherited them from Dogar.

Some scrolls, maps, and medallions lay on the numerous boxes that were being used as tables. It looked like a scientist, not a soldier, lived here. Serra often joked about that.

The newly minted and only caster in the army's ranks could've had her own tent. But she lived together with Nero, and because of this, their tent would often go up in flames. Then they'd be laughing and hugging, fixing it together and patching it up, and that's why their tent was so colorful.

"I don't believe that the King would have sent us to the border," Nero grumbled and then sat down on a bunch of skins, rags, and mats.

This pile of refuse was what passed for Hadjar's bed.

"He would've sent us," Hadjar objected. "If he had no idea how unprepared we were."

"How could he not know? People have been singing songs about it all over the Kingdom for three months now!"

"Ordinary people sing those songs, but the ass of his Majesty sits in a high tower in the Palace. The voices of the common folk are never heard up there."

Nero snorted. He took out his pipe and filled it with tobacco. He patted his clothes and found no flint. Hadjar filled his own simple, carved pipe with tobacco as well. His pipe was dear to him; it was a memento. He used his flint, lit it, and then threw an extra flint he had at Nero.

They both inhaled and exhaled thick puffs of smoke.

"Should we send a messenger?"

"If you don't regret spending the money," Hadjar shrugged.

"I don't give the healers all my money, unlike you."

Hadjar only smiled. He was, as always, broke. He always gave the doctors and scientists his entire salary, buying a variety of ingredients needed for the Technique that strengthened his body. It was worth noting that the result had been quite noticeable thus far.

His skin was almost as strong as stone. In any case, even the strongest strikes from practitioners below the level of the Bodily Rivers left no trace on him. The warriors who'd managed to cultivate meridians in their bodies could leave deep cuts.

Even Nero's punches felt much weaker now. They were still deadly, but Hadjar could feel his progress.

"Do you think it'll be a waste of time?" Nero asked.

"Absolutely," Hadjar nodded. "Why do you think the King doesn't know the whole story and is sending us to war? And why we're at war with The Black Gates in the first place?"

"With Balium," Nero corrected.

"Don't be so naive, buddy. Balium is the cash cow of The Black Gates. If you start a war with that kingdom, you will have to fight the sect as well."

Nero thought about it for a moment and then shrugged.

"I won't argue with that," he said, producing another ring of smoke. "If it turns out that the generals have forged the message...They'll be staked alive, at best."

"If they did it and it's found out, sure," Hadjar added. "I have a feeling the king's going to have a lot of trouble on his hands soon, regardless."

The friends looked at each other. People were afraid to say it out loud, but rumors had spread throughout the Kingdom that a rebel army had appeared in the mountains to the northwest. Some had presumed that they would be led by the 'true king'—Prince Hadjar. But most figured that one of the friends and generals of the late King Haver was in charge.

They were most likely going to try and conquer the capital.

Perhaps Hadjar should have joined them, but... he was going to seek his justice in a different way. And his path required something more than the iron medallion of a senior officer.

He was waiting to receive a General's jade medallion. That would be the next step on his path to vengeance.

"I smell..." Nero pretended to sniff. "The Lascanians'

involvement in this sordid mess."

"I'm not gonna argue with you. I'm sure they've bribed some of the generals."

"Definitely. Besides, Balium is situated a bit too close to the nomads," Nero suddenly jumped up and nearly dumped his tobacco onto Hadjar's bed. "I think, my friend, that our Spirit Knight intends to take revenge. He's probably responsible for all of this."

"The Lascanian wouldn't dare fight us while we have the librarian."

"I don't trust the Darnassian, either. He's a very unreliable old man."

"Everyone loves him," Hadjar reminded his friend.

Nero looked at his friend sternly and then grinned knowingly.

"Except you, buddy. Except you."

"I don't like the way he looks at me," Hadjar replied evasively.

"Do you think our good-natured old man is not interested in women?"

"I think…"

Hadjar didn't finish his sentence because he'd heard the noise of his tent flap being opened.

When Serra, the dark-skinned beauty wearing light clothes, came inside, she immediately froze. Two steel daggers, glittering in the lamplight, were at her throat.

Hadjar and Nero stood shoulder to shoulder, ready to strike down whoever had dared to come inside.

"If you don't want to sleep with me, all you have to do is say so," she shrugged and was about to leave, but Nero caught her by the elbow.

"Sunshine of my life," he said, imitating the accent of the merchants from the southern seas. "I'm ready to love you without stopping, until the harvest festival begins, and love you everywhere, even here."

"Not here," Hadjar interjected dryly.

"You see, the senior officer is against it. I can't argue with my commanding officer."

The tent was quiet as Serra continued to look expectantly at the two friends. She knew they were hiding something. Nero and Hadjar were keeping quiet about it. They were two roguish, but reliable, companions. However, one of them was more than a friend to her—he was at least a lover. Nero wasn't supposed to know about her other thoughts.

The less a man knew about a woman's true feelings, the better for both of them. Love was a far too unpredictable and ethereal feeling to share it with someone who was just brightening up the cold night hours for you.

Maybe Nero felt the same way about her.

Hadjar only rolled his eyes. These two were so alike…

"Okay, well…" Nero blurted it out. "They tried to kill Hadjar."

"When?" Serra was surprised.

"Last night," Hadjar replied.

"And the day before," Nero added.

"And four nights ago."

"And last week, too."

"Twice."

Serra stared, dumbfounded, at the two fools who hadn't thought to share such important information with her.

"General Larvie," she finally guessed.

Serra knew that nearly six months ago, Hadjar had taken Colin's, the son of Spring Town's General, head. Nero had told her that the animosity between him and Hadjar had arisen at first sight. Their relationship had been so complicated that only the death of one of them could've resolved it. But Colin's father, the General of Spring Town, and the whole Prefecture along with him, disagreed.

"First, they sent killers at the Bodily Nodes level."

"The whole range, too. Stages one through nine," Hadjar nodded.

"Then they sent killers at the level of the Bodily Rivers."

"Yesterday, they sent an assassin at the Formation Stage. It was difficult, but I handled him."

Serra snorted and whispered a soft, "Here kitty, kitty..." The skins which served as a bed for Hadjar stirred and a white kitten crawled out from under them. She crossed the space that separated her from the warm, gentle hands in several jumps.

Serra straightened up, petting Azrea, and the white kitten was purring in her arms.

Traitor, Hadjar thought amusedly.

"When were you going to tell me about this? And why does no one in the camp know about it?" She asked angrily.

"The hired killers belonged to the Ax clan," Nero explained, "They've probably got a lot of tricks for euthanizing unwanted witnesses."

Serra grumbled something unintelligible. Holding the kitten in one hand, she got a yellow talisman out with her second hand. Something whispered, she swung it upward, and it melted, literally having soaked into the air.

"What will that do, Serra?" Hadjar was indignant. "I didn't ask you to do magic in my tent."

"I don't need your permission nor your request, Hadjar. You may be a senior officer to everyone else, but you're a friend to me. That's why I want to know when you're attacked next time"

Hadjar and Nero looked at each other and spread their hands almost simultaneously. When something occurred to Serra, it was impossible to stop her.

"The Bodily Nodes. The Bodily Rivers. The Formation Stage…" She whispered softly, going through the various levels. "So, today they'll be sending a practitioner at the Transformation Stage after you!"

"Today," Hadjar shrugged. "Or tomorrow. Maybe the day after tomorrow. Who knows?"

"And you're talking about it so calmly? It's a fucking Transformation level assassin!"

"Honey," Nero tried to hug the caster around the waist. "Don't worry about the bully. He'll be all right. These raids will stop soon enough."

Serra looked at the annoying jerks. They were being slightly evasive.

"May all the demons of hell get into my bed!"

"Darling, there's not always enough room in there even for me."

Serra only hissed in response and Nero immediately went quiet.

"Are you going to the General's castle? You're not fooling me! I see right through you! Do you realize that's suicide?"

"Suicide would be to just sit around here and wait for when the Ax clan sends a true cultivator," Hadjar clenched his fists.

Serra sighed and put Azrea down. She snorted indignantly, upset at the imminent parting. The white kitten, waving her tail to convey her annoyance, dived back into the skins and was soon peacefully asleep.

"I'm coming with you."

"Serra…"

"Honey…"

"It's settled!" The enchantress shouted.

Nero and Hadjar only sighed. Arguing with the woman was useless.

"When are we leaving?" She asked.

"As soon as the artifactor brings us our new blades."

The girl swore in a language unknown to Hadjar.

"So, you kept quiet all this time. You knew and still said nothing," she stated angrily and turned around, going to the door.

"Honey," Nero followed her, but his hand was slapped aside.

"Don't even think about it," Serra hissed. "You'd better find another bed tonight."

After saying her piece, she walked out.

Nero sighed dreamily and smiled, following after her...

"She's amazing!" He whispered, almost licking his lips.

Hadjar didn't know what Serra was like as a beloved, but he knew that she was a reliable friend. He had never suspected until now that he had not one, but two true friends in this world.

It was a wonderful feeling.

Azrea meowed with slight indignation.

Hadjar smiled, pulled out a piece of jerky from his pocket and handed it to the voracious kitten. She immediately began to devour it.

Okay, three friends.

To be continued...